Sylvie
Denied

Sylvie
Denied

Deborah Clark Vance

Flower Press
Cincinnati, Ohio

Sylvie Denied

Flower Press
Cincinnati, Ohio

ISBN (paperback): 9781662902925
eISBN: 9781662902932

Library of Congress Control Number: 2020942040

In loving memory of my parents
who continue to inspire me.

1972-1973

WEDDING GIFT

The impulse to move to Italy had come to Sylvie during a meditation. She hated the underlying violence of America—chicken-hawk politicians with their battle cries, premature deaths of young men, protestor beatings—and wanted to try living somewhere else. Having grown up under the constant warning of nuclear destruction—air raid sirens, duck-and-cover drills at school, classmates whispering about their fallout shelters—she figured she may not have much time if the chance of nuclear destruction was so real.

She'd been in Italy a year before meeting Enzo, who intrigued her as soon as she saw him because his look was more casual American than polished Italian. He was working on an advanced degree and supported himself making leather goods. Sylvie made him teach her how. Soon she was showing him how to streamline his operation by making reusable patterns. In a matter of weeks they were spending most of their time together. She luxuriated in his company when they were together and longed for him when they weren't. To her, their synergy and her intense feelings spelled love.

She was cutting a pattern and he was attaching a cow-hide strap when he blurted out that he wanted to have a family someday. "You're the first man I've known who said he wanted children," she replied.

Truly, she'd never discussed children with a man. But last year in Mantua, she saw her 28-year-old friend Patrizia panic about her waning fertility as her male friends said by age twenty-three a woman was too old for marriage. Such pressure troubled Sylvie too, although she wasn't raised to be a woman who dreamed of motherhood but rather one to finish college and have a career. In fact, her mom had never exposed her to newborns, and children misbehaving in public always prompted Mom to mutter, "Lousy little kids." Whenever Sylvie had asked Mom why she'd had children when they clearly annoyed her, she replied, "Society expects it."

Now Sylvie told Enzo, "I'm not ready to have children, if I ever do."

"Ready?" Enzo said. "Capitalist hogwash! Children enrich life—they are life! You just need some extra food and clothes and you pack him up and bring him along. Think what fun with a little baby playing around!" He pulled her close and gazed into her eyes, reminding her how long she'd yearned to escape suburban artifice and plunge into life's core, to feel its pulse, to be more in her body. She'd experienced such exuberance in Italy where parents included children in ways unthinkable in Sylvie's suburban American world. Children were often seen eating at restaurants late into the evening, attending adult parties, listening in on their parents' conversations, so she was starting to see them as life-affirming rather than an obstacle to her career plans. She enjoyed discovering these cultural differences with Enzo.

"Well," she said, "if I'd ever be a parent, it has to be in an intact family like how I grew up."

"Of course," said Enzo. "And if we're to be married, that doesn't mean we'll stop traveling."

"Of course," said Sylvie.

When she said she'd want a religious ceremony, he said, "Fine, but I don't believe in the Catholic God." And she'd replied, "No problem; my faith doesn't prescribe any image of God." He planted kisses all over her face. "I've never known anyone as substantial as you. Or as good. I love you. I don't deserve you."

"You're fishing for compliments," she'd murmured.

But Sylvie wanted to take Enzo to meet her folks back in the States to ask their frank opinion: Did they see a problem in him that she didn't? A reason she shouldn't marry him? After all, they'd been critical of practically every boy she'd ever dated. Of course, they hadn't had the chance to criticize the ones on motorcycles she'd sneaked out with. But they'd liked Saul, her first lover, who had introduced her to marijuana and LSD. She sighed to herself and shook her head; so much for their judgment.

Sylvie suggested they go visit her family during Thanksgiving. She wanted to cure Enzo of thinking America's only cuisine was hamburgers. Plus she missed the traditional menu of turkey with bread stuffing, cranberries, sweet potatoes and pumpkin pie, while Mom and Dad, her brother Jim, Aunt Hannah and Uncle Willis all swapped stories, arguing about the details and laughing about the situations and characters they described.

Before leaving for the States, Enzo said, "I can't go to America and not meet the indigenous people. I will write my dissertation about their role in the economy." She thought they'd each accomplish something in the States, whether or not they actually got married.

* * *

In O'Hare airport, Enzo kept staring at people. "Tipi mai visti!" he exclaimed, meaning, "Types never before seen!" His marveling at human diversity unsettled Sylvie, who was starting to find him less worldly than she'd thought. When the cab dropped them at her folks' three-story Victorian house, his expression showed surprise. She laughed as he gaped in astonishment at squirrels on the lawn then chased them across the street, even jumping a fence trying to catch one. Thinking how her dog Molly did the same thing made her laugh harder, especially when the squirrel circled its way up a tree, leaving Enzo gazing up, wondering where it had gone.

Thanksgiving morning Enzo kept asking when Mom would start roasting kid and baking lasagna and when the relatives would show up. At noon, he complained when her parents opened measly cans of soup. And finally, during dinner he asked *sotto voce* why her parents were excitedly calculating how much would be left over for sandwiches. Sylvie took his point and didn't argue.

The next day as Dad enticed Enzo to come admire his gadget collection, Sylvie and Mom took Molly on a walk.

"Tell me why I shouldn't marry him."

Mom looked askance at her. "What good would it do? You always do what you want anyway."

So Sylvie proceeded to plan a small reception for the next weekend and lobbied Mom's friends to lend her a wedding dress.

Sylvie and Enzo were pleased with the simple ceremony attended by long-time family friends, officiated by two Bahá'í witnesses. Aunt Hannah lent her own lacy white wedding dress which fit perfectly. Sylvie wore her long hair up and adorned with flowers. Enzo had brought the black suit his Babbo had bought him and wore it, as usual, with

11

no underwear. He'd also secretly managed to buy a couple of gold wedding bands before they left Rome.

Jim brought his new girlfriend. The Connors from across the alley were there—Camille Connor played a flute sonata—but Sylvie's other friends were still mostly away at college. Notice was too short for Aunt Iris and Uncle Simon to come from Vermont, but Iris sent a card and wrote, "Remember that what matters is what you do with your marriage, not who you marry." Her philosophizing always intrigued Sylvie. The one blaring sour note was when Dad shook Enzo's hand and said, "She's your problem now!" Mom wasn't present to correct this ill attempt at humor. Sylvie seethed over it.

Fortunately Uncle Willis was in good form. Sylvie had known Enzo would enjoy meeting him—he'd made a hobby of studying indigenous tribes and even wrote a book about the Lakota's battle with Custer. Willis recounted how he and Aunt Hannah would drive west looking for artifacts and researching in small-town libraries near the Wildrose Reservation. Now he surprised and delighted them by offering the use of his Datsun station wagon as a wedding gift to go visit Indians.

Family friends all hugged them goodbye after the reception, as did Jim's girlfriend. Dad shook Enzo's hand. So did Jim before awkwardly shaking Sylvie's. Her parents kissed her cheek.

The newlyweds accompanied Willis and Hannah to get the Datsun then drove to a run-down hotel where they pored over maps for hours.

Sylvie said, "Probably Willis thinks we'll go to Wisconsin Dells." Though she'd never been there, Mrs. Connor went every year and sent picture postcards featuring men wearing feathered headdresses. "Too bad Wisconsin doesn't really have reservations. The closest ones are probably in South Dakota."

"So we'll go there."

"What?! It's eight hundred miles!"

Enzo said, "Didn't Uncle Willis give us the car for our honeymoon?"

"It's one thing to offer a car to drive to Wisconsin. South Dakota is hundreds of miles farther!"

"But it's a present! Who gives a present and dictates its use? That's unheard of!" His voice rose. "*Che cazzo!* Willis is a sophisticated man!" She knew her parents were unaware of protocols—especially proper behavior at crucial moments like births, weddings and deaths—and took Enzo's point. "Otherwise why would he tell us about Wildrose in South Dakota?"

And since Aunt Hannah said honeymooners aren't expected to disclose their destination, in the morning they took off westward toward South Dakota.

HONEYMOON

When they wanted to stop that night, they saw neither hotels, nor towns nor even houses, so they parked behind a row of trucks beside a barren field and unrolled their new sleeping bags inside the car. The temperature topped out around freezing. When Sylvie awoke, the car was as dark as night. A sudden jolt of realization awakened her fully, sweeping her with the panicked realization she hadn't worn her diaphragm, and tailing that fear was the certainty she was already pregnant, their energetic love-making all but assuring it. She calmed herself wondering if it would be so bad to bring a child into this screwed-up world. After all, she wanted to feel more alive and connected as she fled not just violence but mediocrity. Maybe motherhood would connect her with life on this death-filled planet.

She watched the vapor of her breath settle on the windshield, mirrored by the layer of sparkling snow crystals outside. She wore a knit hat, sweatpants, two sweaters, two pairs of socks and had wrapped herself tight in her sleeping bag, wriggling out now and putting on boots to go out and pee. The trucks were gone so she squatted on the soft shoulder. She remembered her family driving to

Yellowstone Park in the days before expressways and she'd declared South Dakota her favorite state because it had mountains and horses, bright blue rivers and dark green forests. It was spectacular. But now she shivered, depressed by the grim white fields stretching toward the horizon.

Before leaving Chicago, they'd bought groceries; Enzo, oddly fascinated by supermarkets' oversized packages, bought cartons of cigarettes, loaves of bread, jars of orange juice, rolls of toilet paper, jumbo-sized bags of potato chips and marshmallows. Opening the back hatch, Sylvie retrieved the jar of instant coffee, a cup, a mini-box of sugar-coated cereal, and a stainless pot she filled with snow. She set the pot on the stand and lit the Sterno disk. When she was little, Dad would celebrate winter in the Vermont tradition by pouring warm maple syrup on snow, until the government warned that snow contained nuclear fallout that could rip up your insides. But now she had no choice. When the snow boiled, she removed her gloves to stir in coffee crystals and warm her fingers on the cup. She ate cereal out of the box, drank juice from the jar then melted more snow for washing her hands, drying them with toilet paper.

Enzo took the wheel when he was up and drove all morning, saying he'd never seen such empty spaces. When the map told them they were near the Wildrose Reservation, he pulled over at the sight of a hitch-hiking man with long black hair and a deadpan face who ambled to the car and climbed in, reeking of alcohol.

"Where are you going?" Enzo asked.

"This road is good."

"I want to talk to Indians. The real Americans," Enzo said. The man didn't reply, but as they approached a cross-road with no signs, trees, buildings or anything that distinguished it, the man gripped the doorknob and said, "I'll get out here."

Enzo pulled over. "Is this the reservation?"

The man released the doorknob. "OK, you keep going. You go talk to Strong Hawk. Very, very wise man." Then he ducked out of the car and walked backward, bobbing at them before turning down the crossroad.

Enzo said, "I heard Indians are alcoholics. I hope we find a sober one."

"Do you realize how many stereotypes you have? You also say the Indians are an oppressed proletariat ready to rise up."

Enzo said, "That's social science, not a personal stereotype."

"Not everyone is Italian, you know. Or even European."

At an intersection where a small sign indicated Wildrose Reservation, Enzo turned onto a two-lane road of bumpy, cracked asphalt. Along both sides lay rusting cars, some with flat tires, others at such odd angles Sylvie couldn't figure how they'd ended up that way. She'd been right in wanting to leave the States, she thought. This place proved its violent nature, its enduring abasement of those most vulnerable.

Enzo observed, "Don't they have mechanics out here?"

"Please stop it," she said.

They drove through barren snow-dusted plains dotted with naked trees until reaching a row of angled parking spaces. Unpainted clapboard buildings—two tourist shops and the post office—comprised the town. Enzo kept the engine running to stay warm while Sylvie entered the larger store called, with little imagination and a nod to tourists, "The Trading Post." Tables were laden with necklaces and bracelets of Venetian glass beads, an array of turkey feathers dyed in gaudy colors, silver jewelry and

HONEYMOON

Wildrose souvenir key chains and ashtrays. She visited the other store and found shelves of books and spinning metal racks of postcards presided over by a white man in a plaid shirt and bolo tie sitting on a stool behind a counter. She picked up two postcards and a few books about Lakota history and took them to the counter. Through the window she saw Enzo standing by the car smoking.

"That's a good book, but here's some better ones." The owner-proprietor-cashier walked her to the bookcases and pulled out one on the Lakota and Cheyenne. Sylvie wondered how he was allowed to operate a store on the reservation.

"Have you heard of Strong Hawk?" she asked.

"Of course," he answered. "James Strong Hawk."

"How can I find him?"

"Funny, that guy's becoming famous. Stay on this road, go 'round the first curve, cross the bridge, then go about ten miles to another big curve. There's a sign in front of his house with his name on it."

She carried her purchases to the car. "Why didn't you come inside?"

Enzo shrugged. "Wanted a smoke."

They followed the directions until there at a curve where the road turned sharply left stood two small houses, a modular house and another house pieced together with found objects like an art installation—wooden crates, car windows, sheets of corrugated metal, tree trunks holding up the roof, even a pair of antlers. A sign between the houses read, "Strong Hawk's Paradise." While Enzo kept the motor running, Sylvie got out and approached the modular house where behind a tree she glimpsed a tall man at the water pump, standing very straight with his back toward her, clad in a green army jacket nipped at the

17

waist. Approaching, she asked, "Excuse me, do you know where I can find James Strong Hawk?"

From behind he appeared youthful, but when he spun around, his leathery face incised with deep wrinkles surprised her. His untied bootlaces dragged. As he mumbled a reply, she saw he was toothless. She asked again and he replied, "I'm James Strong Hawk." His eyes pierced hers then and he looked at Enzo, who took the cue and got out of the car. "I knew you were coming," he continued. "This I learned from a vision. The white man is coming to learn about the Indian. Yesterday one left. A magazine photographer. Took many pictures. Today you come."

Enzo approached, grinning broadly. Sylvie imagined his pride in sensing the importance of visiting the indigenous Americans. And she believed that hearing the experiences of as many people as possible would bring her closer to understanding what's real in life.

Indicating the modular house, James said to Enzo, "You fix the chimney, you can stay in there, the one the government built. It's no good inside. Heat escapes. I built the other, the one I live in." He took a tube from his coat pocket. "Here." He gestured to Enzo to help him pull out an extension ladder stashed alongside the house and lean it against the wall. Sylvie went to warm up in the car from where she watched Enzo shakily scale the ladder, crawl up the roof and creep toward the metal stovepipe. (Later, he confessed he'd feared slipping on the snowy roof.) He dipped into his pocket for the tube of roof sealant James had handed him and squeezed it around the stovepipe. James meanwhile carried a stack of wood inside the handmade house, then returned to steady the ladder when Enzo descended. They followed James, who climbed into the back seat of their car and said, "Drive into town."

Some miles later, he directed them past the shopping area and down a road they hadn't noticed before. Passing more broken cars, James said, "Indian cars. No brakes." Sylvie understood the poverty and hoped Enzo wouldn't ask about mechanics. James continued, "My grandfather lived during very bad times. Gave up his bow and arrow for gunpowder. Gave up feathers for wool. We kept our children from boarding school. My son was destined to be a spiritual leader like me. My wife wanted to protect the water line with our daughter. We're all born in water."

James hurried them to a windowless building and sprang out of the car before Sylvie could ask more about the water line. He was ready with a shopping cart when she and Enzo caught up. They followed James down narrow aisles shelved with processed goods, as he tossed bags of chips, boxes of cereal and cans of soup into the cart, occasionally stopping to greet friends. Sylvie deplored the limited food selection and hoped reservation residents grew their own produce. Passing the refrigerator she asked, "Don't you want apples? Carrots?" and James picked up bags of each. At the register, he motioned Enzo to pay for the food. Sylvie figured they were buying it as payment to be his guests.

Back in the car James sat erect, hands on thighs, shifting as though his body didn't quite fit in the car. When they reached his land, James indicated the modular house and repeated, "The government built this." He picked up kindling and logs from a stack outside the door to bring inside and directed Enzo and Sylvie to arrange the food on a Formica table near the kitchen. The house's living-dining-kitchen room and bedroom could've fit in a cargo container.

"The food is for you," he said and stooped to build a fire in the wood stove. Sylvie felt sorry she'd misjudged his hospitality.

James returned the next afternoon ready to be interviewed. He settled on a threadbare chair, stuffing oozing from its seams, springs poking through its seat, a woodblock and a brick serving as front legs. Both Enzo and James spoke English as a second language so Sylvie interpreted between them. After Enzo's first question, James sat as he had in the car, erect and looking into the distance. Several seconds later Enzo repeated the question and suggested Sylvie hadn't translated correctly.

"Give him time to answer," she said.

James sat in silence.

Enzo insisted, "You didn't tell him what I said! He didn't understand you!"

James exhaled a long sigh. "The European doesn't know how to listen," he said. "He should open his mind to the Indian way. The European brings war, but the world needs relation-making ceremonies."

As Sylvie interpreted, Enzo sat speechless. James continued, "I was born into a starving world. My family ate whatever gophers, rabbits and squirrels we caught. We foraged for turnips, berries and roots. That was the European gift to us. The white man still covers us in blankets of sickness."

Enzo said to Sylvie, "Tell him I'm against colonizing."

She did and James replied, "Let the Indian way colonize you." Sylvie laughed when he said, "The Statue of Liberty should be in San Francisco harbor facing east, welcoming the white man to leave." He went on. "I found the 1868 Treaty in my grandmother's trunk. She didn't know—she couldn't read. How long had it been lost? It proved the conquerors knew we were a sovereign nation. They stole from us and hid their crime. They appointed ambitious tribesmen as our ambassadors and bribed them into selling our land."

Enzo said in his limited English, "I see indigenous Americans aren't the proletariat. I'll say this in my paper."

Sylvie interpreted and James replied, "We're going to Washington to present our grievances."

* * *

Enzo drove faster than he should through a blizzard all the way to Chicago, stopping to sleep at a rest stop. All the way, they talked excitedly about how different Wildrose was from anything they'd seen. When they got to her family's house, Mom was furious they'd been gone so long and livid about the miles they'd put on her brother's car. Sylvie at least wanted to explain how hairy it was driving in this blizzard, but said nothing, thinking she wouldn't listen. And she wanted to remind Mom that if she'd had a problem with Enzo, she could've said so before the wedding.

"Your behavior has consequences," Mom said. "You're making big decisions now, some we may not support. Dad and I want you to know this. Now you go out and clean that car!"

The streets were paved with ice. To wash the car, Sylvie and Enzo carried buckets of warm water that by the time they got to the alley had cooled and froze into a layer of ice as she poured it onto the car. Mom came out to inspect and when she deemed it clean enough, Sylvie drove it to Uncle Willis's house, determined to walk back home and share things she'd learned, like how cultural differences are really about one's world view and go way deeper than language and fashion and cuisine.

Two blocks away, she braked to avoid a VW speeding down the cross street but skidded and hit it, denting the Datsun. She walked over to tell Uncle Willis, who acknowledged the irony of her long trip ending this way. Then went back home where she withered under Mom's rage.

COPPING THE VAN

Back in Trieste, a letter from Aunt Hannah was waiting for Sylvie, commending her and Enzo for having actually been invited into Strong Hawk's home:

> In all the years your uncle and I traveled west to do research, we never had such an opportunity. Good for you!

Her aunt's praise heartened her, considering all the grief she'd gotten from Mom.

* * *

Sylvie had been fascinated by the idea of living in a vehicle since her second-grade teacher read a book to the class about orphans living in an abandoned boxcar. Then in high school she heard an echo in Thoreau's call to simplify. She longed to step outside of society, thinking that then she'd discover what's real. Far now from those first yearnings, she and Enzo were walking in Trieste and saw a van with English tags and a "For Sale" sign inside its windshield.

"Don't often see foreign tags around here," she said.
"True," Enzo said. "Tourists for sure."

"Maybe we should spend our wedding money on it? It's a caravan we could live in while traveling."

They hunted up and down both sides of the street, popping into cafés and osterias where Enzo called out in heavily accented English, "Who owns a van with English tags?" until finally two middle-aged women and two blond young men hunched at a table, dipping brioches into cappuccinos, stopped and looked up with leery expressions. Even from the doorway, Sylvie could tell from their facial muscles that they spoke English. Encountering English-speakers in Italy always made her a little homesick. Though fluent in Italian, she missed the familiarity of her native tongue.

"Do the dickering," Sylvie whispered. "I don't have the knack." Something very Italian she had yet to learn. So while Enzo descended on them, Sylvie went back down the street to admire the van with its windows and curtains and a rounded front end like Mickey Mouse's car.

Soon they all converged, Enzo walking beside Mum in her flat black shoes and silver helmet of tightly curled hair, a no-nonsense woman who, it turned out, had just traveled Europe with her two grown sons and her friend. Sylvie felt the heat of Mum's gaze through thick-rimmed glasses, making her self-conscious of her repurposed clothes—the long skirt fashioned from an India paisley bedspread and a white peasant blouse made from her mom's old damask tablecloth.

The others caught up. "Back in New Zealand we mostly have Fifties cars," the older son was saying. "Imports, you know. But this one's like new." Sylvie pictured streets full of rounded twenty-year-old cars with tiny windshield wipers, broken springs and moldy upholstery, chugging black exhaust across that green island. The son stood out among Italians with his wheat-colored hair, vague blue eyes and six-foot height. Sylvie had heard some of Enzo's ethnic jokes aimed at the "rubes" from beyond Naples and wondered if he—who considered himself progressive—ever recognized his chauvinism. For him, Italy was the world's cultural center, Naples its hub. But since she'd also been taught to view Chicago, USA this way, she was patient enough with him to be both amused as well as appalled by his cringe-worthy stories about American GIs who, after heroically freeing Naples from the Germans, were so gullible to have bought wristwatches with flies inside, ticking until soon after they were purchased. Enzo stereotyped all Anglos as gold mines. Sylvie had left the States, sickened by its culture of violence, the sacrifices of her peers in a hungry, hopeless war and relentless materialism, and expected—wanted—Italians to be different. And she believed Enzo *was* different, meaning detached enough from his conditioning to get beyond it.

The younger son said, "We saved a lot by driving instead of taking trains. Bought it in London and drove all through Europe." Mum's rumpled traveling companion put her arm around the young man and guided him to the background, effectively shushing him.

"It's a Bedford utility step-van," said the older son. "With windows, as you can see."

The two sons had done ingenious work in the van, creating headroom high enough to hang hammocks for themselves while Mum and her friend slept on the floor. They'd done it by cutting off the steel roof to use as a template for molding a fiberglass one that, when propped up by spokes on one side, stood higher than the original, with latches to lock it down when they drove.

"It's been a wonderful car, hasn't it? Quite comfy," Mum said.

Enzo walked around it, kicking the tires, opening the hood, peering through the windows, and then huddled with Sylvie to decide a price. How much is a car worth? Sylvie wondered. What if it's also your home?

Enzo turned and said, "We can offer two hundred American dollars as soon as we sell some purses we made."

Sylvie accepted his estimate, still unaware of how much he'd spent on all the junk food and curios after their ceremony in the States. They shook on the deal, Mum handed over the keys and as insurance took Sylvie's passport number and her parents' contact information.

That evening when Enzo returned from delivering finished purses to clients, Sylvie asked, "So how'd it go with the New Zealanders?"

"C'mon! They were cheating us," he said. "Where was the paperwork? Where was the lawyer? It's all illegal. If we hadn't shown up, they'd have abandoned it."

"But we gave our word! And ways to contact my parents!"

"Don't bother about any of that," Enzo said.

"But we aren't thieves, Enzo."

"Yes. But we shouldn't be duped by thieves. You're just too trusting."

"Maybe so. But you didn't even ask me. And we're married now, so what you do reflects on me." She used to scoff when Dad had said such things to her as a teenager thinking that only what she did reflected on her. Now she understood.

* * *

Enzo's friend Vittorio came to convert the van into livable space. He brought wood scraps to build a counter for a camp stove and a plastic dishpan and a space for an 8-track radio-tape deck and speakers. They all laughed at the toilet idea—a funnel inside a push-pedal wastebasket above another hole in the floor. To heat inside when they were parked at night, they installed a little kerosene heater with a stovepipe poking through a hole in the cab roof. Sylvie imagined Dad's outrage: With its gasoline, kerosene and propane for cooking, the van was a moving bomb.

They drove south to Naples so Sylvie could meet Enzo's parents who'd consented to the marriage without having met her. She'd visited Naples before knowing Enzo and remembered it as hellish with its heat, bus strikers parading outside the train station, men's eyes level with her breasts claiming the right to gaze, and a seawater-garbage stench. And when she'd bought a calzone from a street vendor, she wondered how something so savory had come from such stinking chaos. But now she entered tidy, tasteful homes, staying with his parents and visiting a different aunt and uncle each day where they served dishes with flavors new to Sylvie—fried eggplant, sautéed fennel, roasted red peppers stir-fried in olive oil and garlic, pasta with mussels, panzarotti filled with buffalo mozzarella, lasagna and freshly grated Parmesan, pastries and strufoli. Enzo's nieces and nephews bombarded Sylvie with questions about American pop culture. Each uncle or aunt slipped money into Enzo's pocket. Each bragged that Enzo's father—his *Babbo*—had almost become a lawyer before the war interrupted his studies, and added sadly that his Mamma was a bit nuts, observations that clashed with Sylvie's who found Babbo pretentious but warmed to Mamma's humor.

"Why do they talk like that about your Mamma?" she asked Enzo.

He paused. "She's talented, yes. But in Italy, men rule." She knew that adage, sometimes amended with "except at home."

"But not you," she warned.

"No *cara*, we are equal."

26

As they gathered at Uncle Salvatore's dinner table, a pretty young woman arrived with a Panettone Christmas cake. Everyone greeted her warmly and invited her to sit.

"Thank you, no," she said. "I just came to say hi. I heard Enzo was here."

"Yes," said Aunt Lina, "and his new American wife, Sylvia."

Enzo took Sylvie's hand and led her to greet Pina who said, "Nice to meet you, Sylvia," and kissed them each on both cheeks. "You realize how lucky you are to marry this man?"

"I'm the lucky one," Enzo said, putting Sylvie's hand to his lips, a gesture Sylvie thought corny but cute.

After Pina left, the family gossiped about how she'd gone north to Trent and gotten involved with radicals.

Enzo said, "She fell in love with one of the Red Brigade."

"Cool!" said his nephew. "But aren't they dangerous?"

"Not really; they're careless. And not so bright."

"We always worried about you alone up there, Enzo," Salvatore said.

"Such a shame your parents sent you away," Lina said. He'd been sent north at age fifteen. His parents had thought he boarded at school but he moved out of there at age seventeen into an apartment with Vittorio and Fabio who'd dropped out.

"Why'd they send you away?" asked the nephew.

Enzo laughed. "I was bad. The schools here didn't want me."

Salvatore said, "The priests didn't like some of his questions."

"You were too smart for your own good," Lina said.

"How can you be 'too smart?'" asked the nephew.

"Let's drink to that," said Enzo.

"But our boy will soon be Doctor of Sociology!" said Salvatore. "And for Napoletani, the north isn't friendly. Eh, Enzo?"

"I don't let them push me around," said Enzo.

"That's my boy. You know it was Garibaldi who moved our factories north to strengthen the border?" Salvatore reminded him.

"Yes, Uncle. I've educated them many times."

This glimpse into Enzo's past filled Sylvie's heart with pity for his younger self and annoyance that his parents hadn't known how to deal with him. She liked how his family emoted, uncensored, while hers sparred intellectually with a quip or a rejoinder. She was glad his extended family supported him.

* * *

As they were returning north in their van-home toward Enzo's university in Trent, Sylvie asked, "What about that Carnevale gig?"

Enzo's friends at Ristorante del Porto in Trieste, four hundred miles from Trent, hired him yearly to produce a children's puppet show during Carnevale.

"You're right! I forgot that's tonight!"

"God, you need a secretary!"

Enzo turned eastward at the next interchange to veer off toward Trieste. The increased speed made the roof pop up and strain against its latches so Sylvie went to sit on the floor in back to clamp it down with her hands and hold tight. Such effort wearied her arms and the rushing sound of tires lulled her to sleep until the roof whooshed over and banged the outside of the van, breaking loose its hinges and bouncing onto the road.

"Oh, no," Sylvie cried out, "I fell asleep!"

Enzo pulled onto the shoulder. "Help me move it. Big ticket for leaving stuff on the highway."

Her heart still pounded. "I'll open the back."

"No, let's leave it on the shoulder."

"Will it be here when we return?" she asked.

"We don't need it," he said.

Though dubious, Sylvie understood the urgency of getting to the gig so Enzo's friends wouldn't think he'd cheated them. Maybe they'd lose more money by not doing the puppet show than they'd gain from saving the roof. She moved to the front seat, breathing deeply, detaching, deciding not to worry about it.

They arrived forty minutes behind schedule. The banquet room chairs were pushed aside to make space in the middle where children screamed and bounced balloons to the lighthearted music from Fellini's film "8-1/2." Sylvie distributed sweets provided by the restaurant while Enzo, who had at least remembered to pack his puppet box when they left for Naples, set up his stage with puppets he'd carved from wood, painted their faces and costumed. The children settled when he blew his mouth trumpet and opened the curtains on his little set. He enacted a story of an innocent man setting out to make his fortune who is robbed and beaten. Soon he meets a beautiful maiden crying alone, lost in the woods. He helps her find her way home which turns out to be a castle because she happens to be a princess. The king lets them marry at a big festive wedding. Sylvie was enchanted by his ability to do all the voices and introduce funny animal characters. She circulated among the guests exclaiming how great his show was.

After three energizing but exhausting evenings, they went out for the city-wide Mardi Gras celebration, heading to Bar Svizzera, Enzo's friends' favorite hangout. As they were stopped at a red light, a group of costumed people waved and called from the sidewalk.

"*Eii*! Enzo, drive us in the parade!" It was forming up ahead.

"Do you recognize anyone?" Sylvie asked.

"Climb in!" Enzo called. She was impressed by how many people knew him wherever they went. He could talk to anyone, swapping stories and practical tips. Sylvie went to open the back door and did a double-take—amazed the stereotype had traveled so far—as she saw someone entering through the opening where the roof used to be, dressed as an indigenous American with war paint and a single feather in a headband. Three men dressed as women and three women in ball gowns clambered in through the back and climbed up to join the Indian on the cut metal edge, all legs dangling inside as they blew kisses first at Sylvie then at the crowd. Sylvie saw her friends Pino and Giustina in the crowd and waved them over. They caught up and walked alongside for a minute then Pino yelled that he'd watch from the sidelines.

"Hey, put this on!" said Vittorio, passing Enzo a pair of black-rimmed plastic glasses, with a big nose and bushy mustache attached; Enzo left it on his lap as he drove. A woman reached down to hand Sylvie a long, red wig and a silver sequined eye mask which she donned right away.

"*Basta*—enough of this! Go to Bar Svizzera!" shouted Vittorio. "Turn here!" (Later that evening in Bar Svizzera, a college student from Houston would tap Sylvie and ask under his breath why so many Italian men dressed like women.)

With a jerk of the wheel, Enzo broke rank and turned the corner, nudging aside a sawhorse roadblock, and drove down the boulevard sidewalk. The passengers shouted and whooped encouragement. He continued, aided by young people dressed as a pirate, a princess and a gorilla who cleared trash cans and café chairs from his path.

"Oh, no; look out!" Ada laughed. The Indian reached down to raise the volume.

Two traffic cops in white helmets and gloves and blue uniforms were corralling them on both sides. The window crank was stuck, so Enzo opened the door to yell, "*E' Carnevale, ogni scherzo vale!* It's Mardi Gras time, all jokes are fine!" and maneuvered around the officers.

One officer shouted, "Show me your registration!" running and grabbing at the door as Enzo slammed it shut, barely missing the officer's fingers. Sylvie feared this would add to Enzo's offense.

Enzo abruptly pulled over, removed the key, opened the door and leaned out to say, "It's in back. I'll go get it."

He wormed through everyone's dangling legs and put on his mask. Not knowing what to anticipate, Sylvie decided to jump out and watch from the fringes of the milling crowd. Ada hopped off her perch on the roof, opened the back door and everyone else pushed out and encircled the van, including Enzo in his new face standing beside the cops, a hand cupping his chin, the other propping his elbow. Only the Indian remained on the roof's edge as a tape of Fabrizio de Andre singing "Un Matto" rang out.

Sylvie was surprised by Enzo's anarchy and fascinated when the officer, not recognizing him with that ridiculous mask, sought him by peering through the windshield. It reminded her of old stories like "Robin Hood" or "The Prince and the Pauper" when all anyone had to do was change clothes and no one recognized him. Enzo and their passengers melted into the crowd and headed to Bar Svizzera. With the van's English tags, all the police could do was impound it, but everything was closed for the holiday. As if playing out a Carnevale farce, the cops drove away, and later Enzo and Sylvie reclaimed the van—their van.

RULES

Sylvie awakened to the reality that her morning quea-
siness, fatigue, bloated abdomen, two missed peri-
ods—heck, even her increasingly tight pants—affirmed
her pregnancy. It had happened surprisingly quickly and
she wasn't prepared, despite having intuitively bought in
Wilmette two New Age books about pregnancy and natural
childbirth. She silently laughed at the thought of entering
"virgin" territory. She felt like a ticking time bomb. He was
ecstatic. Sylvie mourned over giving up their van home but
resigned herself to the fact that pregnancy changed everything. And she wasn't ready for any of it.

They'd gone to Trent after Carnevale: Enzo got serious about his dissertation and about finding a place to stay,
but so far all he found was the floor in a friend's apartment.
He had plenty of data from Wildrose, supplemented by
Uncle Willis who continued to show his forgiveness and
love by sending articles about the Wounded Knee stand-
off clipped from the *Chicago Tribune* and the Mohawk's
Akwesasne News. Sylvie translated what she deemed necessary, in the process becoming more expert than Enzo
about the Lakota, though he knew sociological theories for
interpreting it. When news of the Wounded Knee stand-

off soon broke, Enzo's professor got them both invited to speak on a local radio station as experts.

Sylvie was settled in Café Miraggio, translating the articles while Enzo attended classes. One day Enzo entered with Stefano and his friend Teresa. While the men went to order coffees, Teresa sat with Sylvie.

"Is this a wanted pregnancy?" she asked.

"It is. But hard to get used to."

"I'd die for my children," Teresa said. "I never said that about my husband even when I loved him." Sylvie couldn't imagine ever feeling that way about Enzo.

As the men approached, Stefano was lamenting how people always grabbed him to complain, "Doctor, it hurts here!" So he'd bought an old house up in a medieval mountain village, where he found peace to work on research about freckles' relationship to skin cancer.

"Why not stay there? You need a roof; I need help with English. I'm often in Rome so it's usually empty. I've modernized it."

"Oh?" Teresa rolled her eyes. "The walls are insulated with hay, the entryway floor is dirt."

* * *

The walls and streets of Nogare were formed of round stones dug from the nearby stream, and covered with sun-bleached plaster, its winding passageways donkey-cart wide, its link to the world a dirt path, paved during the war to ease collecting its silver ore.

When Enzo drove to Trent for class, Sylvie translated articles for Stefano and strolled through the village where she met townswomen who, in black widow's weeds, gathered at a spring-fed fountain to scrub clothes with bars of brown soap. She loved how over time they gathered around her pregnant belly and mothered her, alarmed that she lived so far from her own mother. Sylvie tried to reassure them this wasn't so unusual in the States. Olga and Griselda gave her a garden plot planted by a family whose white Persian cat had gone missing and its helpless pelt on a clothesline scared them back to the city.

Each townswoman guarded her secret site where porcini mushrooms—more valuable than wine—burgeoned after spring rains under pines in oak forests. So Sylvie was honored when Olga and Griselda taught her to scavenge for mushrooms nicknamed "big umbrella" and "fart." They also taught her to find snails, nettles, onions, dandelion, rosemary, chamomile, elderberries and hops, all smelling as real as earth. They warned her to bang sticks against tree branches to dislodge camouflaged venomous snakes. To Sylvie's horror, in spring they tied mist nets in trees to trap migrating thrushes, luring them with berries and caged females, then pulling down the chirping, writhing nets to disentangle delicate wings and claws. They pan-grilled songbirds so tiny they disappeared in a bite like a cookie. Germans who seasonally migrated to bird-watch fumed when they read the osteria's menu, recalling frustrated hours in spring, holding binoculars, awaiting the homecoming.

The townsmen had been ordered to extract ore rather than to soldier, and did so until the mine collapsed, leaving a village of widows who carried on, forging bonds as tough as mortar. The two surviving men were an alcoholic on a bender that awful day and the priest whom the townswomen sustained. They said, "He's drunk a lot, too, but we need a priest."

"He conducted the funeral of that wounded Russian. Remember? Just after the war he showed up."

"Yes, we kept him alive a while. Couldn't understand him, though."

The women took Sylvie under their wings. Olga taught her to make soup, sauce with abundant fresh basil and vegetables in oil and garlic and often fetched the daily milk Sylvie ordered from Victoria's cow, the town's only one. With her supply of raw milk, Sylvie wanted to learn to make cheese so she and Enzo visited a creamery where they bought rennet for hard cheese and made ricotta by adding lemon juice to the leftover whey. One evening, Stefano brought home a hedgehog he'd just killed with his car. He skinned it in the bathroom sink then took it into the kitchen to chop up and sauté with garlic and instructed Sylvie to slowly stir broth into rice to make risotto. Sylvie smiled to herself, remembering her disgust with her friend Giulio in Mantua trying to kick a hedgehog to death. Had she grown more daring? Practical? Desperate? She saw no other wild animals and concluded the Italians had devoured most of them during the war.

With some trepidation, Sylvie had written Mom about her pregnancy. She was relieved and not surprised when Mom replied, avoiding any reference to it at all.

Dear Sylvie,

Now it seems Nixon's lawyer and others have lied to investigators so I'm beginning to understand why people get fed up and start marching. I'm not sure if Dad voted for him and hope I never find out, but practically everyone else did. You probably were smart to get away.

Sylvie noticed how Mom was better at talking about impersonal things than her feelings about personal matters. Did she do that too?

Olga and Griselda visited only when Stefano wasn't there. They said they'd peeked through his windows and shuddered at the portraits he painted in Day-Glo orange, screaming chartreuse and black. What kind of doctor painted like that, they asked? They taught Sylvie a set of rules for pregnancy that seemed to her akin to breathing and feeding hunger pains, unlike Mom's and Gramma's artificial rules for table manners, knocking on the bathroom door and thanking a compliment. The rules had been breathed into daughters by their mothers and none dared transgress them or even experiment. Data supported them in the form of tales: the aunt who almost died from washing her hair during the *quarantenna* after childbirth—the forty days of abstaining from water; the sister's illness from putting her hands in cold water; the grandmother who miscarried after sitting on a cold stone. They gave Sylvie dainty baby clothes, wrap-around two-part cloth diapers and woolen undershirts to protect her kidneys from cold draughts. Sylvie imagined their traditions stretched back to the fringes of prehistory where women knew how to forage food and cure their families. They taught her how to mother. She felt like an initiate in a long tradition of womanly knowledge.

Enzo offered rules he'd learned—an uncle with a high fever who was by an open window when someone opened the door and the cold draft of air killed him. And the gardener in Naples who said menstruating women shouldn't touch growing things lest their toxicity kill the plants.

"I can't believe you'd repeat such obvious sexist bullshit," Sylvie said.

By the time she showed in the sixth month, Griselda encouraged her to visit the ante-natal clinic, and in her seventh month, insisted she not travel down the mountain because of the change in air pressure. So she focused on translating. An article in *Akwesasne News* mentioned mothers passing to daughters—from uterus to uterus—the knowledge of the water ceremony and how this "water line" broke when children—daughters—were sent to boarding schools. This was the water line Strong Hawk had mentioned.

* * *

Voices drifting through air and footsteps clapping on cobblestones awakened her. She'd grown so heavy that from lying on her back she had to shift her belly to the bedside, let her legs roll off, push herself up and slide her feet into slippers, a patient old couple waiting on the floor. Though she preferred walking barefoot, the women's rules forbade it. She sat dizzily then stood up and shuffled into the kitchen, leaning backward for balance, and opened the tap to fill the teakettle, careful not to splash her hands as Griselda had instructed. Books were piled on a chair, draped over with clothes, a crumb-covered plate burrowed under an Olivetti typewriter. Olga had told her to lie down when her back hurt—just seeing the mess pained her. While rinsing the terracotta pitcher, she recoiled at the ripe film of yesterday's milk, and didn't notice Olga, face scrubbed to a chapped rosiness, radiant as she stood with one hand clutching the wire handle of a metal pail half-filled with fresh milk. When Sylvie looked up, Olga was stepping back to knock on the open door from outside.

"I came earlier but no one answered," she said. "Your milk's been in the barn all morning. I covered it, but the flies . . ."

Before her heaviness and sleepiness increased, Sylvie would visit the barn early, and once saw Victoria stick her finger in the milk and flick away three flies. Olga insisted she drink lots of milk, but sometimes thinking of it turned her stomach.

"Thanks so much."

"You sleep late, eh? But just you wait. When that baby comes . . . ." Olga's self-assurance was humbling. She'd spent her life in this little village yet nothing daunted her, whereas dust, laundry and dishes overwhelmed Sylvie, the world traveler. In her eighth month, the women cleaned the house while she stood awkwardly sponging the kitchen table, watching them barrel past, stooping, crawling, lifting furniture, scouring walls and floors.

The next morning, Sylvie went to return Olga's milk pail. She breathed in the scent of tilled earth arising from the hot fields as she walked along the cobblestones that lay like rows of solid bubbles even after centuries of hooves and feet had worked to flatten them. Coming through a dark passageway, she entered the bright piazza and tripped on a cobblestone's humped back and the pail flew from her outstretched hands as she stumbled. Olga and Griselda were perched on a ledge, the tiny vines of their calico aprons extending up from the stones. Relieved she didn't land on her belly, they heaved a loud sigh as from a single breast, then laughed.

"We always fell down, too," said Griselda.

"When I was pregnant, I fell down a whole flight of stairs," said Olga.

"Maybe by the time I'm used to all this weight, the baby will be born," Sylvie said, leaning sideways to pick up the pail.

"Yes, and you'll be carrying the little one in your arms instead," said Olga.

Sylvie was about to sit when Griselda gasped so loudly that Sylvie jumped up, expecting to find a snake slithering behind her.

"No! You might lose the baby if you sit on that cold stone!"

Sylvie's heart pounded. "I could've lost it from fright just now!" Olga folded up her sweater to make a cushion for her.

"Just beware of the extremes," said Griselda. "Hot and cold."

Sylvie wanted to rebel against all these restrictions but, without facts to counter them, didn't dare. Besides, she admired Griselda and Olga. They'd never sit in Café Miraggio and discuss whether the economy balanced on women's backs. But who in Café Miraggio could do what they did, bring forth life out of soil, prune grapevines and tie their branches to trellises, gather wood into bundles and sling them over their shoulders, scramble up the hill and out of sight on spring days when porcini were growing in their secret places, move quick and sure, like rabbits darting home?

When Sylvie was eight, Mom handed her a seed packet bearing pictures of bright blue morning glories, suggesting she plant them by the arbor. Smiling, Mom said, "Read the instructions." Sylvie took the seeds outside, poked holes in the soil with her finger and dropped them in, not knowing she'd planted them too deep, and quietly despaired when they never surfaced. She never mentioned it and Mom forgot about it. And when she planted seeds in the garden Olga gave her, she regarded the seedlings with awe, as if she'd performed a miracle. But no, it's the spirit of life pushing through the earth as the spirit of life was in her belly. Where Mom struggled underneath male definitions, these women, growing out of their village stone, knew how their femaleness fit not just on the planet but in society. It was as if they included her in their water line.

WAYS OF LIFE

Sylvie hated to admit her homesickness, but by summer she'd grown determined to observe a Thanksgiving in Italy.

"How do you say cranberries in Italian?"

Enzo toked his cigarette. "What is cranberries?"

"Those berries we had for Thanksgiving."

He blinked at her, exhaling smoke.

"Well, do they have turkeys here?"

"*Tachini*? Of course. I heard about a disease where their feet turn black but are sold anyway," he said. "It's probably easier to get a live one than a butchered one."

"Let's get one now so it'll be fat by November." She'd entered new territory, having only just accepted the argument that if you're going to eat meat then be honest enough to kill it yourself.

A few days later, Enzo came home with a large crate in the car. "I brought you a surprise." When he opened the lid Sylvie stood facing a large bird.

"Is that a goose?" she asked.

"What goose? It's a turkey," he laughed. "You should know. Turkeys come from America."

"Turkeys aren't white." Sylvie pictured the turkey she'd colored in third grade, with its tail fanned out.

Enzo sighed. "Turkeys are white or turkeys are black, like hens are white or black or brown. There is a difference? You should've told me before I drove all the way to Caldonazzo to get it for you. There's a restaurant where they keep them in a pen. This was the biggest. A male." She was touched that Enzo had hunted down a turkey for her, thinking how Dad always fell short when trying to surprise Mom with gifts.

Sylvie found a spot outside Victoria's chicken coop where she sprinkled feed on the ground and poured water in an old dish. Whenever a bus came up the hill, it honked at every turn, and each time it honked, the turkey she named Tomaso shot back, "loodleloodleloodleloodle loodleloodleloodleloodle" in a downward scale. When she heard hens screeching and the turkey gobbling, she'd lean out the window to see chickens pecking at his food while he circled in a dither. She'd rush out and shoo the chickens into their pen, but still they reached their necks through the wires and bullied him. Twenty pounds of feed were gone in several weeks, but Tomaso had shrunk.

You have two and a half months to make him grow," Enzo said, "or you won't have much of a feast."

Sylvie prepared a little leather collar she slipped around his scrawny neck and led him by a leash, holding feed in her hand to coax him to where he could scratch for food. Leaning slightly backward to accommodate her belly weight, she shambled along cobblestones and up the hill toward the commons. Because she was walking backwards, she didn't notice Olga at the fountain.

"*Buon giorno, signora*," called Olga, beaming a quizzical smile. "What are you doing?"

"The chickens taunt my turkey and won't let him eat, so I'm taking him to the commons."

"I see," said Olga.

"Enzo bought him for Thanksgiving. It's a feast back home with roast turkey." She wanted to rest her feet, but there was nothing except cold stones around the fountain and with Olga there, she wouldn't sit down. "We need to start our own family traditions."

Olga stopped scrubbing and wiped hair from her eye with the back of her hand. "My daughter-in-law says turkeys contain seven different cuts. I've never had it."

"We only have it on holidays because it roasts all day."

"We don't do that here," said Olga. "Isn't that a holiday about Indians?"

As Sylvie considered how to explain Thanksgiving, she felt silly portraying it as an interracial day of peace; she couldn't explain how indigenous people, before the genocide, had contributed native dishes to commemorate the survival of colonists. "It's to celebrate the harvest." Her face turned red. "And memories of good family times."

Olga stared at her, shaking her head slightly.

Sylvie said, "But I must go or Tomaso won't get breakfast."

"Who is Tomaso?" asked Olga.

Sylvie blushed. "The turkey." She hesitated. "Maybe I shouldn't name an animal I plan to eat."

Olga looked perplexed as she resumed washing clothes.

* * *

She'd been walking along the cobblestones when a car drove up and parked by their house. The driver was a man with unkempt hair beside a waifish woman, a small child in the back. Recently Enzo had received a letter from Fabio, a friend from Trieste who'd been living abroad. He'd explained how Fabio had been arrested during the Paris demonstrations and was kicked out of France for breaking a store window and stealing a fur coat as a political act—so typical of people then, so-called anarchists who couldn't get beyond materialism, Sylvie thought. She approached the open car window. The man's transparent blue eyes followed her movements, grinning through gritted tobacco-stained teeth.

She asked, "Are you Fabio? and Nicole?"

Fabio's face darkened.

"Enzo's in town. Want to come in and wait?"

"No," Fabio said and turned the car around, spinning the tires and kicking up rocks and such dust that Sylvie had to jump back. The engine puttered down the mountain, echoing as it descended the road that unraveled toward Trent. She hadn't imagined Fabio to be so daft but chastised herself for judging him. Maybe he'd forgotten about his letter he'd sent saying they'd be in Trent?

Sylvie went to the door when she heard cars approaching that evening. Enzo came in first, pulling her aside. "Fabio's terrified of you," he whispered. "He thinks you're a witch!"

"Is he crazy or what?" It was logic, not witchcraft that had clued her about Fabio. Besides the letter, she and Enzo were the only outsiders in town and the only ones with visitors. And he fit Enzo's descriptions. She wouldn't have thought them crazy had they just met now for the first time, except their rotting teeth made them look crazy.

"In Amsterdam, there was this woman with a little dog," Fabio said, plopping onto a kitchen chair. "She walked down the street holding this dog and the dog spoke to me."

Enzo winked at Sylvie. "And what did it say?"

"It spoke in Dutch," Fabio said. "I don't know."

Nicole gave their son Emile crayons and paper. Settling down in a kitchen chair, she recounted how they'd performed live sex on stage at an Amsterdam nightclub.

"Friends watched Emile for us," she said. "But it's OK if he sees what we do. It's natural, after all."

Fabio described their trips to Afghanistan to buy trinkets. And probably hashish, Sylvie suspected. Their attitude shocked her, but she tried to focus on their good qualities. They seemed like caring parents but as they described their travels, she judged them lazy, seeking warm places where they could live cheaply and get high.

After dinner, Nicole laid out a sleeping bag on the floor for Emile and when he fell asleep she shared travel woes with Sylvie. The men meanwhile walked up the hill by the woods and returned much later, obviously high. Fabio said they'd buried LSD in the woods Enzo could dig up later.

Sylvie seethed. "Did Enzo tell you his theory that using drugs supports the Mafia? And that LSD was invented by the CIA for mind control?"

A shadow passed over Fabio's face. Nicole fidgeted. Enzo laughed and said, "'A foolish consistency is the hobgoblin of small minds.' I am high and I am literate. Literately high. Highly literate. I channel Ralph Waldo, Sylvia's transcendental hero whom I'm transcending."

Enzo had broken his promise not to use drugs. Sylvie wanted their guests to leave. And they did, next morning.

* * *

Approaching her due date, Sylvie worried about not getting to the hospital on time because of their car problems. They couldn't afford repairs so when the parking brake went out, they parked in first gear, wedging a stone under a front tire to brake it. After first gear failed, they'd park on a decline, using the stone to keep it from rolling downhill. To start it, Sylvie put it in neutral and Enzo picked up the stone to get the car rolling and as it gained momentum, Sylvie popped it into second gear. Anyway, when she started feeling contractions, Enzo was ready. As she hung onto her seat, he picked up the rock then rushed back to jump into the driver's seat and hurtled down the mountain.

At the hospital a doctor examined, admitted and assigned her to a room with three other women in various stages of labor, each in her own agony. One, in fact, moaned loudly and before long was screaming, "I want drugs! *Mamma Mia! Madonna Mia! Dio mio!* In Florence they give you drugs! Take me to Florence!"

When Sylvie's pain grew stronger and more regular, she tried a method she'd read in her New Age pregnancy and childbirth book, to control pain by singing. When she felt a contraction, she started singing, "Both Sides Now," her favorite song by Joni Mitchell. When she reached the end of the first verse and sang, "but clouds got in my way," the distressed woman shouted, "*Madonna mia, stai zita per favore!* Please shut up! *Basta!* Enough with the singing!" Though hurt, Sylvie complied. Soon nurses appeared and wheeled out the woman.

"About time," said one of the other women. "We've listened to her scream since yesterday." They later learned she had a Caesarean birth.

After shockingly intense pains, Sylvie's labor quickly culminated. Pregnancy's weirdness and wonder finally made sense when her body actually spewed forth another and she gazed into its eyes and felt the full weight of its existence. When the doctor held up the baby and exclaimed, "*Che bambina bellissima!* A beautiful baby girl!" Sylvie beheld a frog-like being, broader at the shoulders than the rear, its nose and ears flattened in the birth canal, a creature newly arrived from an alien realm. Sylvie thought that by mothering this child she'd be tidying up a little corner of the world. Though a stranger, the baby felt intimately close, having been inside her, feeding on her, pulsing with her heartbeat, using her blood, excreting into her body. It was true—this baby *was* life. And now she—Diana—was out in the world, after being hidden, except for the bulbous belly and the rippling, fluttering kicks. Caressing Diana's downy head, Sylvie realized from now on she'd have to weigh the impact of every choice on her, a habit begun during pregnancy.

She and five other mothers—four older than thirty and a teenage mother of identical twins—shared the recovery room, three beds on each side. The babies were brought from the nursery only at feeding times and she and the teenage mom were both tutored in breastfeeding.

She learned something else too. When she complained to the woman in the next bed over about the pricking, throbbing and bleeding she felt the woman said, "Oh, that's from your episiotomy. They like to sew you up tighter afterward. For your husband."

How dare they!

When Enzo had dropped her off, the staff instructed him to return the next day. He stayed at his friend Massimo's who had offered his place in town for when Sylvie was released so they wouldn't have to subject the newborn to the altitude change. Now he arrived with flowers and held Sylvie's hand to go to the nursery window. As a nurse held up Diana behind the glass, Enzo squeezed her hand tighter and smiled so broadly his face practically cracked, but when the nurse brought Diana closer, he backed away, his face ashen, and bolted out the door and down the stairs. Sylvie was dismayed when she later learned he and Massimo had been dropping acid which kept Enzo awake chanting all night, frightening Massimo's boy. Massimo, of course, kicked him out.

But when Enzo took them home, Sylvie saw the crib he'd made of maple wood sanded as smooth as flesh. He'd worked on it for months at Massimo's house. She thought, this is love, or as good as love.

* * *

No one was in the fields; lights were on inside the houses. Sylvie had been sketching on a hill in the commons and now followed the path down to the cobblestones, leading Tomaso on his leash, sketchbook under her arm and Diana in a pouch on her belly. Her intense love for Diana all but overwhelmed her. She spoke to Diana when she was awake, watched her when she slept, sometimes shook her to make sure she was breathing, and ached for her when they were apart. She determined to guide this child to be a healthy individual who would help make the world better.

She could see Olga descending ahead of her, a basketful of kindling on her back, just reaching the fountain where Enzo now stood. He had gone this morning for his dissertation defense which, as far as Sylvie knew, wasn't open to observers. Anyway, he hadn't invited her. Sylvie clearly heard their voices through the still air. Olga stopped, one hand steadying the basket, the other on her hip, and said, "I just saw Sylvie chasing the turkey." Sylvie's hands were occupied so she couldn't wave and didn't want to startle Diana by shouting.

Enzo asked, "Do you think my wife may be a little . . ." He tapped his forefinger on his forehead. Considering his recent behavior, Sylvie thought, what nerve!

"Not crazy. Maybe homesick. That turkey seems important to her."

Sylvie arrived just as Enzo was saying, "The darn thing is shrinking! It's too dumb to eat by itself!"

Sylvie said, "That's why I brought him out to feed him."

"*Cara*, I think it's time!" Enzo said, reaching down and picking up Tomaso by its legs.

"What do you mean?" The scrawny bird gobbled frantically. "What are you doing?!"

"This is important for us," he said. "Let's finish carrying out our plan—becoming completely self-sufficient."

"Put him down!" Her shouting awoke Diana, who started crying, so Sylvie tenderly took her out of the pouch to cuddle and coo to her.

Olga petted Diana's head and laughed. "The man must be hungry for turkey!"

Enzo called back, "You can't make your dinner be your pet!"

Sylvie followed as fast as she could but Enzo took such long strides she couldn't keep up. The turkey was flapping its wings and making such a racket that everyone peered out their windows. The collar was still around its neck, the leash dragging behind. Enzo pushed open the door and entered the work room and, holding the turkey at arm's length, reached into a box beneath the work bench for the hatchet.

Sylvie caught up. "You're jealous of my relationship with a turkey!"

"Don't be silly. This was always our plan. That's why I bought the damn thing." Gripping the turkey upside down by its legs with one hand and a hatchet with the other, Enzo hesitated.

Sylvie controlled her rage so as not to upset Diana. She pictured Thanksgiving dinner, her family talking and laughing around the table, eating their special dishes. She wanted that. She missed them. But she'd also grown fond of the turkey and couldn't imagine eating him, despite having entered this project believing she should be able to kill meat if she planned to eat it.

She ran through the kitchen carrying Diana to the bedroom and put her in her crib then stroked her head as she fell asleep. She pictured Enzo laying the turkey's neck on the tree stump he used for chopping wood, cringing when two blows brought silence. Minutes later, she heard water running full force and, sobbing, she went to the kitchen where Enzo was drying his hands on a towel. He turned to her and said, "Tomorrow we have Thanksgiving."

"You bullied me! You killed Tomaso when I was too weak to stop you! You're just like those fake revolutionaries, like Fabio, who want to overthrow everything and be in charge, expecting their girlfriends to cook for them."

"C'mon, Sylvia. I saw how your family does holidays. Ours will be better."

He tried to hug her but she pushed him away. "You savage! Is this your 'fantasia,' your beautiful life? How phony can you be?"

"We'll start our own holidays. Let's celebrate the grape harvest."

She resisted his embrace, saying, "I get that Thanksgiving is hypocritical. But you can't assume it's meaningless! And if you expect me to detach from my traditions, you have to do the same."

She'd roast this turkey if it took all night, so its life wouldn't be wasted. But Enzo's heartlessness—to Tomaso and to her—climbed to the top of the list of the unforgivable.

PRIMAL STEW

After a few months, Stefano wanted to move into his house with Teresa. So Enzo and Sylvie packed all their stuff, fastened a tarp over the van's open roof, put Diana in back in her portable cradle and drove to Enzo's folks' home in Naples.

Mamma and Babbo declared Diana the most beautiful baby ever. Mamma declared, "She doesn't have my blue eyes but maybe she'll be as blond as I was."

Enzo went with Babbo to his office, Diana went to sleep and Mamma got out knitting needles and yarn to finish a baby blanket. As Sylvie sat with her, Mamma told about her secretarial job during the war at Alfa Romeo, the flagship company of Mussolini's Institute for Industrial Reconstruction.

"Babbo trusted everyone but me, the fool," she said. "But I've endured because I figure out what's going on."

"Wasn't it scary to have Nazis in charge?"

"*Eiii*, Babbo was a Fascist, an army lieutenant stationed on the railway. What did you think? If you didn't join the party, you wouldn't get such a job. Even now, if Enzo wants to get ahead, he must join a party. Besides, the Germans were polite. They showed class. It was like life under the king. People had manners then. When the Germans were gone, the rats rose from the gutters and took over. It's not good when commoners take over. That's why my children have had to leave."

She lost her place and stopped to count stitches. "Everyone said Babbo's heart attack was natural, but he was only forty. I knew better. They'd put something in his coffee." Sylvie wondered how many of these stories Enzo had heard as a boy. "It was *I* who kept this family from being trampled in the gutter by pigs! I made good money as a secretary. Typed a hundred words per minute and no mistakes. I bought the best typewriter I could afford and slaved night and day while he sat like a lump, never even changing his pajamas. He just shuffled around in slippers. We scrimped, we eked by for six months before he was well enough to get up. My children grew used to austerity and quit nagging me to decorate the walls."

Sylvie had already visited Mamma and Babbo's two houses that underscored their mutual hostility and dis-unity—this stark one in Fuorigrotta with its dining room table, stiff wooden chairs, bare floor and walls, in each bedroom just an armoire and a bed with a plain white bedspread. The kitchen held only appliances and a small Formica table. No cabinets, books, or cleaning supplies. Cords hanging from ceilings held bare light bulbs. Then there was the beach resort. Mamma had hoarded her severance package from Alfa Romeo until she heard about the new Marenostra development on a wide, sandy beach north of Pozzuoli. She bought a sixth-floor condo there with hand-painted ceramic tiles, a crystal chandelier and a balcony overlooking the sea, furnishing it with a sectional sofa, mahogany dining table and even a Murano blown-glass chandelier. No two places could look more bipolar. Sylvie thought of her parents' readiness to outdo each other with quips—a different kind of emotional disconnect. How much of their parents' dynamics did she and Enzo share?

* * *

Enzo's brother Giancarlo and his family came to visit from Germany. While Giancarlo's wife stayed at her parents', he brought their daughter Alba to meet Enzo's family and see his folks. The day had begun sweetly. Mamma prepared barley coffee mixed with warm milk for Alba, its aroma wafting through the corridor. At breakfast, Babbo put his hand on Giancarlo's shoulder and said, "Alba, I'm his papa."

"No, he's MY papa!" said Alba.

Babbo said, "Girls are naturally illogical."

Babbo's pomposity grated on Sylvie but she restrained herself—besides being his daughter-in-law, she was now his guest.

* * *

After dinner, Sylvie stood on the balcony overlooking the courtyard, eyes closed and head thrown back, gripping the railing. This four-story building was one of a group of identical buildings within a black cast-iron fence where roses, hortense and a glossy aucuba hedge corralled a triangle of grass. Smells of the fishy sea, diesel fuel and rotting garbage mingled with voices echoing through the thick breeze. Enzo paced in the dining room behind her, then stood beside her at the railing, an arm around her shoulder.

"I need to go out. Meet me when she's asleep."

"Wait. Did I tell you Babbo cornered Mamma in the kitchen and swung at her? He had her up on a chair screaming. Do you think that's OK?"

He squeezed her shoulder. "Put her to sleep—she'll be fine."

"Tell me you think it's wrong," she insisted.

"OK, it's wrong."

She told him Babbo had done something else disturbing. Yesterday when Giancarlo was out of the room, Babbo stuck out his tongue at Alba and she stared back quizzically; sticking tongues out was considered an obscene gesture, a prostitute's invitation. At lunch when Giancarlo was clearing plates, Babbo did it again and Alba smiled at him. Then when all were seated for dinner, Alba initiated the game and Babbo confronted Giancarlo, "What are you teaching that child? That's disgusting!" Alba buried her face in Giancarlo's side and cried. Sylvie retorted, "You're the one who taught her!" and Babbo had replied, "How dare you! Get her out of my sight!" Giancarlo had said, "Sylvie's right. I didn't teach my daughter this!" and scooped up Alba and left.

Sylvie now said, "How can we leave her with them?"

Enzo said, exasperation in his voice, "She'll be asleep." He started pacing.

"Speak to him. That's crazy-making! He's been trying to pick fights with me, too. He insisted the US Congress is uni-cameral. No, I said, there's the Senate and the House of Representatives. He kept arguing and then said, 'You should listen to me—I know!' So ridiculous!"

"He's an old Fascist. What do you expect?"

Hadn't Mamma said that exact thing? "You should be outraged!" Having observed Babbo, she felt compassion for the boy Enzo; but now the adult Enzo needed to step up. Why didn't he worry about leaving Diana in a strange environment with his crazy parents? Even if he's used to them, surely he knows they're unstable.

"Sylvia, come here." He embraced her. "Let's keep calm for the few days we're here. Everything will be fine." He kissed her deeply and turned to rush out the door, without telling his parents their plans. Sylvie chased after him, but he'd already disappeared down the stairs. She hurried to the balcony and leaned over the railing, but he'd already turned the corner.

She fetched a dining room chair and set it between Diana's bed and the window and prepared to read *What Was I Scared Of*, a story she'd recited so often she could read the words while her mind wandered.

"Well, I was walking out at night and I saw nothing scary/ For I have never been afraid of anything. Not very."

The droning rhythm and hypnotic repetition in this Dr. Seuss story made her put the book down and close her eyes, feeling the need to meditate, reconnect with herself. What would Diana do if she, Sylvie, disappeared?

Diana dozed off. Sylvie turned out the light and sat peering outside. Tires screeched and hooted and teenage boys' voices cracked on insults. When Diana's breathing had deepened, Sylvie tiptoed through the hallway. Passing her in-laws' bedroom, she heard them talking against television noise. She went to the dining room where the telephone crouched on a corner table. It was ten o'clock. She picked up the phone as it began to ring.

"Enzo? Where should I meet you?"

"At Cine-Astar. Remember how to get here?"

"Viale Val d'Agosto, right?"

"Yes. Next to the travel agency. I'm waiting outside."

She felt the urgent need to be a self, independent from everyone's pressing needs. Diana would be asleep and safe from her in-laws. She peered in the bathroom mirror to tidy her hair, then went and tapped on her in-laws' bedroom door. Babbo was yelling above the sound of a television show, "You do it all the time. Why?"

"If I'm such a bad cook, do it yourself."

Sylvie tapped harder.

"Come in," they both called. They lay in bed with light from the black-and-white television making shadows dance on their faces. Italian words flowed from an American actor's mouth in a sitcom she didn't recognize, a wealthy single dad and his servant, parenting two kids.

"Enzo just called from the movies. He wants me to meet him there."

"That boy! Why can't he act like a responsible man for once?" said Mamma.

Why hadn't Enzo told them before he left? "We haven't been out together in a long time. I hardly ever called a babysitter."

"You poor things. Why don't you move here? Diana should live near her grandparents."

"Maybe someday." She hesitated. "He's waiting for me. The movie starts in ten minutes, so I wanted to tell you so you wouldn't worry. Diana won't wake up."

Babbo threw back the covers, revealing his blue-and-white striped cotton pajamas. He muttered, "I'll walk you there." With effort, he shifted his weight to the edge of the bed and put on his slippers.

Sylvie stood up. "That's OK; I know the way."

Babbo stood up. "*Cara*, this is the city. Young girls can't go out at night alone. I'll take you."

Sylvie looked to Mamma for help, but her eyes were fixed on the TV. What kind of protection did this wheezing old man think he'd be? Sylvie stood frozen, unable to protest. Could she justify running out the door, escaping Babbo's ideas of propriety and overcoming society's pressing will? The feeling of freedom that had thrilled her moments ago drifted off like a leaf down a well. Her hand on the doorknob trembled as she watched him put on his shoes. Nothing she said would convince him she'd be OK alone on the streets. He'd probably say she'd been lucky so far. Babbo was unpredictable and she feared what he'd do if she crossed him again.

"Forget it. I didn't mean to trouble you."

Tears burned her eyes as she returned to the bedroom. She lay down, angry and frustrated, the voices of young men walking freely as she had done at night in a distant girlhood, in another world, their voices in the fresh night air throbbing in her head. At last she turned off her reflections about unknown peoples' lives and directed them indoors where the even breathing of her sleeping daughter drowned out those other sounds.

* * *

Enzo said he'd had discussions in a bar last night about Italy's dismal job market, even with his degree. And Mamma insisted he'd need to join a political party, preferably the Christian Democrats currently in power.

"It's bleak. Everyone's emigrating to America, Australia or Germany like my brother," he said. "But hey—I know a place that's sort of Utopian, an international artist community. I was there when it was forming, before I was an artisan."

"Why haven't you mentioned this before?"

"There's the draft, don't forget, so I must leave Italy." He put his arms around her and pulled her close. "But you should see this place."

Sylvie was happy to leave that toxic house for a Utopia.

They drove all the next day until reaching the coastal highway to the Italian Riviera and pulled off the road to look down at the sea. Sylvie imagined herself as a pinpoint on earth. If she disappeared here, who would know? How long would it take her parents to find out she was gone? The Mediterranean waters lifted her heart and carried it into and across the Atlantic to the coast past Boston, up and around into the St. Lawrence Seaway past Quebec and into the Great Lakes all the way home to Wilmette.

UTOPIA

Enzo couldn't remember how to get to his so-called Utopia but knew it was near Arma di Taggia so they stopped there at a restaurant, a classy one with white linen tablecloths and waiters in black. Enzo said they still had some cash but Sylvie didn't think they had enough to pay for full dinners.

"Here's how much we had when we left Naples," she said, "and here's how much we've spent."

"Don't worry about it," Enzo said, waving his hand dismissively.

She ignored him and ordered rice with butter and Parmesan. At the end of the meal she was aghast when Enzo offered the waiter, as compensation, a portrait painted by his wife. The waiter balked and fetched the manager, who couldn't resist Enzo's argument that his wife would some-day be as famous in Italy as she was in the US and reluctantly accepted. Sylvie was mortified. Enzo had just simultaneously flattered her and pimped her, acting like she was his property. Worse, he didn't seem to see any conflict with this and the progressive ideals he was famous for in Trent.

"Wait," she interjected. "I have drawings in the car. I'll pick one for you." She selected one of the archway in Nogare.

Afterward Enzo said, "See? That's what it's like to live as an artist."

"You must be kidding. That's the kind of Utopia you were talking about?" she asked. "Next time volunteer yourself." Like a man, she thought.

They got directions at a gas station that took them up a steep road that curved back on itself so sharply Enzo had to make a three-point turn just to follow it up to Old Bussana, an ancient stone city overlooking the sea. The steeples of Chiesa St. Egidio shot up above its sanctuary, now just an empty shell. They parked at the end of town overlooking fields of red carnations, a barrier blocking cars from driving down the cobblestone streets lined by houses, each a gallery with a resident artist. Bougainvillea lavished stone walls with translucent pink petals. Palms and rubber plants adorned balconies. Beyond the portico, a man sat on his steps smoking and Enzo asked who was in charge.

"Talk to Giovanni—the first house by the parking area. He's our unofficial mayor."

When they found his place, Giovanni was just sitting down to eat boiled potatoes and cherries and invited them to join him. He described how the International Community of Artists, born a decade ago, had continual struggles with local governments.

"There's no government here—I just have seniority." He forked potatoes out of the pot onto plates which he passed around. He peeled potato skins with his fingertips, eating as he went. Sylvie mashed some for Diana, who ate some with her fingers and slathered some in her hair.

"We've built everything, even installed electricity ourselves. The earthquake hit on a Sunday morning a hundred years ago, killing everyone at church. Two thousand died. Survivors felt guilty—they'd played hooky from church and later said the pious had sacrificed for them. But others said the Church had become corrupt so God destroyed it. Anyway, they went downhill to found another Bussana."

He turned toward Diana and held out the pot, saying, "Want more?"

Diana turned her head toward Sylvie's shoulder as if trying to hide.

"Prostitutes and thieves from Sanremo found hide-outs up here. So Sanremo sent men up to dynamite the ruins to make it unlivable. It was a pile of rubble when we got here ten years ago. But we artists came and rebuilt with the original stones. Whatever we insure is legally ours for ninety-nine years. We sell to tourists who think if you live here, you must be good."

"Are any buildings available?"

"The livable spaces are taken but there are spots where someone could rebuild," said Giovanni. "Oh! I know a possible place."

He put the dishes in the sink then led the way through the narrow streets. Almost every house displayed oil paintings in their windows. He took them to a corner house that stood across from Trattoria Belfiore, a restaurant with an outdoor terrace full of tables and chairs.

"A French priest lives here only during the summer drought. You'll see why when we get upstairs." They passed through two dank downstairs rooms, each with a narrow window. Upstairs was an open terrace with a covered kitchen. They gratefully took it and settled in.

* * *

They agreed Enzo would watch Diana while Sylvie went out to sketch the ruins. Enzo found a clothesline up in the kitchen which he tied across the small front courtyard and pinned her drawings onto it. She was thrilled when she sold three drawings the very next day, enough to go to the market down the hill and buy food for a few meals.

While she sketched, Enzo explored the town with Diana on his back. In Naples he'd retrieved a harmonica that years ago he'd stored in his old bedroom. He didn't know how to play it properly, but would suck in and out on it, interspersed with impromptu lines of poetry he invented. When he arrived at the street where Giovanni lived, he set on the ground a paper hat made out of a page from Sylvie's sketchbook, and expressed no surprise when people tossed in money.

During the afternoon dinner hours one day, Sylvie was inside finishing her drawings with colored pencils when Enzo entered with groceries, Diana on his back.

"How about cooking up some of your delicious *spaghetti al pomodoro*? I also got mushrooms for risotto. And fresh basil and onion and tomatoes for our favorite salad."

"Jeez, you must be hungry!"

"I'll feed Diana while you get started on that."

"OK, and if you can, sell some drawings."

"Beautiful," he said, and kissed her.

He fed Diana, put her back in the backpack and took off. Sylvie started chopping the vegetables and boiling water on the two-burner stove they'd brought inside from the van and set up downstairs. She relished this time alone when she could create some art and loved being able to make something from nothing and sell it. After a while she took a break to see how Enzo was doing but couldn't find him. She returned and finished cooking, then left everything on the table next to the stove and went back up the hill to look for new vistas. Later in the afternoon she found Enzo and Diana at home. The food was all gone.

"You could've saved some for me."

"I'm sorry. We'll go buy more." She was happy for more time to finalize her sketches.

The following morning Enzo shook her awake. "Giovanni wants to see us."

All the way to his place, Sylvie anticipated receiving another warm welcome, pleased to think maybe he wanted to be friends. But he shocked her when he looked at Enzo and said, "Everyone in town wants you to leave. Tomorrow." Enzo wouldn't make eye contact with Sylvie. Giovanni said, "Did you think no one saw you with Diana on your back, taking orders and serving food? Did you think the owners of Trattoria Belfiore wouldn't mind?"

Enzo said, "My wife's an excellent cook. Did anyone complain?"

"Wait. What?" Sylvie said.

"If they reimburse me for my expenses, I'll share the profit," Enzo said. "They could've asked us directly."

She was trying to absorb this, appalled—outraged—at how Enzo had used her without her knowledge. Violence of a subtler type.

Giovanni nearly laughed but said, "That's not all. Your harmonica playing gives a bad impression. And Sylvie undersells everyone."

Sylvie protested, "But they're just drawings, not oils."

Giovanni said, "You have until sundown tomorrow."

"I get it," Enzo said. "You call yourselves anarchists but you're just playing. All you care about is your business! We helped your business! We showed hospitality. We kept people from leaving town."

"Tourists want souvenirs and if they can get cheap ones, they will," Giovanni said. "This is the town's will, not mine."

Sylvie understood they'd broken rules but asked, "Why didn't anyone speak to us about this? Such a small community could be more friendly." Weren't those the universal rules of the counter-culture? This situation reminded her of when Miss Poppy fired her, saying she didn't fit in.

* * *

They drove all the way back to Naples and found a letter from Dad waiting for them:

Dear Sylvie,

In case you're interested in moving to Vermont, it's my turn to use the old homestead as your Aunt Iris seems to be struggling with it. You can live there if you pay the mortgage and insurance. Come here first to get oriented.

Dad

Sylvie had worked hard to acculturate into Italy and wasn't thrilled to go live in that gloomy house. Besides, Italy didn't pretend to be something it wasn't, unlike the homeland she'd left.

Enzo hugged her tight and said, "Having that house would be like owning an island. We can use it as we please. And I should get a good job in America."

She sighed, thinking maybe he'd help her make sense of it.

STATES

Enzo had seemed more relaxed in O'Hare than last time. He even said, "Nice hair" to a black man with a big afro who signaled back a peace sign with his fingers. But Sylvie felt awkward introducing this baby she'd conceived and birthed and nursed. It was proof of her body and its parts, something she thought Mom didn't acknowledge.

"Mom, meet your granddaughter," she said, proudly handing Diana to Mom while she removed her coat.

"Maybe I'd better not; I think I've picked up a cold."

Sylvie had expected such an annoying reaction. "Mom, this isn't just some 'lousy little kid.' She's your granddaughter!"

"I'm too young to be a grandmother," said Mom, already cradling Diana.

"Yeah, right," Sylvie muttered under her breath.

Mom and Dad suggested they stay a month as they requested social security numbers for Enzo and Diana and paperwork for Enzo's resident status. Sylvie was used to her parents' deadpan expressions but now their awkwardness saddened her, especially compared with Italian effusion. Jim, though, was surprisingly helpful. He found a temporary job for Enzo at his friend's small furniture-making company.

Although as predicted, Mom was embarrassed by Sylvie's breastfeeding, lacked any infant-care wisdom and balked at holding Diana, still she invited friends over, all of whom were thrilled to hold a baby again. Neither Mom's nor her friends' behavior surprised Sylvie, but Sylvie understood they all were surprised by her. "Of all the young women I expected to see married with a child, Sylvie, you're the last," several said.

"I agree," Sylvie smiled. "But with the war and all, I felt tired of death."

Aunt Hannah hugged her. "I think you're great," she said.

At the dinner table, Mom and Dad told about their trip to Burlington after Gram died, when Dad had to meet the estate executor with Aunt Iris. "Hannah and Willis offered to drive us in their Winnebago," Mom said.

"And their friend Albert. Hannah's known him since Ted Serios. Remember who he was?" Dad asked.

"How could I forget?" said Sylvie. "Enzo, this was a man who took Polaroids of his own thoughts."

Enzo asked, "How is that possible?"

Dad chuckled. "Good question. Scientists from Field Museum tested him. They gave him their Polaroid cameras and loaded their brand-new film in Hannah's living room. Serios got soused first. Hannah said he'd feel 'ready,' aim it at his head and click. They couldn't explain it. Whatever they asked him to photograph, Serios produced it. He was accused of fraud, though no one could prove how. That made him drink more."

Mom said, "Hannah volunteered at the Illinois Society for Psychical Research. That's where she learned about Serios."

"The point is, though, Albert is a psychic," said Dad. "Now I'm just telling you this so you know how someone else reacted to the Burlington house. It's not a palace. But it'll be better than wherever you've been living." Dad sipped his favorite vermouth martini with its olive and plenty of ice. "We pulled up in front of the place—you saw it, Sylvie, when you went up from Boston?"

"Yes, covered with vines, a big pine tree in front. I told you about it, Enzo."

"I planted that tree when I was thirteen," Dad said, rattling the ice in his glass. "Anyway, Hannah parked the Winnebago in front of the house and we all opened our doors to get out but Albert wouldn't budge. He said, 'That place has bad vibes! Sell it!' and refused to go inside."

Sylvie translated "bad vibes" for Enzo.

"This man thinks the house is haunted?" Enzo asked.

Dad held his glass in both hands and grinned. "Albert was a bit squirrelly."

"Squirrelly, all running around, *si*?"

Mom said, "His mind is."

Sylvie said, "*Pazzo*."

"Ah, crazy," said Enzo.

* * *

The Burlington house was as dark as she remembered, red the color of dried blood on a scab spread over layers of chipped paint rippling along the clapboards. The pine tree towered above the slate roof, its trunk pressing against the porch gutter, its breadth blocking any ray of sun that could brighten the gloom inside. It should've been felled but Sylvie couldn't fathom killing such a big, healthy tree.

She'd supposed having had relatives here would make her an insider with the locals so she was taken aback when neighbors greeted her coolly. Once when she was out front with Diana, Mrs. Grady said from across the street, "You're Ella Morgan's granddaughter? We hated her! Thought she was better than the rest of us." Mrs. Grady squinted her eyes. "Everyone said she trained her cats to hiss at people."

Jim had once said Dad likened Sylvie to his eccentric Aunt Edith who'd lived with him and his mother and sister. But as for eccentricity, Dad should talk! Unlike Illinois men, he rode a bicycle and tipped his fedora at all he passed. He visited garage sales and, despite Mom's groans of protest, brought home curios he considered bargains. He loved old tools, especially mysterious ones that he'd stock in his workshop, readying himself for any problem. His collection included the first electric pencil sharpener that swallowed up pencils it never returned, and an electric ice cruncher that spewed ice around the kitchen. Their performance appealed so much to his sense of the absurd that he produced them at parties and roared with laughter at their uselessness. Jim said when he visited Vermont, he saw a lot of Dad-like types, standing around a farm implement lying rusted in a field, contemplating it, scratching their heads. Since Dad had always seemed alien in Wilmette, she'd expected Vermonters to welcome her as one of theirs, but instead felt treated like a foreigner, like in Italy. It was as though everyone belonged to separate species and each intuitively knew its kind. Except me, she concluded.

* * *

Sylvie was surprised that Enzo struggled so much with settling in. He kept expressing annoyance that Americans didn't do things the way Italians did. And his hopes for using his Italian degree, equivalent to a Master's degree, were dashed.

"They say I must take some of their undergraduate courses. Undergraduate!"

"Maybe they want to give you more time to learn better English?"

"These idiots are so backward they don't realize what sociology is about!" he fumed. "In Trento we exposed power structures. Here they want to make people conform to them."

He bought a newspaper on Fridays when job ads were most plentiful and soon was hired as evening manager at just above minimum wage at a restaurant specializing in pizza.

"What a frigging stereotype!" Sylvie complained. "You're a professor for cripe's sake."

"It's as conservative and authoritarian here as in Italy," he said.

Fortunately the house contained all the necessary housewares and they'd brought baby clothes from Nogare and from Mom's friends. But Enzo's job expected him to wear white collared short-sleeved shirts. During a thaw they walked downtown to JC Penney's and bought the shirts plus striped bellbottoms for him and corduroy plaid stovepipes (not her style, but only two bucks) for her.

"You'll iron them for me," he stated on their walk home.

"Why? You don't know how?"

"I'll be at this stinking job all evening." He flicked his cigarette butt into the street. "This is what women at home do."

"And girls are born knowing this? Have pity on your daughter!" To Diana, Sylvie said, "Don't worry, Sweetie. You can be whatever you want." To the dour Enzo, she said, "Is it the house that makes you want to play this authoritarian role?"

"Quit being so masculine," he said.

This was another of his stereotypes. She wondered if it comforted him to revert to his familiar culture. Anyway, she wanted to stay home with Diana and be her first teacher. So she assured him she'd take on the task, deciding to approach ironing as an adventure. "But enough with the name calling. You're better than that."

She'd imagined the power of their love would bring them closer, but now it seemed Enzo just wanted to claim his role as *paterfamilias*. Besides calling her masculine he found reasons to call her stupid: "Don't you know how babies should be dressed?" "Don't you know about drafts?" He even suggested she give up her "silly beliefs" and love him more than God. She ignored his name calling just as she'd ignored Jim calling her shallow when she was younger, Dad calling her nutty and Mom calling her scary.

"My family liked to call me names. It won't get you anywhere," she said. "You should just deal with your culture shock."

Their lives split into rhythms different from the camaraderie of doing craftwork: Enzo slept days, worked evenings and joined co-workers afterward at their favorite bar, the Millard Fillmore. Sylvie spent days with Diana and evenings drinking tea in the kitchen with lights out, listening to the CBS Radio *Mystery Theater*.

After a few months of paychecks, they bought an old car he could drive to work.

Keeping house felt to Sylvie like playing with real tools. She visited the hardware store for supplies, smiling to herself when she remembered Enzo saying, "This wallpaper makes me feel like I'm being attacked by the inside of an old lady's purse." When she described the house's interior to store employees, they advised her to rent a floor sander and wallpaper steamer and sold her polyurethane and paint. She and Enzo steamed off ten layers of wallpaper, down to the house's earliest days, then painted the walls white to enliven it inside.

"We could build a doorway at the top of the stairs to isolate ourselves," she suggested.

"Yes, but then we'd have to give tenants another way to get upstairs." They postponed this project, which meant tenants would pass through the first-floor hall on their way in and out the front door. For privacy they'd lock the French doors to their living room; the back door would be their entryway.

She reached out to her old friends as if for a lifeline to a familiar reality:

Dear Janis,

Here we are in Vermont. I thought I knew cold—Chicago, you know!—but the weather here is deadly! No one's outside so it's impossible to meet anyone. But we have a place to live here in the US, that's almost our own. I need to learn so much! Enzo already knows so many practical things but I feel free-floating and disconnected. Bail me out!

A reply could take weeks, so she sought solace in the voices of ancestral women in the attic trunks. When Diana slept, Sylvie went up and read beneath the bare light bulb whose glow was swallowed by gloom, looking for clues about her family and their lives. She read letters, cookbooks and seed catalogues that inspired dreams of flowers and vegetables, relieving her from winter. Soon she'd chip away soil in the frozen yard and bake it on cookie sheets to sterilize it, an idea from the nineteenth-century *Queen of the Household*. Then she'd plant seeds in cut-off milk cartons and place them near all the sunny windows, whether on sills, tables, the toilet tank.

Another trunk was packed with lace-making magazines featuring intricate patterns, along with shuttles, cotton thread and delicate spiderweb tatting that seemed impossible despite the instructions. Patterns for underclothes were complex and cumbersome with their buttons and laces. In the quietude, she visited that era where a life spent producing goods and recycling byproducts required knowledge of the natural world. Those women grew food and herbs and used chemicals to make potions and medicines. She hungered to know what they knew.

And she pieced together family history, reading old IOUs and receipts—for a camera, a candlestick, a necklace and a watch—that seemed to have been signed by Gramps. A letter from Aunt Edith to Gram alarmed and puzzled her—she set it aside and would ask Aunt Iris.

Sometimes she'd hear Diana stirring and find her standing by herself with one hand on the rail of the crib, batting the other against it. She'd go pick up her chuckling baby who would snuggle against her as she carried her upstairs to sit on the rug and play with toys while Sylvie sat with her back propped near a window where a shaft of sunlight spilled in. Odd how Diana's dependency made her happy, while Enzo's increasing neediness made her forlorn, even angry.

After these attic forays she'd break the spell by tuning the radio to local stations that lagged behind the rest of the country. "Hooked on a Feeling" played all the time. Her once-favorite singers Joni Mitchell and James Taylor had grown commercial. If "Seasons in the Sun" by Terry Jacks came on, she switched off the radio—American music had grown stupider while she was in Italy.

* * *

Funny how the sunniest days happen when cold air cuts the lungs like glass shards. The moisture in her nostrils froze, her eyeballs stung, her lungs ached. She felt like a lone life form on a hostile planet but told herself the cold was invigorating. She dressed herself and Diana in long underwear, two pairs of socks, pile-lined boots—and finally understood Dad's compulsion for wearing hats. She put Diana on the sled to walk through the snow, smiling at the memory of when they'd found the sled in the garage. They'd bundled up Diana, sat her on the sled and headed off. And when Sylvie turned around to check on her, she gasped to see her two houses back, lying in the snow like an overturned turtle, padded by all her clothing. She and Enzo, laughing, rushed to rescue her.

When Sylvie got home, Enzo was just leaving and quickly kissed her and petted Diana's head. Sylvie watched through the front door curtain as he clunked down the icy stairs, touched by his struggle to adapt his Mediterranean blood to this cold. In his big, blue parka and oversized hiking boots from Helping Hands, he seemed so vulnerable she detested herself for feeling relief about his going out.

Today they'd coordinated so she could drive to Aunt Iris's for dinner. Uncle Simon would be out. Sylvie changed Diana's clothes, packed her dinner and loaded the booster seat into the car.

Iris decorated in Colonial American style, with oval braided rugs and pine furniture, an iron lamp with a dark green calico shade. Beside the swept fireplace, black iron tongs stood cold and a cloth doll lay in a pine cradle, its black mouth a few stitches, its eyes little dots of black thread. Bunches of dusty dried flowers sprouted from a ceramic jug on the mantel.

Over cups of tea, Iris held Diana as she told stories. "Aunt Genevieve was childless with lots of artistic energy.

She found Burlington society dull and took up art and painted wonderful watercolor landscapes."

"Like the one Dad has," Sylvie said.

"Is there something melancholic about it?" Iris asked, "Genny wanted to leave beauty in the world. Uncle Roscoe was deaf as a post. Imagine how isolated she felt, not to share the least feeling with him. She was so pleased when Edith wrote her." She paused and looked out the window. "Edith's husband Clarence was an inventor, with grand ideas, disorganized but kindly. After he died, Edith tried selling his patents, never suspecting the craftiness of businessmen. She showed one company his inboard motor designs and they asked to borrow them over the weekend. On Monday they returned them, saying they weren't interested. Edith later realized they'd copied them. They built the motor by the end of that year."

"How cruel!" Sylvie said.

"Edith said widowhood exposed her to a brutal world. She was poor except for that broken-down house." Iris poured more tea for Sylvie. "But she learned to make repairs. She even crawled on the roof to fix the slate tiles. Then she hatched the idea to rent rooms."

Sylvie had seen photos from the Great Depression and didn't need to ask how dismal it had been. After a moment, she said, "Can you explain this letter I found: Edith wrote to Gram, *Aunt Genny's dying wish was that I take the house. She left a tiny bit to you for which I'll pay $100.*' Gram must've been desperate to accept that."

Iris sucked in a breath. "They both lived on the edge, didn't they? I don't think Mother ever knew Edith cheated her. The irony is she'd probably have sold her share anyway just to pay for Edith's work around the house. To Edith's credit, she felt guilty in the end. I shouldn't sit in judgment, especially since she was always good to me, but I think willing the house to your Dad and me was a tremendous growth for her soul."

This comment about the soul reminded Sylvie that Iris had become a Buddhist when Uncle Simon was stationed in Japan. "Isn't it odd that Gram, Edith and Genny all died in that house? No wonder Mom and Dad's psychic friend felt bad vibes there."

"Yes, Mother was bitter. Edith surely felt guilty. Genny was lonely and frustrated. None of them were happy," Iris said.

When Diana awoke they all sat down to dinner, Diana in her booster seat.

"What about those IOUs from Gramps?" Sylvie asked.

"Oh, he made us so mad! He was brilliant you know, but couldn't live with Mother. With his radio program on Negro achievement and her using every racial slur . . . ."

"Dad said Gramps impoverished himself so Gram wouldn't come back."

"Yes! And he'd visit us and swipe the camera or a necklace and leave an IOU."

"Actually I saw those IOUs—I guess he stole from you?" She'd heard Dad grumble about his father. "So what do you think about Gram leaving? Should she have tried to stay with him?"

"Oh, Sylvie, it really hurt your dad and me, leaving our father in New York. He was so much fun, so creative. We weren't any better off, including Mother."

* * *

Sylvie was up, sipping coffee and reading the paper in the kitchen when Enzo called to her. He had lifted Diana from her crib and was setting her on her feet, then took her hands and guided her steps across the floor.

"Now you try," he said, letting go her hands and leaving her standing. Diana balanced with arms outstretched in front of her, concentration on her face. Together they watched her wobble across the room.

"Good girl! You did it!" they kissed Diana and hugged each other. Enzo said, "Isn't it fantastic how a person has the urge to grow?" Sylvie's heart swelled with love for them both.

When it warmed up, Sylvie would carry Diana in her backpack to the corner park. A woman often emerged from a house across from the park with a girl about Diana's age, and would bring her to the swings where Sylvie was pushing Diana. Sylvie and this woman, Linda, got to talking and within a week they were planning to meet at the park which soon evolved into visiting each other's homes. Sylvie enjoyed how Linda was interested in and informed about a range of things. When the subject of healthy food came up, Linda said, "By reading labels I realized the healthiest snack is Milk Bone dog biscuits."

Sylvie did a double-take to make sure she wasn't kidding.

"Claudia loves them! Come over and I'll treat you."

U.S.A.
1956-1970

THE REAL WORLD

In Sylvie's hometown of Wilmette, residents felt safe from disruptions that, if they arrived, came on the Chicago "L" to its final stop on Linden Avenue. Majestic elms and robust oaks draped the streets and elegant houses beneath their canopy. On the west side, Holsteins grazed and farmers harvested sweet corn, tomatoes and pumpkins, while the east side's successful business and professional residents knew they lived in the best place in the country. This is where Sylvie grew up.

Sylvie had a favorite spot inside—a window seat on the landing where the stairway turned. She liked to sit there and watch dust motes float in a beam of light, knowing they were souls, something she'd heard about in a Sunday School song. Once when Mom was on her way upstairs Sylvie asked, "Where do I go after I die?"

Mom stopped, regarded her, answered, "*I* don't know," then climbed the stairs. But Sylvie had seen souls so she knew.

An event when she was five—now walled off like a splinter encased in hardened skin—molded her outlook forever after. One warm summer evening, a month before school started, she practiced riding her blue Schwinn twenty-inch two-wheeler and made a sharp U-turn at the corner and crashed to the sidewalk. She frowned at the scrape on her leg, knowing her house in the middle of the block was too far for Dad and her big brother Jim to see and come help.

Righting the bike, she saw a man rushing toward her, maybe one of the teenagers from down Gregory Avenue whom she sometimes saw when she and Jim rode bikes through the alley. He wore a white tee-shirt and khaki pants, walking as fast as he could in his penny loafers. As he neared, she saw his pants were unzipped and his large penis was hanging out and now he loomed over her and told her to suck it and put his enormous hand inside her underpants, the ones printed with yellow bows and the words, "Monday's child is fair of face." In those few minutes, to whatever he demanded she answered, "No!" thinking he couldn't hurt her if she didn't obey, would realize his tricks failed and would give up and go away.

"No!" Sylvie said, looking into his sad face.

As he ran off, she thought she'd outsmarted him by making a plan and holding her ground. She walked her bike home. Dad and Jim were nowhere in sight. Mom was in the living room.

"I saw a man's penis," Sylvie said.

Mom asked nonchalantly, "Oh? What did you do?"

"I've seen Jim's so I knew what it was."

Mom's hand shook as she flipped a page in her magazine. Sylvie stood waiting, expecting her to shout out with anger or surprise. But Mom said no more. To Sylvie this meant she had seen a strange and maybe dangerous bit of life her parents didn't know about. They also didn't know about souls. Sylvie started thinking she knew more than her parents about how the world really was.

Anyway, she had friends to play with so she tucked away the incident, and only brought it out to examine now and then.

One such friend was Lori, who shared her love for horses. When they were horses, Lori always wanted to race the Preakness in the circular alley behind her house; she was Seabiscuit and won every time. But this didn't bother Sylvie because she wasn't a thoroughbred. She knew horses didn't care about winning but loved the feel of running and jumping. She leaped over hedges into neighbors' yards and nibbled leaves off bushes. Maybe she wasn't a horse when she climbed into maples along the streets, but maybe she was when she jumped to the ground from low branches. Being a horse was the closest she came to being a bird. Trees in the alleys helped her get onto garage roofs at homes where kids didn't live and adults paid no heed to the back. And there she flew. And as a protection for this freedom, Sylvie made sure to wear shorts underneath her dress to keep anyone from putting his hands in her underpants.

MONEY WORRIES

The morning Dad left for what would stretch into a year at Ft. Lee, Virginia, he stood at the back door as usual and sang out to Sylvie, "I blow you a kiss"—as he kissed his palm and blew—"across the room." On his way out the door, he really kissed Mom whose tears troubled ten-year-old Sylvie.

She asked, "Are you crying?"

"Of course I'm crying!" Mom said.

It was the only time Sylvie ever saw her cry. Mom had always been solid and sure and taught Sylvie and Jim not to cry but to take charge. Dad, a World War II veteran and reserve officer, had responded to a call to serve as the United States prepared for a showdown with the Soviets who'd walled in the communist side of Berlin.

Ten-year-old Sylvie would miss walking with Dad to buy newspapers and pipe tobacco, playing "Stinkfish" by avoiding cracks and sidewalk emblems, and walking along the canal searching for turtles and finding golf balls Dad bartered at the concession stand for Cokes and candy bars for her and Jim. But maybe, after all, she was getting too old for these things.

Dad's absence created money worries since the family had bought a new and bigger house. He was self-employed and his service obligation would cost him more than half his business. He'd asked Mom to handle clients but without technical knowledge she couldn't give detailed answers. As income dwindled, Mom launched a belt-tightening campaign. So if Sylvie left a room, Mom swooped in and turned off the light or the TV. On Sundays she'd fry one strip of bacon for each. Against the onslaught of Mom's harrying about waste and economy, Sylvie would withdraw to lie on the grass to watch ants and birds and consider how they arranged their affairs without money. How ridiculous that people who are supposedly smarter than these creatures need money to live! She became thrifty and stoic and learned to knit and sew clothes that Mom's sewing group admired.

But in her social world, Sylvie's homemade attire marked her among peers who were increasingly conscious of fashion and boys for whose attention they competed. Some praised her skill, others were jealous and others made fun. She wasn't sure what caused her friends to shun her just two weeks before summer vacation—when she greeted them in the hall, each turned away. They didn't decide to end the silent treatment before break, so Sylvie imagined a lonely summer. She needed a plan because if she sat idly, Mom would drum up unpleasant tasks for her. She sewed clothes and baked cookies or socialized with Jim if he'd let her, and Bobby, the slightly mad boy across the street.

Once she rode bikes with Bobby to a vacant lot. They parked in the alley and Sylvie tiptoed barefooted around broken glass as Bobby scattered dark green plastic army men on his way to the grass.

"Wanna see something cool?" He took matches out of his pocket then set each toy on fire. Sylvie was fascinated by how fire quickly turned each toy into a dark puddle but also frightened by this boy who enjoyed doing something so alarming. Coughing from the black smoke, she said, "I have to go."

"Wait! Why?"

Rushing to her bike, her left foot stepped on smoldering plastic and she stifled her cry so Bobby wouldn't know she was hurt. She pedaled home pressing on her left side only with toes, and lurked behind Mom's back so she wouldn't see her limping and make her explain what happened. Thereafter she hid whenever Bobby called.

She vowed to become more informed about the world, beginning with Ann Landers' advice column in the Chicago *Sun-Times* her parents subscribed to. Since she wanted to know what had made Dad leave home, she eventually graduated to reading the news, trudging through distressing stories about the Berlin Wall, Russia, Communism and Cuba, interests that would later dominate her thoughts.

Two weeks into the summer, Lori dared break her vow of silence and confessed they'd all agreed at Caroline's party (where Sylvie hadn't been invited) to give her the silent treatment because she and Caroline both claimed to like the same boy. Sylvie overlooked Lori's betrayal because they had fun together. One day they walked to the beach and found red flags warning that swimming wasn't allowed because of high waves. No one sat guard to check for membership tokens, the lifeguard stands stood empty and no one was in sight. They both preferred wavy days when they could body surf and today Sylvie wanted to ride those waves so badly, she ignored the warnings and led the way toward where private homes north of the public beach backed onto the lakeshore. They dropped their towels in the tall grass and ran to the water, wading until waist deep and gliding to shore on waves. While awaiting another wave, Sylvie glimpsed a distant beach cop heading their way. They darted out of the water and into the grass, not considering that even if he hadn't seen them running, he'd follow their footprints, which he did, and took away their tokens for two weeks and Lori's mom kept her away from Sylvie.

LITTLE BOOK

An elm shadow swept across her cheek and onto the cool lawn where Sylvie lay chewing the white flesh of a grass blade, looking up at clouds whose shapes evolved out of the billowy white, an old man's hooked nose and pointy chin, a rabbit with a body that grew longer then pulled apart like taffy, a shark with an open mouth that curled and crumbled. She was thinking about how at night she could see so many stars and knew they were suns like Earth's sun and wondered if there were planets like Earth with people like her. She'd learned in Sunday School that God was great and could do anything.

The fresh smell of earth filled her head, binding her to it, until pierced by the only thing that could rupture such peace.

"Sylvie! Come in here!"

She let her head roll over and face the window where Mom's voice hurled out.

"Sylvie!"

A bowl to lick? Chocolate? She pulled herself up from the grass and headed inside, moist blades clinging to her thin legs, pressing into her skin a pattern of sticks and flattened lawn.

The girlish ruffles on her mother's black-and-white gingham apron drooped like wilting petals as she furiously beat cookie batter in a bowl. She said, "Sylvie, there's something I want you to do."

"Gee, Mom. I was relaxing."

"That's silly. You're too young to relax. Your whole life is a relax."

"So?"

Mom said, "So, go up to my bedside table and look in the bottom drawer. There's a little book there I want you to read. Then come back and tell me."

"I don't feel like reading."

"Just do it. Or I'll make you feel like it."

The girl dragged herself to the stairs, imagining that Mom had been sitting there concocting this chore because Sylvie was having fun being idle and this was calculated to spoil a perfect afternoon. She trailed her toes on the carpeted steps and streaked her fingertips along the wall up the stairwell.

Dust particles danced in the afternoon sun like fairyflies, and cedar and lily-of-the-valley scented her parents' room. In the drawers in Mom's bedside table, Sylvie sifted through a pair of white gloves, a box of wax ear plugs, paperclips, pens, notepads, playing cards, dice, postcards, and a jar of face cream. She paddled through loose photographs, bent sheets of stationery and pencil stubs and found a thin booklet with a line drawing on its lime green cover and figured that must be it. Its title, written in script, was *How to Avoid Probate*. She took it to the chair by the window and sat down to read, scanning through text about money and wills, taxes and trusts, yawning at every page, making little sense of it. She worked through the tough words, and after a while put it back in the drawer and went downstairs.

Mom held a steaming tray of chocolate chip cookies in her black oven mitt. She asked, "Do you have any questions?"

Sylvie replied, "Is someone going to die?"

"Where does this funny question come from?"

"That book you made me read."

"*Made* you read?" Mom took a spatula from the drawer and lifted cookies off the sheet and onto a plate to cool. Mom had fostered in Sylvie a love of reading by reading to Jim and her when they were little, especially animal stories—*Dr. Doolittle, Wind in the Willows*—and gave Sylvie books she could read like *Black Beauty* and *Beautiful Joe.*

"Oh, I bet you read the wrong one! Go look again. You'll know when you find it."

"Can I have a cookie?"

"After you find the book."

"Can I lick the bowl?"

"No, it'll give you worms."

Sylvie hauled herself back upstairs. This time the drawer's charm was lost in a jumbled mess. She stirred its contents, not sure what she was seeking that she hadn't yet seen. At last she found another smaller pamphlet. She took it to the chair. Every other page showed a drawing sketched in acid green ink. Sylvie had been worried one of her parents was about to die but now found this new information equally disturbing, especially the line drawings displaying cutaway views of the insides of private body parts—a picture showed how the one enters the other and how the seed finds the egg to make a baby. Sylvie felt the hair on the back of her neck stand on end. Is this what that man wanted to do to her? She was aghast that Mom hadn't warned her right then about the danger; she now felt truly on her own. She flipped through each page in a daze, then stumbled to the desk drawer and crammed the book back and fled to her room. Behind her closed door, she squeezed her eyes together and asked God why He'd given men such power.

"Sylvie!" Mom called from the foot of the stairs after Sylvie had been upstairs nearly an hour. "Did you find it?"

"Yes." Mom had done this with Dad. How could she let him put that thing in her! And how could I be eleven and be popular and tell dirty jokes at slumber parties and not know about this? Do my friends know?

"Come get a cookie now."

"No. Thanks."

The image so offended her that she prayed a phrase she'd learned listening to the *West Side Story* soundtrack, when Maria has learned Bernardo is dead and prays, "Please make it don't be true!" with such passion, it must have had an effect. But when Sylvie returned to the kitchen ready to set the dinner table, she understood by Mom's interest in her reaction that this booklet was serious. All Sylvie ever shared was that she had read it, which seemed to satisfy Mom, oblivious of Sylvie's distress.

She now understood Jim's dancing around last year, saying, "Dad told me all about the birds and the bees."

"What's that?" she had asked.

"Making babies."

"Tell me!"

"Naw. You're too young. You wouldn't understand."

Sylvie lay in bed at night watching squares of light move across her wall. She'd recently realized the light originated with car headlights driving by, reflecting onto the wall by her mirror. She recalled noises from her parents' room that had awakened her—Mom moaning, the bed tapping the wall, Dad grunting. When she combined the pamphlet's clinical diagram with this actuality she was catapulted from blissful ignorance into awareness of a parallel world.

During those fretful times, Sylvie concluded she could change her attitude by playing with her perceptions. She even tested this: She'd walk up the hill from the beach concentrating on convincing herself she was walking down instead. By fooling herself this way, she didn't feel tired. When it was a month before summer break, she pretended summer was four months away and that each week was a month and the months were whizzing by. Once she felt she had mastered Time and Space, she used this technique for conquering Fear of Death and Loneliness, by concentrating and wearing away their edges until finally accepting them.

JANIS

Sylvie met Janis when sixth grade started. She admired Janis's spontaneity and was proud to be the only one who could make her generate a laugh that surged from deep inside like an engine revving up. They became inseparable. Janis joined Sylvie's Girl Scout troop which alienated Sylvie from the other girls because nobody liked Janis as much; but the two of them laughed together as neither laughed with anyone else. They laughed during the movie on menstruation with the broken soundtrack and the narrator's voice sounding like a monster croaking "men-stroo-ay-shun" in slow motion. The other girls turned solemnly to shush them so they could maturely learn how to prepare for the coming big occasion. At slumber parties they joked about the old black-and-white Bela Lugosi and Lon Cheney and Vincent Price horror movies on TV while the other girls were geared to be frightened. When Janis slept over, she went to church with Sylvie where they laughed during the sermons or at how somebody buttoned his shirt or pursed her lips. They laughed all through school assemblies presented by 4H and Junior Achievement. They never only giggled, they laughed.

They were both good with words and invented a game they called Pass, designed after a game Janis knew where one person draws a head and folds the paper over and passes it to the next person who, without seeing the head, draws the torso and so on. Instead of drawing pictures they wrote half sentences which combined to create whole stories, blending their two voices to poke fun at everybody they knew and everything they knew about. Then they would read them to each other and laugh until they were in pain and choking and blind with tears and their bladders threatened to burst from all the Wyler's lemonade they'd drunk.

The laughter brought them closer, so sometimes at sleepovers when everyone else was asleep and only Janis stayed awake to share secrets, Sylvie talked about being molested, and over time heard more examples whispered in the dark at slumber parties.

"Linda said her older brother used to make her take off her pants and let him feel her."

"I can't believe a brother would do that."

"Yeah, but she got strong enough to fight back. After she broke his arm he left her alone!"

"Remember Pam? Her brother would hold her down and let his friends go to second and third with her."

"Why would he do that? What a jerk!"

THE BIG PICTURE

Dad returned the summer before Sylvie entered seventh grade. He still invited her and Jim on walks but Sylvie said she had too much homework. When he asked if she wanted to see the Galapagos turtles Mr. Papatonis kept upstairs, she was sad that Dad would think a teenager, such as she now imagined herself to be, would be interested in turtles.

Though she didn't want to see big turtles lumbering through someone's house, she was curious about the neighbors. She'd begun studying them when figuring out which garages would attract the least attention from their owners should she jump off their roofs. There was a man who put "Keep Out" signs around his yard, and when his next-door neighbors built a tall fence, he moved the signs up in the trees. There was the man with three missing fingers who told kids he'd lost them to the alligator he kept in his bathtub. She was haunted by the woman who was burning a pile of leaves in the alley and when Sylvie passed by, the woman shrieked, "Step a little closer and you'll get burned!" Sylvie had understood it as a threat, but Janis helped her realize the woman was using sarcasm and so was the alligator man. Sylvie didn't get why people would say the opposite of what they meant.

Mom did her own study of neighbors. After dinner when it was darker outdoors than in, Mom took walks, allowing their dog Molly to run off the leash. Once when Sylvie went along, Mom slowed her pace and said, "Look at the pictures on that wall in there." She was looking through someone's living room window. Sylvie peeked, trying not to be obvious.

"They're all crooked," Sylvie said.

"Isn't that funny?" Mom asked.

Passing another house, Mom said, "Mrs. Fiske invited us all for coffee and I saw a blue ribbon stuck to her lamp. She said each week she awards first prize to something: the lamp, the sofa, a picture, the bannister."

"Is she crazy?" asked Sylvie.

Mom laughed. "Let's walk down the alley. I want to show you a backyard." It was fall when most flowers had faded, but here were pink, blue and yellow flowers along the sidewalk to the back door.

"They're all plastic," Mom said, laughing. "Mrs. Connor says she never has to water them."

Sylvie laughed too. She thought this was odd but maybe not crazy exactly—it had a certain logic. Mrs. Connor also plucked out all her eyebrows and drew new ones, higher up on her forehead, giving her a surprised look. She's brave, Sylvie concluded.

But school was serious. That year, her teacher, Mr. Cook, required the class to present news articles each week. Sylvie reported on stories about Cuba and Russia—Berlin having been forgotten—troubled that one country would want to kill everyone in another. One morning the white-haired principal Dr. Arnold solemnly entered the classroom. He stood in front of the class, gazing at his clasped hands, and said in his alien Southern accent, "I'm here to announce to you . . . that the president of the United States .

.. John F. Kennedy ... has been ... assassinated." He blinked back tears as he looked helplessly toward Mr. Cook.

Sylvie understood his words. Should she feel surprise? Terror? Surely David seated behind her, who once asked if her family had their fallout shelter yet, would feel safe. She looked toward Janis two rows to her right and when they caught each other's eye, they burst out laughing in that room of solemn, freaked-out classmates. Presentation by the awkward Dr. Arnold of such grave news struck Sylvie as funny. He dismissed school early and students obediently climbed onto buses that carried them home where presumably their families would help them deal with this tragic news.

Sylvie found Mom busily filling up buckets of water in the kitchen and rushing into the backyard to dump them on Molly who was in heat and coupling with a neighborhood dog Spot who only had to scale the three-foot-high fence to reach her. The horror of seeing her pet dog stuck to Spot and Mom frantically trying to break them apart disturbed Sylvie more than the news of the president being shot. She angrily concluded that female bodies, whether bitches or girls, were not private but open to the world. She knew her parents didn't understand this threat and couldn't cope with her angst about it. She'd have to fend for herself.

She left Mom to her chore and went inside to watch TV where President Kennedy was soon pronounced dead. Saturday morning when she and Jim usually watched cartoons, instead they saw suspected assassin Lee Harvey Oswald surrounded by men in suits and fedoras as an assistant on each side held his arms and ushered him down a hallway crowded with more men who seemed to be reporters and guards, maybe Secret Service. Then they saw someone approach Oswald and heard the shot followed by anguished reporting right there on live television, with all those people standing around.

"Did you see that guy?" she asked Jim. "How come they didn't stop him? I don't believe it."

"Yeah," Jim said. "Why do they have all those G-men standing around?"

"They must've noticed him!"

"Only an idiot would think all those officials couldn't stop that one guy from doing something so obvious."

Sylvie was overwhelmed by the question of whether adults were clueless or just pretended to be. But she remained aware and did what Mr. Cook called "getting the big picture."

WILD THINGS

Every summer Sylvie went to the beach as much as possible, usually walking with Janis, toting the tiny Japanese transistor radio Dad had given her while Janis brought playing cards. They laid out their towels and friends arriving later would park nearby. Sylvie tuned her radio to WLS-AM which made her feel connected to a bigger world. Those confident in their figures, like Janis, wore two-piece bathing suits, attracting high school boys, one of whom taught them sexual words for improbable acts which Sylvie figured he made up to shock them. Another talked about the fun of drinking, even of getting drunk. He introduced them to Danny, muscular and with a cute smile, who had just moved to town and quickly attached himself to Sylvie, to her bewilderment. When he walked her home and they sat on the porch, Sylvie tried to get him to talk. He surprised her by pulling her close and kissing her.

The next day she scrambled when she heard the phone but Mom got there first. "Hello?" she said and after a pause passed Sylvie the phone saying, "He called me sex kitten!" Sylvie took the receiver and heard Mom go into the kitchen and repeat to Dad that Sylvie's new boyfriend just called her sex kitten, and they laughed. Her parents

didn't try to stop Sylvie from seeing Danny, but they and
Jim teased her, especially after finding the 45 RPM record
of "Wild Thing" Danny had left by the mailbox. Arriving
home from the beach one Saturday, Sylvie walked inside
to hear, "Wild Thing, you make my heart sing, you make
everything . . . groovy. . . " playing loudly on the hi-fi and
her parents laughing that this boy considered Sylvie sexy
and wild. Confused by their conflicting messages, she
endured their mockery.

One day she went home with Danny. He asked her to
wait outside and not move while he ran inside. Annoyed
after waiting so long, she ventured in to find him sitting
feebly on a chair holding up his mother's head to drink
coffee he'd made. Sylvie's scalp crawled as she realized
Danny's mom wasn't just lying drunk under the table but
was also naked. Her heart ached for him.

She found respite in her best friend Janis who showed
no concern for other people's problems. They created
mayhem together. When Mom went to the hospital for a
procedure and left Sylvie "in charge" of the kitchen, Janis
came over to "help." They made chocolate pudding and
climbed out the window onto the front porch roof to eat it.
Janis asked Sylvie to get her a napkin and when she went
inside, she decided to lock the window trapping Janis outside. They laughed from both sides of the window until
Janis started removing her top and Dad got a call from Mr.
Larson across the street. Later, the girls conjured many of
their escapades with code words, like "chocolate pudding
on the roof" or "goldfish" (the time Janis convinced her
little sister she had swallowed her goldfish).

Sometimes during summer they would meet and
roam after midnight. With Dad snoring like a mower and
Mom wearing earplugs and eyeshades encased in her cav-
ern of sleep, Sylvie tiptoed down the stairs, avoiding creaky

boards. Molly stirred in her closet bed, rattling her tags as Sylvie slipped through the kitchen and out the back door, fixing the lock button for her return. She maneuvered two blocks to Janis's, hiding by trees at the sight of headlights, searching the ground for pebbles to ping at Janis's window. Sometimes she hoarsely whispered her mom was up and to wait by the door till she crept down to let Sylvie scurry to hide in the basement. Once they heated a can of mushroom soup on the stove and the smell woke her mom who appeared at the door just after Sylvie had scampered downstairs. Janis doubled up laughing, unable to answer, "Who's with you?" Sylvie felt free and in charge when at last outside they'd wander, the antique streetlamps so dim they could walk past someone and not clearly see their face.

FETAL PIG

Sylvie and Janis were in the same high school biology class where students got to pick lab partners and they chose each other. They watched films of cross-eyed microscopic worms and laughed silently, shaking so hard they couldn't hear the narrator. They struggled to focus their microscope on the moving object that often turned out to be an eyelash or the slide glue. Once when dissecting a fetal pig, Janis clapped her hand to her mouth and spit her gum into it. She went to stick it under the desk, but Sylvie nudged her and pointed with the scalpel to a spot in the pig's cavity, on the upper right. Janis molded the gum into a kidney and nestled it in place. They sat back, satisfied, then glanced at each other, bit the insides of their cheeks to keep from laughing, and raised their hands.

Mr. McComb, short, bald and earnest, darted over to their table where they sat with quizzical looks on their faces. "Girls?"

Sylvie asked, "Mr. McComb? What's this?" letting go of her cheeks to speak, then clamping down again. She pointed to the gray latex wad camouflaged among other organs. Mr. McComb poked at it with his scalpel, wrinkling his forehead.

"Why, that's the, um, that's the . . . ah, er . . . that—looks—like . . . that appears to be the—ah, the testes!"

Still biting hard, they nodded, eyes fixed on the gum. Janis mechanically wrote "testes" on their pig chart, and Mr. McComb skittered back to his desk to announce clean up. Sylvie put the pig in its plastic bag of formaldehyde that over the weeks had mixed with floating pig essence to make a gray gravy. The bell rang. The girls continued biting their cheeks until they got to their lockers and let go and doubled over with laughter. Sylvie had canker sores for a week.

Sylvie had already learned from Dad, teachers and textbooks that science wasn't girl territory, so she took other classes more seriously than biology with the scatter-brained Mr. McComb. In English when reading Thoreau's challenge to simplify, she vowed to become self-sufficient. Upon turning sixteen, she got a summer job at the Jewel Food Store and saved almost every cent, vaguely thinking it'd help her become independent. Yet money was the root of most problems and she had begun to despise the idea of it. She shopped at rummage sales, intending her wardrobe as a protest against the obsession with wealth and status.

She hungered to know about the world and with Mom's blessings rode the L on weekends to the Art Institute with Janis or Lori and to Orchestra Hall when Aunt Hannah gave her tickets to piano recitals. Both places had a sanctified air.

But from the train she saw a poverty she'd never seen before and felt a tug on her conscience. Her parents complained money was tight, but it wasn't like this. She felt sorry and wanted to do something to make things better so she joined the after-school social services club where students traveled by bus into the city to tutor low-income kids. Saul Hermann, a thin boy with terrible posture and little muscle, was involved. He awed her with his eloquence and she was touched by how his mop of kinky hair weighed down his head and hunched his shoulders. He was bookish, the opposite of the type of boy that typically appealed to Wilmette girls.

* * *

Sylvie and Janis sprawled on the bedroom floor drawing colored pictures of the bodily systems of the fetal pig.

Sylvie said, "I've been bothered a lot about something."

Janis stopped drawing, brushed her chestnut hair away from her eyes and looked up. "Nothing ever bothers you!"

"I told you about seeing Danny's alcoholic mom under the table. That bothered me."

"Yeah?" said Janis. "What else?"

"Sometimes I get this feeling that I'm not really *there*."

"You mean, like no one hears you?"

"Sort of. More like my body is separate from my *self*. Like my self is missing."

"Oh!" Janis said, "You have to meet Bill Cole! He talks about stuff like that."

Sylvie had been labeling the intestines and put down her pencil. "OK. Introduce me." She hoped Janis was right that this guy might have insight about her feeling.

The following week per Janis's arrangements, Sylvie and Bill stood awkwardly appraising each other. Sylvie was struck by how he, a senior, seemed more man than boy. He said, "How about if I pick you up Saturday?"

He arrived in a Mustang convertible and charmed Mom with his perfect manners. He drove Sylvie up Sheridan Road and showed off his finesse navigating the ravine's S-curves. The October sky was clear and blue while brown leaves scurried across the road.

Sylvie said, "Janis said you'd understand when I told you sometimes I feel like I'm not really there."

"Oh yeah! Alienation. Later I'll tell you ways to deal with that." They were having too much fun to dwell on it now.

When Bill's friend came to town, Janis and Sylvie double-dated with them to attend the senior dance. But first, they all went to a party at the Hermanns'. One of the few things Sylvie remembered about that evening was guzzling a tumbler of vodka and ginger ale Bill handed her. Her other memory was lying on the floor laughing as the Hermanns' dog nipped at her. They never got to the dance. Because Sylvie kept throwing up in and on Bill's car, he drove her to Janis's house (her parents were out) to sober her up and so Janis could dress her in clean clothes before taking her home.

Sylvie woke in the morning, reeking of vomit. Pain pounded her head. She burned with shame as she pulled back the covers and saw the strange pair of red and blue plaid corduroy pants and lacy white blouse she wore. She heard Mom creaking the floorboards outside her door and called, "I'm sorry, Mom."

Mom in her faded bathrobe opened the door. "You damned well better be! Your days of dating upperclassmen are done!"

It took Mom a week to track down the Hermanns who said they'd been in Europe and knew nothing about the party but they pressured their older son Michael to reveal that they'd gotten the alcohol from a gas station attendant in Glencoe who bought booze on request for them. The Hermanns pressed charges against D. J. Brown who was arrested and held in detention.

At school, Sylvie was mortified to hear rumors Bill was spreading about how he'd scored with her. Was that his antidote for her alienation? That jerk had used her!

Boys stopped her in the halls and said, "Hey, Bill told me about your wild date."

"Yeah? Did he also tell you I threw up ham and peas all over his car?"

Another said, "Hey, party girl! Go out with me?" and she replied, "Sure! Mind if I throw up ham and peas in your car too?"

Another said, "So you like going down?" and she retorted, "Did Bill tell you? My dinner liked going down all over his lap."

"I'm getting even," she told Janis. "Wanna help?"

Janis laughed at its craziness and said she'd do it, so in biology class when they were supposed to be working on their report, they cut the ears off the pig—dry and bloodless they looked like pink triangular crackers. On a piece of plain white paper, Sylvie used her non-dominant hand to disguise the handwriting and wrote, "Dear Bill, Bail me out! It's all your fault. Signed (in blood) D. J. Brown." To simulate blood she used a red ink pen. She put the paper on the floor and moved it around with her foot, thinking letters probably got dirty in jail, and folded it around the pig ears. She addressed the envelope to Bill's house, wrote "City Jail" as the return address, and dirtied the envelope too. Should they get caught, she made sure to implicate Janis by having her fold the letter around the ears, put them in the envelope and seal it.

Some weeks later Janis heard from Bill's brother that Bill received a letter and had been afraid to leave the house for two weeks. For a long time after that, all the girls had to do to collapse in laughter was say, "Bail me out!"

ANTI

During spring break in eleventh grade, the church youth minister convened Sylvie's group to tell them civil rights pacifist leader Martin Luther King had been killed and to discuss what that meant, especially since Rev. Bradford had marched on Selma with King a few years ago. Mom and Dad's silence about the assassination supported her view that they lived in a bubble, whereas some of her friends had seen King in Hubbard Woods a few years ago with their parents.

"Everyone around here is so pleased with themselves," she told Janis. "They think they own the world and are better than everyone else."

"Well, we are lucky," said Janis.

"Sure. And we can all act like there's no child molesters on the streets in broad daylight."

Janis said, "Oh, let's just go on the roof and eat chocolate pudding!"

Sylvie was sorry Janis didn't care but couldn't help laughing.

At school the activists among the tutoring group wanted to address the assassination. Some knew sympathetic adults who also wanted to organize and by the end of the week People to Overcome White Racism—POWR—was born. Saul Hermann was involved too. She cringed when he teased her about getting his brother Michael in trouble. The first meeting was at the Hermanns'; she was relieved they were so gracious. She sat on the polished floor trying to listen to the discussion but was distracted by Saul sprawling on the rug, flipping through albums. Judging by his floppy hair and secretive expression, she knew he smoked pot, something she wanted to try. Maybe he even took LSD.

During lunch period she started sitting with Saul and POWR members. They decided to protest the Jewel Food Store chain's plans to raze black Chicago neighborhoods to build stores and import suburban white employees. Adult members had explained this is how racism looks when it's just part of "doing business."

Clear weather ensured a good turnout for their protest in a local Jewel parking lot. They passed out leaflets informing shoppers they were supporting a racist company. Most accepted the flyer or just kept walking but some reactions outraged Sylvie: A man asked, "What's a nice girl like you doing this for?" A Lincoln Continental with tinted windows drove to where protestors stood holding placards, its push-button window inching down to reveal a woman with coiffed white hair who creaked, "You're all a bunch of assholes!" Sylvie loved the chivalry of her math teacher, Mr. Chachem, slight with frizzy red hair and pressed clothes. When a man yanked at Mrs. Chachem's sign and she yelled at him to let go, puny Mr. Chachem scurried over and punched him in the nose.

In the locker room between gym classes, Sylvie saw Camille, who revealed what she knew of a darker side to student-teacher relationships.

"I need to tell you about that teacher, Mr. Snider, who's in POWR," she said. "He's been handing me these gross letters when he gives back my work, asking me to pose for him."

Another classmate was bragging about sleeping with the new English teacher, Mr. Madison, who also led after-school "sensitivity encounter groups" at his home, supposedly to help students become more open and honest. He insisted that in order to get the most benefit, everyone should strip, turn out the lights, sit in a circle and feel the people next to them. The social services teacher was fired for climbing into bed with a boy on the Appalachia service trip during break. One of Saul's friends slept with a married woman who donated to POWR. Though Sylvie was scandalized, she tried not to be.

* * *

Mom hosted her Stitch-and-Bitch group, who sat mending at the dining room table where the light was best. Sylvie studied in the living room, ready for when they asked to "borrow" her "young eyes" to thread needles. She didn't have to wait long.

"Honey, help me out, would you, dear?" Mrs. Fiske was fumbling with a very small needle.

Sylvie took it from her. "It'd help to snip the thread so it's not frayed," she explained, doing so.

"Sylvie, Camille went on an exchange to Quebec last summer," Mrs. Connor said. "Have you thought about something like that?" Despite how Mrs. Connor plucked out all her eyebrows and planted plastic flowers in her yard, her daughter was cool.

"Not really. Did she like it?"

"Loved it! She and her host family still write each other."

"We should look into it," Mom said. Intrigued, Sylvie started researching Quebec.

* * *

Rev. Bradford cited Christ's non-violent message in anti-war sermons and was enrolling black families in their church, inspired by King's claim that Sunday morning is the most segregated hour in the country. But the church, like everything else, had grown combative. As more black members attended, fewer white ones did, until finally the laity held a vote of confidence. In reaction, Rev. Bradford resigned.

"It's all bull!" Sylvie told Mom. What makes these people think they're so great?" She quit too.

Soon after, she received a letter from Aunt Iris.

Sylvie Dear,

I hear you've decided to leave your church. I always thought you were an old soul and trust you've been prompted to embark on a spiritual journey to find the Truth. Maybe your dad told you I did something similar as a young woman.

* * *

They were studying the *Myth of Sisyphus* in Mrs. Bolan's English class. Sylvie liked how Camus said to be aware of your motives and remake yourself in every decision. That's what she'd do! How often had fear—of the unknown, of gossip, of being wrong—motivated her? Somehow she didn't associate her molestation with sex and no longer feared sex but did fear the disruption of pregnancy. What if she flirted with that fear by losing her virginity? But with whom? Saul! She considered him a reasonable friend and was attracted to his brooding dark side, like Danny's. That dark side was another fearful thing she sought to overcome.

On an afternoon when Saul's mom was out, she and Saul lay half-naked on his bed. She pulled away from his urgency and said, "I don't want to get pregnant."

Saul lay back, sighing. "But that's what rubbers are for. You can't take a shower in a raincoat."

"Where did you read that? Ann Landers?" She'd read in Ann Landers that even with rubbers it was possible to get pregnant. But in that moment against the feel of his skin and amid their desire, it was all the convincing she needed.

Triumphant about conquering that silly fear, she took every opportunity to do it with him again.

* * *

That summer, Sylvie went on the student exchange in Quebec that Camille had done, living with a French-speaking family in Montreal's Outremont section. She attended classes and gained confidence in her ability to get along in another language. The Francophone parents were interested in leftist politics: The mom took her daughter and Sylvie to the Swiss Hat and the Asociacion Espanola on Sherbroke Street, with its red-and-white tablecloths and flamenco dancers, where authors often appeared and spoke. Sylvie was captivated by speakers—known in the States only as draft dodgers—who lectured on what they'd learned about the politics of Vietnam.

Back home at dinner Sylvie said, "My French teacher always said they don't speak real French in Canada. But we all understood each other."

"Good for you!" Mom said. "Canadians are so civilized."

"*Ah, oui*," said Dad.

"I had a friend from Canada," Mom said. "A race walker. She'd roll up her clothes into little balls when she packed."

"Where is she now?" Sylvie asked.

"Oh, I broke up with her brother which made her mad so I never saw her after that."

"*Ooh-la-la*, Mom!"

"Your mother became smitten with me," Dad said, sipping his martini.

"And you know, French is the language of diplomacy," Mom said, looking askance at Dad.

Sylvie recounted the draft dodgers' talks and asked, "Wouldn't you rather that Jim went to Canada than Vietnam? That's what I'd do. This war is a farce."

Dad expressed his disagreement so vociferously that Mom said the arguing was giving her ulcers as well as migraines. Jim as usual didn't engage.

Sylvie usually told her parents exactly where she was going, but when Saul's parents were in Europe, she arranged to spend the night with him, concocting a cover story with Janis. Saul had gotten some LSD, something she feared but was curious about. He said she'd need at least twelve hours to come down from the high. Before they took it, he shared advice from his brother Michael who'd had his first acid trip with a guide: "You'll see things as they really are, so just accept it. Being rigid will freak you out because it means you're stuck or uptight or judgmental." The drug gave her a heightened sense of beauty, what seemed like a hyper-awareness of how everything fit together. But she knew she shouldn't do it again.

* * *

During the final weeks of summer they explored downtown. They bought secondhand clothes at the Maxwell Street flea market and went to the Festival of Love in Lincoln Park, a "be-in" of anti-war and pro-civil rights protests ahead of the upcoming Democratic National Convention. As they waited to cross Eugenie, a police van drove by with a cop on the back bumper shaking a fist and yelling at them, "We're going to get your ass!"

Shaken, she turned to Saul, "Do they think we're someone else?" He shrugged.

They popped into a bookstore where the cashier said, "I'm all for you Yippies."

Now Sylvie was offended at being stereotyped. "What the heck are Yippies?"

"Y-I-P. The Youth International Party."

When they were out the door, she asked Saul, "What do you know about Yippies?"

"Just that they know how to publicize. Shit, the Festival of Life? It's all street theater."

In Lincoln Park, they passed groups of young people playing instruments, singing, juggling, picnicking, giving speeches, sunbathing, smoking pot and making out. Some chanted "OM" and played drums, others invited people to help send peaceful vibrations and love to Mayor Daley who seemed anxious to batter them. Theater, yes, but also life affirming. She relished the array of flashy, free and inventive clothes, wild hairstyles, unusual behaviors that showed maybe you *can* do anything! Throughout the park, speakers expressed outrage that their generation was dying in a senseless war, detailed how the draft exploited poor, uneducated minorities, derided artificial ways people interrelated, demanded psychic liberation, and criticized consumerism. Someone in camouflage shouted, "Who do you think is fighting this war! It ain't the children of congressmen. It ain't the silent majority's children. It's black folk!" Some New Trier boys too had drifted off to Vietnam. One never returned, another came back an old man and took a job pumping gas.

Walking to the L, Sylvie shivered at the sight of military tanks and cops in riot gear behind a police depot. And later, when watching the convention on TV with Saul and his parents, none was surprised to see police clobbering protestors and subduing them with tear gas.

Mr. Hermann said, "It's a tactic of Italian fascists: infiltrate a peaceful demonstration, provoke a violent reaction from the police and blame the protestors."

"Isn't that illegal?" Sylvie asked.

He replied, "First Amendment protection."

"It's dishonest," Sylvie concluded.

* * *

After Saul left for college in Boston, Sylvie faced senior year more focused on the world outside school walls than within, as the curriculum seemed detached from reality. She helped organize talks and "teach-ins" for POWR, and was excited when the new Social Service Club advisor Mr. Evans invited her to join an experimental cultural exchange project in which he and his friend Yvette, a white social worker, would pair white suburban students with black Western High students in Chicago to co-tutor disadvantaged children. Sylvie and her partner Althea agreed they'd teach phonics to their three fourth graders, although the school was teaching sight reading. They quickly saw results.

But after two months, Yvette said she suspected the white students' motives. Staring sternly at the assembled students, she said, "Do we all know what the King assassination signifies for our community?"

"Yeah, we're at war," said a Western High boy, "against the white man who keeps us in the ghetto."

"And sends us to Vietnam," said another.

"What do you white kids have to say?" asked Yvette.

"Racism is a huge problem," a New Trier boy said, "but isn't it also racist to lump all white people together?"

"That's bullshit," said a Western High girl. "Just more excuses not to do anything."

"It's a question of who's got power," said another New Trier boy.

A Western High boy said, "You come down here, throwing money around 'cause it makes you feel better. But if we had that money, would you sell us a house? Could we go to your schools? You can go back to your suburb and forget about our problems."

Their argument made sense, but Sylvie believed Yvette had inflamed her students. Wasn't their goal to build bridges? Sadly Mr. Evans pulled them out, pessimistic of the project's success.

"I feared this would happen," he said, adjusting his eyeglasses. They had stopped at a diner on the way home. "Yvette called last night and said she was worried for your safety."

"Don't you see she was stirring up trouble?" Sylvie said.

Mr. Evans took a breath. "We don't know what went on when we weren't there."

Sylvie wasn't convinced. "C'mon, guys. I don't believe this! I got along well with Althea."

A boy said, "Yeah, but maybe they told Yvette they didn't want us there."

Mr. Evans said, "I hope you all learned something, in any case."

Sylvie said, "Yes. Not to be afraid to do what's right."

FACE-OFFS

Dad had convinced Sylvie the East Coast was an intellectual seedbed, so she was excited when Boston U. accepted her and thrilled to be assigned to a room in a sophisticated brownstone on Bay State Road with two other women. To personalize her space, she went alley-picking as she'd done in Wilmette where she'd gathered framed pictures, a wicker chaise and the green corduroy curtains she'd refashioned into a dress. Now she found a large cardboard box and filled it with a green rug, coat hangers and a pink metal wastebasket decorated with two poodles. The box blocked her view as she carried it, so when the man appeared, it was as if from nowhere.

"Hey, you're insane to carry that."

"So how should I get it home?"

"I'll carry it."

"Then you must be insane."

"Right." He took it from her.

"You shouldn't have to carry my stuff."

"I want to. Hey, what's your name?"

"Sylvie."

"Mine's Rocky." When they got to the Student Union, he handed back the box. "I'll look you up someday."

At home she dragged the box upstairs to her room where her roommate Bertie stood, bending at the waist and sweeping her hair from sky to floor. Dad's word "wispy" aptly described her.

"What are you doing?"

"Hair exercises," Bertie replied. Her sparse hair exposed a white scalp.

"I've brought a surprise." Sylvie dragged the box into the room.

Bertie looked into the box, grabbed the wastebasket and said, "I'd love to throw trash in this!"

Sylvie went to fetch their other roommate Karen who was visiting across the hall, sitting on the edge of a bed, gripping her throat with her left hand while hugging herself with her right, gently rocking back and forth, epitomizing another of Dad's descriptions, "A slender reed on which to lean." She was from a small Connecticut town where weekend fun happened in a mall parking lot. They returned together to find Bertie lying within her bed frame, her mattress thrown into the middle of the room and bedclothes tossed onto Sylvie's bed. Sylvie would tell Dad she didn't find the East Coast to be an intellectual seedbed.

In bed at night, Sylvie would look out the window and through the wrought-iron fire escape. Traffic dribbled along the expressway below. Across the Charles River, a grassy park with ducks and sailboats promised days of idyll. But that scene was overpowered by neon lights reflecting in the water the cold blue "Jordan Marsh Furs" and smaller "Cain's Mayonnaise," corporate messages that made her feel lonely and small. Last year she'd seen protestors—even innocent bystanders—beaten by Chicago police. And before that, Chicago police murdered Black Panthers in their beds and King was assassinated while minding his own business. By the time presidential hopeful Robert Kennedy had been killed, she was so numb she barely reacted. Boys her age were being drafted and coming home maimed unless they saved themselves by fleeing to Sweden or Canada. Though as a woman she wouldn't be drafted, she too felt like a war victim. Was this the country she'd sung about in school, the one she'd pledged allegiance to? Was it redeemable? Or should she move somewhere better?

In the library one day, she discovered *The Diary of Anais Nin* lying on a table and checked it out. Though she admired Nin's artistry, it bothered her how Nin recorded her experiences at the expense of living and feeling them. But Sylvie recognized she sometimes behaved similarly, especially with her project of overcoming fears, and realized she'd done so for as long as she could remember— maybe since "that day." She vowed to live in the moment. To experience. To feel.

* * *

Students were talking about the huge anti-war march in Washington. Saul said they could stay with his dorm-mate's family in Bethesda and one of Sylvie's professors who was driving there agreed to take them in her VW beetle. Saul, who was taller, sat in front while Sylvie spent the six-hour trip in back next to the professor's farting dog. Since it was a free ride, she didn't complain.

Missing the friendship she'd shared with Jim before his male posturing derailed it, she'd written him about the upcoming march, hoping to convince him to oppose the war. But she felt betrayed when she learned he'd shared her letter with their parents despite her asking him not to. Dad wrote:

Sept. 1969

Dear Sylvie,

I was sorry to learn you intend to go to Washington to watch the demonstrations as we worry about this. I particularly do not want you to go to this one. The last one was rather safe for a witnessing but this one has the earmarks of both sides being polarized and wishing very hard for violence to occur and there you and others would be in the middle of something you only know a bit about.

Naturally you won't agree as to who knows most about what you are doing, but the disturbing thing is that little can be accomplished by large groups milling around. Assembly is easy but everyone is lined up one side or the other. You aren't going to convince anyone to change his mind by your being there and you stand to get hurt. You'll spend a weekend away from your studies where you can be heard as a voice working to correct inequities but that requires a dedication to long years of study etc.

Dad

Mom included her letter, saying, "Every decision you make affects everybody." Their pleas seemed old-fashioned, their advice boilerplate: Besides, at the rate the world was self-destructing, she didn't have time to spare, and certainly not "long years." Mom continued, "Jim said he's going on a charter bus to Washington for the demonstration but will spend his time at the Smithsonian." She felt sad for Mom and Dad believing everything everyone says because they themselves didn't lie. And sad that she'd lied to them.

In D.C., she and Saul joined crowds streaming out of the Metro station, funneling into a line forming for the march. She joyfully chanted with the crowd through town, believing the demonstration would change minds. Passing the White House, barricaded behind a row of parked yellow school buses, rumors rippled through the crowd that young Tricia Nixon was peeking through the drapes, inspiring the hope in some, like Sylvie, that she sympathized with the marchers and would persuade her father to end the war. She and Saul veered off with others upset by the Chicago 7 trial to protest in front of the Justice Department. She was surprised to find such a small faction, making them easy targets: Police tossed teargas canisters at them, but they ran, covering their noses with the kerchiefs that had been distributed. Only her eyes stung a little.

REAL WOMEN

Sylvie had called the number in *The Phoenix* classified ad and a woman gave her the address, so on Tuesday evening she hitchhiked there because it was faster than the subway. After days of not seeing Saul, she managed to conjure only a hazy image of him.

Lyn answered the door wearing faded Levi's and a men's embroidered Guayabera shirt. She led the way upstairs where women sat in a circle on metal folding chairs or floor pillows. Sylvie nodded hello and sat beside Lyn who said, "Last time, Jean, you were talking about the rape. I'm wondering how far you want to go with this?"

"I don't know. But I don't want my husband to find out. He'd never believe me."

"Are you kidding? If I told mine a story like that, he'd beat the crap out of me," said a woman married to a cop, flicking ashes into a blue jar lid.

"But Jean," Lyn continued, "besides your husband believing you seduced your rapist, what about *your* feelings?"

Jean paused then said, "I'm sorry, but I don't want to talk about it now."

Lyn nodded. "What we as a group can do is give sisterhood, and that should be a comfort. But we also have to keep raising our own consciousness and that of our brothers. This is all about learning. Most women spend their time talking about their clothes, hair, makeup and boyfriends. Wouldn't that tend to make us feel intellectually inferior? Aren't the ads geared toward making us think we must be attractive because our life job is to get a man? Why shouldn't men spend all their time becoming enticing? For that matter, why should anybody?"

Some women shifted in their seats. "That's easy for you to say in your ivory-tower world, Lyn. But we're out there with real men," said the woman in make-up.

"Oh yeah? What's a real man?" said Lyn. "If we knew what men thought they should be, we could support them. But if a man doesn't know who he is, how can we help him from remaining a child?"

"Are *we* supposed to know?" said Make-up Woman.

A woman who Sylvie figured to be about twenty-five spoke up. "Since you've mentioned children . . . ."

They all laughed.

". . . I've been losing my mind. I used to be an artist, but now I'm a mom."

"That's an old theme," Lyn said. "When you have family responsibilities, it's tough to reconcile that with your urge to make art."

"Lyn, this is one time I'm going to disagree with you. My mind is totally involved when I make art. It's not an urge."

"Point taken," said Lyn.

A braless woman with pendulous breasts beneath her peasant blouse said, "We let men be assertive because we're sorry for them. They can't have babies. Creating and developing human lives is the most important work of art anyone can do."

"Barb, I'm glad you said that," said Lyn. "Women have always been subjugated because they have the

119

babies. Because of that role they don't shine out in the history books."

Barb continued, "But if we proved we could do the same as men, if not better, where would that leave them?"

"Why should I care?" said Artist Mom.

Make-up Woman said, "I'll tell you why. If men all stayed home and raised children while we were out politicking or painting, they'd all become impotent. Or do you think we'd eventually become aggressive enough?"

"That's absurd," said Jean. "Women attacking and raping helpless men, like dirt attacking a shovel to make a hole in it."

"Listen to yourselves, sisters! That's a trap," said Lyn. "It's what Marx called 'wearing your chains willingly.' We are our own oppressors."

The murmuring stopped. Everyone gaped at Lyn in anticipation.

"I want men to understand women and treat us fairly," Sylvie said. "I remember when my brother asked me—maybe I was thirteen—whether I thought of myself first as a person or as a girl. And I said, as a person and he said he thought of himself first as a boy."

Lyn said, "Because he recognized the power boys had."

"I mean," Sylvie continued, "I always thought of myself as a human with a mind, and then a body."

"You're lucky if you didn't internalize those messages that said otherwise," said Make-up Woman.

"Yeah," said Artist Mom, "like girls can't roughhouse, play sports, get dirty, be loud . . . ."

"I always thought of boys as just so sad," said Mrs. Cop.

"Me too! They didn't have friendships like we have. They always seemed so burdened," said Barb.

"It's those cocks they have to carry around," said Artist Mom. Laughter swept around the circle.

Lyn said, "Who here has a son?"

A few hands went up.

"We have a responsibility to raise our sons differently."

* * *

After spending a night together, Sylvie and Saul faced off across the room, arguing the pros and cons of protesting. Sylvie accused Saul of abandoning his ideals which made him so angry he clammed up. Thereafter, he made excuses not to see her. She reminded herself she'd wanted Boston with or without him, but couldn't deny his role in her choice. So it angered her when, at the movie theater in Harvard Square one Friday night after she and Karen sat down, she spotted his halo of frizzy hair. They moved up to sit right behind him. Sylvie squirmed her foot through the space between the seat and its back and poked him, knowing he'd pretend not to notice. Karen couldn't stop laughing so she moved farther back. Sylvie grabbed hold of his seat back, leaned forward and kissed his neck. When he turned his head she could see, even in the flickering movie light, his scowl. After the movie he invited her to his place. Karen caught her eye in the lobby, winked and slipped away.

As soon as she was settled on his bed, Saul said, "Sylvie, my shrink suggested I cut down on seeing you. He says it'd be better for me to go out with other girls."

"Women."

"I think he's right. Better for you, too. We've been together too long. We're just used to each other."

In this moment when she knew he was breaking up with her, she went over and put her arms around his neck and said, "I know what you're going to say."

121

"That's the problem," he said, pushing her away. "You know me too well. It keeps me stuck."

"Yeah, blame me that you're stuck," she said, backing off. "I thought you were more than this." She felt like a stereotype—the first boy she'd slept with was dumping her before Christmas break. She hated herself for being a cliché. And was stung by his heartlessness.

* * *

After her anger cooled, she realized how free she felt from Saul's moods. And she liked regaining the time she'd spent waiting for his calls and traveling to Cambridge. Even during high school she'd been wrapped up with Saul and now regretted how much time she'd devoted to him. She spent her newfound time in the library randomly exploring subjects that interested her, and while wearing headphones in the record area, she'd leaf through books while listening to Coltraine and Monk. Sometimes she'd pick up books and papers left behind on the table which is how she discovered Wittgenstein's tautologies and Clifford Geertz whose anthropological research inspired her—she'd be a participant-observer in life! The world is a big research project. Maybe she didn't need college classes to structure this for her—she just had to do it.

Meanwhile Bertie said she was having a spiritual awakening, "searching for her inner beauty." She'd decided to become a vegetarian one day, and on another she wrote out and distributed fake $100 checks. Sylvie smiled, reminded of last summer's Be-In at Lincoln Park.

One Saturday after midnight, voices singing "Happy Birthday" wafting through the open windows wakened her.

"Sylvie! C'mon join us!"

"We're having a birthday party!"

Curious, she dressed, ran downstairs and opened the door to see a group of students including Jeff and Alan from her classes. Rocky and his girlfriend were with them.

Sylvie asked, "Hey, remember carrying my alley stuff last fall?"

He concentrated. "Yeah, the trash-picker!"

"Whose birthday?"

"Anyone's! Ho Chi Minh's!"

They roamed the streets without the purposefulness of demonstrations. Such freedom reminded her of her night roamings with Janis, without fear of being caught.

OLD MAN CACTUS

After winter break, Sylvie returned to her conscious-ness-raising group.

"Does anyone have anything else to share?" Lyn asked.

"The guy I'm living with won't marry me," said a mousy woman.

"So, why do you want to get married?" asked Lyn. "Marriage is part of the patriarchal society."

"It's the only way to protect your rights," said Artist Mom.

"Ditto," said Mrs. Cop.

"No, it's legal prostitution so he can get sex whenever he wants it," said Lyn.

"So? It ensures you're not the only one financially responsible for your babies. Believe me!" said Jean. "Don't listen to those free-lovers out there. They're full of it."

"No one's authority is better than your own. No one has the right to slough an opinion on you, and you don't need to accept it without scrutiny," Lyn said. No one dissented.

"Something else," said Mouse.

"Donna?"

"What I want to know is, how do you tell a man what you like in sex? I mean . . . "

"Or what you don't like?" said Barb.

"Good thing to talk about," said Lyn. "And it's the talking about it and being aware of other women's experiences that support all of us."

"I think it's a good question and I don't have an answer because I don't know what I like. I've never found out," said Jean.

"Same here. They always want to be in charge, even in bed," said Mrs. Cop.

"I'm too angry right now to take this on," said Barb. "There's nothing he could do to please me."

Sylvie cleared her throat. "This will sound trivial after all that."

"Honey," said Lyn. "Women always excuse themselves. Believe me, your voice matters."

"Thanks. My issue is typical, probably. I came to Boston because my boyfriend wanted me to."

"You're not the only one!" said Barb.

Sylvie smiled. "He said he couldn't live without me. He threatened to drop out and come home, he was so depressed. I thought he might kill himself if I didn't come here."

"You rescued him, in other words," said Lyn. "Go on."

"We've been together two years. Right before Christmas he said his shrink thought he should break up with me."

"Why?"

Sylvie choked up. "His shrink thinks he's a case." Saying this out loud embarrassed her so much she giggled. "He's even given lectures about Saul's classic symptoms. He told me a little of it—Oedipal complex and everything."

Lyn said, "Dear Sigmund. The major misogynist and oppressor of women in the 20th century."

"Yeah," said Peasant Blouse. "Can somebody tell me how I can convince my analyst I really *don't* want a penis?"

Laughter bubbled around the circle.

"Hey, if you change your mind, I know where you can get one. My husband's going to lose his if he doesn't quit cheating on me."

More laughter.

"What did you do when he dumped you?"

"Nothing. Cry. And I did real bad on fall exams. Then I remembered how he's into symbolic things, like rings and stuff."

"Typical English major," said Peasant Blouse.

"So I looked for a symbolic memento. He'd asked me to buy him a cactus at the Haymarket. Luckily, a guy was selling them so I got this tall narrow one."

"Phallic!" called out Peasant Blouse. "Perfect!" Several women laughed.

"Yeah. 'Old man cactus.' Its spines were white and hairy."

"So what did that accomplish?" asked Mrs. Cop.

"Probably nothing. Maybe something to discuss with the shrink. But it made me feel better."

"No small achievement," said Peasant Blouse.

* * *

March 1970

Dear Sylvie,

Any day now you will be receiving a box of cookies made by loving hands at home. These cookies are valued at about $2000.70. The 70 cents is postage. Savor every bite.

I packed up the box yesterday just before Grandma came by to have me drive her and her car to the car wash, then the supermarket and then the post office. Because there was a no-parking zone in front of the post office, I parked in a no-parking zone, left the keys in the ignition and said, "I'll be right back." I was, in less than 5 minutes. She'd already pulled forward into a recently vacated space, and had floored the accelerator instead of applying the brakes, resulting in her corrugating a 1966 Buick that creased the rear end of a Chevy which put a dent in the trunk of a Thunderbird, which is to say nothing of what it did to Grandma's Pontiac. The woman in the Buick said, "I saw her in my rearview mirror. I couldn't believe she wasn't going to stop." Hannah suggests we write a testimonial to Pontiac about what great pick-up the car has. Grandma was ticketed, relinquished her drivers' license and goes to court in 6 weeks. If this makes you feel a little ill, pass the cookies around to your friends.

Sylvie smiled at this letter, realizing she used to have trouble perceiving Mom's irony. The cookies arrived with another letter where Mom said she was learning to make buttonholes and blind hems on her sewing machine and had tried a yoga class and found it strange and had started reading the new magazine *Psychology Today* which made her wonder if the roommate Sylvie wrote home about might be violent. Aunt Hannah sent a separate letter saying she took Mom to hear a psychic talk about predestiny.

"Listen, Karen," Sylvie said. "My aunt says the psychic world is true. She did my chart and says I need to beware of 'psychic fallout' and should stay away from drugs because they add to it and that confuses the collective consciousness."

Karen said, "Interesting way to say 'don't get high.'" They laughed.

"But then she says her friend was murdered at a Spiritual Frontiers meeting, then the murderer killed himself, so she felt endangered."

"But does she say the murderer smoked pot?"

"No," Sylvie said. "But she seems psychic and wants to warn me."

"Like I said, it's a new angle."

On a morning they were late for class, Karen and Sylvie decided to hitch a ride up Comm. Ave and climbed into the first car that stopped, Karen in front. Based on his plaid shirt, Sylvie figured the driver was thirtyish and predicted he wasn't a student. "Na na Hey hey" by the Pioneers came on the radio. Sylvie heard the driver say something, the volume rose suddenly and Karen cried out, "Oh my God!" and twisted around as though trying to climb into the back.

The car stopped at a traffic light and Sylvie said, "Thanks, we'll get out here," and hopped out. Karen was fumbling so Sylvie opened her door and yanked her out as the driver was pulling away.

"What was that about?"

"Didn't you see? I was looking ahead and heard him say, 'How d'you like my circumcision?' so I turned and saw his thing hanging out."

"Oh crap!" Sylvie said, recalling Hannah's warning about psychic fallout.

"I won't ever be able to listen to that song again," said Karen.

"Glad it wasn't something we liked!" They laughed but Sylvie felt the confusion, fear and bravery of her five-year-old self. She asked Karen, "Are you OK?"

"Because of that loser? He was pathetic."

During class the day after the second-largest anti-war demonstration in New England, someone suggested they discuss the ensuing riot. The SDS and Weathermen had hosted an assembly featuring William Kunstler introducing the movie about Bobby Seale, the eighth defendant of the Chicago Seven, who'd been gagged and bound to a chair during their trial. Some frustrated individuals left and threw rocks at windows in the Hotel Commonwealth, drawing police to Hayden Hall where they waited outside for more troublemakers. Sylvie hated when people turned free speech into disorder.

Mom wrote: *"Mother and I took her car out to get an official estimate of repairs on Friday and it will come to $415. This makes the cookies worth even more than $2,000.70."*

GRAM

The break-up discombobulated her. She wrote to Aunt Iris about how it made her distrust her instincts about people, especially men. Aunt Iris wrote back:

> Sometimes it just doesn't matter who you love, but it's important _to_ love. It might not really even matter who you marry but what you do with it . . . . Why not come up for a visit?

Sylvie wrote back to arrange a date, and on a Friday boarded a Greyhound to Burlington, settling behind a bearded man with long brown hair whose shoes were off and his feet on the seat. Her backpack beside her, she unbuttoned her Navy peacoat, leaned against the spotty window, and unwrapped her long scarf to ball up to cushion her head.

As a girl, Sylvie had met Gram when the family drove east to visit. She remembered the vine-covered porch where hostile cats hid and mewled. Years later Gram visited on Thanksgiving and drank too much and threw up at the table, eliciting both gagging and mirth in Sylvie and her brother. She was different from her other grandparents, Grandpa in his yellow stuffed chair, Grandma in the worn pink brocade, sipping Old Fashioned cocktails and sherry. Grandma collected wise sayings she copied into a notebook and shared with Sylvie. Some were Biblical, others poetry, some German sayings she'd learned as a child. Out of a sense of duty, Sylvie had decided to take this trip to get to better know Gram and give her a chance to know her granddaughter. Maybe Dad's stories and her memories didn't do Gram justice.

She brought sunflower seeds and dried dates to eat on the way, but the diesel fuel fumes wafting through a window turned her stomach. She opened *Crime and Punishment*, despairing that she'd selected this book to write about for class. Reading and motion rocked her eyelids closed, and she fell asleep and dreamed Saul and she were walking over a river on a bridge that dead-ended and Saul approached as if to push her off. Her chin settling into her collarbone jerked her awake.

The bus shot through a tunnel of maple trees hovering like ghosts along both sides of the road. Dried leaves clung like desperate animals to their branches, lichen painted their trunks. Beyond them, black shadows huddled in green spruces and faded grass tarnished the ground. The lack of billboards made Vermont seem beyond human reach, a relief from the staged and prim Back Bay Fens. Sylvie stretched her legs underneath the seat in front of her, then let them relax. The man ahead of her sat sideways, the corner of his eye trained on her.

"Everything's dead now," he said. "It's pretty in the fall." She felt him searching her face a bit too intently.

"Actually I'm thinking how colorful everything is. Those branches end in red and orange buds."

"If you say so. You in school?"

"Yeah. You?"

"Stayed in long enough to not get drafted. Then the lottery happened and I drew a high number."

"Cigarette?" she tilted her pack, holding it so there'd be no chance he'd touch her fingers, and he took one. She saw fluidity in him, a warmth in his eyes like a veil over a secret fire. He held his head and moved his hands with grace. She guessed he was about twenty-two but there was something old behind his eyes.

"College was supposed to be intellectual," Sylvie said.

"Isn't it?" he asked, a smile playing on his lips.

"No. It's like I paid all this money and still have to teach myself."

"Hey, that's life."

"I sit in on classes at Harvard where my friend goes. The difference between my classes and theirs is mine are taught by nose-picking young women rather than haughty old men."

He laughed with real pleasure. "Which do you prefer?"

"The women, I guess, just 'cause they're women."

"Chauvinist," he said. "But I know what you mean. In a way I wish I hadn't graduated."

"Why?"

"Because the system serves the State and they hide their real goals."

"Which means . . . ?"

"They don't tell you that you're learning to be a worker bee, to sit and take orders and produce papers. Who wants that kind of life?" He reached over the seat and tipped back the book cover so he could read it. "Dostoyevsky? Man wants the freedom to break traditional barriers and define himself."

"He really makes me think," Sylvie said. "Have you read *Brothers K.*?"

"Yeah. Alyosha left the priesthood for freedom so he could decide whether or not to accept God and was the only Karamazov to survive. It's kinda like Camus."

The man turned to face forward, enfolding into his own world again. As the bus left the interstate and turned westward, she looked out at clusters of purple brick buildings set behind a wide lawn, paths winding through huge maples, students wearing down jackets and hiking boots. She saw leaves that had looked brown at first were actually gray, copper, golden and rose.

After saying goodbye to the man who continued north (and briefly musing about joining him), she adjusted her backpack and shuffled behind other exiting passengers. She followed the map Aunt Iris had sketched to get her from the bus station to Gram's. Delicate clapboard houses perched against the Church Street sidewalk, looking as if the spindles supporting their porch roofs would give way any moment. Amid melted snow, fragile skeletons of last summer's marigolds and chrysanthemums, surprised in full bloom by frost, crouched in the small front yards. Droppings of dozens of dogs were the only clues to live bodies.

Down Gram's street, Sylvie saw where a white pine jutted past the house's three stories toward the sky. A vine curtained the front porch, its old growth turned to wood, its tentacles choking the lathe spindles, gouging the clapboards, blocking sunlight, covering the porch save for a vault-like opening at the stairs. The red paint and white trim were weather beaten and flaking. Gram and her sister had raised Dad and Aunt Iris here, confining themselves to the damp basement and the gloomy first floor while renting the upstairs to strangers. Would Gram be watching for her through one of the windows? She ran to the bottom of the stairs then up the steps and knocked, waiting a moment before giving the door a push. Then she stopped, frozen.

An odor, like a forgotten time, overcame her and filled her with a puzzling sadness. As from the depths of a deep pool, she heard it, a voice that creaked the way a door creaked.

Gram called out, "Come in!" more commanding than inviting.

The dust smell enveloped her. Trapped stale air crept upstairs and down, hugging walls, floors, beds where Dad and Aunt Iris used to sleep, sliding down the bannister, over the eighty-keyed piano and under its wires, through the grandmother clock, the china knick-knacks, the stuffed chairs crammed together, the kitchen shelf filled with cans, through heating ducts to the attic trunks of papers and clothes, down the basement floor littered with butternuts and horse chestnuts from backyard trees. As the door opened, this dusty air poured outside as if freed from a tomb.

"Come in!" the voice croaked again.

Sylvie followed the voice across the entry hall with a wide stairway and through French doors into a living room. The wood moldings and floor swallowed the light, and the shade cast by the monstrously tall pine tree Dad had planted added to the darkness. In the next room, originally a dining room, Gram perched on a Queen Anne brocade chair, her feet flat on the floor, arms caressing wooden armrests as if attached to them, long fingers flicking. When Sylvie bent down to kiss her baby-soft cheek of perfumed talc, Gram grabbed her chin and pulled her face down to return the kiss. Then, lifting off the straps of her backpack, Sylvie sat across from Gram and a potbelly stove. In the living room she could see an oil of a young auburn-haired woman looking coquettishly at the painter.

"Course, you're not as pretty as I was. I had such beautiful hair—not dirty blond like yours—and so many beaux you couldn't count 'em. Why I married your grand-father, I'll never know."

Sylvie gaped at her. She hadn't before heard laments of marital unhappiness, except in the women's collective, and was only aware of one divorced family in Wilmette.

"And don't you look like your mother!" she accused, gazing beyond Sylvie and out the window, flicking her fingers. "You staying long?"

"Couple days. I have to be back at school Monday."

"Be sleeping upstairs?"

"Yes, thank you."

The front door closed and Sylvie heard footsteps. "Halloo? Here comes lunch! Anyone hungry?" Aunt Iris appeared with a paper bag emitting savory smells.

"Doesn't she look like her mother?" said Gram.

"No, Mother. I think she looks just like you," said Aunt Iris whom Sylvie hadn't seen for maybe ten years. She hadn't realized how beautiful she was, with a beaming face and curly black hair. Gram was glancing over her shoulder and out the window, as if she hadn't heard. Iris embraced Sylvie and asked about her trip.

After they ate the quiche, Iris said, "Come see my old room? Mother, we'll be back shortly."

Sylvie followed Iris, who floated gracefully up the wide staircase, nearly choking on the mustiness.

Iris said, "It's so good of you to visit. Your grand-mother has spoken of nothing else for days."

"Could've fooled me. She hasn't said two words."

Surrounding a square hallway was a bathroom with a claw foot tub, a door leading to the attic and four bed-rooms—three with a tarnished brass bed, faded Oriental rug, dresser, bedside table and lamp and the fourth con-verted to a kitchen. Iris's old room wore a thin hand-stitched quilt of tiny hexagons.

"Oh, she's just shy." Iris flipped on the light switch in her old room. "I know she misses your dad a lot. And doesn't know how to act around young people." She flopped onto the springy mattress.

"This room was my home-sweet-home for a whole year. And before and after that, a series of tenants lived here and shared the kitchen and bathroom. Mother moved us here to live with Aunt Edith when your dad was thirteen and I was fifteen."

Sylvie looked out the front window at the porch roof and the street below. "Where else did you live?"

"I moved to New York before the war and visited here whenever I could." Iris hopped up and led the way into the next bedroom. "They talked a lot about the past, how Edith had sat with Aunt Genevieve as she lay dying in the living room."

Inside the second bedroom, Iris opened a door to show Sylvie the bathroom with a new shower. "There was at that time another roomer here, Simon Anderson."

"Uncle Simon?" Sylvie knew Dad never liked Simon, thinking his beautiful and talented sister could've done better.

"Yes. We married. He was in pharmacy school, one of the few men not away at war, but the army took him soon enough."

"Who's Genevieve?"

"Your Gram's aunt. She moved here with Great-uncle Roscoe as a newlywed. She was a real artist—your dad has one of her watercolors." Iris bowed her head a moment, then lifted it, her eyes distant. "She died in this house, you know. So did Aunt Edith."

Maybe that's why this house felt so airless. Maybe dying in a place fills it with the last emotions of the dying. She tried to decipher the house's feelings. Depression? Disgruntlement?

"You're probably tired. I'm sure we'll have plenty of time to talk."

After Gram had gone to bed in the dining room and Iris had left, Sylvie settled into the back bedroom. She lay in bed for some minutes, then got up to explore the attic where black brass-edged steamer trunks lined the walls. Time felt suspended there in the quiet. She tiptoed to one of the trunks, pulled open its latch and recoiled as a mothball smell assailed her. She rifled through embroidered handkerchiefs, lace curtains, tablecloths, doilies and antimacassars. The next trunk brimmed with seed catalogs—so many kinds of green beans! Handwritten letters and postcards filled a third trunk. Thin spidery lines drawn in fountain pen covered some on top. She picked one up and read:

Dearest Ella,

I hope my letter finds you well. Am having a wonderful time with our Aunt. What a sense of humor she has, and so much spunk! We took easels and paint boxes into the fields and she taught me fundamentals of landscape painting. Mine of course was not fit for viewing. But what an eye she has! I wish you could see how she translates the homeliest of scenes into a luscious watercolor!

The weather is hotter than expected. Aunt Genevieve says you just never know. It really is rather a wilderness, but Burlington society has everything anyone could want—choral groups, soirees, dances.

Your doting sister,
Edith

She swished them around a little then picked up a couple of typewritten letters:

March 20, 1959

Dear Mother,

I hope you are well. Things are rolling along here. We've just closed the deal on a bigger house so when you next come to visit, you will have a bit more space. As the kids are growing, they seem to require more room for all their assorted equipment. Of course, the piano didn't quite fit in the den on Maple Ave., but now the kids will be able to play clinkers and our delicate ears won't suffer so much.

A jolting letter helped her understand her place in the family hierarchy.

1950

Dear Mother,

I'm sure I told you of the Blessed Event we're expecting. Actually, it did come as somewhat of a surprise, as financially with the new house, etc. it's not the best time for a new arrival. But we'll manage. Phyllis was quite blue about it for a while because she had worked hard to get back her figure and fit into her old wardrobe. I've promised to buy her a whole new one. We're kind of stuck on names. Any suggestions?

Well, that sums it up. I won't be coming your way this year because of the baby and hope you understand.

Love, Dean

* * *

Iris arrived early to help Gram wash up. They were in the living room when Sylvie came down.

"Did you sleep well?" asked Iris.

"Yes, I looked through the trunks last night and have so much to ask."

Gram fixed her eyes on Sylvie's and finally said, "I always knew you were trouble. You were such a naughty little girl!" Gram turned to look out the window, fingers flicking.

"Mother!" Iris reprimanded.

Dad sometimes related how Sylvie had offended Gram during their visit. She'd begun piano lessons and thought she knew something about pianos that Gram would be pleased to know—that hers was special with its mere eighty keys. But Dad said this had insulted Gram.

"I was five. I barely remember."

Sylvie was irked by Gram. She understood now why Dad grumbled ahead of his dutiful Sunday phone calls. He'd recounted how when he was stationed in the South before being shipped off to Normandy, Gram visited and wanted him to put her in a nice hotel and drive her around at a time when gas was rationed. Her beauty had accustomed her to being fawned over. Dad told how Gramps had been excited to show the family a farmhouse he'd bought in Connecticut and drove there with Iris and Dad in the rumble seat. When they arrived, Gramps idled the car as Gram yelled, pounded the dashboard and even swatted at him. Dad couldn't hear but Gramps, never stopping the engine, turned the car around and drove home. After that Gramps grew aloof, no longer catered to Gram and took low-paying jobs that interested him. Sylvie admired him for this but regretted he and Gram couldn't find a way to work things out because it created a troubled childhood for Dad. Gram packed the kids in the car and moved throughout New England, using her sewing skills and fashion sense to make and sell hats. Unable to manage money, she amassed debts and left towns before creditors caught up, forcing Dad and Iris to enroll in a new school each year. They moved about until Aunt Edith sent a letter saying Genevieve had left them the Burlington house.

To atone for past offences Sylvie asked, "Gram, remember when you used to make dolls and stuffed animals?"

Gram eyed her piercingly. "I remember giving you a doll and you said you didn't play with dolls. That's what I remember."

If Gram had any affection for her at all, Sylvie couldn't tell. And she was sad Gram was hard to love.

STRIKE!

Just before final exams, news erupted of student protestors killed by the Ohio National Guard. Death was creeping closer! Her college joined the national student strike against the war, with professors canceling exams and the college canceling graduation though dorms stayed open for a few weeks.

Mom wrote: *I went with Mother to court Monday morning. It was sort of funny. She was nervous as a cat but managed to walk up to the bench when her name was called. The woman she hit was there too and the judge asked her to give her story first. So she went through the whole bit about how Mother hit her and how she lost many valuable hours as a result and how she could have been killed. Then he asked Mother if she wanted to add or say anything in her defense and Mother said, "No, she's absolutely right, that's exactly what happened but I plead not guilty of negligent driving." She wound up being fined $15 and got her drivers' license back. When we left the courthouse she said, "The sun is shining in my heart even though it's cloudy out."*

As Sylvie walked to a rally, a straggly-haired man bounded out of nowhere and said, "If you're not building bombs, you're not in the revolution," then disappeared around a corner. She'd met other people like this, dumb and scary. They advocated the same tired ideas but under their leadership. At the rally, a speaker with shoulder-length hair and a faded green army jacket shouted from the top of the lecture hall steps.

"No one on TV ever criticizes Nixon," he told the crowd. "Have you noticed? Does he condemn pollution so we won't notice the murder and lies of Vietnam? When he's through Vietnamizing the war, there'll still be three hundred thousand Americans there. Have you noticed no one on TV is allowed to say Peace? Come on, let's all say that dirty word: Peace! Peace! Peace!"

It was Rocky. Scanning the crowd, his eyes connected with hers and he grinned.

"I love it when you talk dirty! Peace! Peace!"

The crowd was shouting now, raising their fists.

"What do we want?" he cried.

"Peace!" they screamed.

"When do we want it?"

"Now!"

Rocky put down his mic as marshals directed everyone toward Commonwealth Avenue to head to City Hall. When he descended the platform, she approached him and asked, "Why are we marching to City Hall? What can they do about Vietnam?"

He cocked his head.

"Are we going to talk to Mayor White?"

"Great idea!" he said. "We'll ask him to strike with us!"

Chanting continued all the way there. Rocky made a parody of "Give Peace a Chance" by changing the lyrics to, "All we are say-ing . . . is take off your pants!" as if affirming that youthful hormones inspired protestors. She cringed at how he kept combining sex and politics. But she broke away with him and ran to one of the doors of City Hall. A bored-looking guard let them in.

"Whoa, that was easy," Rocky whispered.

"Surreal," said Sylvie.

On the directory they found the mayor's office number where another guard ushered them into an elegantly furnished room. Mayor White grinned as he stood to greet them and said, "I can tell you're surprised how easy it was to get in here."

Rocky and Sylvie nodded.

"I maintain an open-door policy," he continued. "What can I do for you?"

Rocky said, "We wanted to ask the city to join our strike against the war."

Mayor White said, "Well, a strike isn't an easy thing for a city. Nor for a college, by the way. The city provides a great deal of services I can't ask our citizens to go without, like garbage collection, schools for their children, and fire and police protection."

Sylvie admired this. She bit the insides of her cheeks to hold back laughter and looked at Rocky, indicating with her eyes that he should say something, but he wrinkled his brow. Mayor White stood and they followed suit.

"But I want to thank you for thinking of me. I'm very honored." He walked them toward the door and shook each of their hands. "And I support your principles."

Once outside they exchanged looks then burst out laughing about the unlikelihood of what they'd just done.

* * *

Sylvie wrote home:

May 1970

Dear Mom and Dad,

I've told you about the student strike. I'm hanging around to see what develops. I don't think I'll be back here next year.

You've written about the Bill of Rights and due process. Maybe I don't know as much about them as I should. But I know enough to know the legal system isn't working.

I don't think the income in the US lower class being higher than England's middle class, as you point out, means they have a better quality of life. So they have cars and televisions. What makes that comforting? They've bought themselves little presents to make it all seem not so bad? I don't agree TVs make life better. But Mom, maybe you're the type who should hire a maid and go to work so you'll have the money you want and won't complain about being unhappy all the time.

Though worried about demonstrators' growing hostility, she and Karen attended a bigger march near Harvard Square. Rampaging schoolboys threw rocks at store windows and started fires. An advancing wall of police hurling tear gas impelled the students. Sylvie led Karen away from that chaos into a dorm that she knew from roaming with Saul was connected to an underground tunnel and in there too was a stream of demonstrators. As they ran, Sylvie saw a man ahead of them—a hunting knife tucked into his belt—and tugged Karen's sweater and pointed. More psychic fallout? They slowed until the man was far ahead then backtracked against the crowd and found a stairway that opened out to a street across from a diner.

Inside she noticed Saul, slouching in a booth, drinking coffee with two other guys. She barely recognized him, his hair cut short, his face flaccid. She strode to their table, Karen trailing behind.

"Sylvie! I never imagined to see you in this fiasco. So, you're still demonstrating?"

"You're not?"

"No," he said coolly. "I've been reviewing my participation in all this . . . adolescent acting out."

She stood speechless a moment, then just turned toward Karen, rolling her eyes. They found a booth on the other side of the café and waited for the streets to calm.

"God, everything about him has changed," she said. "He's become a pod person!"

Karen said, "That weasel was the love of your life? Give me a break!"

"He just called me immature!" Maybe he blurred sex and politics—like Rocky?

Karen said, "For believing in something? Trying to make change? You're a model citizen!"

They headed home, walking along the river along with other stragglers, and somehow ran into Rocky again.

"Hey, fancy meeting you here!"

"Crazy as ever," Sylvie said.

"Anyway, glad I ran into you. We're organizing in the high schools. Wanna help?"

* * *

The strike closed classes. Sylvie loved the impromptu "teach-ins" where she learned about the war's illegality, corruption of elected representatives, draft evasion, institutionalized racism and the possibility of violent revolution. She was disappointed that other students preferred partying. Rocky told her his group was educating high school students and she could teach them feminism. And he introduced her to SDS members who were screening students to go cut sugarcane in Cuba with the Venceremos Brigade. They said, "Schedule an interview. We'll contact you if you're accepted."

Why not? She'd change her charted course. She'd filter through the mess of society and connect to the earth, like she belonged to it and on it. It didn't make sense that she could forage in alleys and had a free will that animals lacked but felt more dependent than an animal would. She yearned to get unstuck.

Back in the dorm room, Bertie had drawn big round freckles on her face with eyeliner and was donning a floppy purple hat. She burst into singing, "Que Sera, Sera" and at bedtime she pulled out her nightgown collar and looked down. "Just checking. Yep—still there." Sylvie admired how Bertie tested various ways of being.

BACK IN THE LOOP

Dad picked her up at O'Hare, only grunting hello until they exited the parking lot. "I trust you had nothing to do with the boycott nonsense?"

They passed franchises with huge plastic signs shaped like hotdogs, buckets of chicken and hamburgers. Ducking Dad's question, she asked, "Isn't that the first McDonalds?"

"First of its chains," Dad said.

Wires strung buildings together in an unending shackle until by Wilmette, houses sat like separate islands facing wide brick streets. Sylvie had been groomed in suburban protocols, like safeguarding her social personality and jockeying for position to promote her potential success. North Shore-bred professionals attended college and then got a position—something prestigious and lucrative, fun and perhaps meaningful. She now understood such freedom from chaos was maintained by power that excluded the "wrong" people. Instead, she felt drawn to the vitality in that chaos beyond these people, this quiet street, this big house.

At home, Sylvie settled with Mom on the screened-in side porch, enveloped in greenery, presided over by the comforting bend of the tall elms, twists of the oaks and accommodating crotches of maples, like the ones from which she used to jump. Daffodils had browned and shriveled as lilac buds swelled. Mom lamented that "junk birds" in the yard had come up from Evanston, which made Sylvie wince at its class overtones. She was eating a bowl of creamy millet and waiting to drink her cup of peppermint tea, both of which made Mom discreetly gag.

Sensing Mom was in a receptive mood, she said, "I told you about the women's group I joined."

Mom said, "I've enjoyed Stitch and Bitch."

"C'mon, it wasn't like that. We analyzed things, not just gossip."

"Like?"

"Like men. Like how we never really see their power over our lives."

Mom lifted the tea bag from her cup and plopped it on the saucer. "Did it occur to you these women may have an axe to grind?"

"What do you mean?"

"Why do you think women join such groups?"

"We discussed politics." Sylvie picked up her bowl and moved to the metal-framed sofa.

"But why would you want to hang around with man-haters?"

"I didn't say they were man-haters."

"These feminists want to blame men for everything. Weren't they, um, unattractive, mostly?"

Sylvie looked out across the alley at the dead top of a silver maple reaching gray bony fingers through its green branches.

"No! God, Mom, I can't believe you're saying this!" Mom had never emphasized the importance of women's looks before.

Mom said, "The ones you wrote about sound confused. Aren't any normal people involved?"

"What's, quote, 'normal'?"

Mom said, "Probably they never get dates . . . ."

Sylvie wouldn't even acknowledge that comment. "By the way, I'm thinking of going to Cuba on the Venceremos Brigade. I can't fly direct but could leave from Canada. I wrote Senator Percy to protest the travel ban."

"You did what?" Mom's voice rose. "You'll be blacklisted!"

"He didn't seem to think so. He sent a sympathetic reply."

"You'll never get a job!" Mom shouted. "We won't pay for your college and have you throw it away like that!"

"Then I'll pay for it."

"Great!" Mom said. "Get your own loans from now on!"

Mom held up her newspaper, blocking her face. Sylvie reached for the *Wilmette Life* on the table and flipped to the classifieds where she saw one for a file clerk. She'd work until saving enough to get to Cuba. She recalled what women in the Collective had said about job equality but because she never pictured herself doing office work, she hadn't understood their issues. Indeed, her notion of jobs was distorted: Mr. So-and-So on Greenwood worked for Standard Oil and she thought he ran a gas station. Mr. Who's-It on Chestnut owned parking lots, so she pictured him as the attendant. Even Dad's job made her sad, based on what little she understood of it. He'd proudly show her and Jim the ball bearings and thermocouples he drove all over the Midwest to sell. She imagined him hunched in dark offices reeking of fuel and trying to sell these things to crumpled men. He'd return home bearing trinkets bought at truck stops that touched her heart with their inanity. She displayed them in her room to show her appreciation for his attempt to communicate with her. The world was a pathetic, lonely place.

She went on the interview and was hired to start Monday.
Mom received this news blandly. "I'm not sure I can
spare the car every day."

"I'll ride my bike." It was still in the garage.

* * *

Her job was to load mail into a cart, wheel it through
the building and file it. She liked not being fastened to a
desk and enjoyed meeting people who seemed friendly,
including fellow underlings with whom she ate lunch. On
Tuesday her supervisor said she was the most efficient
worker she'd ever had. But on Wednesday the personnel
director summoned her.

"There've been complaints," Miss Poppy said. "The
men are distracted."

"By what?" She couldn't connect this criticism with
co-workers' friendliness, forgetting that adults could act
like sixth-graders.

Miss Poppy's face was stone. Single-hipped in her gir-
dle, nylons shining on her legs, she was part of the machinery.

"You need to wear a brassiere," she pronounced.

Sylvie was amazed at how little it takes to disrupt
a pattern; she was a foreign object, human with hair, no
deodorant and so flat-chested she couldn't understand the
hubbub. "Well," she said, "I'll buy one after I get paid."

Tight-lipped, Miss Poppy coupled her hands on the
desk. "You'll wear one tomorrow."

Hadn't Dad said she'd need to toe the line in an office
job? Doing her job, yes, but how dare they tell her what
underwear to wear! And who are these men who are "com-
plaining?" Why would anyone notice her small breasts?
Are offices that uptight that any jiggle is unbearable?

On her three-mile bike ride home, she stopped at Lyman's for some Rit dye. At home she dug deep into her underwear drawer and found an old bra, took it to the basement where she poured orange dye into the machine and tossed it in.

Over the orange bra she wore her sheer, white long-sleeved peasant blouse with red embroidery so they'd see her compliance with their dumb rule. Then on Friday, she wore a seersucker blouse and gray corduroy skirt. Miss Poppy called her back into the office.

"It doesn't look like you're going to work out here," she said.

"Why?" Sylvie asked. "I wore the bra."

"That blouse doesn't even look as if it were pressed this morning."

"It's seersucker. You're not supposed . . . ."

"I'm afraid you just don't fit in."

Sylvie drew herself up. "Don't you think it'd bother *me* if I didn't fit in?" she said. "Aren't *I* the best judge of that?"

Miss Poppy glared back, then stood and showed Sylvie the door.

Sylvie rode home on her bike, crying the whole way about what she saw as petty and unfair. She hated conforming to such rigid standards. But that was how it was.

She tried again and found something at Easton and Associates, a small advertising agency where she'd type letters and answer the phone. Since learning about war profiteering in Vietnam, she'd been suspicious of the corporate world. But there was something stimulating about the realm of men in suits and cologne and the occasional women in tailored dresses, hosiery and heels. Her own wardrobe was the same as ever, but she also wore hose. On the train she sat with legs primly crossed at the ankle and hands perched on her lap.

Three men were on staff besides the owner, Mr. Easton. She was mystified when Richard, his eyes fixed on her through coke-bottle lenses, lisped that hers was a "fine Irish name" and when George, aristocratic in his impeccable suits, boasted how he'd make a killing with miniature replicas— cheap-looking trinkets— of the fifty-foot-tall Picasso sculpture in Daley Plaza. She felt sorry for him having such a pathetic scheme. The rotund office manager, Ron, fresh from college, only impressed her with his lack of talent besides his Bachelor's degree.

Sylvie's job was secretary-gofer. Her letter-writing finesse soon impressed Richard and George, who both asked if she'd like to try writing copy for radio ads, which she did. They used her copy with minor editing to fit their hard-sell format. She believed they'd inform Mr. Easton who'd recognize her skill and maybe promote her, but soon saw they claimed her work as theirs. It depressed her to realize she'd never get credit or compensation.

A forty-ish man who boarded the train on Davis Street always sat beside her when the seat was free and showed an interest in her job aspirations. She said how she really would prefer something more creative.

"Maybe I can introduce you to people," he said. "I know high-earners who might be good resources." He called himself Jerry Dawes and asked her to meet him for lunch. One day she agreed to meet him at a diner where she found him planted at a table, cupping a half-eaten Reuben sandwich, a worm of sauerkraut on his chin.

"I'm almost through," he greeted.

"I thought we were meeting for lunch."

"Oh. Yes. A burger? What?"

"Grilled cheese. I guess. Or soup."

Dawes checked his watch.

"Am I late?"

"Late? No."

Another dark suit behind Dawes—heavier, grayer, similar glasses—leaned over and said, "So this is . . . ?"

"Oh, um . . . ."

"Sylvie," she said, growing suspicious.

"My special friend," he added.

He watched her eat until she put her spoon down and said to him, "Why do you keep staring at me?"

"Why are you eating?"

She laughed. "This is my lunch. We're having lunch now."

He lowered his voice. "I've booked us a room nearby." He reached for her hand. "That's why you've come."

"Oh, yeah?" She pushed over her water glass and watched it flow onto his lap. What had she done to make him think she was sexually interested in him?

He still smiled at her when he boarded the train, but she smirked and looked away.

SPIRIT

She found it meditative to walk through the bustling Loop during lunch, mulling over her future. Most of the political activists she'd met were clueless. As she was thinking this, she recognized the man dressed in black passing out leaflets for The Process Church of the Final Judgment. He was one of Bill Cole's friends. Predicting a brainless conversation, she hid by pulling her long hair over half her face. Further down State Street, Hare Krishnas in yellow robes danced and clanged finger cymbals on the sidewalk, making it difficult to pass. One reminiscent of Bertie, chick-like and with a similarly small head, blocked her path. His thick lenses made his eyes look small and far away.

"Everything is spirit. This is all illusion," he said.

Sylvie stopped, intrigued. "You think everything is spirit?"

"Yes."

"Are you spirit?" Sylvie's brazenness surprised her, but she couldn't curb her curiosity about what made people tick.

"Of course. And so are you."

"Is spirit stronger than your body?" Mom had always said her mind was stronger than her body—this guy must have figured out that part at least.

"You seem to understand our message. Would you like . . . ?"

"Then why do you wear glasses?"

When she passed a few days later, he wasn't wearing glasses and didn't approach her. She laughed to herself, thinking maybe he couldn't see her and pleased he might have listened to her.

Another day, she walked down West Diversey to the address in the phone book and saw the brass plaque announcing The Urantia Foundation. Mr. Connor had once lent her parents *The Urantia Book* which purported to have been written by extraterrestrials. Sylvie had read some of its thousands of razor-thin pages and recalled several of its ideas; one surmised that if a particular frog hadn't been able to jump so far, then humankind wouldn't exist in its present form. She was intrigued by, "Animal parents love their children. Civilized man loves his grandchildren." Would Urantians consider Gram uncivilized? Behind the entrance, a bare lightbulb dangled from an electric wire. She ascended the stairway to a locked door where no one responded. It freaked her that someone had taken the trouble to publish this complex book but no live person was available to explain it.

She passed banks and brokerages and on Washington St. she saw a storefront filled with pastel eight-by-ten prints of Abe Lincoln and George Washington, light beams streaming from their heads. The sign above the door announced the "I Am Temple." Inside, a smiling woman in a grass-green dress behind the bookcase greeted her.

"What is this place?" Sylvie asked.

"We are a religious activity that affirms life. We meditate on the violent consuming flame." Behind her hung a picture of a pastel Jesus.

"Can I read a pamphlet?"

"You must first read the first book."

"That seems expensive," Sylvie noted, then, "That's a pretty dress."

"Green is the color of precipitation," the woman said.

"Is it going to rain?" Sylvie asked.

"Soon," said the woman. "You'll notice we avoid the negative."

From behind a door in the back of the store, Sylvie heard a chorus of shouts and approached as close as she could, feigning interest in books inside the case. Through a crack in the door, she saw a rotunda. The chorus, "I AM, I AM, I AM!" echoed from upstairs. She couldn't imagine this little woman shouting like that. She loved how these odd spiritual groups—like glimmers of hope in a funhouse mirror—nestled throughout the Loop's commercial machine.

She returned to the counter and noticed a lower-priced book. "Can I buy that book first?"

"You must buy the one I indicated," said the ever-smiling woman.

Sylvie was sad this place seemed more interested in selling than explaining.

* * *

One Friday, Sylvie crumpled into a chair on the porch with Mom. "No, I haven't met any nice boys downtown. I just meet leering men on the train."

Mom sipped her tea. "I don't think that women's group did you any good."

"A group like that'd do you good, for sure."

"Women's lib is a plot by men to get women out of the houses and into the offices so the men can stay home and have the good life, working in the garden, playing with the kids, cooking a meal now and then."

"I can't believe you're saying that! You hate being a housewife."

"Maybe I complained when you were younger."

"Maybe?! You convinced me to never get into your line of work!" When Sylvie and Jim were younger, Mom sometimes called them "lazy louts" who never helped around the house and left the dirty work to her.

"It's easier now that you're out of the house."

"I see. What you hate is having a daughter. Thanks, Mom."

"Oh, quit being so dramatic," Mom said. "You see for yourself what a grind it is going to work."

Sylvie bristled.

"Advertising might be a good field for you. You're creative. You'd have fun."

Before getting married, Mom had been editor of a magazine for the hairdressing industry, writing and posing for articles about makeup and hairstyling. She'd told Sylvie she loved the work but the topics were stupid.

"Mom, even though Jim says I'm shallow and only think about fun, how can I and why should I? Boys die in Vietnam and people like you and Dad sit around and let it happen. Anyway, advertising's made us a country of mindless consumers."

"Why do you have to reject everything? It's easy to criticize. What do you propose?"

"Anything but being a depressed housewife." She immediately regretted her harshness.

"As I said." Mom readjusted her glasses, picked up her book and flipped a page.

Sylvie retreated to her room upstairs where she could look into the treetops. She was misinterpreting everyone!

She'd thought Saul loved her, but he only needed her. She'd supposed the so-called revolutionaries were sincere but they played games for glory. Her filing job had said they liked her work, but really only cared about her looks. She'd thought Mr. Dawes was supportive but he only wanted to get laid. She'd believed Malory and Mulligan wanted to help her career but they used her work for their benefit. She longed to find sincere people who saw things as they were and said what they meant. She'd been navigating uncharted waters since her childhood trauma: Authorities were clueless. Truth was out of reach.

* * *

One Saturday she walked to Gillson Park and lay on the sandy beach, inhaling the sweet lake air, watching clouds drift. As a gull soared overhead, she mused that if everything had been given to that measly bird to make it happy, then why not to people? She'd encountered all those groups downtown seeking such contentment.

On her way home from the train on Monday she approached Gillson from another direction, riding her bike down Linden. A block from Gillson she stopped at the Bahá'í Temple and its gardens. She circled around the building reading inscriptions above the doors and was struck by, "The source of all learning is the knowledge of God." Though she'd learned to be kind and to give back to the community, she'd never specifically connected learning with spirituality. Entering the sanctuary, she found more inscriptions in the alcoves. Sunlight streamed through the high filigreed ceiling as she strolled, the sole visitor in the stillness. She came to the quote, "All the prophets of God proclaim the same faith" and felt an "aha!" of recognition.

She'd always believed this. She sat in the middle of the row of seats in the sanctuary, closing her eyes to ponder. She felt like her body held two selves wandering through two parallel worlds—one had been asleep and the other half-awake, one obvious and the other hidden.

She followed the stairs down to the foundation hall to find someone to talk to—despite the temple's prominence, she'd never met a Bahá'í—and left with books and a phone number. She walked along, reading about the soul as a mirror and felt her heart swell. The tenets of this faith clashed with much of what she'd learned about the order of things, politics, competition, gossip, success. She rode across to Gillson near the pier, laid down her bike and removed her shoes to leap along the sand, splash through the water and then plop down to inhale the lake. Like lightning, her consciousness had shifted.

She'd always believed that if she found answers to her deepest questions about life, it'd be a simple matter of adjusting her behavior. But although this new dimension she'd discovered challenged her deepest notions, she wore the same clothes and had the same tastes. Friends and family seemed to see her as the same person with some new trait they didn't like, brushing away her new notions. "C'mon, let's get high!" was like a taunt, since now she avoided intoxicants. Not that things she'd grown up believing were all bad, but she wore a new perspective that set her apart. Her old friends judged her by the old rules, charged her with criticizing them and stopped calling.

She'd felt alienated before her conversion but now felt like an outsider even—no one seemed to detect the disruption she felt. She didn't know how to click her new life onto the old one, how to merge the two different directions of her internal world.

ITALY
1971-1972

TRANSPLANTING

Sylvie had grown up believing she should get a good job to get a comfortable home. But what if you hated your meaningless job and shallow coworkers and the compromises you'd make for money? Life must be more than that. Now she was learning to sit quietly and connect to something within. She'd already decided to change direction before spending three more years of study without a goal: Knowing what to study presupposed knowing what kind of job she wanted which she couldn't imagine. She'd given up on Cuba but still wanted to flee her birth world with her new sense of self to explore who she truly was in a place where she couldn't rely on conditioning. Even with her new faith starting to order her thinking, the old rules ordered the world and were hard to avoid.

She'd learned in Quebec she could speak French well enough, so she found catalogues in the library with places to write for information about studying in Europe. She was disheartened by immigration restrictions in France and Belgium but thought, why make language a barrier? Italy was more accommodating, plus it had a university in Verona specializing in literature and another in Trieste for translators and interpreters. And Italian is related to French, after all. So she borrowed Berlitz tapes and bought a beginner Italian textbook at Kroch's and spent evenings studying every day for six months until she felt ready to quit her job and leave. She wanted to be able to think—even dream—in a second language, and see the world through its fresh lens. She wanted to be of another culture. Italian it would be.

Her new Bahá'í friends held a going-away party at Rex's place where, in homage to Rome, they put a rented plastic fountain in the hallway that, when filled and plugged in, lit up and water cascaded down its tiers. Sylvie gave away surplus clothes and books and was encouraged when friends said, "Bahá'ís are everywhere. They'll help you out."

She wrote to the school in Verona which replied that she could attend classes before enrolling. And she wrote to the Bahá'í Center in Rome saying she was interested in studying in Verona and wondered if they knew any nearby Bahá'ís. They sent her Mariella's name, a woman living in Mantua, a half-hour from Verona by train, who said she could host Sylvie while she got settled.

She packed books into the red hard-sided suitcase Mom had given her as a high school graduation present, and stuffed clothes and her sketchbook into Dad's old canvas army backpack. Because of the strong dollar and Italy's low cost of living, Sylvie calculated she'd saved enough—including what she'd planned to use toward college tuition—to live frugally for a year or so.

But when Mom chided, "Maybe the Pope will kiss your ring," Sylvie gasped. Mom had always encouraged her independence. Well, here's the result.

"This religion makes sense to me, Mom. Sorry you disapprove."

"Well, I guess college isn't for everyone."

Sylvie replied, "Jeez, that's so cliché! Did you read it in Ann Landers? You know that's not me."

"No, Sylvie. I'm afraid I don't know at all who you are."

How cold! Mom didn't try to stop her or suggest alternatives or promise a safety net. Her woeful conclusion was, "What good would it do? You're nineteen. You're going to do what you want anyway."

To which Sylvie retorted, "If you didn't want me to travel, why'd you get me a suitcase for graduation?"

Despite her opposition, Mom led the motorcade of friends escorting Sylvie to O'Hare. Everyone promised to write; Mom gave her a package of super-thin airmail stationery.

NEW WORLD

Through the scratched airplane window, Sylvie looked down at the landscape of clouds thinking how she'd always loved watching their changing shapes from below. Up close they're all the same. But the shapes of buildings, cars, trees, and people down below had crisp edges, defined clearly as if drawn with penciled outlines.

In the airport she was amazed to realize the many eyes boring into hers were actually looking *up* at her. Inhaling the sweet outdoor air, she tuned in to the music of the language which she partly understood unless people spoke too fast.

She took a train from the airport to the station where she bought a ticket to Mantua. While awaiting departure, she watched some steam engines chugging in and out. She climbed into her train car and sat in a compartment across from an old man. During their three-hour trip, he spoke slowly and loudly. She could understand much of what he said about how the Gonzaga family had settled Mantua because they liked how the rising mist from surrounding lagoons veiled the city from enemies as it now did from tourists. Approaching the city hours later she saw how it was an island in a sea of flat farmland, like much of Illinois. She'd soon realize how few tourists visited there—Americans among the least—and just how much she stood out.

Mariella was expecting her. Striking in her knee-length tweed skirt and hair in a French twist, she welcomed Sylvie with a kiss on each cheek and led her to a comfy bedroom. Sylvie took a little break and lay down. How strange to be on another continent, in an unknown culture. She put away her things and then returned to the living room for tea. Sound ricocheted off the apartment's marble floors and concrete walls, making the rooms feel like a cold lecture hall, something Sylvie would never get used to in Italy. Mariella's English was poorer than Sylvie's Italian and Mariella spoke slowly. But after two hours speaking Italian, Sylvie could hardly stay awake.

Mariella was a retired teacher, widowed and childless, and loved to entertain. On Thursdays she invited friends over and served tea and sugar cookies along with a discussion of spiritual topics. A regular guest was Luigi, a thin, earnest public works employee, who usually brought his nephew, a high school student named Sandro who was fascinated by Mariella and now by Sylvie too.

Within two weeks, Mariella had found her an apartment in a recently renovated building on Via Cocastelli where outsiders lived. On a street too narrow for vehicles, Sylvie was buzzed through a massive door into a courtyard with stairs on both sides. There she signed a twelve-month contract for a one-bedroom apartment. She moved in the next day and slept on a pile of clothes she'd arranged on the floor.

Mariella had told her about Upim, a department store where she could buy housewares. On the way, she admired a hardware store window display of red-handled tools balanced on a black ladder, unlike typical shop windows back home with items jumbled amid dust balls and dead flies. Its artfulness inspired her to decorate with flair but she needed to do so on limited funds. At Upim, she bought kitchenware, bath items, a lamp and a bed with a thin mattress that were delivered the next day. She bought large pillows and black twill fabric to make slipcovers for seats to put on the kitchen floor. On the way home, she stopped at the hardware store for nails, a hammer, small cans of paint and a brush. She collected orange crates left for trash pickup on the curbside and used them to make shelves for clothes and a bedside table and to build a platform for her new two-burner stove, its propane tank positioned dangerously nearby. She finished decorating by taping pen-and-ink drawings to the walls.

Ascending the stairwell one day, she met Karl, a German who spoke English better than Italian, lived directly above her and offered to share his fridge. Sylvie spent evenings with him, talking and listening to Brahms and Grieg piano concertos on his tape player. She guessed he was gay, and once he knew she knew, he spoke freely about what physical qualities attracted him to men, like a strong neck. He seemed gawky and uncomfortable; six inches taller than the average Italian, his height always became a conversation topic. He dressed meticulously in bland clothes that looked like they'd shrunk a half size. His khaki appearance made him seem airy despite his height but his silence added weight. His teasing about her crate furniture evolved into their play-acting at being filthy rich and bored to tears, just living cheaply to be quaint. He told her about the other neighbors—a Dutch couple, Lucas and Eva, who also spoke English, and three Turks whom no one could understand— who, like him, worked at the local electric company. The final tenant, a single woman on the first floor, was reputedly a prostitute, something Sylvie thought was just gossip.

Once Sylvie visited a gallery show with Karl. They were looking at a painting of three ducks flying in formation with arrows pointing in the same direction and he burst into uncontrolled laughter and ran outside, to the displeasure of other attendees. Sylvie followed and said, "I'm learning that some rules are arbitrary and maybe silly, but people need them."

It took him a while to calm down and say, "That makes sense," then started laughing again, and Sylvie joined in.

During Mariella's Thursday evening conversations, Sandro peppered Sylvie with questions about US pop culture and started visiting her after school, eager to practice English. He complained of his conservative parents and drab home life. Sylvie fed him tea and bowls of peanuts from the farmers' market, sometimes splurging on a box of cookies and a jar of Nutella to spread on them. She always insisted he teach her more Italian.

Sandro also explained the intricacies of the train schedules which helped Sylvie plan trips to Verona where the university let her audit classes in Italian, French and English. In a bookshop near the college, she bought an Italian grammar book and a *Scientific American* with articles in those three languages which she used to study vocabulary.

One day, two students she recognized from class boarded the train and stood holding ceiling straps. "*Scusi.* You speak English?" the man asked in English. "I'm Carlo. She's Rachaela."

"Yes. How could you tell?"

"Your clothes."

"Not stylish?"

"I like your clothes."

"I also," said Rachaela.

Carlo said, "Would you teach me English?"

"You already seem to know it."

"Not enough."

"OK. Will you teach me Italian?"

They agreed to meet in cafés after class. They wanted to show Sylvie the area. Carlo said, "The more things we do together, the more English words you can teach us."

They drove her to Lago di Garda where sentinel cypresses guarded country roads, fat plane trees with cropped limbs lined the streets, and forests of pines grew in straight rows—so different from Illinois' convoluted oaks and tall elms whose long branches collectively embraced entire towns. Human dominion was clear: Hills were molded and trees cropped and captive. She felt like a raw substance from a less civilized place at risk of being shaped. They exited the highway and followed a lakeside road, stopping to visit the monastery and some caves, to climb hills behind a shepherd and his flock, even to row in the lake.

She said, "There are no isolated places in this country. Are Italians ever alone?"

Carlo laughed, "It's a state of mind, *Americana*. We don't have the luxury of physical isolation."

Sylvie invited Rachaela to visit and Rachaela invited her to the Ducal Palace to see Mantegna's paintings, considered the first *trompe-l'oeil* in the history of painting, and the wing built to scale—low ceilings and doorways, smaller steps—for the little people whom the Gonzagas had brought to court, wrongly believing it'd cost less to feed them. She also took Sylvie to the Basilica of St. Andrea where white pigeons roosted on the roofs. Or were they doves? Rachaela's priest friend showed them hidden rooms containing oil paintings, furniture, gold and silver, and from the dome they could look down into the sanctuary and over the rooftops of Mantua—sights, Rachaela said, Mantuans never even saw. Sylvie was pleased with herself for having penetrated so deeply and quickly into a foreign culture—if she could do this, she could do anything.

Rachaela and Carlo invited her to join them and other friends at an outdoor café where, to Sylvie's horror, Carlo picked antennae off snails plucked from jasmine leaves hanging from the pergola over the tables. Carlo's friend Giulio invited Sylvie to lunch the next week at his parents' country house. While the garlicky tomato sauce simmered, they went outside to see the gardens. A hedgehog crossed their path and Giulio immediately kicked it with his work boots until her screaming made him stop. It got away and he said, "But why? It's good to eat." Back inside when she noticed caged birds, Giulio said, "Do they eat these in America?" By the time he served the pasta, Sylvie had lost her appetite.

Back in her apartment, Sylvie thought about how she could reinvent herself here. No one knew her so she could take on any persona. Instead, she wanted to find who she truly was, untethered by the expectations of family and friends. What were her actual qualities?

And here she was interacting with people who had completely different expectations. She'd assumed Italy was entirely sophisticated and so her friends' crudeness puzzled her. She supposed people had to learn to survive during the war, but Carlo's and Giulio's mindless cruelty to animals shocked and saddened her. Did such behaviors stem from cultural training, or were they based on inner compasses?

TRANSLATING

After not seeing Eva for a week, Sylvie ran into her in the courtyard.

"Nothing goes well," she lamented. "We drove to Genoa and Pisa last weekend for a holiday and it rained constantly! And someone broke into the car and stole our radio and camera."

"How awful!" Sylvie said.

"And my work project is two months behind schedule because of how Italians do things. They don't ever seem to work! So we must be here at least until winter."

"I like all the holidays here, and the relaxed attitude about working."

"Easy to say when you're not on a schedule," said Eva as each turned toward opposite stairwells. "Anyway, you must come for dinner."

Sylvie did go that Saturday and so did Karl. After dinner, Lucas, who'd been "twelve years a sailor," told a story.

"A priest from Ta-hee-tee . . . you know where is Ta-hee-tee? who one day he came on board. And we was always smoking, drinking, playing poker, because that's what we do to make the time go by. And, you know, I don't mind anyone who's got his own religion, Catholic or whatever. Well, this priest was twenty years in Ta-hee-tee and he come on board and came over to us so we couldn't play poker. And he come again a second day. Fourteen days he come, then one of us says, 'Look. We don't mind you coming around but we're going to go back to playing poker because that's what we do.'

"'Fine,' says the priest, 'And why'd you stop?'

"So we start playing poker and he plays too, and good he was. Naw, he didn't use money but played for cigarettes—hey, he used to smoke and he'd drink with us too. And he played good poker. He told us twenty years he'd spent out in the bush-bush there civilizing people. Why, he had people there from the bush-bush and they didn't know how to use a fork or a knife. And he civilized them. He said that after he civilized one man, he'd come to him and say, 'Priest, I want to be a Catholic,' and the priest said that man was a better Catholic than one whose parents shoved him as a baby off to church each Sunday."

Sylvie said, "Boy, I can relate to being stereotyped—people think blond American equals mindless drug-fueled free-love hippie." She thought Lucas was criticizing her teetotaling.

* * *

Sylvie continued attending classes in Verona, sometimes socializing with Sandro and Rachaela and sometimes Eva and Lucas, and saw Karl every day. Otherwise, she stayed in her room, reading newspapers and magazines with dictionary in hand to learn Italian, sketching still lifes and views through the windows, praying and meditating, corresponding with friends. Janis had gone to an artists' colony in Mexico and met a guy from California she now lived with. Camille never wrote. Lori was at U. of Illinois. Jim sent advice about how best to talk to the parents. Uncle Willis wrote about news. Aunt Hannah wrote about the spiritual world. Grandma sent love and praise. Mom and Dad bemoaned how she'd abandoned her studies.

But her world became transfigured when she heard Patrizia outside a travel agency speaking perfect English to a British tour group. Sylvie waited at the edge of the crowd and when Patrizia was alone, she went up and said hello. She was about thirty years old with a mature self-confidence, a serene expression, speech measured and calm. She dressed smartly, a silk scarf tossed loosely around her neck, and a flowery perfume hovered around her. They exchanged addresses and made plans to get together when Patrizia was off work. With Rachaela's approval, Sylvie invited Patrizia to join them for an organ concert in St. Andrea where they sat behind the altar beneath the organ. Patrizia deemed it a marvelous experience and showered thanks on Rachaela and told Sylvie how delighted she was to have met her.

* * *

Sylvie was pleased to receive one of Jim's rare letters:

Dear Sylvie,

I consider it my duty as your elder brother to tell you of the plight of Camille Connor. Her parents are dismayed that she allowed herself to be violated, something likely caused by her alluring clothing. And since our aged parents are pathologically unable to discuss such delicate matters, I take it upon my shoulders to insist that in your innocence, you not invite similar unwanted

*attention, particularly there among hot-blooded
Italians where you're so far from home. Apparently,
Camille won't submit herself to the humiliation of a
public trial . . . ."*

She was often amused by his mock formal tone, but he
used it to mask his sexism. Poor Camille! It's bad enough
the Connors blamed her for being raped, but how awful to
broadcast it. And how appalling that her brother would be
so unenlightened. She was sure he didn't know about her
being molested—and would he say her five-year-old self
had asked for it? She ripped the letter into tiny shreds and
flushed it down the toilet.

Sylvie continued attending classes but needed a job.
Patrizia advised her to interview at a company that should
appreciate native-born American English, but the company didn't have enough foreign trade to need anything
but rudimentary English and instead wanted someone
with meticulous Italian. Sylvie had known it was beyond
her reach but went anyway and left feeling foolish. She
next interviewed at the Shenker School of English two
hours away up in Bolzano where the director-teacher John
from London took her out for coffee.

"Italians are easily insulted," he offered. "They're ego-
ists. But there's no confusion about sex roles here as there
is in England, and in the States too, from what I can tell."

Sylvie hesitated. "Yeah, women are tired of being second class."

John chose another controversial topic, scandals
about US atrocities in Vietnam, and said that in the British
army, each soldier is free to use his mind and make independent decisions.

"You mean, like deciding to raid villages? Or kill officers?" She regretted the outburst, but couldn't help it.

He slowly sipped his coffee then confused her with his reply. "America is as odd and foreign to us as the Soviet Union."

She was speechless. How could this be? All her history classes had stressed the US's British roots, but this Brit disavows any relationship.

She assured John she'd consider his offer to teach in Balzano so he loaned her a tape player and tapes of the Shenker method, designed to teach English phonetically and aurally. When she got it all home, she realized she'd need to teach with a British accent, and smiled to herself thinking how John didn't even really think they spoke the same language. When she played the tapes in her apartment, "Heah we ahh," rushed out her open window and rang through the courtyard.

Though Sylvie needed the income, she felt obligated to her year's lease and didn't know how or whether she could break it. Besides, she had become so comfortable in Mantua she sometimes thought if she could sustain herself in her little room, she'd never leave it. Plus she needed to investigate the program for interpreters and translators and decided to hop a train to Trieste in the morning.

On campus that afternoon, students kept steering her to the office of an American English professor named Bruce. When she finally found him, he greeted her with, "Don't see many Americans here. In fact, I could use you. How'd you like to visit my class tomorrow and speak English?"

This was a style she understood—direct and to the point. "What should I say?"

"Just have conversations. Whatever comes up." He added, "And please be my guest tonight."

The classroom discussion was fun. Sylvie occasionally turned to Bruce to translate some words. One student asked about jazz and rhythm and blues and was impressed when Sylvie said she'd seen B.B. King in Chicago, prompting another student to joke about the famous Italian mafioso Al Capone, whose gang had terrorized Chicago. A woman wanted to know if Americans ate anything besides hamburgers which Sylvie countered by saying she'd come to Italy a vegetarian but had difficulty finding whole grains and rarely saw anything but overcooked vegetables in the trattorias. After the class, she told Bruce she wanted to apply to the school for interpreters.

"If you do, you're welcome to stay with me until you get settled," he promised.

* * *

Back in Mantua, Sandro came over after school and invited Sylvie to walk to Palazzo Te. They encountered Karl in the courtyard and Sylvie asked him along. The two men hit it off so well that by the time they'd reached the castle, she'd been watching them jealously. They strolled together throughout the rooms, gazing at frescos, oblivious of the heat and the crowd and her.

The next afternoon, Sandro appeared at her apartment when Karl was there and asked him. "So, young man, you are infatuated with America?"

"Yes, especially rock music."

"Do you also like German rock music?"

"Not as much, really."

Karl laughed. "Why don't you come to my apartment and I'll play some for you?"

"Maybe someday," Sandro said, between sips of tea.

Sylvie said, "Maybe today, because I need to leave soon."

She never heard about the visit but knew it had been successful because on Monday when the buzzer rang at the gate, she looked out her window and was surprised to see Sandro who walked up the stairs past her door and straight up to Karl's apartment. She felt snubbed. She was glad that two people became friends through her, but also felt used. She wondered whether Karl, given the chance, would also try to monopolize Patrizia.

* * *

Patrizia stopped over and said, "I came to invite you and Karl to meet me Saturday at Bar Venezia. I have an idea to share."

"What is it?" asked Sylvie.

"I'll tell you Saturday."

On Saturday they found Patrizia at an outdoor café table dressed in tailored slacks, sunglasses and a silk scarf. She said, "In Rome I consulted a psychic astrologer who said we'd all met for a reason, not by chance. I've thought about this," she said. "We each come from different countries and I met you both on the same day outside my agency. It must be something to do with work. But what? I asked myself. Well, Mantua is ready for an international shop."

"I have a full-time job," Karl said. "How would I fit into this scheme?"

"I want to sell items I find while taking tourists abroad. I'm sure you could import things from Germany."

"And me?" asked Sylvie.

"You can be sales clerk. Maybe sell your drawings."

Sylvie was intrigued but doubtful. The shop would anchor her, besides helping her support herself. But she wanted to study in Trieste. This feeling butted against Patrizia's belief their meeting was fated, with which Karl concurred. But how could they make enough sales in

Mantua? At least Patrizia would buy the license and pay the rent and they'd chip in when they could. Out of friendship, Sylvie felt unable to refuse.

Patrizia asked, "So you'll do it?"

Sylvie and Karl nodded.

"Wonderful!"

Patrizia planned a celebration at her country house and invited them, Eva and Lucas, Carlo and Rachaela, Sandro and Giulio and others of her friends. She had lit a wood fire in the fireplace and set a candelabra on the piano where Alberto was playing when Sylvie arrived. Maybe his lack of training brought him more pleasure than her laborious studies did her. She who had studied piano twelve years felt diminished by this man who claimed to be ignorant of music but who seemed nearer to its essence. When Sylvie complimented his playing, he said, "*Tu sei la musica!* You are the music!"

"Oh, please!" she said, sensing she'd given him too much credit.

This party was unusual for Sylvie. Patrizia had friends of all stripes; Sylvie heard a communist and fascist argue heatedly and then joined in song around the piano. She met Monica, a petite widow from Venice, where she'd moved after marrying. She claimed to have telekinetic powers. "Visit me in Venice," she said, "and I'll show you." Sylvie was fascinated, but Monica might be crazy. Still, this presented a chance to see more Italian life and it'd be great to have a guide in Venice.

The world here moved along without talk of Vietnam and little notice of US politics. The subject hadn't even been raised in Bruce's English class. It felt odd to see her native land from the outside. Someone at the party asked if they had rock music in the US and if she'd ever heard of the Beatles. She was about to say, "That's ridiculous," because rock music was invented in the US, when Karl said, "You know, the Beatles first became popular in Germany."

"Fine," she said, "but Europeans learned about jazz and big band music when American troops were here."

At times she felt like a free-floating spirit linked to other spirits, passing through a maze like a three-dimensional board game, surrounded by people who'd forgotten where square one was and that it's just a game. Only when laughing with others did she feel really at home. She wanted to find the right love, someone she could laugh with, who could relax with her and her friends without trying to prove anything, who'd fit in with her family, though she wasn't even sure if *she* fit in with them.

Patrizia continued her plans, learning who they needed to see for a permit and setting up appointments, the first of which was at the licensing bureau. They were ushered to a sofa where they sat while the bureaucrat stood and spoke. Suddenly a crash brought all their attention to a central point. The chandelier hanging from the ceiling had fallen to the floor, missing the man's head by centimeters. Patrizia blanched and said, "God's trying to tell us something."

Or, Sylvie thought, this is a warning sign that the idea's crazy.

Undiscouraged, Patrizia threw another party where she planned to announce their shop and ask everyone to help brainstorm a name. Later in the evening, Sylvie noticed Patrizia moodily watching Karl and Sandro huddle together as though they were alone in the room. When Patrizia caught Karl's eye, she beckoned him and he obediently came and stood beside her. Sylvie was close enough to hear her ask, "Are you gay?"

Karl smiled sheepishly.

"I asked you a question," Patrizia said. When he didn't answer, she called out, "The party's over. Everyone leave!" With some confusion, guests gathered their things and poured out the door, still talking and laughing. Karl filed out and stood among them smoking. Sylvie overheard comments about Patrizia's unpredictable moodiness.

"Creative people are like that," mused Alberto.

But Sylvie suddenly realized Patrizia had fallen for Karl and maybe wanted to marry him. She was at an age Italian men deemed too old to marry and might've seen Karl as a last chance.

The next day Patrizia stopped by. "Why didn't you tell me about Karl?"

"I didn't think it was my place. I figured it out myself and you always seemed more worldly than me."

"You both deceived me! And you knew I was in love with him!"

This jolted Sylvie. "I guess there's different rules here. Back home, we consider sexuality someone's personal business." She considered apologizing but didn't think she'd acted wrongly.

"I'm done with you both!" said Patrizia. "No store, no parties. No friendship."

DINNER

Sandro had stopped by last week to invite Sylvie to his parents' for dinner. She headed there now and as usual when she walked through Mantua's streets, women in bland fashion of fine wool coats and dark leather shoes stopped talking and dug gazes into her. She averted her eyes toward a bistro window, blindly gazing at white tablecloths in a hollow room where silverware sparkled and vested waiters plied berry-topped tarts. Blue shadows skulked on walls outside where white peeked through brown plaster papered with black-worded death notices.

Turning onto Viale Cavour, she saw herself in window glass. She used to pay little attention to her appearance, but was trying to look less American, with some success. She found the address and pushed the button next to the name that matched the one she held. The buzzer let her into a courtyard where ficus trees in terracotta pots stood in a triangle of sunshine. Sandro waited at his door next to his mother, who surprised Sylvie with her youthfulness and her modern tailored dress.

"*Prego, si accommodi*," she said, and Sylvie replied, "*Permesso*" in the ritual that seemed as foreign as a Japanese drama.

"Ciao, Sylvie," Sandro smiled boyishly, his eyes frantic. He escorted Sylvie to the dining room where a Murano chandelier hung above a table covered with white damask cloth which barely covered the ends but draped amply on the sides. Sandro's father entered, rubbing his hands together, and sat at the end farthest from the kitchen.

"*Mangiamo!* Let's eat!" he said, scooting his chair in close to the table.

Sandro's mother reappeared carrying a stainless-steel pot and large bowl. She gathered everyone's pasta bowls and ladled mostaccioli into each with a dollop of Bolognese sauce. Sandro lined up noodles on the tines of his fork then sucked them off one by one. His father slurped and his mother seemed to be just pushing food around her plate. Sylvie caught Sandro's eye and almost laughed out loud. Instead she grabbed her water glass and drank.

"So, why did you come to Italy?"

"It's so beautiful," Sylvie said. "I came and saw it, and decided to stay . . . ."

"*Veni, vidi, vici,*" said Sandro's father.

". . . and I wanted to find a new language to think in," she finished, puzzled by his reference to Julius Caesar.

"No one wants to learn Italian," said Sandro's father.

His mother just looked at her like she was out of her mind. "That's an odd notion, wanting to think in another language."

"It's interesting. There are things I just can't say, and things I can say better."

"Fine, but why Mantua? It's so far from everything," said Sandro's mother. "Nothing ever happens here."

"That's why I like it," said Sylvie. "My friend Camille's in Rome. I wanted somewhere smaller."

"Wouldn't you be happier in a city like Florence or Milan?"

Sandro said, "My parents wish they lived in Milan."

"So, why don't you move?" Sylvie asked.

"No," said Sandro's mother.

Sandro said, "She'd be too far from her mother."

"Too expensive," said Sandro's father. He clanged his fork in his plate and shoveled food into his mouth then dabbed his mouth with a napkin. "Sandro? We need to go to Uncle Flavio's to get the car."

"But Sylvie's here."

"She'll be here when we get back. It won't take long."

"Sylvie, do you mind?"

"We'll have coffee," his mother said. "Just the women."

Sylvie was angry. "It's OK," she said, rolling her eyes at Sandro and sighing in disgust. After he'd met Karl, Sandro had visited her only twice. She felt so hurt when she saw him that she could only speak to him in monosyllables. He'd been her first home-grown Italian friend here and now she never saw him, so enrapt was he with Karl. The two of them treated her like a stepping stone. So this invitation had made her happy. He must recall how he had begged her to come to dinner, a casual friendly sort of meal. Sylvie blamed Sandro rather than his mother for being a poor host. As he disappeared behind the door, he winked at her. His mother led her to a sofa in the living room and sat on a chair opposite.

"Yes, Milan is much bigger. People are richer there." Sandro's mother poured espresso into a demitasse and balanced a little spoon on the saucer. "There used to be special houses for women who earned their living in ways that are now considered illegal."

"You mean, like prostitutes?"

"Yes, exactly." She gave a little smile. "And they had doctors on staff."

Sylvie settled against the sofa. "Interesting," she said. "Even here in Mantua?"

Sandro's mother sniffed. "Without doubt, though it was before my time. But the point is that when anyone got sick or had a problem, they could take care of her."

She felt awkward alone with Sandro's mother and wished he would come back. She hadn't met people like her. The young people she met talked about music and movies. She read newspapers to keep up with subjects that wouldn't have interested her in the States, like provincial government news, because it was important to know the culture and learn new words. She wondered if prostitution were a current topic here.

Sandro's mother took a saucer herself and sat with her back straight. "Everyone got good care," she said.

"That's good," said Sylvie, slowly stirring the sugar. "In my country there are many who don't."

"I'm sure that's so," said Sandro's mother. "Your country is young. And a bit wild, if you'll pardon me."

Sylvie swallowed. "I suppose you're right."

Sandro's mother set her cup down and said, "Sandro does nothing anymore that he used to."

"Really? What does he do instead?"

"As if you didn't know." She glowered, her face darkened.

Sylvie considered his moped, his interest in English, rock music, America. "What?"

"Whatever you do at your house with boys!"

"But he hasn't been to my house in weeks!"

"Sylvie, you're beautiful. You know he's attracted to you. But don't misuse your charm."

Sylvie's spoon clattered to her saucer, the cup trembled in her hand. "What?"

The mother smirked. "No need to pretend, dear. My sister-in-law sees him come out of there every day."

Sylvie's voice rose. "Your sister-in-law? What are you talking about?"

"She shops at the produce man on your street. They keep her informed."

Sylvie couldn't deny Sandro used to come out of her house daily, and at nineteen he was only a year younger than she. Would she have seduced him had his visits continued?

"If you don't want Sandro visiting people, why don't you speak to him?"

"Oh, I have! He's in your power now."

Suddenly she realized Sandro's mother had actually insinuated that *she* was a prostitute! She'd been ambushed! She felt mortified. If she denied this accusation, she'd have to explain the truth. With the evidence she could give, the woman would be a fool not to realize Sandro and Karl were lovers and Karl could be arrested. She glowered back at Sandro's mother, like the women did to her on the street.

"I guess I'll be going," she said, getting up. "Please give my regards to your husband and Sandro."

Sandro's mother tranquilly sipped her tea as if nothing untoward had happened. And Sylvie wasn't yet sure what had. She passed the funeral posters on the amber-colored walls and gazed into the hardware store window thinking the red tools on the ladder in the display looked silly. The lights down the alley were out, and rain was falling. Shutters clapped lonesomely. Her heart pounded as a silhouetted fedora hat and the glowing tip of a cigarette lunged toward her from the darkness but then came the gentle apology, "Scusi, eh?" Around the corner, a helmeted man parked his cycle outside and entered a cheerfully glowing bar. Then a long street, lights spent, an abandoned building with broken windowpanes. Grand junipers loomed like large hungry animals, reaching for her, then leaning back instead. Dirty water poured through downspouts into the street, making bubbles like tadpoles slithering over the cobblestones. Carlo, Rachaela, Giulio and Sandro visited at all hours. Sylvie didn't consider that though she didn't sleep with any of the men, she still might appear promiscuous, especially since an alleged prostitute lived on the ground floor. She hadn't expected Europe to be more prudish than back home.

Back inside the courtyard, Karl's light was on. She knocked on his door.

"I had dinner at Sandro's," she said.

"It was pleasant, I hope?"

"No. He left me alone with his mother and she rather pounced on me."

"Oh, dear," said Karl. "What about?"

"I thought you might know," she said.

Karl stood up and paced and fumbled in his breast pocket for a cigarette.

"Now that you mention it, I suppose I do," he said. "He caught something. From me, most likely. His mother found out after he went to the family doctor."

"And he blamed me?"

"Sylvie, what could we do? I could go to jail."

"You seduced him?"

"On the contrary, my friend."

The next afternoon, Sylvie heard a long buzz upstairs in Karl's apartment. Then her own. Probably Sandro. She heard a voice outside the courtyard calling, "Open the door!" Was it for her or Karl? Sandro's mother's spies would be watching. Sylvie went upstairs to Karl's apartment. She knocked and waited, then pushed the door open. Papers, empty bottles, a book and some hangers littered the floor. A shirt hung on the shower head. The bare mattress stared back at her. Karl was both a liar and an outlaw. He had fled for his own safety. Should she leave too because of one woman's opinion? But if Sandro's mother found her guilty, then so did her family and friends. Sylvie was no longer an anonymous outsider.

She'd come to Italy disillusioned with her own country, whose reality belied its promises, and gained more understanding of the world, including that human deceit and self-interest were everywhere. Karl and Sandro had used her. How could she still consider them her friends? But Karl hadn't asked her to cover for him—she did that herself, following a friendship honor code he clearly didn't share. Maybe her problem wasn't that she didn't understand the culture but that she didn't understand the geography of her own heart. She'd run away toward a new beginning but found the same stuff taking new shapes. What was she failing to see?

* * *

She flew back home. Her parents said she could temporarily live on their third floor. Dad clarified, "We've raised you to be responsible for your decisions. You've made some doozies lately." Mom said they enjoyed their empty-nest lifestyle and expected Sylvie to act like a grown-up, pay her own way and leave soon. Sylvie had expected this, since her parents compared her with her peers who were progressing nicely.

She found an evening job as a waitress and arranged for Boston to transfer her credits. Then she registered in a university degree program, declaring a French major, and crammed a year of course credits into two quarters, still with the goal of attending school in Trieste.

Her year in Mantua had stirred her to her core. Over there she'd felt suspended between cultures. Though she'd immersed herself into Italian life, her obvious foreignness branded her as an outsider. And she'd spent hours alone studying Italian grammar, comparing articles in *Scientific American* in English and French, reading French and Italian poetry, viewing mannerist art in Mantua's castles, praying, meditating, scrutinizing her beliefs and pondering her future. Maybe she'd failed socially. Maybe she'd been insensitive and brash. But she'd also made friends and entered their worlds.

Back in Chicago she was peeved by classmates who seemed locked in small worlds, but as much as she wanted to progress in her studies, she also wanted to make friends. Both her Bahá'í friends and childhood friends seemed distant—or had she been so saturated by a new hybrid cultural self that no one recognized that she was still the same person? She needed to integrate the dueling systems working inside her. Her new faith and Italian-ness had entered her veins and her nerves while her upbringing still flowed through her lymph.

Mom and Dad accused her of having ruined her life by veering off the charted course and said they didn't see how she could possibly succeed. Succeed how? she wanted to know. When she told Mom her plan to return to study in Trieste, Mom heaved a big sigh and said, "It's your life. But try not to screw it up any further."

Sylvie spent hours in the library looking for ways to go back with a defined purpose and found that for University of Trieste's school of translating, she'd need to pass the entrance exam in French, the international language of diplomacy, which would serve as her main language. She telephoned the Italian consulate in Chicago for an official translator to translate her letter of application, as the school required, and got the name of a woman in New York to whom she mailed her letter and her original high school diploma and a check for $50.

And Bruce wrote her back:

April 1971

Dear Sylvie,

How wonderful that you want to study here! My students still rave about the time you spoke to the class. You certainly may stay with me until you get settled.

Sincerely, Bruce

By summer she had enough credits for admission to the University of Trieste and had saved enough to support herself for maybe a year, given the still strong dollar. She'd live frugally and earn money teaching English. The university wrote to thank her for her application and advised classes would start November fifteenth. She bought her ticket and quit her job. Mom and Dad didn't comment.

PARRY AND THRUST

She landed in Milan, feeling quite at home. In fact, the city seemed almost too familiar, too predictable, too much like big cities anywhere. But Trieste was something else—a little more German and Slavic, even a bit Venetian. And distrustful.

She dragged and pushed her suitcase five blocks from the station to Bruce's apartment, stopping to rest every so often. People stared, as usual. Bruce answered the door and at first seemed not to recognize her.

"Oh, Sylvie! Let me help you." His voice was flat. He easily carried her suitcase into the hall.

"You can stay here tonight, but then you'll need to find some other place," he said, looking across the room.

"I thought you said . . . ?"

"Yeah, sorry. Things have changed."

He helped her get settled and made some calls. Finally Giustina, a former neighbor, and her boyfriend Pino agreed to take her in. Sylvie wasn't surprised—that's how youth culture in Europe and the States was the same.

In the morning, Pino picked her up. "Bruce got fired. He put some moves on a boy in his class. The college kept it quiet though. He's lucky he wasn't arrested." He laid on his horn and cursed. "Do you like Joan Baez?"

Though Sylvie knew she should welcome Pino's chatter, she was struggling to get used to her disappointment and it annoyed her.

"Sometimes. But I prefer singers who write their own music."

"I'm a musician, you know, not just a mechanic," he said. "Sometimes I perform in the piazza."

"You mean Piazza Unita? It's the biggest piazza in Europe!" She'd read about how it was an example of Fascist grandiosity—an immense public square embraced by massive buildings.

"Big means lots of people," he said. "If you sing with me we'll attract more people. Italians like Americans."

She was looking at shop and street names, trying to locate useful places and memorize the way back to Bruce's.

"Can't do that," she said, "but I'll help with English pronunciations. And maybe lyrics."

"It's folk music. Who cares? Even Bob Dylan doesn't have a voice."

She hadn't enjoyed the time she'd sung a solo in church. "How about if I help you practice?"

Clearly he expected something for his hospitality. "For starters."

Pino's apartment was up five flights. Sylvie stayed in the loft with its bathroom toilet that flushed only by pouring in a bucket of water. She could stand on a chair to reach a trapdoor and climb onto the roof where she could sit and watch boats in the harbor—the Adriatic Sea ultimately connecting her to home.

The following day she walked to the university's main office and announced her purpose to a series of clerks. After much paper shuffling, they found her letter of interest but hadn't received her documents. She was welcome to attend classes but wouldn't receive credit until the documents arrived. Now what?

If she had a job, that would help her settle in and tolerate the wait. She went to a café and sat outside to work on an ad publicizing herself as an English teacher. Guistina helped put it into the Sunday edition of *Il Piccolo*.

Near her ad was another by a "Mr. Zingaro"—not "Sig." but "Mr." Since Zingaro means gypsy, she wondered if it was a pseudonym but the name and the title aroused her curiosity. It described an international society to help young people. If it provided any income at all, she could do this while waiting for responses to her ad. She couldn't just sit around waiting for documents to arrive and school to start.

Sylvie found her way to the hotel where an assistant named Giorgio handed her forms to fill out: She put Camille's name—who might still be in Rome—as someone who'd known her for at least three years. When Giorgio said they knew Camille, that she'd worked for them but was in Greece and returning soon to rejoin them, Sylvie was just happy to feel that home connection and didn't question it. Giorgio explained the job was selling magazine subscriptions door-to-door and showed Sylvie a glossy *House Beautiful* clone, saying since they didn't advertise, they had to sell it this way. The job paid commission, and travel and expenses would be covered for trainees. Not wanting to be prejudiced about such jobs based on similar ones in the States—and recalling a letter she'd received at her parents' address where Camille mentioned how much money she was making—Sylvie decided to go with them to Pordenone, a city flush from lucrative employment at its America airbase.

At the end of the interview she met Mr. Zingaro (alias Giuseppe somebody), a short, bald man in a cream-colored suit and crisp shirt. He was the mastermind of this operation and had final say about hires, but wouldn't be accompanying them.

When she told Pino her new plans, he expressed disappointment that she wouldn't sing with him the following weekend, which she hadn't agreed to do. Relieved to escape his constant insistence, she packed provisions for a month, planning to return in time for school. She met the others at the hotel and they all climbed into a white Rolls Royce. During the ninety-minute car ride, Sylvie thought about all the twists and turns in just the week since she'd arrived. She always prayed and meditated and weighed every little decision but never discerned whether any path that opened had attracted her soul or was a random coincidence. She took people at their word and kept an open mind.

Though a bit cramped, Sylvie was happy to find she had a private bathroom. Before turning in, she peeked out her door and noticed a fellow trainee's door was open, so she went over to talk. He introduced himself as Delyo from Luxembourg who had joined the company six months ago. She was amazed to see *Mein Kampf* on his bed. She quickly said good night and excused herself. Each step carried her deeper into something murky but she'd come this far and needed an income.

In the morning after she gorged on an American-style breakfast, Giorgio drove her, Delyo, Franco and Marco to Pordenone. Sylvie was paired with Franco as her mentor. After ringing doorbells that went unanswered, they were invited by an elegant woman into a spacious living room where Franco opened a briefcase containing various magazines, praising each as the woman perused it. He explained subscription costs and handed her forms to fill which she read carefully and said, "This mentions a contest."

"Oh, don't bother about that," said Franco.

"Sorry. I'm not interested," she said, standing to lead them out. Embarrassed, Sylvie also arose while Franco stayed put and told the woman she was making a mistake and would miss her chance to win big. The woman continued to the front door, followed by Sylvie, who looked at Franco and then headed out. They hadn't been upfront about this job.

Franco caught up with her and said, "Don't do that! I was wearing her down!"

Sylvie wanted to quit but felt bad about stranding Franco and at the next house she silently endured his presentation. Back outside, she said, "Who wants a chance to win a magazine subscription? That's nuts. It's embarrassing."

Franco said, "Everyone loves to gamble because everyone is greedy."

Greedy is a choice, she thought.

It was time to join the others to drive to lunch. When all were in the van, she said, "Giorgio, based on this morning, I'm not interested. Can you please take me to the station?"

Giorgio said, "Quitting because of Franco? He has the brain of a fifteen-year-old."

"Not about Franco," she said. "I don't want a job based on lies."

"He's the liar," Franco said.

"Everyone lies," said Delyo.

"I'm not everyone," Sylvie said.

"Don't you know how much money you can make?" asked Marco.

Annoyed, she said, "Please drive me to the station." It was a mile away and her luggage was awkward.

"Anyway," Delyo said, "why shouldn't we exploit stupid, weak people?"

Giorgio smiled. "Tell us what you'd do differently, then I'll drive you wherever you want."

Sylvie said, "Franco doesn't think customers see through his bullshit, but I'd just be honest." Suddenly she realized that having an American with them gave them greater credibility.

Delyo said, "That'd never work."

"I'd always heard Americans were naïve," Franco said. "It's true."

Giorgio said, "Your friend—Camille?—she was quite successful with us."

Sylvie said, "Oh, stop! You don't even know Camille. That was just to deceive me."

Giorgio laughed. "Ah! You're catching on."

Had she been arguing with them for an hour? She said, "Please, just drive me to the station."

Giorgio said, "Open the door, Franco, and hand over her things."

While Franco put her bags on the sidewalk, she climbed out, saying, "Of course you'd even lie about driving me to the station."

They sped away. At least she'd eaten well this morning. She found her way to the station by following landmarks they'd passed, cursing them and herself for getting sucked in, and saying silent prayers for strength as she lugged her bags.

It was late afternoon. The train to Trieste had a layover near Venice. She had Monica's address, whom she'd met at Patrizia's party, not far from the station. She got directions and found her way through the rain. Monica greeted her warmly.

"Hurry, come in! It's starting to pour out! You must stay for dinner!"

"That's very kind, thank you, but my train leaves in an hour."

"You can't leave in this storm. Stay and I'll show you Venice. Didn't I promise that when we met?" She was widowed and had just sent her daughter off to college and said she felt lonely. "Have you seen Patrizia since you left Mantua?" Monica asked.

"No," said Sylvie. "Have you?"

"Sadly, no," said Monica.

Sylvie was relieved to leave that subject. Rain slashed against the windows and the winds picked up. As they were finishing dinner, the power went out.

Monica said, "If conditions are right later on, I can demonstrate my telekinetic powers."

"What is that, exactly?" Sylvie asked.

"I can make objects fly off the shelf and back on again," said Monica. She closed her eyes and Sylvie waited in the semi-dark room for a dish to fall off a shelf. After some minutes she heard Monica's breathing deepen and slow, so she tiptoed into the spare bedroom. Soon Monica awoke and appeared in the doorway.

"I guess conditions weren't right but I assure you, it happens."

"That's OK," Sylvie said, recalling her Chicago lunch-time walks.

In the morning, they found all trains canceled because of trees and debris on the tracks, so Monica, as promised, provided a tour of Venice. The water level was high from all the rain, and debris floated in the canals. It was a magical place and a bit unnerving, never knowing what was around any corner. They sat at a small café where Sylvie enjoyed a cappuccino and Monica had tea.

In the morning, Monica said she'd telekinetically moved a cup at 2 a.m. but hadn't wanted to awaken Sylvie. Sylvie suspected Monica made up stories to get attention but was grateful for her hospitality. In fact, she thought the deranged ones on this trip were Mr. Zingaro's bunch, not Monica.

BOUND FOR TRIESTE

On the train platform, a young man wearing blue and gold argyle socks sat atop a luggage wagon, hugging his knees as he smoked and looked down the tracks. Sylvie was touched by his socks' gaudiness. His short-sleeved cotton shirt, navy blue with white lines woven through it, hung untucked from baggy khakis, making him look a lot like a frumpy American. His shirt lifted up when he stretched his arms overhead and she could see how his pants were pulled to overlapping with a handmade leather belt. Except for his bushy haircut, he looked like a kid from the 1950s, like one of her playmates who hadn't quite grown up. He seemed more relaxed than Italian men she'd met—maybe a sign that he was less judgmental and more mature? He had a rugged attractiveness, a playful "I don't care" aspect. She found Italians more mature than American boys, but still juvenile. By contrast, Saul was flaccid and non-athletic, non-physical—a complete bookworm living entirely in his head.

She felt his gaze as she climbed on board the train. She found space in a compartment across from two uniformed soldiers chatting together, their eyes trained on her. She sat looking out the window and as the train

jerked to a start, she saw a reflection in the glass of someone entering the compartment and taking a seat by one
of the soldiers. It was him, the man in what looked like
hand-me-down clothes. He introduced himself as Enzo
and passed around bread, salami and provolone. Then
he took a cloth clown from his pocket—a present for his
friends' new baby—and made it somersault down his
chest. Sylvie, whose world hadn't included men interested in babies, felt stirred by this man, though Mom's
"lousy little kids" phrase popped to mind.

Enzo regaled them with stories, making them laugh
when he said, "I was kicked out of the Catholic school and
the public *scuola scientifica* for asking them to explain
how Mary could be a virgin? I mean, I understand why
the Catholic school, but not the school for sciences." His
deep eyes sparkled.

"C'mon. You knew that'd happen," said the soldier
who kept pushing his glasses back up onto the bridge of
his nose.

"I expected my teachers to reward my inquisitive
mind. Then my father discovered the Istituto Nautico in
Trieste." His diploma in navigation qualified him to be a
ship captain who could look forward to serving three com-
pulsory years in the navy.

"You'll never last in the military," said the other,
pudgier, soldier, "with questions like that!"

To Sylvie, Enzo said, "Your president Nixon is the
biggest hippie in the world, right? He's theatrical, he defies
social norms—all he needs is bellbottoms." As they discussed Vietnam and war in general, Sylvie was impressed
by how better informed they all were about US politics
than most Americans she'd talked with. She admired
Enzo's energy and indifference to others' opinions of him.
They shared a history of protesting. He was refreshing after

the deception of Mr. Zingaro's crew. They both got off in Trieste and continued talking as they walked.

"My great-grandfather owned all the taxis in Naples," Enzo said, "but died with nothing."

"Why?"

"They were horse-drawn. A little invention called the automobile put him out of business." His openness made her feel like she'd known him a long time. "That's a lesson for us all. If such rich and powerful men hadn't tried to monopolize, they wouldn't have lost everything. They could've shared the wealth."

He reached for her suitcase and she let him carry it. As they walked, she stared at his black hair, remembering Mom's insistence there was no such thing as truly black hair, that it can only be dark brown. Maybe Mom had never actually met anyone with black hair? She studied his movements and expressions as she assessed whether he lived in the same psychic and emotional world as she.

"I've never known an American," he said, "just Italians who move over there. I warn them not to get drafted."

"That's even tricky for American-born boys," she said.

"There shouldn't have to be any military, especially not a navy."

"My dad says the same thing about the navy. He was in the army. Landed at Normandy."

"A hero, no?"

"Funny. I always only argued with him about war."

"I'm sure I argued more with my father," he laughed. "He supported Mussolini."

Enzo kept his legal residence in Trieste but worked toward an advanced degree in sociology in Trent and was about to start his dissertation. As long as he stayed in college, he wouldn't be drafted.

They arrived at a bar where he asked her to join him in greeting friends and sharing a glass of wine. "I'm non-alcoholic," she said. "Keeps the mind clear."

"C'mon, just one."

"No, thanks." She wasn't in the mood to enter where she knew she'd be the only woman, especially because American women were considered sexually free. She didn't want to be stared at or have to explain why she wasn't drinking wine.

"Please wait here for me?"

She waited outside each of his haunts and they continued walking when he rejoined her. She believed they shared an opposition to how the world was—its politics, its social rules, consumerism. And they agreed that how they lived their lives was key to changing the world.

Enzo reassured her with, "I don't use drugs. It's fun, but I don't want to support the Mafia." He reached for her hand and put it to his lips. "People with power want a zombie population they can control."

"You're kidding, right? You don't think people have a choice?"

"We think we're choosing, but the selections are pre-determined."

Sylvie was reminded of Camus talking about one's responsibility to make conscious decisions. "What about the choice to simply get along, to compromise?"

He was leading her up to his favorite spot, a bench by Castle San Giusto on the hill overlooking the city, now in its evening clothes. "Sure, we choose war and peace at every level, and culture usually gets in the way."

"Maybe not if there's love," she said. She thought he looked at her with hope. But reviewing this moment later, she thought maybe it was pity.

"I had to come north. It was a forced decision. Here they see me as an outsider, not as good as they are. Even in

Trieste! Such a backwater they don't even speak Italian! Do you understand their dialect?"

"I don't understand anyone's dialect."

"Well, the Fascists converged here after the war, to create their own state. What simpletons!"

They compared their elder brothers—Enzo's had left seminary to enter the army— "He must need regimentation and solid answers," he said. They mused about whether their frustration with their brothers had driven them to deeper action. She inhaled the pungent sea air as she looked out at boats in the harbor, then up at the starlit sky.

"Do you wonder about God?"

"Of course. Any sane person would wonder what life is about. But I don't think our minds can do it. Just our spirits can."

"That's what I believe too!" said Sylvie. Talking to him was an adventure that could lead anywhere. She was smitten.

He put his arm around her and then jumped to his feet. "I feel like singing!" he exclaimed and burst into a song in Neapolitan dialect, "*Quanno sponta la luna a Marechiare pure li pisci nce fanno a ll'amore*" of which she understood little. "C'mon, sing with me! You say you came here to study language—I'll teach you all the language you need to know. *Dai!*"

"Oh!" she said. "I learned "Funiculi Funicula" in English in fourth grade!" and sang that.

He responded with "*Ah, che bell'o café.*" When she sang, "O Sole Mio" he marveled that she knew the words in Italian.

"My brother and I used to goof around with old songs—I played piano and he sang horribly off-key and it made me laugh so hard because he didn't realize. But you have such a nice voice."

"I've performed in many operas, you know."

"That's fantastic! Which ones?"

"*Aida, Cavalleria Rusticana, Turandot* . . . ."

"I'm impressed."

He laughed. "Actually, we were extras. We just stood in a crowd, held flags, stuff like that. For money, of course. Though I also love the music."

They talked and laughed and sang all night. He said, "I've had such a good time with you, Sylvia. I'm taking you to breakfast," and led her downhill to a piazza outside a convent. Toothless street people with rheumy eyes shuffled behind them and stood propped against a wall. In the center of the courtyard was a heavy, black iron-studded door with a small sliding panel at chest level above a small ledge. When the clock struck seven, Enzo went to the door and tapped on the panel. It slid open. Beyond was blackness.

"Sister, we are two poor students without money to buy food," he intoned. The panel slammed shut. Sylvie was sure they were in trouble but moments later the panel opened again and two hands appeared and set two cups of sugared cappuccino and two crusts of day-old bread on the ledge. The tubercular old men shuffling behind them drew nearer.

Enzo whispered, "Keep away from those germy guys and take your food quickly." They carried their breakfast to sit on a stone ledge by the fountain and dipped the crusts into the lukewarm cappuccino and sucked on them.

"This is something the church does for students too?" She felt uncomfortable about possibly stealing from the indigent.

"They've known me since high school, like a son."

She'd never seen anything like this back home and knew nothing about how the Catholic church operated.

He walked her to Pino and Giustina's and told her he was going to Trent where he was finishing up his degree in sociology, but would see her when he returned. Sylvie continued spending days studying for her entrance exams, checking to see if her documents had arrived, and teaching English to a young man and an older woman, each of whom brought a high school textbook that helped structure the lessons. At night Pino strummed his guitar and sang, "He's got the whole world in his hands."

"C'mon!" he urged.

She joined in, then said, "You've got the beat wrong" and showed him the syncopation.

"Nice," he said. "So you can sing and I'll accompany you."

Sylvie laughed. "Besides me not singing in public, I think you need something more contemporary." She didn't like how he expected this from her.

At night Sylvie liked to sit up on the roof, inhale the sea air and look at stars in the sky and boats in the harbor, feeling connected to Spirit. She thought about her goals and about how Enzo shared her desire to make the world better, a desire rooted in their woundedness.

Enzo came to Pino's when he returned and invited her to his apartment to see his leatherwork table. She admired his ingenuity in earning a living doing a craft, and exclaimed over the elegance of his products despite her qualms about using animal skins.

"I'm vegetarian, you know," she said.

"I show respect for the animal by making sure its whole body is used."

This gave her a chill but he had a point—leather was a byproduct of a carnivorous diet. She repressed her misgivings and a few days later asked him to teach her. She found leatherwork like making clothes, something she knew. He gave her simple tasks and she caught on quickly. His handbag designs combined fine Yugoslavian kidskin for the bag and stiff Italian cowhide for straps, tops and bottoms. He showed her how to use the nineteenth-century iron stamps he'd gotten from an old Florentine who claimed to have worked for royalty and had taught Enzo the craft. Sylvie hammered patterns on the cowhide with stamps shaped like a flying bird, a fleur-de-lis, a grape leaf and paisley. She admired how Enzo mixed aniline dyes to gently tint the cowhide in green, blue and red chiaroscuro abstract patterns. She used her clothes-making skills to create cardboard patterns for the purses he designed, even copied purses she'd seen in shop windows. She was sort of following in Gram's footsteps.

Several weeks after the placement exam, she got a letter announcing the happy news that she'd passed. But it also said they hadn't yet received the documents she'd sent from home months ago. She could attend classes but wouldn't earn a diploma without proper enrollment.

This grieved her so much she spent an entire day walking all over Trieste thinking, stopping at park benches, lingering over cappuccinos in different cafés. At first she was angry and wondered if the translator had ever sent anything. She was angry at the postal service. She worried about spending time in class and nothing to show for it. Or did she really need official proof of her skills?

Her plans crumbled under rejection and deceit, from Bruce turning her away to Mr. Zingaro and his bogus employment. But she'd also met Monica. And Pino and Giustina who were generous, though Pino expected something from her besides rent. Were they also a little crazy, or was this the Italian spectrum? She believed her inner self sought its course, and after so much effort to get this far, she couldn't turn back. Grandma used to say, "God doesn't close a door but He opens a window." Was meeting Enzo that window? He was kind and smart and fun. Besides, he'd said, "I can teach you expert Italian."

* * *

When Enzo went to Trent for his studies, Sylvie spent evenings up on the roof, wondering about where to take her life. As always, the constellations and the water were as familiar as home. She found herself missing Enzo, someone she'd connected with, someone sincere.

So after a few weeks when he invited her to move in with him, she said, "I'm happy to take the living room. That doesn't mean I'll sleep with you." He'd insisted at first that the more they knew of each other the better friends they'd be, but after she didn't meet him for dinner the next day, he accepted friendship on her terms, adding that he'd never heard such a request from a woman.

"I don't get it, but OK."

"We'll see how it goes," she said and threw in her lot with Enzo.

HOSPITALITY

Enzo praised how her innovations streamlined the leather work, allowing him—them—to make five times more purses than he'd ever done alone. They agreed to find a way to earn a higher profit. And as leatherworking would be Sylvie's sole income, she decided to use the money earmarked for classes (that she doubted would ever happen) so they could buy enough leather for ten purses. She'd figure out later how to finish college. Now she'd be a participant observer, as she'd decided in Boston.

"The leather dealer in Ljubljana says kidskin costs less at the tannery in Skopje."

"How far is that?"

"Maybe a week to hitchhike," Enzo said. He took her hand. "I want to travel with you. Traveling reveals your true self—so we can learn about ourselves together."

"It sounds like fun," Sylvie said, recalling hitchhiking in Boston. "But Yugoslavia is communist. Is hitching allowed?"

"Probably they shoot hitchhikers." He laughed and pulled her close. "But I promise I won't let them shoot you."

The next day they walked through the guard station into Yugoslavia and quickly hitched a ride all the way to Split. Enzo knew from previous trips to Ljubljana and

Dubrovnik, tourist destinations with facilities, that they shouldn't have trouble finding food and lodging, so they weren't prepared for an absence of shops and paucity of forage besides the ripening pomegranates. While standing and waiting for rides, Enzo sprang up and swatted at their purple globes that fell and rolled into the brush. He picked up one of the fruits and stabbed it with his pocketknife to pop out slimy red seeds which he dropped into Sylvie's cupped palm. She pecked at them with her lips but spit them out, shocked by their sourness. Enzo leaned against the stop sign and sucked out seeds then tossed aside the empty husk. They'd been standing there for hours.

"Hitchhiking is selling. Make it easy for your customer," Enzo pronounced. "When the driver stops, you must ask him face to face." She was impressed he'd reasoned through such details as insisting they stand near a crossroad where a driver would naturally stop. Finally a car pulled over.

"It's your turn," he said, wiping his blood red hands on his pants.

Sylvie agreed that since the drivers were men they'd respond more readily to her. Striding to the open window, she proffered a map to the driver who poked his finger at a word near the blue space of the sea and said, "*Je vais qua. Io vardo qua.*" Though he spoke imperfectly, Sylvie understood where he was going. Waving "c'mon" to Enzo, she dragged her backpack like a dead cat and squeezed into the back seat, Enzo in front.

"This is new road," the driver said, mixing Italian and French. "Not many in my country know how to drive. Few cars." Apparently enjoying this captive audience, his head bobbed to look at Enzo and, swerving into the left lane, twisted toward Sylvie then jerking the car back when he remembered he was driving.

"Where you coming from?"

"I'm American," Sylvie said. Enzo wriggled his back against the seat. Why did this guy make him nervous?

"Ah. America!" The driver twisted toward her. "I have few company. Never American. I am military, back from vacation. In Belgrade. Visited mother, brother."

The road was a thin ribbon stretched along a precipice, clinging to the side of sloping rock, dodging every gully, hugging the massive land above the sea. Rounding the corners hurtled the car from bright sun to cool shade. Everything looked closer on the map where you couldn't see the mountains or feel the curve of the coast so it took longer than expected to drive to points that on the map seemed a short leap. Looking at the rocky slopes whipping by made her dizzy.

By the time they saw the sign with the name of the driver's town, Sylvie had watched the orange sun completely melt into the sea. "You won't get more rides tonight. You come my house," the driver said, speeding down a dark road where low buildings cowered behind a long, barbed-wire fence.

"My work!" he said, and saluted. Some miles past acres of fence around what looked like an army base, he turned down a street lined with little white houses facing the sea, and pulled in front of one.

"You come in, eat, sleep," he said.

Sylvie said, "Thanks, that's very kind." What choice did they have?

The driver hopped out and ran around to the passenger side. Bowing from the waist, he tapped his heels together and held the car door for them. Enzo indicated they'd like to look at the sea.

"Sometimes you see dolphins," the driver said. "Have a look. I go inside."

A single light atop a pole cast shadows back onto the row of houses. Sylvie sat cross-legged, her knees touching the tops of large rocks piled along the shore. She inhaled the fishy breath of the sea, a black mass married to the sky. Hearing the lull of waves creeping up and back carried her to Lake Michigan. The stars were pinpoints. She found Cassiopeia, the throne of stars like a lazy W, and felt linked to all the other nights and places where she saw it spreading out.

"We made tracks today, huh?" she said.

Propping an elbow on his knee, Enzo squatted, cupping one hand around the fire of his wax match and lighting his cigarette. Afterward, he flicked the white cylinder into the water and they watched it bob on the surface. Their host, a backlit faceless silhouette framed in the doorway, called, "Hellooo!" Enzo returned Sylvie's gaze then strode through the shaft of light streaming at them like a headlight. Sylvie shuffled behind, curling her toes to keep her moccasins from slipping off. She disliked Enzo's behavior—the inbred imperialist attitude that he sometimes accused her of. She considered their host, now wearing a blue paisley shirt and khakis, just an individual, not a hostile agent. The sweaty smell of boiled cabbage wafted into the night air. In quick hen-like movements, he ushered them into a closet-sized kitchen.

"Please," he said, sweeping his hand through the air above a square Formica table ringed with coffee stains.

"Oh yes!" He leaped from the room in one step, returning with three wooden folding chairs. He handed one to Enzo and opened one for Sylvie.

"Who is hungry?" he asked, rubbing his hands together. He lifted a stack of chipped white plates from the sink and put one in front of each of them along with a bowl of cabbage. "I love boiled eggs," he said, taking a pot off the burner. "Cake too. Eggs and cake."

He put the pot on the table, scooped out two eggs, and let one roll off the spoon onto each plate. He got a loaf of bread and a bottle of red wine from a cupboard that was otherwise empty. Enzo put their salami and bouillon cubes on the table.

"One day I ate twenty-eight eggs," their host said, flashing his fingers to show how many.

That must be unhealthy. Sylvie ripped bread from the fresh loaf. "What do you do in the army?" she asked.

Enzo spat his eyes at her. Her face flushed.

"Lieutenant." He ate several eggs then left the room and returned hugging a shoebox which he set on the table, untied the string and ceremoniously flattened his palms alongside the lid and lifted it. Tightly packed photographs popped up. He picked up a photo, looked at it, smiled, then gently passed it to Enzo who glanced and dealt it to Sylvie. He passed another and another, each of someone posing in the middle of the frame against a blurry background.

"My brother," he said, whether a man or woman smiled back.

After handling a dozen photos, Enzo leaned back to smoke. When the lieutenant left for more, Enzo said, "*Che stronzo!* What a turd!"

Sylvie found their host ill-mannered by American standards, but who knows what's usual here? "I suppose you know so much about Yugoslavia?" she scolded.

The lieutenant brought out photos that curved together as if molded around a toilet paper tube. He looked at each, then laid it on the table and titled it: Mother. Friend. House.

Sylvie began to recognize faces. "I'll guess this one. Mother." She wanted to show friendship to this man who had opened his home to them.

"No. Mother's sister."

"Your aunt," she said.

"Mine aunt," agreed the lieutenant.

Enzo took a cigarette from the pack of Zetas on the table. His cheek twitched, his eyes narrowed. Sylvie suddenly understood a joke staring at her—the worst cigarettes in Italy are the national brand called Alpha, a word usually designating the best of something. Here, they make no pretense and call these awful cigarettes Zetas, the last letter, the end of the line. "Ha!" she said, covering her mouth when both men looked at her.

The lieutenant packed up the box, pushing the lid on and tying a string around it. "I get more," he said and carried it away.

Enzo leveled his chair and leaned forward. "Don't be such a chatterbox!" he hissed. "Can't you see he's crazy? He's trapped us here. We don't know his motives!"

Sylvie mentally replayed the evening. Minutes ago everything *was* fine, but after all, what did she know about this man?

Enzo whispered, "Stay calm. Act like everything's normal."

This time his words shifted her perception. Now fear churned her stomach as she saw through Enzo's eyes: He had watched her get sucked in by the lieutenant who now brought another box. She studied his face, weighing Enzo's judgment as they viewed more photographs. His brother. A house. Himself in uniform. A woman. The figures stood stiffly in the center of each square. Their smiles changed to mocking leers. The faces became the same face, his face, wearing different disguises. Sylvie's head whirled. She had seen so many tiny black-and-white squares. Would he test to see if she could remember who was who, holding a gun to her head?

She regretted saying she was American. American women were known to be easy, especially blond, braless ones wearing jeans, wire rims, and an India print peasant blouse. She should've kept quiet, as Enzo said. Now it was too late. But then she wondered, where's the line between culture and crazy? Between crazy and violent? Or, for that matter, between violent and culture? Mrs. Connor in Wilmette was a little crazy, plucking off her eyebrows. Monica in Venice was a little crazy and might even be violent. Who knows? Patrizia had sent everyone out of her party and her friend Alberto said she was creative. Or was she unstable? Sylvie continued her mental list—protestors miming and juggling at Lincoln Park, the woman in green "the color of precipitation" at the I Am Temple. Even she and Janis were crazy when they sent pig ears to that jerk Bill. And her roommate Bertie, whom Mom worried was dangerous. John in Bolzano who believed in witches. Mom and Dad probably assumed she, Sylvie, was crazy for joining a new religion and running off to Italy. Aunt Hannah who did horoscope charts—lots of people would call her nuts. Sylvie thought if she treated people with respect, they'd respect her too and she'd be safe. They'd know she was sincere.

It was after midnight when the lieutenant looked at his watch and said, "I must go work soon. It's OK. You sleep my bed."

"We can sleep on the floor here," Enzo said.

The lieutenant was adamant. "No! I here. You there."

Furniture was crammed into the bedroom. Sylvie wondered why he had a double bed then saw the lace curtains that bespoke a woman's presence. She undressed under the covers and put her clothes under the pillow and curled up.

"He's nuts, you know."

"Just lonely, I think."

"Ah, Sylvie. You're so naive!"

* * *

A door slammed. It was raining, half-light. Sylvie was disoriented at first, but the lieutenant, just home from work, peeked in.

"When I wake, I drive you to the road," he said. He entered the bedroom, took something from a drawer then went to sleep on the couch.

Toward noon, hunger awakened her. "Enzo," Sylvie poked his shoulder. His head moved, hair haywire on the pillow. She lay alone with her fear, spawned by Enzo's. How can he sleep so calmly? She shook his shoulder to rouse him. They went outside and followed the street along the splashing sea, looking for food and a way out that avoided the army base. Giving up, they went back inside, wet and hungry, and when the lieutenant returned, he repeated last night. Eggs. Bread. Wine. Zetas. He made espresso then sat down to dig into the photos, him and his brother looking stupidly at the camera. Enzo smoked and drank, brooding. We're prisoners, Sylvie thought. He's torturing us.

After they went to bed. Sylvie heard the lieutenant come get his uniform from the hanger. She lay concentrating on not moving, conscious of every muscle. She itched all over. She felt the lieutenant looking at her, maybe heard him whisper her name. He seemed to linger a long time. She heard his footsteps cross the floor, stop, start again. The front door closed.

Enzo woke up as the car pulled away. "We'll go tonight, before he gets back." He closed his eyes again, breathed evenly, and was soon asleep. Sylvie couldn't stop worrying that they wouldn't wake up in time. She wanted to leave now and sleep by the roadside.

When Enzo woke her, the streetlights were off and the sky gray. They picked up their backpacks, eased the door shut and stole down the street along the shore. They saw a flash of white, a car turning the corner at the end of the street behind them.

"He saw us! Run!"

ANIMAL SKIN

They scurried through a side street to the main road and kept running. If the lieutenant were pursuing, they'd lost him. Maybe that hadn't been his car. Sylvie felt sorry as she pictured him unlocking his door, stung to find his new friends had left without thanking him or exchanging addresses or even saying goodbye, and sitting down alone to his eggs and photographs. She felt foolish. She wondered about the lace curtains. Enzo was often right about people's motives. She hadn't really grasped how frightening people could be, especially nice, kind ones. But maybe he's wrong. She'd trusted Enzo's gut feelings for months but he didn't trust hers. His oddness made them paranoid.

At the highway they plopped down and leaned on their packs. The sun had risen above the trees and shone warmly by the time a green Fiat van picked them up. The back compartment was flattened and covered with backpacks, some bearing Canadian flag decals. Sylvie felt at home and talked about her stay in Quebec.

They got out just outside Titograd near the Albanian border where dark-eyed children in dirty and colorful clothes peered from behind the border patrol station where the road curved up into Albania.

"Don't talk to them," Enzo warned. "Don't even look at them! That shows you're an easy target. In Naples, they stalk you like prey and pick your pocket."

"Seriously? They look like child-sized old men just trying to survive." The children beckoned them until sharply summoned by adults.

Sylvie's feet were cold as they continued into the wilds looking for a sheltered place to settle for the night. Following a gravel road up a hill, they came upon a cluster of small, boxy buildings, the first shops they'd seen in hundreds of miles. Doorways were draped with cloth or beaded strips. One shop had a meager supply of sausages, some in a glass case, others dangling from the ceiling. Enzo pantomimed for one. As they then approached the next shop, a bearded man with pant legs stuffed into the tops of big, rough boots emerged with a loaf of bread, several wolf pelts slung over his shoulder. This was wilderness. Outside this hamlet, they followed the road until they saw a group of trees atop a grassy hill.

"That looks sheltered and secluded," Sylvie said. The grass was slippery approaching the trees under whose cover they removed their packs, spread out the sleeping bags and lay down to gaze up at the Milky Way. Sylvie regarded Enzo's nose silhouetted against the sky.

"Look how many stars!" he said.

She reached over and stroked his face and he turned to smile at her and took her hand and held it. She heard a wail far away. Then another echoing. Then another closer.

"Listen!" she hissed.

"Wolves," he said. "Don't worry," he turned, his eyes peeking open. "Don't you think I'll protect you?"

Though she trusted his intuition, she didn't think he could protect them from wolves. She watched him fall asleep and shimmied herself in her sleeping bag to cuddle against him for warmth. He rarely complained about feeling cold. She should've had his blood since she'd lived in colder places. Her feet jammed against the bag's bottom as it slowly slid foot-first down the hill during the night. Lying next to Enzo in one of the wildest places on earth, she realized how little she knew him. She knew he appreciated her sensibilities and she admired his creative mind. Aren't these qualities of the spirit? Was there more to love than these things? How close could two people possibly hope to become?

They awoke to cowbells and bleating goats. Inside the bags, they warmed their clothes and dressed, uncurled and emerged like butterflies from a chrysalis. They packed their gear and followed the sounds to a farmhouse. Enzo said a lone woman would not seem as threatening as a couple so he waited on the road while Sylvie knocked on the door. A pink-faced young woman in black and calico answered, sun wrinkles around her eyes. Sylvie mimed drinking from a cup, tilting her head back. The woman raised a finger and disappeared inside. She reopened the door, one hand clutching a glass bottle of goats' milk and the other a chunk of cheese. Sylvie took the food and held a palm open, three coins sitting in it: The woman took just one. Sylvie was heartened by this exchange, each side trusting the other. She carried the food to where Enzo sat on the grass across the road and returned the bottle after they ate.

They put on their backpacks and returned to the road that ultimately became a clean, wide street. As there were neither sidewalks nor cars, they proceeded down its middle. They were well into Titograd when Sylvie heard giggling and shuffling. She spun around and was amazed to see a group of children in school uniforms, chanting and skipping behind them.

"Queen Elizabeth!" said one, and the words rippled throughout the group. Did their blue jeans look exotic? A little girl about ten years old skipped up to Enzo with a piece of paper and a pen.

"You are movie star?" she asked in Italian.

Enzo smiled and signed a thin black scribble autograph on the paper. The crowd swelled. Enzo and Sylvie exchanged looks and laughed as they kept walking.

"Eastern European women love Italian movie stars," Enzo bragged.

"Don't let it go to your head."

Two mothers had joined the group. Sylvie pointed to the ground. "This road goes to Skopje?"

"Ya," one nodded. "Skopje."

Enzo saluted as the group turned the corner.

"Whenever did you hitchhike through Yugoslavia?" Sylvie asked.

"Never."

"Some idea!" They both laughed.

They continued until the road ended where it met railroad tracks and a mountain path that paralleled the tracks before disappearing among trees up a steep slope. It was still morning but the sun already dipped behind the hills. Puzzled, they looked back toward the street that had deposited them there. As there didn't seem to be any other way to head east, they waited, stymied.

A herd of sheep appeared as if from nowhere, tiptoeing along the path across the tracks. Two men, the older one on mule-back, shepherded them. Both wore patterned wool sweaters, woolen knit caps and sheepskin coats that might have been the herd's grandparents. Through gestures and broken French, the younger man communicated, "No trucks come here. You come with us." The one on mule-back got off and motioned to Sylvie to get on. At first she refused and kept walking—she didn't feel right riding while he was on foot. But he kept walking, too. When she looked at him, he pointed to the mule, then at himself and shook his head no. So she climbed on and rode. The shepherds hiked silently, stabilizing themselves on the steep trail with walking sticks. Their minds were precision instruments in a shepherding machine as they led the herd that followed as one body.

A hand tapped her foot. The younger shepherd was handing her a fat salami sandwich. She'd been a vegetarian but was practical enough to realize if the only available food is a sausage, that's what she'd eat. She thanked him. Lone snowflakes appeared, drifting gently onto their clothes. The shepherd produced an umbrella, opened it and handed it to Sylvie who again thanked him.

The higher they went, the colder it got. One shepherd indicated they'd continue higher into the mountain. When they heard the distant honking of an approaching bus, the other pointed up through the woods, repeating something with urgency, motioning them to run that way. So they scrambled up the hill and ahead of the bus that honked at each bend in the road. They flagged it down and it screeched to a stop. The driver shook his head at Enzo's offer of coins and waved them aboard.

"Those shepherds were a godsend," Sylvie said. "And this bus."

They found seats in the back of the cold, smoky coach, passing rows of men singing along to a concertina. Enzo soon joined the singers, offering Neapolitan songs as the concertina followed his lead and others snapped their fingers and called out. Sylvie listened to the clucking, nasal, whirring vowels of a Slavic tongue. She was touched by how Enzo jumped in and they welcomed him. The singing and snow continued even as the bus began sputtering and finally gave up in Businje where everyone filed out to cram inside a cold, narrow tavern to await another bus to rescue them. Enzo spoke with fellow passengers who knew some Italian. He learned that the tannery was in Pec, not Skopje.

The driver of their next bus dropped them in Pec and they waited on a park bench in the brisk dawn air. The streets remained empty until a sweeper appeared. Enzo hailed the man, pointed at his leather belt and looked questioningly. The man pointed down a street and counted five on his fingers. Enzo saluted and he and Sylvie followed five blocks to a large, one-story, windowless building with one windowless door. A man in a suit responded to their knock and greeted them warmly in French. He communicated that he could only sell in bulk to wholesalers. Still, he invited them to tour the tannery and ushered them through the building, passing rooms full of pelts in various stages of tanning lying in piles, some blue from uric acid. Sylvie breathed through her mouth to avoid the ammonia stench. This was the climax of their costly trip.

"Enzo, think about how everyone helped us the entire time, really," she said.

"Helped? Or did we use them for our purposes?"

They found a hotel where they were given an overpriced unheated room with a lumpy bed covered with a threadbare blanket, transom windows above a ten-foot wall, and a bare bulb dangling from the ceiling. Sylvie went to the manager's room to ask for heat and when the door opened, she felt heat pour out. All she understood from his gesturing was that he hadn't promised any heat.

"This is how you treat guests?" she asked in English. "In the USA you'd lose your license!" The proprietor looked at her, blinking, until she stomped back to their room.

"Who's using whom?" she asked Enzo.

He had set up the little Sterno camp stove on the bare floor to boil water with bouillon and sausage in it.

"You're amazing," he said. "A real trooper."

They kept the Sterno burning to huddle beside long after they'd eaten, then climbed into the thin, lumpy bed and made love.

The money they'd planned to spend on leather bought them two bus tickets back to Trieste.

U.S.A.
1974-1978

FLOWER KILLER

Dad had telephoned last week to announce he was coming to Burlington to officially sell Sylvie the house. Now, after checking into a hotel near the airport, he drove his rental car to pick up Sylvie and Diana for lunch and then to the lawyer's.

After they'd ordered, Dad said, "Tell me about the deal you made with the New Zealanders."

Sylvie was distressed that they'd contacted him. She'd dreaded having this conversation. "Oh, yeah," she said.

"They say you owe them $200?"

"That was the agreement. It was a van. They'd created a roof. You'd have liked it, I think." She wasn't going to rat out Enzo. "But it didn't last long."

"OK, but do you owe them $200?"

The waitress came with their order and refilled their water. When she left, Sylvie said, "I guess so. We intended to pay it but they left before we had the money."

Dad looked at her hard even as she turned to busy herself with Diana. She could hardly stand her embarrassment.

"Here's what we'll do. We'll send them a check for you and work it out in the details of the house sale." He gazed steadily at her. "And no more shenanigans. You're in the adult world now with adult responsibilities."

Sylvie was starting to feel relieved that it hadn't gotten really ugly.

"So, a toast. We're putting you on the deed as one-fourth owner."

This was news. "You, Mom, me and Enzo?"

"No. Jim."

"Why Jim?"

"To make it fair."

"Why's it fair? Jim doesn't live here and fix it up."

"I'm not arguing about it, Sylvie."

After lunch, they went to the lawyer to sign the papers. Dad said, "Tonight I'm visiting my old army friend Dr. Otto Shuster at your aunt's house." He bent to awkwardly peck her cheek and patted Diana's head. "And just so we're clear, this is your final launch. Don't think you can move back home. You're on your own now, so tread carefully."

* * *

She knew how hurt Enzo was to hear about the house transaction. Still, she said, "Are we ready to fix the upstairs for renting?"

"Really? Let's exploit my free labor for your parents' property? They put Jim's name on the deed, not mine," he complained. "Tell *him* to come do the work!"

"Oh, please! They vouched for your visa and gave you a way out of the draft. That was a big deal for them."

"I'm their son-in-law. They did what's required." He stroked his chin. "Anyway, I'm keeping track of my hours laboring here."

Though she had complaints about her parents, she didn't like him criticizing them. "You're acting paranoid," she said. "Stefano's house wasn't yours and that didn't bother you." "I've stated my terms," he said. "And I want to quit my job."

Sylvie was tired of how Enzo lavished so much attention on himself. Didn't he feel at all changed by fatherhood? "How will we pay the mortgage and insurance? Diana needs a home. And food."

"I'll do leather work again."

"Yeah? What's your source for leather?"

He just looked at her.

"You're being frivolous. You're not a teenager anymore," she said.

He went off to shower. She'd bring it up later.

Sylvie realized she'd underestimated the challenge of marrying someone so different. How could they ever have a united family when their assumptions were so far apart? One thing they'd agreed on was to scorn anything smacking of their middle-class childhoods, but here they were with typical middle-class concerns.

Diana sat on the floor lining up blocks and stacking one on top of another. Sylvie put on a Judy Collins record and retreated to the sink to tackle dishes, her eyes fixed on the stainless steel faucet. As hot water ran, she mused about things her parents had given her, things requiring money, and realized she couldn't give these to Diana. Was that bad? Had those things brought happiness—the record player, the big house, the piano lessons? She hadn't noticed her viewpoint slowly changing until she was where she'd vowed never to be.

She squirted soap into the water and swirled it with her hand to make suds. Doing dishes usually soothed her, the water's steady stream, the rhythm of wiping plates.

She'd focus on soapy bubbles reflecting the pink of her skin, and when she moved her hands the color shifted as in a kaleidoscope, water that imbues so much of life, the water line from uterus to uterus. But now she picked up a dishrag and furiously scrubbed plates, the memory of Enzo's words making her want to scream. She respected his adventuresome spirit but despised that he seemed unconcerned about Diana's well-being.

With a start, she dropped a plate and watched it float down and tap the sink bottom. Had she become Mom already? Housebound with a child, discontented, unfulfilled, not able to communicate with her husband? Mom's depressed voice was in her head, criticizing the family and the life. Hers was the life Sylvie had fought to escape. But in escaping, she'd bungled because she lacked things she'd rejected that would dig her out. She saw how deeply rooted she was in the materialism of her culture and prayer and meditation hadn't freed her of it.

* * *

Before answering the doorbell, Sylvie lifted Diana from her high chair and put her in the backpack. On the porch stood a woman with teased gray-streaked hair, black-rimmed glasses and a loose-fitting dress faded from repeated washings.

"Is . . . your man here?" she monotoned. "Your husband?" She gently patted her hair.

"No, he's out."

"Well," she said, her nose twitching, "he called me about the cat."

"He didn't mention it." Sylvie was willing to support Enzo's interests, to help appease his culture shock. But, a cat?

"I like to screen homes before I place my cats."

"Well, we talked about getting a kitten, not a cat."

"I've got a six-month-old. He loves tuna. Pasta. Sometimes cottage cheese, but not too much."

Sylvie laughed, "So do I!"

The woman eyed Sylvie then peeked around her into the hallway. "Whose house is this?" she asked, patting her hair.

"Used to be my grandmother's."

"Seems I rented a room here once."

"Possibly. She had roomers."

"Wasn't she a nasty one! Had Siamese cats hiding behind those vines growling at people! You'll have to train your child to be nice to the cat."

The woman's lack of manners, making her seem more inept than rude, made Sylvie smile. "Is this six-month-old cat nice to children?"

"When he gets used to them. His mother has had litters in my yard twice every year for twelve years. I had to start screening foster families. A child once choked a cat of mine." She fingered her throat. "May I see your kitchen?"

"Beg pardon?"

"It should be sanitary, you know, for your cat's health."

Sylvie granted her lackluster house-cleaning—dirt settled in nicks of the worn hardwood floor. Grease encrusted the cast-iron combination wood and gas stove. She moved ahead of this woman, picking up Diana's sweater, stacking newspapers on the arm of a chair, removing glasses from the table, conscious of the woman's critical eye, and forgetting for a moment what this inspection was for.

"I have three cats," continued the woman. "A Siamese, almost ten years old. And two others I never placed."

"You have your hands full." Sylvie relished the handiness of such noncommittal phrases.

"If you knew my anguish! I want to go to Florida next winter but not with four cats."

She wondered how hard the woman would push. "Did my husband tell you I'm allergic?"

The woman ran a finger across dusty porcelain plates and tarnished candlestick holders, Sylvie's inherited luxuries. "When will he be home?"

"So you think we'd make a good home?" Sylvie didn't want cats but also didn't like being judged.

"Oh, yes," said the woman.

"He gets home late."

"Have him call," said the woman.

* * *

Enzo came in the kitchen when he got home and greeted Sylvie with a kiss.

"When we were at the park yesterday, kids got off the school bus and ran to the swings and giant slide. Two girls from the block pushed Diana in the baby swing."

"Maybe they can babysit someday." He picked up Diana from her high chair and twirled her around in the air. Sylvie found it adorable when he put Diana on his shoulders and she clutched his hair like reins.

"I don't know—they're a little wild. They run around free until dinnertime. I feel sorry for them—Michelle's parents work and leave her free to roam. Christie's mom's an alcoholic."

"You can't hold that against the girls."

Sylvie used to roam around all day like that, and technically she could run to Mom at home but that wasn't always the case, as with the man-boy who had molested her in broad daylight on a public street, the catalyst that had disrupted her notion of a peaceful world and set her to seeking the engine that made the world tick. She thought about Mom's mothering, and Gram's letters in the trunks

229

and realized she was the next generation foot-soldier in the civilization's slow march.

"I also made friends at the Fillmore—Rick and Brian both just moved to the city with their wives and invited us over sometime. Brian is *simpatico* but Rick wants too much to be a boss. I don't trust him. He manages a garden store. Brian has a carpentry business."

"Well, maybe Brian can teach you some carpentry and you can use it working on the house."

"Maybe," he said. "And I met someone who needs a room. Maybe she can be a trial tenant and just pay expenses."

"Enzo, please don't make deals when you're drinking! That's not something we agreed. Neither is this—some nutty woman came saying you ordered a cat. Don't you think we have enough going on?"

"It's just a little kitty," Enzo said. "Diana will love it."

"Oh, really? I thought you'd want to roast it."

He scowled.

"You have no idea how to care for a pet."

The idea of having to take care of people as well as pets overwhelmed her. She was glad she'd started making friends, even the girls who now followed her and Diana home from the park. They told her about school and their favorite TV shows, played with blocks, musical instruments and dolls with Diana or colored and painted at the dining room table or helped Sylvie in the garden. Sometimes Sylvie let them help make bread or tomato sauce, Diana either watching from her high chair or standing on Sylvie's lap and "helping."

From inside her house, Sylvie could see into her neighbor's living room, the television's cold glare dancing across Mrs. Steele's face. Mr. Steele was a taciturn man who trimmed the lawn like a golf green, with razor-cut edges along the sidewalk which Mrs. Steele swept daily as if against the disorder that spilled over from Sylvie's yard. Starting out on a walk with Diana, Sylvie stopped to chat with Mrs. Steele, whose calico housedress embraced her plump folds as she was sweeping the sidewalk. She left home only once a week when her daughter picked her up in a shiny car.

"Nice day, isn't it?" Mrs. Steele asked, barely lifting her white head.

"We've earned it after this winter."

"Cold up here, eh?"

"The flowers say otherwise now, I guess," said Sylvie.

Like other neighbors, Mrs. Steele remembered Gram without affection, saying her house was called "the dark house." On Halloween, Gram had five apples ready for the five children she recognized and slammed the door on others. Yet Sylvie still wanted to know what Gram had known, how she'd survived back then raising two children. She understood now why, when she'd visited from school, Gram had seemed so bitter. Sylvie wanted to keep collecting details from Aunt Iris. Her link in the chain of womanly knowledge had broken, especially since Mom was so practical and didn't believe in "such nonsense." Sylvie imagined most women knew survival, including Gram as her garden proved. Aunt Iris said that after dark Gram would steal into a nearby field armed with a pair of shears in one hand and a trowel in the other. Sylvie pictured moonbeams glancing off the shears' shiny steel, Gram's shadow the long black figure of a warrior cast behind her. Gram would dig up plants precisely, the sharp trowel slicing cleanly through soil, carefully pot them and line them in terracotta rows on the back porch.

"You should see these little roses when they bloom," Mrs. Steele said, indicating a bush that poked its branches from Sylvie's side of the rusty fence. "I don't think they bloomed last year. They're tiny, and so pretty."

"A wild rose. Iris said Gram started that as a shoot. Did you ever share plants with her?"

Mrs. Steele scoffed. "You got a lot of weeds. Too shady over there." She pointed to a row of gladiolas. "My daughter just planted these. And she's bringing petunias."

Sylvie thought such tropical flowers looked out of place there.

"By the way," Mrs. Steele said, "the men are coming to dig post holes for the fence."

"Would you let me know when? I need to go out and want to be here to make sure they leave my flowers alone."

On walks with Diana, Sylvie followed different routes, studying the frame houses standing equidistant from the street, each with jumbled weeds beneath shaggy bushes, steps up to porches, doors trimmed with dingy peeling wood. As she saw worn fabric pressed against window glass, a still darkness beyond, she smiled recalling her walks with Mom who assessed people by their décor. Amidst the dinginess, plants hung from porch ceilings in twine macramé hangers, their lush vines grazing the railings. She pictured backyards with tidy flowers—spring daffodils, summer marigolds, fall chrysanthemums—whose brave brightness withstood muddy Vermont springs, torrid summers and frigid falls. She tiptoed up steps to pinch off Swedish ivy slips to smuggle home some hope.

Now she took off for the Willard Street Market where she saw Linda who invited her to bring Diana over to play with Claudia while she and Sylvie watched the new *Phil Donahue* show. His interview guest was Squeaky Fromm of the infamous Manson family who had killed Hollywood celebrities and the hippies' peaceful image. Sylvie felt vulnerable to such people because she'd met so many. One of Saul's friends had hitched out west with a Manson woman who claimed to be a witch who just by squinting could disappear the cars that didn't pick them up. They watched the show fascinated and horrified.

But she was happy to be at Linda's house. She appreciated the society of mothers and children, a world hiding in plain sight. She and Linda differed but also had an unspoken, primal bond—that of birthing. Though the greatest physical change endured by humans, it had no formal structure for women who had experienced it. Mothers found each other anyway, especially ones like Linda and her with no other family in town.

Walking home, she noticed a spiraea bush like one back home, covered with lacy white flowers. Once Dad had trimmed the shrub into a big ball while still in bloom, shaving off the flowers bit by bit until just leaves remained, upsetting Mom who liked how it arched naturally. Hosta flowers brushed against her leg, reminding her how she used to pop their flowers puffed full of air. "Is it a poppy?" she'd ask Mom.

"No," said Mom.

"What's a poppy look like?" she would ask.

"I don't know."

She suddenly remembered the new fence posts and was anxious to see how they looked. Looking up the property line, Sylvie saw the old rusty fence and rotting wooden posts were gone. A black dog was lifting its leg on a butternut tree in her yard. Bright shiny steel posts stuck up from cement roots along the property line, the earth between each pole black and raked smooth several feet into Sylvie's yard. Gram's flowers were gone.

She ran and banged on Mrs. Steele's door, shouting her name. "Mrs. Steele!" Sylvie was breathless by the time she answered. "You've ripped up my flowers!" Mrs. Steele must be Griselda's evil twin, so detached was she from life.

"Oh, it was just weeds," she said. "The men did that. Getting it ready for the fence."

"Those weren't weeds! They were the flowers my grandmother planted. Even the rosebush is gone." Those flowers proved that Gram had been able to love something.

"I told you this morning they were coming."

"Where did they put the plants?"

"Oh, they threw them in the trash."

In a fury, Sylvie ran out to the trashcan behind Mrs. Steele's garage, hoping the plants would still have soil clinging to their roots. She could see the barrel out back, exposed to the sun and packed to the brim with wilted plants. Distraught, she was going to salvage the plants anyway and stormed across the yard, feeling as though Gram herself had been thrust into the trash can with the flowers she'd tended for so long.

DOMESTICATING

In the garage, Enzo found an old wooden wagon that he cleaned up for Diana who, when she started walking, liked to push as a parent slowly pulled. This is how they met their other next-door neighbors, Judy and Gary, whose daughter Sunny was Diana's age. Gary, a staff psychiatrist at the university hospital, immediately engaged Enzo in rhapsodies about cities on the Italian Riviera.

How ironic, Sylvie thought, that while she'd been reading ancient seed catalogs last winter, Judy was next door planning her vegetable garden. Now Judy lent her past issues of *Organic Gardening, Prevention Magazine* and *Whole Earth Catalogue* with its tips and sources for self-sufficiency, all of which boosted her study of plants. At the health-food store, Go to Health, she bought an herb handbook, a guide about foraging wild food, another for identifying wildflowers and a vegetarian cookbook pairing grains, legumes and dairy for protein.

On walks with Diana, Sylvie sought places where she could forage like in Nogare and discovered vacant overgrown land on Prospect Street abutting a convent. Traces of old buildings, a forgotten pool, and the ruins of a foundation hid beneath maple seedlings and pokeweed.

Wooded at one side with a meadow in the middle, the land hosted many plants Sylvie recognized. Soon, she was gathering raspberry fruits for jam and leaves for tea, and boneset, motherwort and Joe Pye weed for home remedies. Later in the season, she'd harvest young milkweed pods to sauté in butter, rosehips for tea, and juniper berries to add to sauerkraut. Near a stream she collected pollen from cattails to add to pancake batter.

She passed from the woods into a plowed field where nuns hoed and dug. At the far edge was a grid of garden plots where a sign read, "Gardens for All" with a phone number. Excitedly, Sylvie called when she got home and reserved a plot where every day she'd push Diana in her stroller and garden as much as she could while Diana played with toys on a blanket or napped. She would've enjoyed hearing the nuns' gardening tricks but became engrossed in her own work.

Sylvie wanted Enzo to come along on these walks, knowing he loved seeing wild animals. In postwar Naples, where every obtainable creature had been someone's dinner, his experience with wildlife was confined to rats, feral cats and stray dogs, so squirrels and rabbits were a novelty. Since Sylvie knew he especially liked watching the crows in the tree across the street, she suggested they carry suet to the woods for them. Soon the crows followed them to the woods, signaling each other from treetops. Times like these when they were all together were Sylvie's favorite.

"When we rent, we just need to cover insurance, mortgage, taxes and utilities. The house will pay for itself, but let's make it something friendly."

"Might be interesting," Enzo said. "A cooperative household."

"Yes, where people can feel it's their home, not just ours," she agreed. "You know, if we're good at renting rooms, maybe someday we can rent out the whole house and use that money to buy another property. And so on."

Enzo eyed her. "Ah, yes. Capitalists and their means of production. Is that who we're becoming?"

Sylvie laughed. "Maybe so." She surprised herself with such thinking but wanted to face reality. But really, that's what Gram and Edith had done.

The people Enzo had met soon materialized. Rick and Annie's daughter Florie and Brian and Miriam's daughter Melissa were about Diana's age. Both women grew vegetables, canned food and foraged for herbs and had unconventional childrearing ideas. Miriam exposed her baby, Teddy, to so much sunshine his skin had turned thick and leathery. Incongruously she dressed him in a bonnet, his only clothing besides his diaper. Miriam astonished Sylvie with her recounting of the feast held after her home birth where one of her friends collected the afterbirth and made placenta stew for the guests. As omnivorous as Italians were, Sylvie doubted they'd do such a thing. Nonetheless Sylvie socialized with them both so Diana could have playmates.

Betsy, Enzo's find in the Fillmore, moved in Sunday and spent all day in her room until evening when Sylvie heard her go out. Enzo slept late and Betsy left early each day. It became Sylvie's task to deal with her. It'd be the same thing with a cat—burden's on me, Sylvie thought as she went to collect Betsy's share of utilities, the deal Enzo had made with her. She wasn't there. But early the next morning, Sylvie surprised her in the upstairs kitchen and was amazed how large she was—not just tall but muscular.

"I don't have the money," she said. "Besides, I should only pay one-fourth since there's three of you and I'm not even here twelve hours a day."

The next Saturday, a man—Enzo said he knew from bar gossip that he was married—visited in Betsy's room and they played music and talked loudly, which woke up Diana, whose crying carried through the stairwell. In the morning, Betsy came downstairs to complain about the crying.

"It's your noise that woke her up," Sylvie pointed out.

Betsy replied, "Sorry," provoking Sylvie with her sarcastic tone.

"Besides, you owe us."

"Fine. I only moved here because your old man said it was free." She handed Sylvie $30 cash.

The next day was quiet upstairs. Sylvie went to check and found Betsy's room empty and the bed stripped. A hardcover Rodale's *Organic Gardening* lay on the bedside table. Sylvie accepted it as payment in full.

* * *

They agreed they'd take any renter who handed over cash and hoped they'd get along. Sylvie thought how hard it must be to run a business and be a "do-gooder," a term Dad sometimes used to tease Sylvie about her anti-materialistic notions. She and Enzo still hoped to help build a community.

The first to respond was Timothy Clay, who arrived in a three-piece suit and tie, looked at the back room from the threshold, said, "I'll take it," and counted out two months' rent in cash. Then he added, smiling thinly, "Call me Sticky. Everyone does." His elegant manner contrasted with his pale face and whiny voice. Sylvie felt sad that he blithely accepted the taunting nickname Sticky Clay.

The room with the shower soon went to Gretch, a tall, solid woman who reminded Sylvie of Mum who'd sold them the van. She worked on a bread factory assembly line.

Eddy, a recovering alcoholic on disability, took Aunt Iris's old bedroom. His girlfriend Amy, who constantly twirled her hair around an index finger, spent a lot of time there too. She was a special education teacher who said she moonlighted as a stripper over in Plattsburgh. Eddy said, "She's got the bod for it—trust me!"

The third-floor suite went to Jerome, a bespectacled African American, his freckled, red-haired wife Mary and their baby.

At the end of two weeks, the rooms were filled and Enzo convened everyone in their upstairs kitchen and said, "We hope you'll create community here. Meaning you should share and care about each other."

Mary said, "Anyone can use my kitchen stuff—just clean it and put it back."

"Ours too," said Amy.

Gretch left the room and returned with a small black-and-white TV and set it on the counter, saying, "Just keep the sports to a minimum."

When Sticky wasn't in his room playing his only record, he watched *I Dream of Jeannie* and *Perry Mason* reruns, staring at the set, immobile even when someone came in and changed the station. But it was a start.

One day when Diana was napping, Sylvie headed upstairs to collect rent. Approaching, she overheard the kitchen conversation and paused on the stairwell to eavesdrop. She felt uncomfortable spying but wanted to see how well they got along and felt her presence might change their behavior.

"The entire school district down there is special ed." It was Amy's voice. "It's those long winters. After they do the livestock, they go for their kids."

"That's gross," said Gretch.

"Sad but true," said Amy.

"Teaching beats the goddamn assembly line," said Gretch.

"It's probably not that different," said Amy. "This one guy? I give him paint, a brush and paper, so he paints black until one spot is so wet there's a hole in the paper."

"What can you expect?" said Gretch, slurping. Probably beer from the can.

"Not much," said Amy. "But now I know what moron really means."

"I worked in a home for cripples. I couldn't stand looking at deformed people every day."

Sylvie heard the clink of a can hitting the table. "You sure you're cut out for this job?"

"Do I give a shit? Gotta earn money, don't I?"

"And the school district doesn't care you're a stripper?"

"I cross the lake to Plattsburgh. How'll they find out? You think customers are gonna blab about seeing me?"

Sylvie heard footsteps descending the attic stairs and figured it was Jerome, probably carrying his baby, judging by how he was cooing.

"Hello," he said, his voice trailing as he entered the kitchen. Sylvie heard chairs dragging across the floor. Jerome usually laid out coupons on the table for supermarket contests and put stickers in appropriate places to ready them to mail. He sometimes won first-round prizes which, when they arrived, he littered throughout the kitchen— lemon juicers, plastic tongs and lid flippers.

"Well, *he* doesn't think so," Gretch said.

"'He doesn't think so' what?" said Jerome.

"Forget it," said Amy.

"Doesn't think he needs to earn money," said Gretch.

"Like you know what I think?"

"Then tell me," Gretch said, "why would an able-bodied man like you get food stamps?"

"'Cause I can't get a job," Jerome said.

Sylvie heard the fridge open and shut and the rattling of a paper bag.

"Why not?"

"'Cause I'm black. In this town."

Gretch snorted. "Maybe if you were an honest man, you could get a job."

"Who says I'm not honest?"

"You! You just said you can't get a job because you're black."

"What?"

"But I think it's because you're stupid and dishonest."

"You're calling me stupid?"

Oh no—this is all wrong! But Sylvie waited to hear it play out. There was a pause and smacking of lips. Probably Gretch drinking beer again.

"Yeah, stupid. Because you have a baby and don't have a job."

"I told you, I lost it when Mary was pregnant."

"She should've gotten an abortion. It'd be cheaper than being a burden on the State."

"How dare you! You fat bitch!"

"Besides, there's too many black babies. And it's not fair to mulattos to bring them into the world. They don't know if they're black or white," Gretch said. Sylvie knew how Gretch would say something obnoxious then primly retreat, and imagined her doing this now.

"What difference does it make?" Jerome's voice was rising.

"Cute baby," said Amy loudly. "How old is she?"

"What difference? They won't know which box to check. And anyone who sees them thinks they're black even though *they* think they're white."

"Hi, little baby," Amy cooed.

"You're a bitch," Jerome said to Gretch.

"Indeed I am," she said.

Sylvie walked heavily, audibly, into the kitchen and paused in front of the baby. "She is so adorable, Jerome! I love seeing how sweet fathers can be with their kids." When Jerome's eyes met hers, she saw four hundred years of pain.

Gretch said, "Where's that cute little girl of yours, Sylvie? Looks just like her daddy!" Amy moved toward the TV and turned it on.

"These women in Italy were like goddesses. They taught me how to be a mother. They made me feel so welcome," Sylvie said. "That's how I want this place to be."

Gretch smirked and sipped beer.

ERUPTIONS

Dad called to say he and Aunt Iris were no longer speaking. "It's clear she's pilfered valuables from the house. And she and her no-good husband were living off the insurance from a fire caused by their tenants."

"Oh, Dad; I really love Aunt Iris."

"The lines are drawn. She wants you to know she's siding with that bum of a husband. We'll see if she does the right thing."

Sylvie's eyes welled. Besides Iris's warmth, she was deep. But Sylvie hated Uncle Simon's meanness. Just before they'd posted the ad for roomers, Simon had stormed in the front door and up the stairs and kicked a box of dishes across the floor, screaming, "You and your whole damn family can go to hell!" Aunt Iris had warned how moody Simon was and knew Dad never liked him. Sylvie realized she was Dad's pawn in an old fight.

She dialed Aunt Iris to hear her side of things.

"Sylvie, I'm so sorry. Simon isn't always the nicest man, but I need to be loyal to him."

Sylvie thought of Iris's advice, that it doesn't matter who you marry but how you behave. Had she just wanted company in her misery?

"I understand. I love you."

Iris sniffled and tried to speak but finally said, "Me too, dear."

On the tenant front, Sylvie learned Sticky's routine. When his disability check arrived, he'd buy ground beef and cigarettes. He'd plop the meat into a pan on the stove with the flame set high, then go to his room and turn on his David Bowie 45 RPM record of "Young Americans" and sit on his bed smoking while the burger hissed and crackled. Along with the stench of burnt flesh, Bowie's lyrics wafted through the house: "She cries, where have all Papa's heroes gone?/ All night/ She wants a young American . . . ." After playing it several times, he'd return to the stove, toss out the burnt meat, pull out a cigarette and stare unblinking at the TV. Sylvie laughed about the irony of these romanticized lyrics describing people like her and her tenants with their struggles.

* * *

Annie brought Florie over and said, "Let's walk to your garden. I'll teach you about some herbs on the way." Before getting pregnant, Annie had worked at Go to Health, where she'd learned a lot from a customer called the "Herb Lady" who lived in a trailer in Winooski. "The plants just grow in your yard, if they're what you need," Annie said. She pointed out common herbs—boneset for fever, mullein for coughs, comfrey for healing, motherwort as a woman's tonic and lamb's quarters for stomach ache. "Wherever you see poison ivy, you'll also see its antidote, jewelweed."

"That's so amazing!" Sylvie said. "Why don't people know this stuff anymore?"

"Yeah. It's all out there in the world, for free."

After Annie left, the mail delivered another effusive letter from Janis about her idyllic life in California gold country, the wonders of making jam with fresh-picked cherries, tending bees and gathering honey, milking goats and making cheese, raising her boys and joining with like-minded friends to make music and dance. She always included an open invitation to Sylvie who dreamed of such a self-sufficient life in a friendlier climate. Sylvie had long yearned to absorb folk wisdom about nature that would help her feel at home anywhere in the world. How ironic that Janis had fallen into this life without it having been her goal.

Sylvie noticed a box in the corner of the porch. She lifted the top to find two kittens the cat lady must've left. Man, that cat lady is such a hypocrite, she thought, inspecting others' homes while she herself was so careless as to leave cats unattended on the porch of strangers. When Diana squealed with delight at the sight of kittens and tenderly pet them, Sylvie couldn't bring herself to refuse to keep them.

Following Annie's advice about treating her allergy, Sylvie bought coltsfoot and foraged for mullein to steep in boiling water in a large bowl over which she'd lean, covering her head with a towel that trapped the vapors she'd inhale. Remembering that she'd loaned the bowl upstairs, she headed up to fetch it, holding Diana's hand as she tackled each step. Finally she knocked on the kitchen door which was locked.

"Wait til I'm finished," Gretch yelled.

"Why is this locked?"

"I'm taking a bath." The sound of running water increased, so Sylvie knew Gretch couldn't hear her now. She went into the bathroom to see why Gretch wasn't using the tub. Jerome's baby's cloth diapers were soaking in the bathtub. The urine smell was strong.

"Pew!" she gagged.

"Pew," echoed Diana.

There were clicking sounds at the kitchen door, furniture swishing along the floor, the door flew open and there stood Gretch in her bra, flesh folding over the towel around her middle, fluffing her wet hair with a hand. She'd splashed all over the counter and onto the floor. Water was still rushing down the sink.

"What can I do for you?" she challenged Sylvie, then, "Oh, hellooo, little girl! You're getting so big!"

Diana smiled broadly.

"What's going on?"

"You saw the tub?"

"Yes."

"Well, unless you get a new one or hire professionals to sterilize that one, there's no way I'm using it anymore."

"Where's Jerome and Mary?"

"Probably out spending their welfare check." Gretch backed up and plopped onto a chair. Putting her head between her legs, she continued tousling her straight ear-length hair then sat back, put her feet on another chair, and draped the towel over her shoulders.

"Maybe they're pissed cause I told him to beware the KKK cause I might call someone I know."

"You said what?"

"C'mon, I was kidding. I'm a liberal. I wouldn't do that."

* * *

Sylvie was back downstairs when Jerome tapped on the door. "We're leaving. Obviously." Behind him, Mary carried a box out the front door.

"I'm so sorry. But I understand."

"You got some loonies in here," said Jerome. Sylvie thought it selfishness, not lunacy.

Days later, Stu, a Vietnam vet and divorced dad, moved in with his girlfriend Cindy. His parks department job required him to trim trees either from inside a cherry-picker bucket or while attached by a chain to the tree trunk. On days off, he'd stay in his room wearing headphones with the volume up as loud as possible. Sometimes he'd visit in the kitchen. Cindy was pet sitting her uncle's talking mynah bird and kept its cage in the kitchen where she liked to hang out. Wondering why she spent so much time in the kitchen, Sylvie once asked if everything was OK with the attic rooms.

"Oh, Stu's always listening to music. At night too. Always the headphones," Cindy said.

"What's that about?" asked Gretch.

"Drowning out memories from the war," Cindy explained.

The bird fascinated everyone, especially Diana, who'd stand immobile in front of its cage, waiting for it to talk. Cindy's uncle had kept the cage in his shop against the wall between the phone and the bathroom; this is where it learned its vocabulary. It could say, "Is Joe there?" in a man's deep voice and "Hiyah, beautiful!" in a higher voice, could make a noise like a flushing toilet, and if you asked it, "Where's that cat?" it would meow three times. The bird ate canned dog food mixed with applesauce and would hold it in its beak, shake its head and splatter brown spots on the wall. Gretch tried to get it to make the flushing sounds then, with little luck.

* * *

Sylvie often watched Sunny for Judy and Gary. On a beautiful spring morning, Sylvie sat out front watching the girls push dolls in the wagon and crows congregating atop maples across the street. From the corner of her eye, she could see Sticky rocking in the porch chair, barely stirring when Eddy came out and sat down to read. Sticky's rhythm of chair squeaks and floorboard groans grew faster and louder until Eddy closed his magazine and slapped it onto the floor. Sticky looked at him and asked, "Do you have a cigarette?"

Eddy tossed him his pack which fell to the floor. Sticky bent to pick it up, took out one cigarette and arose to return the pack. "Keep it," Eddy said.

When Sylvie was looking the other way, a man's voice from behind her said, "The one thing I remember about your grandmother, she always had nice flowers."

Sylvie's heart jumped. She turned and saw an older man in a jacket and tie.

"Didn't mean to scare you," he laughed. "I'm Dr. Shuster. Your dad told me to look you up."

She stood and stepped down onto the sidewalk, peering over his shoulder to keep watch on the girls. "Oh, you're who he stayed with recently?"

"Yes. We'd met in ROTC forty years back," he said. "How's your Aunt Iris? And your husband? I understand he's from Italy?"

Sticky's rocking accelerated. Eddy flicked his butt into the bushes and went inside.

"Oh, he's fine," Sylvie said. "But I think he'd like a better job than making pizzas."

"Here's my card," Dr. Shuster said, "Tell him to come see me." She thought of how in Italy, the universe seemed to provide all sorts of opportunities, not all of them good.

After Shuster left, Eddy reappeared. "I keep seeing that guy out here. He looks like someone I saw in the psych ward."

"He *was* in the psych ward," Sticky said. "At Waterbury."

"Better watch out, Sylvie," said Eddy. "He's a scary man. He messed with our minds."

"He's an old army friend of my Dad," Sylvie said.

Eddy squinted at her. "Was your dad at Waterbury?"

"No," Sylvie laughed. "He sells machine parts in the Midwest."

"We're all machine parts but most don't know it," said Sticky.

Sylvie walked Sunny home then brought Diana inside while she started dinner. She lit a fire in the wood stove and placed the stovetop oven over the burner to pre-heat, then took Diana upstairs to visit. Eddy slumped at the kitchen table with cigarettes, dealing out hands of solitaire and saying, "After high school, I was a carpenter. Would've gone to 'Nam if I didn't pull a high number. I dunno. Montreal didn't look so bad."

Stu and Cindy entered as Stu was saying, ". . . and who am I to tell my kids they're misbehaving? Maybe I'm misbehaving but they don't spank me."

Gretch, just awakened, came to hang out in the kitchen which she said helped psych her up for her monotonous night shift. "You know very well you're an adult and know more than they do. If a child misbehaves, he should be spanked."

Stu shot back, "Who says I know more? Maybe they know more but just can't talk. The only difference between them and me is I'm bigger."

"You don't believe that."

"The hell I don't," he said.

"Then it's a good thing you don't have custody. You'd probably raise a couple of savages."

Sylvie chimed in. "Stu's right—how can we progress if we keep repeating past mistakes?"

"Like what?" Gretch asked.

"Like how we treat our kids. Each other."

Gretch said, "Oh, please!"

Stu glared at her. "You're crazy, lady," he said, and retreated upstairs.

"I'd rather be crazy and right than to be sane and stupid like you!" Gretch called after him, and swigged another beer. Cindy sighed heavily.

Enzo bounded in, lifted Diana and threw her in the air. She reached up her hands to try to touch the ceiling— he usually let her get that high on the third try. He said, "You Americans think there are rules for everything in life. You need more *fantasia*, more imagination."

Eddy dealt another hand. "Man, I just enrolled at Vermont Institute for Community Involvement," he said, placing a red seven on the black eight. "College without walls. You oughta check it out, man. You'd be a good teacher."

"My dad was a teacher. The other dads worked in the granite mine," Gretch, now settled across from Eddy, spoke between sips from her beer. "I knew my family was among the intellectual elite in Montpelier."

Enzo chided, "You're saying you were intellectual because your father wasn't working class?"

"Not because we weren't working class. Because I was working *in* class. I was always head of the class. Because Dad discussed world affairs with me and I knew I was special. Everyone was jealous of me too. Even in college." Her coworkers now were younger women whom she'd quiz about their political beliefs, determined to enlighten them by regularly reminding them how stupid they were. She opened the fridge and poked around. She'd told Sylvie she constantly needed to police the food marked with her name because her housemates couldn't be trusted.

"Now I'm thirty years old, working at that shitty bakery. I thought it'd be lovely to smell fresh bread every day. Didn't know until day one they wouldn't let me bake anything. Just watch stuff pass on a conveyor belt and push a button for rejects. Wish I could do that for some people! Sometimes I reject something so I can take it home to eat. Anyone want me to get you anything?"

"Sara Lee cheesecake!" said Eddy.

"Oh, yum! Cholesterol in a pan!" said Gretch. "But I don't work at Sara Lee."

GOING BAD

At dawn when Gretch's steps sounded on the upstairs landing, Sylvie heard loud sobbing and rushed upstairs to find Cindy convulsing in Gretch's arms. Cindy had been waiting to ask Gretch to bird-sit while she arranged Stuart's funeral: He had fallen from a forty-foot-high treetop and broken his neck.

Sylvie brewed coffee and they all sat. Cindy said, "The other night at three, Stu swore he saw you up there, floating, in a long white dress. He even called out your name. I didn't see anything but he said a woman that looked like you just glided through the room about a foot off the floor."

Sylvie said, "You know I wasn't up there." She didn't want to mention that others had also reported seeing ghosts in the house.

"Stu was haunted by Vietnam. You have no idea how messed up he was."

No one believed he'd fallen, especially considering all Cindy's fretting about his moods and memories of 'Nam and yesterday he heard his ex-wife had gone into hiding with their kids. Eddy and Sticky were especially shaken. Even Gretch was at a loss for words. Sylvie grieved too: Stu had seemed like a gentle soul who'd seen hell.

Brian and Miriam, Rick and Annie brought over casseroles. Annie also held an acoustic guitar Brian was teaching her to play. "When I heard about the suicide, I wanted to bring you some soothing music," Annie said. She plucked chords to "Skip to My Lou" and sang off-key in a high, thin voice. Though the music grated, Sylvie was touched by Annie's thoughtfulness. Rick brought cigars, exposing his cluelessness, and the new Joni Mitchell tape with "Free Man in Paris."

"Dammit, Rick. I used to love Joni but this album is a sellout," said Sylvie.

"*Au contraire*," Rick rejoined. "She's successful now. I never even heard of her before."

Annie said, "I totally agree, Sylvie. Rick only likes it now because everyone else does."

"All you hippies gotta evolve sometime," said Rick. Sylvie knew this was sarcasm since they all used to live in communes in the so-called Northeast Kingdom in northern Vermont.

* * *

Sylvie was coming up the basement stairs when she heard the front door creak open and steps squeaking on the floorboards.

"Hello?" she called. The footsteps headed upstairs. She put down the carton and ran up to see a man heading upstairs.

"What are you doing?"

He wheeled around. "Enzo's renting me a room." Eddy and Amy had moved up to the attic.

"I didn't hear you knock."

"He said to just go in."

"He didn't tell me about this."

"I don't see why everyone has to know about it."

"Everyone doesn't," Sylvie said. "But it's my house, so I should, don't you think?"

"Oh, sorry." He descended. "I'm Hank Roach. I know Enzo from the Fillmore. He's told me about this place, like how everyone knows everything about everyone. So I just figured."

"Well, a room's available. Two weeks' deposit. There's a contract to sign."

"I want to see it first."

"Come back when Enzo's home."

"I'll wait for him upstairs," Hank said.

Diana was awake from her nap and calling, so Sylvie rushed off to get her and wait on the porch for Enzo. When he arrived, she asked, "Did you get the job?" Dr. Shuster had promised to create him a special position.

"Not yet." He scooped up Diana, who hugged his neck and kissed his cheek. "How's my girl?"

"There's some guy waiting for you and I don't . . . ."

"Hey, landlord!" said Hank as he came out the front door. "I love it. I'll take it."

"Any time, man. Wait here while I get a contract." Enzo rushed inside.

Sylvie followed and said, "Great that you found someone, but can we trust him?"

"He's friends with everyone. Don't worry!"

"I didn't like how he just walked in."

"Remember, we're creating a community here." He gave her a kiss.

After Hank signed, Enzo said, "I'll show you around."

By the time Sylvie and Diana had walked up every stair step, Eddy was saying, "You could teach at Vermont Institute." Noticing Sylvie, he said, "There's no one like your old man. Smartest guy I ever met."

"Like that's saying much." piped in Gretch. "You've never even left this town." To Diana she said, "How's my girl? You're bigger every day!"

Diana climbed into Gretch's lap which pleased Sylvie, who wanted her daughter to have a sense of what community could be even if Gretch seemed unstable.

"You could get paid to teach there, man," Eddy persisted.

"You want me to teach you? Bring me some weed and I'll teach you everything," said Enzo. Sylvie wasn't amused.

"Man, the shit you say makes so much sense," said Eddy. "Grassroots anarchy. Build a utopia on reason and justice. Like the founding fucking fathers."

"Subversive citizenship," said Enzo.

"What's that supposed to prove?" Gretch asked.

"First you must understand power," said Enzo. "Then you can create a utopia."

"Yeah, like you can do that," said Gretch. "That's just fantasies."

"It's everyone's goal to be happy. But what's happiness? And is *being* or *having* more important? Is living or having lived more important?"

"If death is more important," said Eddy, "how would that be happiness?"

Hank was leaning against the doorway and said, "Kill yourself, man. It'd make me happy."

"Hey, look who the cat dragged in," said Eddy. "I know this guy. Are you moving in?"

"Yep. And who cares what's important anyway?" said Hank. "Screw that."

"No one ever accused you of being a genius now, did they?" Gretch also knew Hank from the Fillmore.

"You think *getting* is important cause you never get any," said Hank.

"A major wit here," said Gretch.

"You're hysterical," Hank raised his voice. "You need it right between the legs." It bothered Sylvie that her judgment of Hank was right.

"Yes. That will make me calm as it always does to women like me," said Gretch. "Hyster, the womb. They used to remove it to fix a woman, make her more logical, more manly, less hysterical."

To calm the waters, Sylvie said, "What's important is getting unstuck from your world, your way of thinking."

"Yes," Enzo said. "To know that the rules are made by the powerful to serve themselves."

Hank said, "The powerful *should* make the rules. What's wrong with that?"

Enzo inhaled a cigarette and blew a long stream of smoke. "Sometimes you just need to be shaken awake and see that it's always 'now.'"

"That's deep, man," said Eddy.

Hank stood up. "Now it's time for the Fillmore," he said. "Drinks on me." To Sylvie's annoyance, Enzo agreed.

* * *

Sylvie had listened to the CBS Radio *Mystery Theater* and was in bed reading when Enzo came home. He'd been drinking and smelled like pot. She was annoyed about this presumption that as paterfamilias he went cavorting while she tended the homefires. But she picked a different fight.

"What are you trying to prove to these tenants?" she said. "Eddy and Hank obviously admire you."

"Nothing is 'obvious.'"

"But are you sincerely trying to help them? It's clear you love the adoration from these lost people."

"C'mon," Enzo insisted, "you know it's just fun. Don't act so jealous."

"Jealous? That's not it."

"I share the attention with you. Look how everyone comes and keeps you company."

"You take their praise too seriously. Besides, I don't trust Hank."

"He's OK; I know him from the Fillmore."

"The bar where you've formed so many deep friendships?"

Enzo slipped under the covers.

Sylvie recoiled. "God! The alcohol fumes ooze out your pores!"

"You don't like it?" He shoved her. She resisted but he was stronger and she fell off the bed. She got back up and he yanked her toward himself. She pushed him away and he yanked her again, laughing. Frustrated, she dragged the comforter and a pillow to sleep on the floor in the next room.

One more for the list of the unforgivable.

RESEARCH

Dr. Shuster offered Enzo a position as assistant researcher of the university/hospital's psych ward patients.

"I'll be able to use my mind," he told Sylvie. "And the pay's better."

"Will they finally recognize your degree?"

"He hasn't said so. But I told him how in Trent we started action research activities in hospitals. He wants to know more." He looked out the window. "He's studying how to get people to push their limits. Said he was in Naples after the war and was amazed by what my people did to survive."

Sylvie said, "Remember how the tenants said how scary he is?"

"You and I know they're crazy."

"Maybe emotional wrecks but not crazy," Sylvie said. "They make logical arguments. They have jobs, mostly. Anyway, what's the research?"

"I'll let you know," said Enzo.

A few weeks into his job, Enzo brought an older grad student, Rima, to meet Sylvie, who enjoyed her company so much she extended an open dinner invitation. One evening after dinner and a few glasses of wine, Rima said, "Falkner couldn't hire Enzo in the Soc. Department since his degree is from a foreign university. So somehow Shuster finagled a way to hire him. There's cross-pollination among social sciences there."

"Shuster's a good man," said Enzo. "He knows about the *scugnizzi's* bravery in 1943."

"Who's that?" Rima asked.

"The street kids who died martyrs planting bombs under German tanks. Naples built them a monument."

Rima let Enzo pour her more wine. "Well . . . be careful, Enzo. And document everything."

"Why? What's going on?" asked Sylvie.

"Can't trust any of them," Rima said. "Falkner has plagiarized some of my work but I can't prove it because I didn't document everything. He stole my research and got it published. He's lazy and dumb and in danger of losing his job because he's high all the time."

"Yes, Falkner is limited," Enzo said. "Maybe that's why Schuster hired me."

"Hired you for what, exactly?" Rima said.

"To observe how people behave before and after treatments."

"What treatments?" Sylvie asked.

"Involves drugs. Strong ones."

Sylvie said, "How can you buy into this so easily?"

"You want a provider. Fact of life."

Rima eyed him.

Sylvie said, "I get that, and I get that you want to do research. But what's its goal?"

Rima said, "Yes, Enzo. That university/hospital connection is a minefield. You need to be very careful about what they want you to do. Something there doesn't smell right." She slowly sipped wine and Enzo poured more. "Still, I'm fascinated by the inpatient community. My study looked at how they create a social hierarchy so I often talked with them. You know, they're supposedly nuts so you can't really trust everything they say but you can tell by the emotion there's something going on. They said certain people would be taken from the ward for long stretches and come back vegetables."

"What did they think happened?" Sylvie asked.

Rima said, "You can never repeat any of this."

"Of course," said Sylvie.

"Shock therapy mixed with drug treatments and isolation."

Alarmed, Sylvie said, "Enzo, is that who you're studying? What're they having you do?" She hoped the paycheck was worth it.

Enzo said, "I'm not supposed to talk about it."

"Oh, bull!" said Rima. "I already know what's going on there."

"He wants me to observe some of our tenants and take notes. He knew them on the psych ward."

Rima said, "Then what? Did he ask you to take anything—drugs, I mean? Does he know you're an acid-head?"

Enzo grinned. "Sometimes he wants me to trip and describe my sensations."

Sylvie asked, "Now who's the naïve one?"

"Why?" he chuckled. "Isn't it a dream job?"

"And it's not funny. Shuster's the nutcase."

After a long pause, Rima said, "So you're sort of baseline since you're healthy."

"But why him?"

"Because he's available and has admitted to dropping acid. That gives Shuster deniability if anything goes wrong."

"Enzo, we'd agreed you'd dropped enough acid."

"Maybe you agreed," he said. "I never did."

Rima said, "Apparently some walking wounded are among your tenants."

"Yeah, they even recognize him and say he's bad news," Sylvie said. "But why would a hospital want to make people crazy?"

"I wondered that too," said Rima. "The US has long been interested in mind control and I think this is what they're doing here. Vietnam ended, sort of, but the cold war hasn't."

"So you think the government's behind it?" Sylvie asked.

Rima pulled closer and whispered. "It wouldn't surprise me in the least. There's so much covert activity in this country. But tell me, how many of your tenants have been in Waterbury?" Rima asked.

"Hmmm. Not sure about Jerome and Mary . . . ," said Enzo.

"Does that seem normal to you? That high percentage in a town this size?"

"Never rented rooms before, so it's hard to say," said Enzo.

"C'mon," said Rima.

Sylvie said, "Eddy says everyone in Vermont cycles through Waterbury."

"Exactly," said Rima. "And apartments won't rent to them."

The following week Rima dropped off her original research paper about psychiatric in-patients forming a hierarchical social structure and Falkner's published journal article she'd smuggled from the library. Sylvie compared the two—if Rima's paper came first, then Falkner clearly had plagiarized it.

"I can't afford to sue," Rima said the next time she came. "But I figured something out. They're behaviorists in that department and think personalities are acquired, not inborn. They're experimenting with breaking them down by destroying their memories and rebuilding new ones by suggesting new histories."

"But that's sick!" Sylvie cried. "It's criminal!"

"Not even possible," Enzo said, stubbing out his cigarette.

After Rima had left, Sticky came halfway down the stairs and said, "Something's wrong with Eddy! I can't wake him up!"

When Sylvie and Sticky arrived upstairs, Gretch greeted them with, "Looks like Eddy fell off the wagon."

"Hank holds cans of beer under his nose," Sticky said. The women looked at Sticky expecting more information. "Said he'd buy some for Eddy."

Gretch said, "Yep. Look up 'demon' in the dictionary and there's a picture of our boy Hank."

Sylvie entered Eddy's room that reeked of alcohol. Eddy lay on top of the covers.

"It's been three years," he moaned. "I thought Hank was my friend."

Sylvie felt Eddy's remorse transmute inside her into rage against Hank whom she saw as not just meddlesome but evil. "I'm really sorry this happened, Eddy," she said.

"Hey, I'm a fuck-up. It's not a secret."

"I'll get you some coffee," she said. And I'm getting rid of Hank.

* * *

Enzo came home hugging a pound puppy, black with a white throat. "She's purebred border collie. For free, since I didn't buy her papers."

Diana ran to the door laughing. "Doggie!"

"Yes, *carina,* all for you. Give papa a kiss!" Enzo squatted down and Diana hugged his neck and kissed his cheek.

Sylvie thought the puppy was adorable but said, "You plan to take care of this one, Mr. Earth Mother?"

"Somebody's got to be one around here." His smile irritated her.

"One, we can't afford it. And two, I don't want the responsibility."

He held the puppy in his lap and showed Diana how to gently pet her. "Her grandfather rescued a baby from a stream by pulling it by the diaper. And think how nice for Diana to have so many pets." To Diana Enzo said, "She came with a name: Farfella."

"Hi, Fafalla," Diana said.

"She'll guard Diana. It's in her blood."

"Then let's get rid of those cats! I've tried everything—herbs, positive thinking—and am still allergic."

"It's a weakness. Get over it."

She could give them away and say they ran off, but didn't want to lie. "Sounds like another of Babbo's fascist theories—sickness as weakness." Sylvie didn't mention that Mom had similar ideas from her Christian Science parents.

Enzo narrowed his eyes, then stood and took Diana's hand. "Let's go introduce Farfella to everyone."

"I just realized—you don't want to be a dad—you just want an audience!" Sylvie said to his back as he went up the stairs, and hated how she sounded. She was angry Enzo made her the bad-guy animal hater. He claimed the right to be boss. She wanted to scream, *But it's me, Sylvie! Your partner!* but didn't think he saw her as anything but Diana's mother while he was the *paterfamilias,* a role that was well-defined in his mind. He could glamorize pet ownership because she was supposed to do the grunt work. She burned with resentment. But later when she saw Diana lay socks and a washcloth on the cats' backs, petting and talking to them, she lost the heart to give them away.

Rather than argue with Enzo, she called Mom. But when Mom answered, Sylvie couldn't bring herself to criticize Enzo. Mom and Dad had never advised her about boys other than Mom saying to let Jim win at sports and not let boys think she was smarter than they. Nothing in her life had prepared her for marriage and she'd never known anyone who was divorced. She imagined their conversation:

"Why'd you say you liked him? I really wanted your opinion," she'd say. *"You'd have done it anyway,"* Mom would say. *"If that's true, then why do you think I asked?"* Mom wouldn't reply. *"And now that I've made this commitment and we have a child, do you think I should ditch him when he's struggling? How is that OK?"*

She couldn't tell anyone about Enzo's abuse. They'd only accuse her of being a masochist who liked such treatment. Besides, how could she ditch him? Aunt Iris had said how hard it was growing up without a father and now they had a child. If she divorced Enzo, he might return to Italy. Maybe the stress of the cold made him mean and they should move somewhere warm?

To Mom she said, "Things are fine. Enzo brought home the cutest puppy." She believed his interest in animals was retaliation against her love of plants, but he merely acquired animals and never understood them.

"It's good for kids to have a dog," Mom said. "By the way, remember when I criticized your women's group? You were right. I just attended one. We talk a lot about how we don't see the power men have over us. It's been quite enlightening." Then, "Your father wants me to ask, when will you be getting your degree?"

Adrenaline rushed Sylvie's head. Mom had buttered her up then bam! Sylvie believed opportunities would present themselves and she'd have plenty of time. "I'm working on it."

"I guess a mother hasn't much say in her children's lives once they're adults. But I feel I've failed."

"Great, Mom. I'm one of your failures? Is that what you tell your support group? And, hey. Why are you hanging around with a group of man-haters?" *Touché*, she thought, remembering how Mom had characterized her women's group. Yet, she also wondered what Mom was trying to say: Sylvie hadn't really investigated Enzo's character before they married. But how could you really know another person? How could you know when they'd crack or crumble? She could've been the one to flip out, to flee, to rebel.

She'd called Mom for advice about dealing with Enzo but ended up wanting to turn to Enzo for help dealing with Mom. She felt torn by these two incompatible people, and her feelings for them were also incompatible. And she felt so overwhelmed—with Diana, the house, the tenants, the want, Enzo's volatility—that she couldn't think about his abusiveness, much less about solutions.

* * *

Sylvie got the mail out of the box. Opening the phone bill, she noticed a long-distance call to a Boston area code, noting the date and time of the call. It had to be Hank's— she was enraged he'd taken such advantage of them. She stormed to the phone and dialed the police to ask how to get a restraining order on a tenant who refused to leave. "Lady, that's what background checks are for. Once they're inside, there's not much we can do. Sorry about that."

She suddenly felt like an idiot for thinking they could create an environment where everyone got along, especially when they weren't interested in doing so, and felt quite alone.

There was also a letter from Lori with a typical Wilmette drift:

Sept. 1975

Dear Sylvie,

Gosh, it's been so long! I got a degree in English, finally, and went back home and got a job reporting for Pioneer Press. Well, it's a start, anyway.

I saw your mom at the Jewel and she gave me your address. She seemed a little freaked about what you're doing. A baby? A husband? Vermont? Anyway, she made it sound really bad. I have to admit, it doesn't sound like what I imagined you'd be doing—you were always the activist and I never understood what you were talking about. And now here I am, wanting to report on events. Watergate really inspired me.

She responded to a tap on the French doors to find Sticky standing there. "Do you mind if I stay with you?" he said. "They frighten me up there."

Regarding this bearded, hollow-eyed specter, she said, "Maybe they're afraid of you too!" She hated this. How foolish it was to expect these people to get along. And all Enzo does is take notes, enjoying the chaos.

"Do you mind if I stay here?" repeated Sticky.

"Sure—have a seat on the steps. Diana, let's see what's doing upstairs." She thought it was good for Diana to experience this little community.

Diana said, "I coming."

Upstairs Sylvie found Gretch in the kitchen and said, "Sticky's all freaked out downstairs."

"He should be, but that's not my fault," said Gretch.

"He's terrified. Asked if he could live with us."

Eddy said, "Sure he is. When he was by the bannister, Hank came behind him and said, 'Go ahead and jump.'"

"That really sucks," Sylvie said.

"You know what really sucks?" Gretch said. "Ronald Reagan will be president someday. Mark my words."

"Here we go," Sylvie muttered.

"Who's he?" asked Eddy.

"The has-been actor who's now the fascist governor of California who said student rioters should be shot on sight," said Gretch. "If he ever becomes president, that'll be the end of civilization as we know it."

Eddy said, "You're saying Americans are so dumb we'd elect a cowboy actor?"

Enzo popped in. "Well, isn't President Nixon the biggest hippie in history?"

Eddy laughed. "How come? He's not peace-loving."

Enzo picked up Diana and held her overhead, mock-groaning, "Oh, you're so big and heavy!" To the others he said, "Not for that," he said. "He's all guerilla theater and counter-cultural. For that, I salute him."

"That's a stretch," said Gretch.

"When did you get home?" asked Sylvie.

"Just now. Sticky was on the steps and told me about Hank so I made Sticky come out to the porch with me to confront him. You know what Hank said? 'Don't hit me, I'm a hemophiliac!'"

"Now *that's* guerilla theater," Gretch said. "And off-the-wall—like Sun Yung Moon who thinks he can take over the government. Those Moonies act like your friend but put you in work camps."

"Anyone who joins a religion is an idiot anyway," said Eddy. "They're just after power and money and caused every war there's ever been."

"Idiots? I've met religious people who are a hell of a lot brighter than you," said Gretch.

"Well, aren't we all weird and strange?" Sylvie said, trying to make peace. "We're all like foreigners to each other."

"What can anyone do with this information?" Eddy was drinking cup after cup of black coffee. "There's no definitions. How can you ever discuss anything?"

"I just mean," Sylvie said, "our upbringing, our prejudices are always there, under the surface." Sylvie turned to Enzo. "Why's Hank still here?"

They started off downstairs, Enzo holding Diana's hand.

"Didn't you give him notice?"

Enzo cleared his throat.

"We need to change the locks!" she said.

Enzo and Diana continued while Sylvie stopped at the foot of the stairs. She could hear Gretch, now talking to the bird in a loud voice.

"Hiyah, beautiful," said the bird.

"Thank you!" Gretch replied. "No one has ever said that to me. People around here are spineless." Amused and curious, Sylvie walked halfway up the stairs to eavesdrop.

Gretch continued, "What do you think? Does being human come naturally? Or do we have to practice? I guess most of us try to do human better. But you know? You'd make a decent human."

"Is Joe there?" said the bird in a deeper voice.

"God, how trite you make me feel! You're as bad as TV. They try to make me want to live at the center of things. 'TV personalities are great influences,' quit kidding me. Influence for what?"

The next day when Enzo came home, Sylvie said, "We need Hank out. Now!" She and Enzo went upstairs and tapped his door. He slept late and didn't seem to have a job. Sylvie figured he must've come from money.

"Hey, come in. Sit anywhere." He perched on the unmade bed and clothes were piled on the chair.

Enzo cleared his throat. "We won't take long. Man, you know it's been great you joined our experiment here but we're shutting it down."

"What!" said Hank. "But you're my family, man. Better than family."

"Yes, brother," Enzo said, "but it's time to leave the nest."

"You can't be serious!" Hank looked like he would cry.

* * *

Sylvie had become less keen on their Saturday walks to the woods because of Enzo's new claim he magnetically attracted the crows who recognized him as a superior person. When she didn't get out of bed to fix breakfast, he said, "You need to be more womanly." He regularly criticized her long strides, her strong hands, her aggressive intellect. "If you don't want to turn out like your mother, you should listen to me."

She shot back. "Do you know how stupid that sounds?" Despite what he presented as progressive thinking and his talk about eliminating prejudices, he still believed women were intellectually inferior, ruled by emotion and intuition. He pulled the covers off her. She groaned and turned over. "Go away!"

"Get up!" he scowled.

"Leave me alone!" She pulled the covers back over her head.

He yanked her by the arm until she was on the floor. "Two minutes. Let's go."

"Damn you!" She ran to the bathroom, locked the door and took a shower. When is it time to get divorced? she wondered. Five minutes later he was gently tapping.

"Sylvie?" as sweet as could be. "Diana's ready. You coming?" She slowly came out and let him hug her. Tomorrow he would bring her flowers with a sappy card and say, "I can't help it sometimes." Now he said, "I'm sorry. I'm under so much stress."

"Probably because you call the family 'bourgeois baggage' and you carry the baggage of paterfamilias. You're conflicted!" The man she fell in love with was one she'd thought would be a good father—had she invented such a man? Had his increasing drug use changed his personality or had she not really grasped his personality before? And though she opposed his using, he was nicer when stoned and hadn't gotten high yet today. How complicit was she?

BY A THREAD

Sylvie walked with Diana to the Grand Union grocery store every Monday, pushing the shopping cart she kept by the garage. Diana picked up rocks and acorns and plucked red barberries to put in her pockets and when she tired of walking, she rode in the cart. They'd gone four blocks when Sylvie realized she'd forgotten her wallet and turned around. Entering the backyard through the driveway, she was confused to find a pickup truck blocking her way. The basement hatch was open and she saw a man dragging a trunk across the basement floor.

"What the hell are you doing?" she called down the hatch.

"Who are you?" said the man.

"That's my trunk. I own the house."

"Naw," said the man. "Hank sold me this."

"Sorry but Hank can't sell you my trunk." She turned and saw Findley's Antiques written on the side of the truck.

"Put everything back right now. Are you Findley? Where's Hank?"

"Yes, Irving Findley. Hank was here a minute ago," he said, ascending the stairs. "Please don't call the police. I didn't know these weren't his."

It was now week three that Hank hadn't paid and hadn't left. Clearly Enzo had lied about giving him notice."

"Show me what's in the truck."

He opened a box filled with the 1920s craft magazines Sylvie enjoyed browsing. "What's that black fabric in the front seat?" It was the long woolen cape Sylvie had planned to have cleaned when she found extra money. "I'll talk to my husband about whether or not we'll call the cops."

"Please don't!" he said. "Really, I thought this was Hank's house."

"That's why I'm giving you another chance," she said. She felt sorry for this man who had just tried to burgle her. Besides, wasn't it all just stuff Gram hoarded? She watched him put everything back into the basement, and took down his license plate number and contact information. But she felt too overwhelmed to follow up.

* * *

When Diana woke up, she and Sylvie went upstairs. Gretch greeted her with, "So, you have pretty new shoes! But look at *my* shoes." They were the sturdy, black shoes Gretch always wore. She was a heavy-set woman with feet that seemed dainty in contrast. "Little girl, these are ugly shoes. And sometimes ugly is best. When you can be ugly on purpose, it means you don't care what others think."

Gretch knew nothing about Hank's activities, nor had she heard of Findley. She was in the midst of downing a six-pack, lamenting that whenever she entered the bakery, her coworkers—high school grads and dropouts—nodded to her but never smiled or said hello. Gretch would clock in, put on her starched white coat, stand at the conveyer belt and mechanically pick up bread loaves and stuff them into plastic bags, over and over. On breaks she said she lectured them, and admitted that her lectures often devolved into tirades.

"At their age, I had more sense. They're immature and brainless and aren't interested in knowing anything."

After everyone else had turned in and Sylvie had put Diana to bed, she could still hear Gretch's Middle Eastern dance music from downstairs.

* * *

After Gretch hadn't been home for a week, Sylvie was on the porch when a cab dropped her off, her right hand wrapped in gauze. She plodded up the stairs and limply fell into a rocking chair.

"I was so tired I fought to keep my eyes open and a couple times actually nodded off. The conveyor belt hypnotized me. I was thinking about my last conversation with Stu. The girls told the boss I was yelling, 'Of course older people are smarter than younger ones.' Those girls just about bust a gut. They're always laughing at me. I missed a loaf and reached for it but the gears snatched my finger and pulled me along. I screamed, 'Turn off the belt!' and stupid Moira says, 'Is she screaming again?' and Shelly goes, 'What else is new? She's going nuts,' and they kept working and laughing."

Gretch had pulled her bloody hand out of the gears and clutched it to her chest, wrapping it in her sleeve, and fell to the floor writhing in pain. Two fingertips remained in the conveyor belt. Moira called 911 and an ambulance came and took Gretch to the hospital. Her parents took her home. Over the next days, an infection beset her pinky and ring fingers and the doctor cut away more centimeters of skin, further shortening her fingers. Now she wanted to sleep.

Gretch's depression grew that week. She said she'd joined the ranks of "them"—the handicapped. An Other. She knitted mittens to hide her hand so no one could know her shame. Sylvie made hot meals for her, knitted with her. But Gretch receded into herself and even vowed to quit drinking beer. All she could see was her own deformity.

"Gretch, don't you see? You victimize yourself with those beliefs about strong and weak."

"They aren't beliefs," Gretch said. "That's how the world is." She moved home to her parents.

* * *

Sylvie insisted on building a separate outdoor entrance to keep tenants out of their space—the French doors were currently their only barrier.

"It'll be good practice for you, Enzo. Maybe you'll build us a house someday." Sylvie invited Brian and Miriam for dinner and asked Brian if he'd help with the project and said, "I'll babysit for you in exchange."

Brian said, "Hey, Enzo's my buddy. I help out my friends and know they'd do the same for me."

Enzo said, "Let's drink to that, friend!"

Over several weekends, Brian and Enzo built an exterior staircase leading up to the back kitchen window which they enlarged and turned into a doorway with a door, then they installed another door on the interior stairs that they kept locked.

Frosts returned in August, starting stealthily at night, blackening tomato plants so their stems that yesterday had borne pounds of green tomatoes now sprawled helplessly on the ground.

"Winter is killing me!" Enzo said. "People get weird." He never thawed out enough to recover from the previous year. Whatever Shuster and Falkner had him doing seemed to darken his outlook. She wondered about his mental state and whether anyone else had noticed a shift in his behavior. Maybe not, since he was so volatile anyway. And besides, they didn't understand Italian.

Sylvie handed him a letter. "This arrived yesterday."

"It's from Babbo!" Enzo opened it and read. "He says Mamma keeps running off. He doesn't know where she goes. He worries about her."

"Is that so strange? She's very independent."

"Everyone knows she's nuts but she's never done this before." He was quiet a moment then said, "This isn't good for his heart."

* * *

With Hank's room cleaned and ready, Susan moved in. She confided to Sylvie she was a recovering addict. "My mother used to dress me up and put me in the yard to play and got upset when I got dirty. I mean, she freaked out. She had me on downers when I was ten. I was in Waterbury by junior high."

Susan was kind to Diana, who enjoyed visiting her upstairs. She would approach Susan's chair and stand, waiting for a reaction.

"Such a pretty dress!" Susan would exclaim. "You look so nice!"

* * *

Winter dragged on. Enzo said he wanted to get aquarium tanks like the ones at the Fillmore "so I won't have to go there so often." Sylvie suggested building shelves in the wide doorway between the living and dining rooms to hold them. He did. And a bartender gave him a tank and lights and guppies. Turning out all the lights except the aquarium lights created a dreaminess. Diana stood and watched the fish at her eye level and when Sylvie played a record, Diana twirled around the room exclaiming, "I happy! I dancing!"

"Diana's got the idea—let's have a whole-house party," Sylvie said. "It's so gloomy in here."

The wheels were set into motion: Eddy, Amy and Susan invited friends but Enzo and Sylvie regarded it more as a sort of work party than a social event. Sylvie invited Rima, thinking she might be interested to experience and maybe explain the house's dynamic. The day of the party, Sylvie unlocked the door at the top of the stairs so people could move between upstairs and down. Enzo borrowed films from the university science department to project on the living room wall and with the sound off, images of microscopic worms seemed like abstract psychedelic art. Rima carried upstairs the lasagna Sylvie made and pizzas Enzo prepared downstairs. Others brought salads, chips and drinks. During the party, Sylvie kept Diana close. Rima enjoyed two servings of lasagna and mingled a while then said she'd stop by in a few days. "Too much chaos," she said.

As guests argued politics, Sylvie realized how it's easy to feel united with diverse people abstractly. But how could she get along with people who not only think differently but in ways she found repugnant, like eating canaries or pulling antennae off slugs? Or lying for financial gain? Or manipulating others to break their vows? Or thinking it's OK to wage war on a distant country because you don't like their government or for white people to be boss, for men to define women? How had the world treated her? How will it treat Diana?

Susan supervised the record player, playing Stevie Wonder, Steely Dan and Springsteen. No one had asked who brought the punch bowl but since it was so prominent, everyone drank some. Eddy said Hank had approached him when he was alone. "He kept putting a cup of punch in my face and saying it'd be good for me. I said I'd had enough of his damn drinks. Then he set it next to me and twinkly-toed away," Eddy said. "Everyone drank some. Except me."

"Hank was here?" Sylvie said. "He wasn't invited."

"I saw him ballet dancing around the fish tanks," Susan said. "Probably he put LSD in the punch."

"What?" said Sylvie. She had a sickening feeling Enzo had drunk more punch than anyone. This punch thing had happened in Boston at a party she'd attended with Saul seven years ago, after Ken Kesey's Merry Pranksters popularized the "prank." But she never expected it now, in Vermont.

"It's obvious. People were tripping their asses off."

Sylvie realized with alarm how dangerous Hank was. His reaction to being kicked out was scary. She'd seen unusual people but hadn't considered this kind of vicious-ness. To add to her distress, Enzo began spending more time with Mickey, a new Fillmore friend, and afterward would come home and tell Sylvie how Mickey criticized her faith. "He says you don't accept Jesus Christ as your personal savior, so you're doomed."

"How do you respond?" she asked.

"He may be right."

This exasperated her. "You're just trying to control me however you can, is that it?"

He smirked and toked his cigarette, exhaling smoke at her. She wondered how someone with her smarts could wind up in a situation so dumb. Well, if you got off your prescribed path and lived in the margins, the old rules may still apply but looked different. She'd been a dreamer, oblivious of ill-intentioned people.

"Tell Mickey I don't accept *him* as a decent friend of our family."

On top of that, sometimes when she was walking to the store, a speeding car passed carrying a passenger who, with middle finger raised, shouted out the window, "I'm going to get your ass!" After several incidents, she recognized Hank.

DEEP END

When Enzo returned from a walk with Diana, he was grinning strangely and staring at Sylvie. Diana kept repeating, "Faffella hurt him's tail."

"What's she talking about?" Sylvie asked.

"The door closed on Farfella's tail."

"What door?"

"The church," Enzo said, eyes wide, lips quivering, brow sweaty. "We need to have a real wedding." He started pacing. "Things aren't going well because our marriage isn't legal."

Sylvie's head buzzed with adrenaline, knowing something was very wrong. "Of course it's legal. We were married in Cook County."

"Not in the church." He glared at her, eyes popping.

"You've always hated the church." She steadied herself despite her rising panic.

"We went inside to look at Jesus on the cross." With mounting terror, she thought only *she'd* noticed this personality change.

"Diana doesn't need to see that! I was thirteen when I saw that image and it terrified me."

Enzo had been a better person in Italy. Here he seemed lost without his language and people who understood him in context. She tried convincing him that drugs created psychic fallout, but he laughed at that.

One evening after Mickey had dropped him off and driven away, Enzo was disoriented. He spent hours mutely staring and smiling, and laughed when she spoke to him. Had he had one trip too many? He didn't sleep for two days and nights and then went out early. Sylvie had spent a typical day with Diana, reading to her and playing Candyland with her, taking Farfella on a walk. She was in the kitchen fixing dinner when Enzo came in, disheveled, desperation in his face. His lips tried to smile but wavered as he stifled tears. She was shocked when he addressed her as Pina, the name of his Neapolitan girlfriend. He picked up a log from the wood pile and launched it toward her but missed. Then he went into the bathroom and ran a bath. Sylvie followed and stared at him from the doorway.

"It's OK; I know what's happening," he said.

He had plugged in the hairdryer and she could see the cord was too short to reach the water. She quietly shut the door. He was acting so strange that she was afraid. She ran to Diana in her bed, shook her awake and whispered, "Let's go see Carrie! Get your boots and wait by the door." Diana dreamily obeyed. Sylvie hurried to the kitchen for the house keys, passing the bathroom just as Enzo opened the door.

He was naked, sobbing, holding the electric hair dryer and turned on the spigots. "I'm filling the tub and using this."

"Fine!" she called, rushing through the house, snatching coats off hooks, scooping up Diana and running down the street to Linda's house and knocked on the door until Linda's husband Harry appeared in his robe, rubbing his eyes.

"Sylvie? Come in!"

"I need help. It's Enzo." She mouthed his name so Diana wouldn't hear. "Can we crash here?"

Linda was padding down the stairs, tying her robe.

"I'm sorry to wake you, but Diana and I . . . ."

"Hey," Linda said, confused.

Sylvie said, "Could Diana lie down somewhere? I'll explain."

"Sure. Diana, come, let's surprise Carrie and I'll read you two a book."

Harry sat down across from her and she described the evening's events, and ended saying, "I feel awful I left him like that. He's obviously suffering."

Harry said, "He threw a log at you and you feel sorry for him? You did the right thing to come here."

Linda returned with a pot of tea and three cups. "The girls are enjoying their impromptu sleepover." Enjoying the peace of this home, Sylvie recalled what Aunt Iris had said, that it doesn't matter who you marry but what you do with it. The "it" wasn't the man, she thought, but the situation—and this is what she was doing with it.

"I don't know what to do!" Sylvie said. "Do people go this crazy here in winter?" She'd never told Linda about the drugs or the abuse. What proof did she have? Who'd believe her?

"They say Vermont has never been this cold," Harry said.

"That figures," said Sylvie.

Pounding on the door interrupted the peace. They knew who it was. Harry went to answer the door.

"Yes they're here. It's late, Enzo. She'll talk to you tomorrow."

Enzo pushed him aside and shouted, "Please come home! I'm sorry."

"Enzo," Harry said, "She asked me to help and I've calmly asked you to leave."

"Easy for you to be calm." Enzo pushed him again. "No one's after you! No one's lured your wife away." Harry blocked Sylvie from him. Linda slipped into the kitchen and called out, "I've called 911!"

Sylvie said, "Hear that, Enzo? Cops are coming. Get out fast or they'll arrest you."

"I'll prove there's people after me!" he cried.

With Sylvie trailing behind, Harry corralled Enzo in the dining room and blocked his way to the living room. Linda came up behind Sylvie, startling her when she said, "Come back to the kitchen." Sylvie did and peeked around the wall and saw Enzo pacing and muttering.

Two officers arrived. One said, "Sir, did this gentleman ask you to leave?"

"He didn't mean it," Enzo said.

"Sir, answer the question. Did Mr. Bonaire ask you to leave his house?"

"Don't you remember what happened, Pina?" Enzo shouted at Sylvie. Her eyes burned with tears, remembering in Naples when Pina had said how lucky she was to marry Enzo. She realized she'd been right about his mental state.

One officer grabbed Enzo's arm. "I'm going to ask you to come with us."

Enzo pulled away. "Get off me!"

The other officer grabbed him from behind and they wrestled him to the floor. One held his arms as the other pulled a straitjacket over his head, forced his arms into the sleeves that they tied behind his back.

"How can you let them do this? Just come home!"

This was too brutal to watch. Diana and Carrie had come downstairs and were peeking around the corner. Enzo saw them and cried, "Diana, help papa!"

Sylvie saw Diana's wide-eyed face before Linda chased the girls back upstairs. "C'mon," she said, "let's go see what's in Carrie's room."

The cops had Enzo face down on the floor, squirming like a fish on a pier. "I didn't do it! It wasn't my fault!" he yelled. As Harry held the door open, each officer dragged Enzo by a tightly bound armpit.

The Bonaires let Diana stay in the morning while Sylvie went to court for Enzo's hearing. First, she went home to get ready. She mechanically noted a broken window pane on the back door and, with no fear or anger left to spare, she only thought of the cost and hassle of repairing it. She called and updated Rima, who agreed to meet her at the courthouse. She was surprised to hear tapping on the back door. It was Eddy.

"Where's Enzo? Is he OK?"

"In jail," Sylvie said. "And no, he hasn't been OK since drinking Hank's acid punch."

"Oh, man. He was in a bad way last night. He was shouting so loud, I came down to check it out and knocked on both doors. He didn't open up so I broke the glass to get in. I'm really sorry."

"I understand."

"He was squatting on the rim of the tub and filling the water and when I saw he was trying to plug in a hair dryer, I ran down and took out the fuse. When I came back up, he was running out the door."

* * *

Suspects in the criminal court sat under guard in the visitors' section. Rima had been watching for Sylvie and waved her over when she entered. Rima pointed out Falkner who, coincidentally, was there on his third DUI charge. He was first up, given a large fine and sentenced to rehab. They saw Enzo, eyes fixed on Falkner, scribbling on a scrap of paper.

When his name was called, Enzo approached the bench, deposited the paper and turned to bow to the crowd, grinning. Some observers laughed nervously.

"What's this?" the judge said, "Get back to your seat." Sylvie watched tearfully as Enzo stood immobile. "Get this man out of here. Take him to Waterbury." This was an emergency commitment order to the state psychiatric hospital. The judge pounded the gavel. As Enzo, now quiet, was ushered out, Rima squeezed Sylvie's hand and put an arm around her shoulder. Sylvie was handed a notice advising how to extend commitment beyond three days.

"Rima, I know this is awful but I can't deal with him now. I can't bring him home!"

"I'm going to sound like a hypocrite, too, after all my criticisms of psychiatry here," Rima said, "But don't you live next to a shrink? Maybe he can help."

Sylvie hadn't wanted to involve Gary out of respect for his and Enzo's friendship. But this was an emergency. She took Diana's hand and they went next door, relieved that Judy wasn't home but Sunny was happy to play with Diana. Sylvie described Enzo's situation, trying to remain objective because she really didn't know if he had a mental illness or suffered from a drug reaction. As Gary read aloud from the manual, checking with her about Enzo's symptoms, his face showed increasing concern.

"I'll sign the commitment papers so they'll have more time to observe him," he said.

Though Sylvie knew Enzo wasn't in his right mind and needed help and was relieved there was a system that would help, she was amazed at how easy it was to take away someone's autonomy with such little evidence. The judge had read the cops' rationale for arresting Enzo based on his behavior, and she now attested that Enzo was a threat to himself and others. So the system removed him from society with no one truly knowing his mental state, just his behavior. Yet she also knew she wouldn't have had this help by saying he'd hit or threatened her because that was a domestic matter. Nothing in this process assuaged her feelings of guilt and betrayal. She was not only frightened by the system's power but also by how efficiently and effectively she'd used it.

Her complicity increased when hospital aides summoned her to come translate. Enzo was in distress and medicated and trying to communicate his mental state in his broken English. How accurate could he be about his confused feelings and thoughts? She thought that since translation was an interpretive art and she had the power to misrepresent him, asking her to interpret was probably not even ethical.

Sylvie found the state hospital menacing, even downright medieval, and hardly rehabilitative. The tenants had described it with dread—the howls echoing through the halls, threats of seclusion for minor infractions, transformation of friends into zombies through over-medication, unexplained removal of offenders by strong-armed orderlies—such authority forced on the meekest of patients while the most menacing flew under the radar and continued their intimidation.

She noted all the snow mixed with dirt into frozen gray mounds along the roads. While in many parts of the country people are happier in spring, Vermonters decried mud season, which often made people morose and even suicidal. She exited the highway, flooring it to seventy-five, reaching over to hold the passenger door shut because the latch was broken and the door swung open on turns. She pulled under the overpass and waited until she saw the car speed by that was following her. Hank had been harassing her and she worried that could be him. She was breathless when she reached the office Dr. Shuster had on state hospital grounds.

"Sylvie, I wasn't expecting you today." He sat at his desk, each hand pinching either tip of a pencil and twirling it.

"I was being followed," she said, the door slamming behind her.

Enzo was weaker than either of them had supposed. As a person of her word, she intended to support him through this illness and uphold her vows in this tough time. She couldn't wait for others to build a kinder world if she also didn't do the work. They'd weathered so many challenges that might strengthen their marriage. Or was only she doing all the work? Was only she accommodating? She thought him a basically sweet person who never meant to hurt her but who couldn't cope outside Italy.

She'd sewn him a shirt, crying the whole time, mourning the loss of her youth, the death of her aspirations. She'd brought it along, an act of kindness for her sick husband. Without her, he was a stranger in this backwater, isolated by geography, weather and hostility to outsiders. Dr. Shuster observed the shirt, eyed her suspiciously and asked, "Why are you here?"

"To see Enzo." Duh.

"I see," he said. His staring unnerved her. "You say you were followed? Why do you think so?"

"It's our tenant. Was, I mean. He's got a grudge."

"Oh?"

"It's a long story." Was he assessing her mental state too? What if she told him she believed they were all spirit and God directed all their lives? Was that an illness in his manual? He could think she was crazy for her offbeat religion, for staying with Enzo.

"Don't be concerned when you see him. He had a rough night. We've had to put him in solitary."

She fell back into her chair. "Oh my God. He's worse?"

"There are no guarantees for this type of thing. Schizophrenia is still completely unknown to us."

This was the first she'd heard this diagnosis. Shuster must have noticed her blanch.

"Paranoid schiz," he said, as if in explanation. He swiveled in his chair and looked at her sideways. "But truthfully, I'm rather worried about you. Have you considered seeing someone? For support?"

"Not really," she stammered. What about all the LSD experiments Shuster had—supposedly—enlisted Enzo for? He must know the connection between LSD and schizophrenic symptoms. She was afraid to ask.

He looked at her another long moment and said, "Here." He wrote a name on a business card and handed it to her. "Perhaps . . . ."

She quickly stuffed the card in her pocket. "Can I see Enzo now?"

He studied her a bit too long, then buzzed his secretary. "Remember, if you need anything, Sylvie," he extended his hand which she took, wishing she'd never met him.

Saying, "Follow me," the nurse led her into a waiting room. She spoke to the guard, handed him the shirt and told Sylvie she'd have fifteen minutes. Sylvie sat in front of the glass wall with a sliding panel. Soon Enzo appeared on the other side, an odd twisted smile on his face. She hadn't planned to talk about their relationship, but it spilled out.

"So you thought you should experiment with your own brain?"

He stared blankly. Then his eyes filled with tears. She recalled sweet things he'd done, his tenderness with Diana. He was having a bad trip. She couldn't—shouldn't—love him after what he'd put her through, but she couldn't abandon him. He put his hands on the glass. "Will you put your hands against mine, please?"

She did. He'd been right about many things, like how the state had its fingers in every part of your life. But he's not rational. Paranoid schizophrenic, Shuster said. But is that what Shuster had done to him? But he was paranoid of the lieutenant in Yugoslavia. If she got drunk, she wouldn't have to think about these things. But isn't that helpless attitude what the powers-that-be want? Or was she paranoid too? If you don't want your mental state to be judged, you must conform. Even praying was considered aberrant, or at best immature.

She visited again on a day when the sky was high and blue and furnished with plush clouds. The snow had melted in sunny places. They laid a blanket on the lawn for a picnic. Enzo, wearing the shirt she'd made. Sylvie saw a woman in her late teens wearing thick glasses approaching and when they made eye contact, she parked her blanket next to theirs.

"I smell a skunk," said the woman. "I love that smell!"

Sylvie said casually, "It's like ReaLemon, that fake lemon juice." Then turned away.

Days later, she called her parents. When Dad answered, she told him some of what had happened but didn't mention Schuster.

"Boy, if there's a way to mess up your life, you'll find it."

"Oh, like I'm doing it on purpose, Dad."

"Can't you settle down and do what you're supposed to be doing?"

"Like what? Get married and have children?"

* * *

288

Sylvie read Diana a story, put her to bed, and then lay down on the mattress on the floor beneath the windows, the curtains brushing against her face, enjoying the smell of sandalwood incense as she fell asleep. Suddenly, loud blasts like a backfiring car bolted her upright, her eyes popping open in time to see a bright spark near the aquariums. As she lay back down, she realized the pumps weren't humming, and sleepily reasoned that a short circuit had tripped the breaker switch. She felt a draft chilling her feet and when she reached down to adjust the covers, something sharp cut her finger. She forced herself to get up to see what had happened to the aquariums. Something crunched under her stockinged feet. She turned on the switch and saw the top half of the aquarium's extension cord dangling in mid-air. Across the room she noticed black spots on the wall—five of them. She went to look closer. They were holes. Bullet holes. A chill ran down her spine as she recalled how she'd been sitting in front of those windows.

She had to get Diana out of there.

A half-hour after she called the police, a patrolman arrived to make a report. Hours later a detective arrived. She was taken aback by his pink jacket and plaid pants, like the host of a children's TV show. They took pictures, measured each hole and chipped away plaster to try to dislodge a bullet, then found the sixth bullet in the front door.

"Can't really tell. They came in so fast they all melted." The detective said they were thirty-eight caliber but without uncovering a bullet, he couldn't trace the gun. When Sylvie wondered aloud if her husband might be behind it, retaliating for the hospitalization and working through one of his friends or a fellow inmate, the detective rolled his eyes and said, "Just go move in with your girlfriends." She recalled the woman in her Boston consciousness-raising group who'd reported having been raped and the police didn't believe her, nor did her lawyer. And her classmate was raped and her friends blamed her for it. Hank had harassed her—it could've been him who shot the house. Or was it a neighbor who hated the rooming house?

Annie, Rick and Florie lived across town and agreed to host her, so she drove there the next morning, bringing Farfella. Rick asked her to park a few blocks away so no one could trace her to their house. She complied but thought he was over-reacting. Or was she too idealistic? She looked in the *Free Press* every day for news and was surprised to find no mention of the incident. Surely this was unusual for Burlington. Reporters didn't find it newsworthy? Daily she called the police who said to call at midnight or at six a.m. or at three p.m. Need she fear for her life? Was it safe to go home? What the hell was going on? The cops had no clues and after a week said sorry, but they weren't equipped for a full investigation, were too busy to investigate and had more important business. What, she asked, was more important than the safety of a citizen in her own home?

Fuming, she resigned to figure it out herself. The shooting had happened on a Sunday so she started over again with the *Free Press* and combed every word of the week's newspapers. Suddenly she noticed a brief article about a person whose name caught her eye. A Henry Roach at 1:13 a.m. on the night of the shooting had been picked up blocks away for a so-called hit-and-run incident. After several calls to the Winooski rather than the Burlington police station, she learned it was, indeed, their Hank. She told the detective he'd been their tenant, was kicked out and had made threats all year. Did they have clues linking him with the shooting?

"We're legally bound to protect the innocent," the detective explained, "and can't wrongfully inculpate anyone."

"What about me and my daughter?" Sylvie asked. "We almost get our brains blown out. Who's protecting us?"

He sighed. Then he explained that hit-and-run in this case meant Hank had rear-ended a cop car on the Winooski bridge then got out of his car—a stolen car—and ran. On the back seat lay a hot thirty-eight caliber stolen shotgun. The detective admitted that when police had questioned Hank just minutes after and a few blocks from the shooting, he'd said, "I was so fucked-up I don't know what I did." The problem, said the officer, was they hadn't read him his Miranda rights and he'd been high at the time so his confession was legally worthless. The officer was sorry, but there wasn't enough evidence to press charges against him for shooting the house and nothing more they could do.

Weeks later, Eddy delivered news from the Fillmore grapevine that Hank had been extradited to Massachusetts to face charges for car theft. Why would Hank, to whom they had shown hospitality, cooked meals, allowed to use their phone and treated as family, want to kill her? She'd wanted a rooming house that welcomed misfits and encouraged them to create a community, but the tenants wanted Enzo to guide them. A slender reed on which to lean. She recalled Boston war protestors saying you couldn't be a revolutionary unless you were so detached you could kill family members. Had Enzo inspired Hank to think of himself as a revolutionary? But Hank was too self-centered to care about social change. He was simply lawless.

Sylvie feared his eventual return. She said to Annie, "Remember I told you about the guy who used to drive by and shout obscenities at me? I never thought he'd go this far!"

"He sounds obsessed with jealousy of you two. Anyone can see your devotion to each other."

"Yeah, my flipped-out husband in the mental hospital. That is something to envy."

Annie paused. "Maybe you're a beacon for this Hank. He envies your strength. He can't have it, so he wants to destroy it."

Sylvie laughed, thinking how Annie liked romance novels. She said, "Really, there's so much drug use among the tenants." Saul used to make a big deal about dropping acid like it was a spiritual event. He even had a guru guide him through his first trip. The acid phenomenon had swept through the culture, making them all guinea pigs in a big social experiment. Everyone was playing with fire. She started spending more time upstairs to keep tabs on the tenants, who were quieter than before, subdued perhaps by Enzo's meltdown. This is probably what Hannah meant about "psychic fallout." Psychic energy had been disturbed.

She received a letter from home in the mail:

Dear Sylvie,

We wait in anticipation for any new hare-brained idea you'll come up with. You are now a partner with us in property ownership that has made you a capitalist whether you like it or not and must be mindful of your responsibility. We've given you a leg up as it seems you've put aside your education to go your own way.

You've been duly warned about the experimental drug lifestyle of the young nowadays and as you are parents now, you two must steer clear of it. Shuster says it's rampant in Vermont now. We won't continue watching out for you.

Dad

SOIL AND ASH

Diagnosed paranoid schizophrenic, Enzo was released. He took Haldol for a few days but said he couldn't sleep or think and it was almost as disturbing as psychosis.

Rima came to see him, very concerned. "Your psychosis came from the acid and whatever else they did to you—I tried to warn you! Shuster tests it on you and boom, you're in the hospital under his care."

Sylvie didn't say so but she felt she'd failed her husband as his interpreter. But yes, his psychosis had needed a remedy. And though she wanted to honor her commitments and give him another chance, his acid experimenting was a betrayal. She didn't trust him to be sincere.

Rima continued, "Disgusting how buddy-buddy psychiatry works with the court! Probably the drug makers too! But I was looking for stuff in the *Whole Earth Catalog* and found this article about treating schizophrenia with massive doses of niacin. Enzo, please visit the clinic and try to get some B_3 shots!"

"Will do. Thanks, Rima, for cheering me up."

Sylvie didn't question that Enzo needed help and she'd used the system to protect herself and Diana. But that didn't diminish the fact that the laws were rigged in a particular way—a man hitting his wife is normal, legal behavior, but a man writing on a piece of paper and handing it to the judge is a lunatic who must be locked up.

Enzo said, "Remember when you said we could rent out the house and buy a place? Let's do that now! We could buy land; I'll build a shelter and maybe we can rent that out too. Brian can help."

According to Gary's DSM manual, this looked like manic behavior and reminded her of her roommate Bertie's grand gestures. But regarding Enzo's suggestion, she thought of her grandmother's saying "In for a penny, in for a pound." If she was going to honor her marriage vows at all, what's the difference if she went all the way, or at least gave it a try? *The Mother Earth News* contained ideas for low-cost shelters. Her ultimate safe haven was Janis's and she vowed to get there soon.

* * *

They studied newspaper ads until they found a cheap five-acre parcel with a water source and nearby power lines. The agent said they could camp while awaiting settlement. They gave notice to the roomers and replaced them with a group of students who signed a contract to rent the house for the whole school year starting now, paying one month's security deposit plus two months' rent upfront. Rima questioned this plan but Sylvie said, "He's his old self. I'm sure it was the acid."

Sylvie was about to hand over the keys when the lead tenant said, "My dad's a lawyer. He says I should ask you to clear out all your stuff 'cause we don't want to be responsible. We need space to store our stuff. Otherwise, no deal."

Sylvie wished they'd spoken up sooner, but they'd made so many preparations now she felt trapped.

So into a U-Haul truck they loaded clothes, Diana's favorite toys, all Enzo's handmade furniture, tools, kitchenware and sundry furniture, and bought a Sears eight-person canvas tent, green with a yellow door and mesh windows that let air circulate when the flaps were up. Its aluminum poles fitted together for the frame and spikes secured guy-wires to hold down the floor. They drove it all to the property.

"Diana, look! We're putting our whole house into a bag," Sylvie said cheerily. "You can learn things like this, then you won't need anyone to help you."

Farfella's nose immediately started working as she explored the area, never out of sight of her family, especially Diana. They pitched their tent and unloaded their things in a clearing fifty feet from the road. The tent accommodated three mattresses and their bureaus filled with clothes. They set up furniture that didn't fit in the tent around a firepit Enzo dug before driving the truck back to Burlington and returning in their car.

Sylvie found solace in the woods and wildlife and loved lying in bed and breathing the forest. Outside, crickets tunelessly whirred. Their stereotype struck Sylvie— they really are carefree, delighting in the summer night. She enjoyed their chorus but not the lone cricket that moved into the tent whose solo was like an unaccompanied recorder aimlessly playing a monotone. She roused herself to hunt it down but anytime she approached too close, it stopped. When she awoke, light was penetrating the tent making it glow like an emerald. The tent she'd loved last night now seemed like a pathetic strip of canvas and a few weak hollow poles. It was like waking up to see a stranger's face on the pillow next to yours.

Enzo went to gather water from a spring that fed the bog near the blueberry bushes while Sylvie searched for firewood. She'd become adept, having built fires for the wood stove in Burlington. She poked a stick into the embers. "Did you think we could actually live here?"

"Not in winter, no. It's good to own land—in Italy it's sold by meters, not acres. But I want to check out the property lines. The woods are so thick it's hard to tell what's what."

Sylvie took Diana to the wet area where Diana giggled as she and Farfella chased frogs and Sylvie picked leaves from motherwort and boneset. In her enthusiasm, she also pulled out ferns from around the blueberries. She'd never noticed how ferns had razor-sharp edges and as she yanked, she sliced her pinky finger. She cried out and flopped on the road and sucked on her finger while Diana played and ate blueberries. Mosquitoes landed thickly on their arms, too many to swat them all. Just across the road and down a ways were the closest neighbors. Children had come out to play and a woman came over and introduced herself as Minnie.

"Did you do something to your finger? Let's see."

Sylvie was still sucking on it. "I'm fine," she said.

"Come over and I'll get you a Band-aid."

Sylvie liked her simple openness. If she lived here, Minnie would become her closest confidante just because she's a neighbor.

When Sylvie and Diana returned to the tent, Enzo was there sipping coffee and staring into the woods. "There's no way this is five acres," he said. "It's more like three."

"How do you know?"

"I've paced it twice, wondering how they could say it's five acres. I can tell the boundaries by the orange flags."

He went off to complain to the agent who said he'd send someone in a day or so and a few days later they heard a car crunching on the gravel. "Must be them," Enzo said and ran toward the sound.

Sylvie fed Diana and heated water for washing dishes. In the peace of the woods, she reviewed how hard everything had been. She and Enzo had begun as friends. He was basically good-hearted and earnest in building a strong family with her. At first, she'd felt a spiritual connection with him, but then it seemed sex substituted for intimacy. Enzo believed it was her task to nurture their marriage and family because after all, she was the woman. After a while, by the end of any special day—birthdays, Christmas, their anniversary—he'd have grown surly and she'd be in tears and he blamed her. And sometimes she'd want to invite friends over and he'd object but then bring home his choice of guests, sometimes ones he had just met. Had he always been a jerk? Had she accepted this as how Italian men are? Was he a devoted husband who loved her or a madman set on destroying her? Or both? If she thought him a madman and behaved accordingly, would he play that role? She'd feel their souls touch and then he'd act paranoid as she suspected his motives. His paranoia and her suspicion flickered back and forth like an electrical charge. She'd spun a web of happiness and love and wrapped it around herself, hoping to draw him in. And though her will and cheerfulness were sometimes strong enough to prevail over him, he was often high, leaving her lonely and sad, which convinced him she wasn't sincere about making a happy home and he turned on her. She felt drained and tired and dwindling.

Perplexed, she made a mental list of Enzo's messages, his rules:

Be sexy, but sexy women aren't trustworthy;

Don't be materialistic, but people who don't spend money are stingy;

Cook well but don't spend money on ingredients;

Be my friend and companion but do as I say;

People should be free to do what they believe, but your religion is ridiculous;

You can't garden because you don't know how. I know how but won't do it.

It added up to a despicable man. Surely her younger self wouldn't put up with this, but she felt duty-bound to care for him.

They drove to the real estate agent to find out the surveyors' verdict. Enzo was right—it was just over four acres.

"False advertising. You said it was five," Enzo said.

The agent's face reddened. "OK, be off by Saturday with all your crap. Or lose the deposit."

Moving all their stuff was a burden Sylvie was tired of.

She went to explain to Minnie what was happening and offered her their furniture. Minnie's face looked as though a light had gone out. She simply said, "We don't have the space," and shut the door.

Enzo said, "Let's burn it. We'll keep what'll fit in the car, especially the tent."

He stoked the still-hot embers and added some branches. They kept most of their clothes and Diana's toys, but tossed onto the fire the end tables with spindly legs, the kitchen table that'd been burnt once before when Aunt Iris and Uncle Simon had been in charge, the dresser whose paint blistered and its eighty-year-old veneer disappeared then it slowly turned to charcoal and dropped a brass drawer pull. They stood at opposite sides, tossing all Gram's haunted things onto the flames. Sylvie threw clothes, plastic boxes that disintegrated before their eyes, curling up into a big black ash that consumed itself. Enzo added projects never finished, dresser drawers, books. They threw in yellow plastic plates like Frisbees. Diana threw a plastic doll into the fire by its arm, backing away solemnly, and minutes later cried to have it back. Everything melted into a black oily pool. The bonfire was so loaded with fuel that its white flames reached as high as the nearby maple sapling tips. Destroying something of potential value felt liberating. The surveyors' dishonesty may have saved them from a reckless plan.

Under the darkening sky, they stood shoulder to shoulder, their faces full of awe at the fire's devastating power. The fire purged her attachment to things. This stuff—that she could've sent Findley to jail for stealing—had caused Dad to break with Aunt Iris. It was every material thing gained during her marriage, a commitment that needed to rise above material things. Enzo wanted her companionship. Was that enough? She looked at his face lighted by the flames, shadows flickering across his brow. It could be the face of a madman. Who was he anyway? He had abused her. And they were in one of the remotest spots on earth, watching their things burn. Sylvie entrusted her and Diana's lives to this person whom she thought she loved, felt she *should* love. But it wasn't like her steady love for Diana.

They put Diana to bed in the tent and read to her and when she was asleep they went outside and made love on the ground in near-total blackness, wordlessly grappling each other. Afterward Enzo said, "Come, let's watch the fire."

The flames had grown as high as the birch-tops, smoke rising in a pillar as if sucked up by the clouds. Enzo firmly gripped Sylvie's arms. "Maybe I should throw you on, no?"

She started to smile, but saw his eyes without light of their own, just reflections of the fire. "What did you think?" he said, gripping tighter. "I'd come back and we'd make love and it'd all be fine again? Did you think I'd forget you betrayed me?"

The fire heated her back. "Betrayed you? I've been faithful. And truthful. Hell, who lied to who?" She wriggled free and hurried into the dark woods to wait until his anger settled and he went to bed. She sat hugging her legs and sobbing about everything she'd lost—not just their stuff but her dreams. Their love. Her tolerance for Enzo.

She quelled her fear and focused on the good things in her life, like Diana. She scolded herself for thinking Enzo would seriously hurt her and accepted blame that she'd had him hospitalized. Now she believed her plan to get to Janis's was her best option because it'd also get Enzo to California, a place where he might thrive without her. Her parents were right—she'd been making her own choices and couldn't just go running back to them.

It started storming and she stole back into the tent and into her bag and let the rain patter lull her to sleep. In the morning, they stonily packed up their tent and remaining possessions, most of it sopping, then stopped to say goodbye to Minnie who said she'd never before seen such a rain.

1978-1980

NOMADS

They returned to Burlington and pitched tent at the North Beach campground. Two campers were hooked to outlets like parasites feeding. The sun left a stain like watery blood on the other side of the lake. Sylvie took Diana to the shore where she tiptoed into the water, followed by Farfella, and ran out, chased by Farfella and waves that slithered as far as they could before recoiling. Digging their feet into sand that felt like a warm bath, they returned to the tent.

Sylvie decided it was time to find a way to get to Janis. She still wanted to see what it was like to live self-sufficiently, using just the earth and her wits like Janis was doing, and could no longer imagine such a life alongside Enzo.

"Let's head to California, Enzo. It's always warm there."

"Brian says Washington's better. Or Oregon."

"Really? Why?"

"California is more expensive now."

Sylvie figured once they were out there, she could figure out how to get to Janis's. "It's like four thousand miles, you know. We may need extra money."

Enzo agreed and said he'd go to the unemployment office to find something temporary. Despite all that had happened, he acted as though everything was back to normal. Sylvie felt the opposite. But besides his parents, she'd never seen abuse except in movies and then thought it was only among criminals. She thought about Stuart's suicide after his wife kidnapped their kids and thought she could never inflict such pain on Enzo, no matter how much she wanted to leave him.

* * *

Canada geese flew evenly spaced like cued-up pool balls above the campground. Enzo said, "They say I can work as an apple-picker, probably because of my accent. They import migrants because locals won't do the work. Go see if they tell you the same."

Sylvie found a shopping cart near the campground parking lot and used it to push Diana. First she walked up North Street to Linda's to invite her to a cook-out at the beach.

"Sounds like fun."

"Come soon. Not sure how long we're there. Enzo's friend Brian can't come but probably Annie will bring Florie."

Then she and Diana went to the unemployment office where cheery orange triangles on brown walls and different plants and pictures on gray metal desks only stressed the room's grimness. Sylvie sat, legs crossed at the ankle, and regarded the leather bow on her flats. She smoothed her hands over her khaki slacks and made sure her t-shirt was tucked in. Diana was in her pink knit dress and white lace-trimmed anklets, her legs too short to dangle. Sylvie thought these clothes gave a good enough impression. Not bad for free clothes. She followed the voice calling her name to a clerk who led her to a green chair, faded black by so many bottoms.

"I see you're looking for something live-in? Like a nanny?"

Sylvie considered whether to mention Enzo's abuse, whether this was where she'd find a way out. But he'd only hit her twice in the past six months—who'd care about that, even if they believed her?

The clerk peered over eyeglasses perched on the ball of his nose. "Bring your own baby?" he quipped. "BYOB . . . let's see . . . ." He flipped through some cards. "There's not much. But the orchards complain they can't get local help."

"To do what?"

"Apple-picking." He looked at the bow on her shoes. "You probably aren't interested," he decided as he shuffled the card to the back.

"Wait! I'll check it out." Enzo's paranoia about having been singled out annoyed her.

Eyebrows raised, the clerk handed her the card. "The pay's not bad. And they have housing." It was unlikely anything else offered housing.

On the way back, she stopped at a payphone near the convenience store and called Rima. "Hey! We're out of the house and at North Beach."

"How's Enzo?"

"I don't know—sometimes he scares me, but I feel so responsible."

"Be careful. The drugs may have lingering effects but who knows what other experiments he agreed to."

By the time she returned to the campground, Annie was helping Florie out of the car and Linda was at the picnic table with Enzo, sipping espresso flavored with her anisette liqueur, and Rima was pulling in. Diana and Claudia were playing inside a tent Linda had set up.

"Enzo made a wonderful spaghetti sauce," Linda said, a bit too cheerily. Sylvie suspected she'd been uncomfortable alone with Enzo, having witnessed his nervous breakdown.

Annie had brought her guitar. "I can't stay long," she said, "but wanted to practice with singers."

"Will you take requests?" asked Linda.

"I'll try."

Annie called the girls to come sing "Skip to My Lou" and "Row your Boat." She was off-key but Sylvie admired her chutzpah. As Annie was about to leave, she said, "Rick didn't want to come. This gives him free time to hook up with a woman I think he's cheating with."

"What an ass," said Linda, then giggled. "Oops! I don't even know him!"

Annie said, "No, but you're right."

When Enzo revealed they'd soon be apple-pickers, Linda said, "Farm workers? Unbelievable. Though Sylvie does like to garden."

Before going to bed, Sylvie emptied a carton of eggs into a pot of water and left them to cool on the picnic table. Growling awakened her during the night and she lay listening, frozen in the dark, a shock of fear shooting through her. The streetlight cast wolf-size shadows onto the side of the tent. She mused about survival and her mind connected to women's social survival, straining to fit into male-defined categories. Saul, Italian men, her job at Easton and the women's collective, Mr. Zingaro. Even Olga and Griselda wore widows' weeds. Then she remembered her molester and the terror she'd never voiced. All these years she'd managed her suspicions and wariness of men bent on diminishing her. Enzo embodied both a promise and a threat. In himself he both incited fear and assuaged it.

She looked toward sleeping Diana then peeked outside to see it was just raccoons eating the eggs. In the morning, she brushed the meticulously peeled eggshells off the table and for breakfast they ate dry cereal out of little boxes. She had visited the rest of that night like a foreign place and awakened a seasoned traveler, remembering how she'd supposed huge creatures were growling outside when it was only oversized rodents. Fear was just a motivator and she'd just have to face whatever caused it, for Diana's sake.

They packed up and drove past Middlebury to Quarry Road, turning at a cracked wooden sign with "Johnny Appleseed" painted in fading script and entering the driveway of a small house. They went up and pushed open the door to see smoke shrouding a figure in a black-and-blue checked shirt at a chipped veneer desk behind "Moe Kress" lettered gold on a black plastic plaque. Two cigars wrapped in cellophane peeked from his shirt pocket.

"The job bank sent us," said Enzo.

Chomping on the unlit cigar, Moe took a pen from a pink ceramic cup shaped like the round contours of a woman's butt—Sylvie was glad she couldn't see its front from where she sat—and took a sheet from the stack of application forms. "So, you have experience?"

"Of course," Enzo lied.

Sure, I've picked apples from the tree behind the garage, Sylvie thought. And the You Pick 'Em orchard Mom took us to.

"Otherwise," Enzo continued, "why would people like us be here?"

"Ha! That's good." Moe tenderly rested the cigar on the edge of the desk and made a mark on the form, then plunged into filling out the rest. Sylvie studied his thick fingers clutching the pen and reduced him to manageable status by picturing him as a first grader.

"They said you provide housing."

The cigar branded the desk with a black crescent. Moe put it in the ashtray then reared back in the chair. "That what you want? Housing?" He looked askance at them.

"Yes."

Plopping down his front chair legs, he caught a cigar mid-roll as it fell out of his pocket, and ripped open the cellophane. "Aha! Well!" he rocked back and hooked his thumb through a belt loop. "We don't have the Fed's OK for kids."

"How about if we camp somewhere?"

Moe spit the tip off the cigar and focused on Sylvie's chest. He bit his cigar, showing his teeth. "Well, since you're *experienced* . . . ." He scrutinized them then said, "Get your car and follow me." He stood up, revealing he was no taller than Sylvie.

They followed him onto the gravel driveway of an old one-room schoolhouse hidden by a screen of maples with leaf tips like rust eating the tree from outside in. With the idling truck excreting blue fumes, Moe strode to Enzo's open window and leaned on the rim. Cigar odor oozed from him like an essence.

"Park behind this place and set up out back." He nodded to a corner where two fences met. "Kitchen and john are inside. Follow the truck when it picks up the crew tomorrow." He pulled his lips back, baring yellow teeth clenching the cigar, touched his forehead in a salute and lumbered back to his truck, stomped the pedal and skidded away, a curtain of dust filling the air between them.

Sylvie got out of the car coughing. Diana rubbed her eyes, Farfella patiently guarding her. Enzo lugged the tent back where the grass looked like ripe wheat, letting the green metal poles clang to the ground. Sylvie recalled their houseful of furniture, roomful of little-girl clothes, garage-full of tools, kitchen-full of cookware; everything remaining was in the car. She'd saved enough toys and books for Diana while she and Enzo picked apples.

Diana ran to the fence, crying, "Horses!" and pointed in the next-door field at them, scabby patches on their hides. She dared herself to scramble over and touch the ground on the other side of the fence where they roamed, moving closer as Diana scrambled back to this side, exclaiming "I beat!"

In the distance a house nestled, snug and safe in an opening among trees with fire-colored leaves spreading into the foothills. While Enzo struggled with the tent, Sylvie called Diana to help carry food inside. Two men were playing poker watched by a woman wearing a crocheted choker. Diana skipped toward a long-haired man picking bluegrass on a banjo. He looked up and winked at her. He wore his plaid flannel shirt like Enzo did, sleeves rolled to the elbow.

Glancing at Sylvie, the dealer shuffled, the cards slapping each other. "You another picker?" Moe was supposed to have informed the Schoolhouse crew they'd be sharing the kitchen.

"Yes. We're camping out back."

In the corner was the kitchen, its sink crowded with dishes. Sylvie too always cleaned up after Enzo, like domestic help, a lower social class. His needs had so shaped her life, she'd lost track of what she herself wanted.

"Help yourself to whatever dishes," the woman called.

The dealer clapped a card down and shouted, "Yes! Ruth, get a beer. Tim's gotta pay."

Tim, the other card player, smiled, making Sylvie wince at the black decay outlining his teeth. Ruth's hands swooped like claws over beers in the fridge. Her large breasts made her look heavier than she was.

"Sorry about the mess," Ruth said.

"Is that your job?" Sylvie asked.

"I'm the only girl here," Ruth said.

"Do they pay you extra?" Sylvie goaded.

"Free beer." Ruth tugged the pop-top. "You don't look like much of a picker."

"I'm not. You?"

"Not many chicks ever work here," Ruth said. "I've been the only one. Only white one." She sipped her beer.

Sylvie squatted to open a cabinet door and clanked through a shelf of pots, scaring up what she needed. By then Diana had come to help. Sylvie set her at the sink with different-sized containers and a plastic bin of water.

"How'd you get into apple-picking?" Sylvie asked as she drizzled oil into the frying pan.

"Dwayne got me started. Moe's his cousin. Dwayne's been doing it all his life."

The dealer, Dwayne, chimed in. "Doing it all my life? Yeah, but not with you, baby. Hell, you don't even let me do it with you every day!"

"Dwayne, shut up. There's a kid in here." Ruth rolled her eyes.

The banjo player began picking a fast chord progression and Diana ran into the middle of the room and twirled around. He strummed faster and faster and Dwayne and Tim clapped to Diana's dancing. "Go! Go! Go! Take it all off! Yeah!"

Enzo came inside and said, "Bellissima, Diana! Beautiful dance. Now let's work on a puzzle." To the men he said, "America is the wealthiest country in the world, no? But I've never seen such ignorance."

The men frowned at him. Sylvie wished he'd used more finesse.

"Dwayne, you're sick," Ruth said.

"I'll feel much better soon's I get that beer."

Ruth hurled it at him. "Pig," she said.

He caught it. "Yeah," he said and belched. "Tim, bring more beer like I told you, burn-out."

Tim wandered into the kitchen and leaned his face so close to the bubbling tomato sauce that Sylvie feared he'd drool in it.

"What's this shit anyway?" he said. "There's no meat!"

Ruth and Tim joined Dwayne who said, "C'mon, assholes. What're you waiting for, Mitch? We're going to town."

Mitch stopped strumming and grabbed the banjo by its throat, snapped it into its case and entered the kitchen. His chin stubble looked like an unevenly mown lawn. His boyishness was endearing and she was grateful for his friendliness.

"I'd eat your stuff, but we kinda do what Dwayne wants." A horn honked outside. "Later, then."

Sylvie was apprehensive knowing Enzo would eventually blame her for Mitch's flirting. She drained the spaghetti, put it on plates and ladled on sauce. When Diana finished eating, she ran around the room in big circles.

"We won't be here long. Can we just try to get along?"

"How do we get along with boorish morons?" Enzo fumed.

The next morning when Enzo and Sylvie went inside to wash up, Ruth was on the table with her feet on the bench lacing up her work boots and Mitch was pouring water into the coffee machine.

"I was gonna come outside and wake you," he told Sylvie, running his fingers through his hair. His eyes, blue and clear like sink water, burned through her. Enzo stepped between him and Sylvie and glowered at her.

"C'mon, let's go!" Tim called.

Sylvie told Farfella to stay in the tent and joined Enzo in the car. He followed the truck carrying the crew members on the flatbed, sharing a joint. Trees, their brilliant leaves refusing to die peacefully, lined the road. In the orchard parking lot, they walked across frozen red mud where rectangles and stripes from boots and tires created a primitive design. They wandered through rows of apple trees so laden with fruit their branches slumped like overburdened beasts. Passing the migrants in the orchard, Sylvie heard a man's voice saying, "These are too green. When I say 'ninety percent red,' do you know what I mean?"

"They ain't no ninety percent red on this tree."

"Keep lookin. Pick red. You don't want me to tell Moe, do you?"

Around the corner they met Dwayne, who told them, "Take this card and go down there." He nodded to where Mitch stood at the foot of a ladder. "He'll tell you where to pick."

Out here the crew weren't the stoned goofballs of last night but acted like they were superior to pickers, despite some pickers' expertise: The Jamaicans amazed with machine-like speed as they sang and picked. The extended family of migrants, too, were experienced farm-workers.

Mitch sat on the forklift waiting to drive bins to the barn. "Hey, woman, grab a ladder!" he called to Sylvie. "Start with this tree."

Enzo said, "Hey, friend. You talk to me, not my wife." His paranoia and possessiveness distressed Sylvie.

Mitch ignored him. "OK, watch what you do." Bushel-sized galvanized buckets rested on the pickers' bellies like metal feedbags, canvas straps looping across each shoulder. "Grab the apple, twist, then lay it in." He pantomimed picking an apple, twirling his long slender fingers in the air. "Don't reach. Move the ladder. When it's full, call us and we'll mark your cards before you unload into the bin."

Each time a picker gently unloaded their forty-pound bucket into a bin, a supervisor punched their card and at day's end tallied and paid per bushel. Pickers aimed for ten bushels a day, but the Jamaicans picked up to fifteen.

The white people from the schoolhouse had the easy, higher-paying jobs as supervisors and "skimmers" who, when a bin reached capacity, removed as much as a bushel of apples per bin to use to create new bins. The original still looked full. Sylvie was appalled to learn the orchard shortchanged the buyers this way.

After two weeks' steady work, Sylvie woke to rain sounding like slow flames on the tent. On rainy days they didn't pick because the managers said touching wet apples could bruise them. Weary and achy, she gathered toys and found Diana inside sitting in a corner playing with puzzles and Enzo reading a magazine.

"Me and Dwayne, we hitched all summer," Tim was saying. He flicked his cigarette ash onto the top of one of the crumpled beer cans on the table.

"Went to Maine and picked blueberries. That's back-breaking, man. Guy down there told us about apples. This place was closed but Moe let us stay. Told him I picked five years, so he hired us as checkers."

"What was your real experience?" asked Dwayne.

"A season," Tim laughed. "Then I got mugged coming here through Boston. Black dude pulled a knife."

Mitch plucked the banjo. "Hell, you were probably asking for it."

"Keep them away from me or I might lose it, man," Tim said, lighting another cigarette.

Dwayne said, "Moe keeps them separate to see how fast the sons-of-bitches are, see what they're worth." Sylvie noticed a cigar, probably from Moe, in his breast pocket.

"How come they get the big house and we're stuck here?" Ruth asked, wrapping hair around her finger.

"Cause there's more of them, dingbat," said Tim.

Sylvie clutched her cup, wondering why people, including her, put up with bullying.

"Niggers shouldn't live in cold places," said Dwayne. "Moe thinks so too. That's why he likes us."

"I heard they ain't working no more til they get paid," Dwayne said as he dealt cards. "And they don't know it, but they ain't gonna get paid." He laughed.

"You think this exploitation is justified?" Enzo asked.

"Oooh, big words," said Dwayne.

Tim put another cigarette to his lips. Sylvie knew these guys were in charge, but said, "Can you quit smoking so much in here? Jeez, we all have to breathe this air. Give our little girl a break!"

Tim frowned at her. "Who asked you to bring a kid in here?"

"Ah, here goes the typical bourgeois American stupidity," Enzo said. "Children are life! And you're just a blot on the earth!" She'd loved how Enzo knew how to shut up the bullies. But then he became one too.

"Yeah?" said Dwayne. "Who asked *you* to reproduce?"

"The kid's your problem. She shouldn't even be here. Besides," said Tim, taking a long drag, "the world's over-populated." He slowly exhaled a lungful of smoke.

Dwayne agreed, "There's enough kids in the world. We vow never to have them."

"Enough Americans, yes," said Enzo.

COLD FRUIT

On Saturday they took Farfella on a walk and spent as much time as possible outdoors. After lunch Sylvie read to Diana and they both fell asleep until the afternoon sunrays brightened the tent canvas, making the inside glow a lurid green on her skin and awakened her to find she was alone. She heard a car engine wheezing. She didn't trust the crew and was afraid they'd lock up and leave. She ran to the schoolhouse, yanked at the door, pounded on it. It didn't budge. Then she turned around and saw Diana at the fence watching the horses rub necks together and Enzo talking with Moe on the driveway.

"I'm afraid it's not working out. They say the kid's a nuisance. And frankly we're not cleared for kids. Sometimes the Feds check and I could get a nice fine."

Enzo said, "So where should we stay?"

Moe considered. "Well . . . we get migrants here. Negroes. You could pitch tent over there if you don't mind being with those people."

Moe waited while they packed. The car was littered with empty potato chip wrappers, juice cartons, grocery lists, store coupons, crinkled maps, beach sand, pebbles and bayberries Diana had gathered. The car felt like home, a steady presence, the trash a reminder of both civilization and wilderness.

"What is this? Cronyism?" Enzo said.

"They want to be with others that look like them," Sylvie said. "They think that means they *are* like themselves." This job was supposed to be an uncomplicated way to earn quick cash but it was a political swamp.

They followed Moe to a big, white Victorian house with green-trimmed windows and shutters and a wraparound porch across from a working dairy farm where chickens scratched along the roadside. Moe pulled over to Enzo's open window, pointed out where they could pitch tent behind the house and drove off.

After setting up and eating sandwiches, they left Farfella on guard duty and took Diana across the street to ask to see the animals. Bianca, a woman in her twenties, introduced her teenage twin brothers as having been "born during a hurricane"—a phrase the boys echoed several times each—when the power went out and they were born in pitch dark and "didn't get enough oxygen." One asked if Sylvie and Enzo were from the big city, saying, "I been there once" and his brother echoed.

"He means Middlebury," Bianca said.

A little boy about nine trailed behind Bianca. She alternately referred to him as her brother and her son. The horror of this chilled Sylvie as she remembered their tenant Amy mentioning an entire school district designated special education because of inbreeding. Even on this prosperous looking farm? Bianca's uncle invited them on a tour and escorted them past farmhands ankle deep in a mud-manure sludge they were raking out, and into the sterile milking parlor that stood empty now since the cows were out grazing. As they left the barn, a waddling flock of geese lowered their long necks and aimed their pointed beaks toward Diana and speedily approached. Bianca's uncle quickly scooped her out of the way.

"I want to see Fafella," she sobbed.

* * *

After Diana was asleep, Enzo stopped Sylvie outside the tent and accused her of flirting with Mitch.

"Is talking flirting?" she said, "I'm supposed to not talk to men? Who do you think you are?"

He slapped the side of her head and she backed off, screaming, "That's it! I'm sick of this! We're getting divorced!"

Enzo glared at her, then turned and went and drove off.

In the morning, rain pounded the tent like someone kicking it, sounding so loud it covered the usual silence except for the crickets, so it took a while for Sylvie to realize Enzo and Diana weren't there. She hadn't heard him return during the night. She peeked through the flap at the empty parking space, then ran into the house to see if they'd gone to the bathroom. All was quiet. She returned to the tent thinking they probably went to the store. After an hour she was panicking; her head buzzed, her heart pounded, her whole body shook. She'd read about estranged parents kidnapping their children.

Her unease grew into a dread that filled her body, forcing her across to the farm to ask to use the phone. With Bianca's permission, despite her mother fretting she'd call long distance, Sylvie dialed Linda, Annie, Miriam, Judy and Rima and only reached Enzo's born-again, pot-head pal Mickey who loved that useless band Pink Floyd and stupidly boasted how his parents were friends with that has-been right-winger Perry Como. He said Enzo wasn't there.

She begged Bianca for a ride to Burlington.

"What can you find there that you couldn't learn by phoning?" Bianca wondered.

Sylvie said, "Yeah, probably Enzo can't manage Diana alone and will hurry back." She thanked Bianca and her mother for their hospitality.

She lay awake all night, pricking up her ears the few times a car passed. Having read stories of parental kidnapping where the aggrieved parent never sees her child again, she was terrified, thinking how her case matched such stories. She'd die if she never saw her baby again! Her sole comfort was that Diana had an American passport so surely Enzo would get stopped at the border.

The next day she returned to make phone calls and then borrowed Bianca's umbrella, intending to hitchhike. She walked along the highway, passing woods and hilly fields, her toes numb in the wet cold. She stoked her fear into anger and fury and then resolve. Maybe she could've been a better wife? More patient? She knew about acid trips. Maybe she should've let him recover on his own? No. He's showing who he is. She'd get away. She'd do it right, no matter how long it took. She lifted her raincoat's hood and stood at a stop sign waiting for a car, getting drenched until she gave up and returned to camp.

On Monday morning, Sylvie woke with a headache. She heard a car outside and looked out to see Enzo lifting sleeping Diana from the car. He carried her to the tent where Sylvie tenderly tucked her in and petted her hair until he beckoned her outside and hissed, "Try to leave me and I'll take Diana where you'll never see her again!"

She'd felt satisfied to have realized how despicable he could be. "Kidnapping my child is vile! You, who everyone sees as this great progressive social reformer." She instantly regretted her words—not because she didn't mean them but because she knew they'd set him off. "Where the hell were you?"

"At Mickey's."

"That liar said you weren't there."

"He's my friend," he said and stormed back to the car.

Enzo had set in motion a new future because starting now she'd find a way to leave him that wouldn't let him kidnap Diana again. She'd bitten off all her fingernails. She'd been supportive while he piled up abuse and lies. She hated his chaos, his cruelty. Even if she had to hide and skimp the rest of her life, she didn't want to relive the panic and emptiness of losing Diana. She'd bide her time, play along, lay low and not resist until the time was right.

She went to find Diana's passport in the bag where they kept documents so she could hide it. It wasn't there. She'd check in the car when Enzo returned, but her car key was nowhere either. She panicked, realizing she couldn't ask him for either or he'd suspect her. He'd been making his own plans.

Sylvie hadn't yet met anyone in the big house. Because of the rain, there'd be no picking again today, so when Diana awoke, they went inside and found the air thick with oily smoke. Holding Diana up to the bathroom sink to wash her hands, Sylvie glanced in the mirror at her thin face, made haggard-looking by her wet hair. Vermont's cold infused her pores like swamp water that petrifies wood. She struggled against exhaustion.

Wanting to protect her innocence, she made light of Diana's trip, asking if she had fun with Papa and said, "I missed you so much!"

"I missed you too, Mommy."

"Honey, make sure you call me every day when you go on trips like that. Papa forgets sometimes." She crouched down and hugged her daughter tight, tears in her eyes.

Exiting the bathroom, Sylvie noticed a woman in the lighted kitchen standing at the stove, her dark hand gripping a spatula to tend fish filets floating in a frying pan.

"Hello?" Sylvie led Diana into the bright kitchen to watch as the woman continued working intently, her face glowing with sweat.

She saw Sylvie and said, "You the ones living back there? Lord have mercy! In this cold?"

"We're used to this climate," Sylvie said, breaking eye contact.

"It's too cold for a child! There's room for you here!" The woman shook her head. "The Lord wouldn't like it if I allowed any child to freeze when they could be warm here inside."

"That's very kind. But Moe said . . . ."

"Pooh! Let Moe be ashamed for keeping you outside. You won't be in nobody's way." She pursed her lips. "I'll show you soon's I can. Sit down. Call me Rose."

Diana's eyes grew large watching the golden mound of fish grow on a plate.

"Go ahead, baby. Take some," Rose said.

"Can I, Mommy?"

Sylvie nodded. When you're poor and without allies, you're at the mercy of everyone's humanity. She was grateful for Rose's kindness.

Rose said, "I don't know nothing about you, but I got a feeling you're good people."

"Thanks," Sylvie smiled. "But why didn't Moe want us in here?"

Rose hesitated. "I s'pose he don't like you mixing with us. Long as nobody knows what he's doing, he can keep doing it."

Rose sprinkled black pepper from the largest McCormick container Sylvie had ever seen.

"I mean it. And I've been places. Mm-hmm. Go on and eat, girl. You look starved."

Sylvie met the rest of the farmhouse crew—several extended families from Florida—as they gathered around the table.

* * *

Enzo returned the next morning. "Mickey hid us because I asked him to," he said and took her hand. "You know how much I love you, Sylvia. You're everything to me." He wrapped his arms around her and pulled her tight. "I can't bear when you say you want to leave me." Sylvie's heart was stony. She wriggled away.

During the next few days, she, Enzo and Diana ate with the migrant crew. Sylvie contributed salads from vegetables Enzo had harvested in Mickey's garden.

"We ain't none of us done apples before," one of the crew, Anthony, said. "We've picked lots of fruit. Apples is the toughest. Peaches are easy. They're like rocks. You just shake their tree or wait until they fall to the ground because they ripen later. Orange trees are easy, too, but snakes hide in 'em. Apples have to ripen on the trees. They're like eggs. They said we can't pick 'em when they're wet because that'd bruise 'em. Worse, though, some ugly people run this place."

"How so?" asked Sylvie.

"Hmmm! Let me tell you something," Rose's husband Fred said. "It's so rainy we can't work. Been here four weeks and only worked two. They guaranteed us work and now they won't pay. Half our crew left last week."

Feeling cheated, some had left, others spent the days fishing in Otter Creek, catching bass, pike, bullhead and pickerel and putting it in the sink. The crew didn't see how they could earn what they'd been promised because soon the fruit would start dropping.

"It's amazing how many tricks they have here," said Sylvie.

Rose flattened her palms on the table and pushed herself up. "Enough chitchat. Forget that old tent," she said. "Let's go get you a bedroom."

Upstairs they passed a room where a man was telling some boys about his fishing. Teenage girls sprawled on a bed in another room, one with hair in rollers, another painting her nails, watching soaps on television.

"You girls done your homework?" Rose asked.

"Yes, ma'am!"

"In there," Rose said to Enzo and Sylvie. "Nice and dry." She pointed to a knee-high door leading to a storage room and pulled open its tiny brass knob. A window at the end let in light. They all had to duck their heads to fit through the doorway but the room was spacious, even with metal bedframes stacked against the walls.

"Thank you," said Sylvie. "This is nice!"

When they were settled on mattresses on the floor, the moon shone on them through the tiny window. The bedframes stacked vertically along the wall felt like a big metal cage.

As the torrent continued, they all got to know each other. The girls braided Diana's hair while watching TV. Everyone welcomed Sylvie, Enzo and Diana into the household and included them in Sunday church service where they sat on wooden chairs pushed against the walls in a circle around the cleared floor space. They clapped as Rose led them in song until all at once she danced in the middle of the room while the others kept the song going and made unusual sounds that Sylvie thought must be speaking in tongues. Rose was a good, kind person and if this is what helped her be that way, so be it.

Enzo played his harmonica after the service. Anthony called out, "Play 'Merry Christmas!'" and Fred said, "That's it! That's 'Merry Christmas.'" Sylvie wondered if they really detected the tune Enzo invented or were being polite. She loved how they found pleasure under these distressing conditions. That's how she wanted to be too.

Saturday Rose invited them to follow her to the laundromat in Cornwall. Sylvie and Enzo had two full loads to wash. When everything was in machines, they went next door for ice cream, then Enzo took Diana back to the laundromat while Sylvie window-shopped with Rose and the girls.

"I married Fred after raising my children," Rose said. "It's a mistake to have children with someone you love."

"I kind of understand what you mean," said Sylvie. "I used to love him."

Sylvie felt people staring, as though singling out her conspicuous white skin amid black people, suddenly realizing her friends were the only black people in town.

She and Enzo drove to Burlington the next day to look up Rima and then have dinner with Annie and Rick. When Enzo wasn't looking, Sylvie slipped a letter into the mailbox. When she escaped, she'd need a refuge.

Dear Karen,

My life is weird, of course. Did I marry a jerk like my old friend Saul? I'm such an idiot! May head your way so don't be surprised. XXOO—S.

Rima met them on campus outside the library. She crouched down and gave Diana a hug. "Oh you're getting so big!"

Diana hugged her back.

"I hope you're all doing well, considering all you've been through."

"Couldn't be better," Enzo said.

Sylvie rolled her eyes but didn't think Rima saw.

"Listen, I'm pretty sure Shuster is using residual funds. That LSD research goes way back. Good thing Enzo left! No telling what damage he could've done."

"Yeah, no telling," said Sylvie, widening her eyes until she knew Rima saw.

* * *

They arrived back in Cornwall later than planned. The darkness felt like being inside a bowl of black. Suddenly the car chugged and wheezed until it stopped dead.

"Out of gas!" Enzo cried, looking at the red needle on the fuel dial. "Shit! I don't believe it!" He coasted onto the shoulder.

Sylvie thought, he'd be asking me how I could be so stupid. Such a hypocrite.

"Diana, honey, wake up," Sylvie said.

Diana jerked awake and whined as Enzo picked her up and carried her, stumbling, Farfella trotting alongside. Sylvie felt like she was floating in the thick blackness, pinholes in the sky the only light until bright light came toward them from behind, turning the road ahead silver and speeding by. They trudged on, breathing hard, so tired she could have lain down and slept right there. More lights came over the hill, making shadows dance. A car passed, slowed down, stopped and backed up. A man with the same hollow cheeks as Tim—the same smirk, the same dead eyes—rolled down the window.

"Need a ride?"

"Thanks," Enzo said, panting as they climbed into the back seat.

"We recognized your dog. You living in that house with the niggers?"

The hostile word frightened Sylvie more here than it had inside the schoolhouse. She felt them watching her enter the house. They tiptoed through the quiet house to the storeroom and through the open window she still heard talking from inside the idling car before it skidded away.

Sylvie was awakened by crunching gravel followed by muffled voices rising through the floor. She nudged Enzo awake and they both left Diana sleeping and hurried downstairs. Rose's face brightened when she saw them.

"Praise Jesus! You're here!" She hugged Sylvie. "Sit down and listen to me."

"The cops were here," Fred said. "They found a burned-up car that sounds like yours. And yours ain't here . . . ."

". . . so we figured you was in it." Rose's eyes brimmed with tears.

"We ran out of gas a mile away," Enzo said. "There was nothing wrong with that car!"

Sylvie asked, "How can it just burn up?"

"A lot of mischief last night," Fred said. "Man who drives our bus, his house was shot up. The guys already hit the road, scared for their life."

"Darlins, we all gotta leave," Rose said. "Just be glad you're OK."

Fred and Rose packed their caravan, with room enough for his girls plus Enzo, Sylvie, Diana and their stuff, including the tent in its case, whom they'd drop at North Beach campground, the only place they could think of to go. Sylvie went to round up Farfella, who usually slept on the wrap-around porch, which is where Sylvie found her lifeless body, another victim of last night's spree. She sat with her a moment and thanked her for her faithful service then ran back into the kitchen for a towel to cover her with.

Fred stopped at their car, which lay like a black carcass alongside the road. The windshield had melted, its glass dripped and hardened like clear amber on the bumpers. The trunk was open and Sylvie saw a pile of smoking threads which must've been the laundry bag they'd forgotten to unload. In the glove compartment, the camera was charred metal. She felt violated.

Rose's words "just be glad you're OK" haunted her. Diana sobbed about losing the doll she'd left in the car and cried now, asking for Farfella.

Sylvie hugged her and said, "Farfella decided to stay on the farm with all her animal friends who love her." She wrapped Diana in her arms and mourned quietly, keeping all the horror to herself.

ANOTHER STAB

It was still rainy, almost cold enough to snow. Sylvie knew she shouldn't be rash and weighed the risk of failing in her escape against the strain of being with Enzo. She dismissed the chance of his seriously harming her; after all, she had focused so much on survival that she felt like an expert. Enzo reminded her of her promise to help him escape the cold but added that he wanted to earn extra cash before they took off, reminding her how her parents had cut him out of home ownership and that he needed to feel solvent.

Sometimes Sylvie thought she was being unfair or cold-hearted. She worried she'd forgotten how to feel. But lying awake at night, she felt the depths of her despair and prayed for the strength to keep her goal in mind.

It would've been convenient to get to Karen's in Boston but Sylvie had never heard back. Besides, her goal was Janis's whose tantalizing letters from California about picking cherries and raising goats, the endless sunshine, the majestic land, always closed with, "You're welcome to stay with me any time!" Sylvie had clung to that promise for years now. She couldn't bring herself to crawl home to her parents, thinking it would stir up more problems than it would solve.

On their third day at North Beach, Enzo returned with groceries, saying, "I found our way out of here." He'd seen a VW van parked on the street, a For Sale sign on its windshield. "The color of marigolds. They're going to drive it over so you can see!"

When the owners showed up, Sylvie and Enzo took turns test-driving the van then made an offer. The title was signed over and Sylvie now knew to have them write a bill of sale. She started packing while Enzo went to the Department of Motor Vehicles to get plates and she asked him to make her a copy of the key, which she never saw. She contacted Annie, who brought over her houseplants.

Sitting on top of all their stuff packed in the back, Diana asked a million questions during the long drive, but not all at once as in her intense probing at home. Eventually she had the grace to fall asleep.

After hours of driving, Enzo would pull over and let loose his rage over some imagined slight, keeping Sylvie constantly on edge. One moment she'd be laughing at his Mussolini parodies, and the next he was pulling her hair or grabbing her arm and pinching hard. He always made his moves when Diana was sleeping and Sylvie muffled her cries, conflicted about protecting Diana from the truth. After all, isn't that what she blamed Mom for having done when she was a child?

They came to a rest stop in South Dakota where Sylvie took Diana out to pee along the side of the road. Alone in the car, Enzo drove around in circles with the side door open, allowing Sylvie's purse to slide off the seat onto the ground and driving over it. She couldn't tell if he was obliviously or purposely crushing it and reined in her anger to protect Diana from perceiving his mania. She stood watching him, fascinated by the horror that must impel him. She watched as though from a distance, just as she now looked upon her molester, the pimply youth in penny loafers and white socks who had invaded her small body, trying to engage her in a horrific act. By masking her fear back then, she had diminished him, banished him. So with Enzo now.

After several minutes, Enzo stopped the engine and rested his head on the steering wheel. Sylvie fetched her purse and looked inside to see her glasses' smashed frames then went back and stood at the overlook and threw pebbles with Diana out over the hill.

"I miss Farfella," Diana said.

"Me too," said Sylvie.

Diana picked up the biggest rock she could find. "I'm throwing this at that farm!"

Enzo came up behind Sylvie and hissed, "Why don't you react? You should growl or scratch with your nails. You should draw blood! You make me feel invisible, like a ghost. Why can't you be more in your body?" He grabbed her arm. "I make you laugh, I make you come. Why don't you suck me everywhere, anywhere? You can be ferocious—do it!"

Whispering over her shoulder, she said, "For a smart man, you're pretty dense." She shook her arm free and turned toward Diana, who was pointing at where her rock had landed.

Enzo said, "You make me lonely. I don't matter to you. You don't give a shit about me!"

He dares to slap me and expects adoration? Kidnaps Diana and thinks I'll forget it? Sylvie was disgusted by his neediness. She remembered how he'd said traveling would help them learn about each other: She'd learned all she cared to. Something stirred inside her, like a larva that'd been buried for years underground before emerging as an adult. She'd sacrificed for this family, repressing her desires and neglecting her talents, so he could pursue a career—which he never did. In return he treated her with abuse and disrespect and kidnapped their daughter. She'd poured so much energy into her marriage and for what?

* * *

Enzo pulled over at an overlook across from Mt. Rushmore. He opened the back door to get a bag of chips and let several of Sylvie's houseplants fall out and stomped on them, breaking their clay pots.

"They're taking up too much room," he said.

"Jealous of my plants? That's pathetic!" Even if she could salvage them, she had no containers. As they drove away, he rolled down the window and tossed out the empty chips bag.

"Oh come on! We have to pick that up!"

He kept driving. "How does it benefit us if we do? It's just paper."

Like our marriage certificate? she wondered. He'd bury her before he'd bury their mortally wounded marriage.

"It's litter—doesn't belong here. What would Strong Hawk say?"

"That's your stupid false consciousness. The government wants you to think it's your job to clean up the earth, when it's their policies that pollute."

They continued through expanses of mountain and plain, seeing neither human nor house. Then, just after filling up at the only gas station in miles, the van sputtered to a halt near St. Regis, Montana. Enzo steered to the shoulder and walked the mile back to the station whose attendant returned with him, examined the car and announced he had no metric tools and couldn't work on foreign cars but would call around for parts. So they spent the night, Enzo and Sylvie in the front seats and Diana stretched out on top of the stuff in back. All around was dark silence, above them the stars, and between them an undercurrent of suspicion. Sylvie's life alternated between reacting to Enzo's abuse and planning her escape. Their relationship was like a chess game, but she didn't think he knew she was playing. She counted on his belief in her naïveté and was sure her oldest friend would take her in.

Seattle was gloomy and billboards in Portland invited visitors to keep moving. She navigated as he drove, unaware that she was aiming for Janis's place. They stopped in Eureka and Garberville where flyers in realty windows advertised land for sale. Sylvie bought a stamped postcard in a drugstore and wrote, "I'm dying to see you" and mailed it to Janis. She also saw flyers on lampposts and fences accusing a Reverend Jones of kidnapping; she thought he could be a criminal or religious man but not both. They stopped to cool off in a river just past Mendocino, the water so frigid Sylvie only waded briefly. A tall blond man at the same spot described the tight community of unfriendly pot-growers there. They skirted around San Francisco and drove east through farmland where vast stretches of dead brown grass dumbfounded her. She hadn't known about California's annual drought.

She drove while Enzo—teeth clenched and body twitching—slept. The heat increased and the open windows allowed the breeze of motion. She headed toward Janis up into the foothills, where stately trees with wide, spreading limbs grew amid the dead grass then entered a conifer forest with massive trees along a road of unimaginably red-orange ground. They were now so remote she wondered how she could possibly elude him.

No sputter or whistle warned before the van choked and lurched. She steered into the weeds at the roadside, smoke hissing out back as the car rolled to a stop. Her ears roared in a silence punctuated by woodpecker taps echoing through the cedars.

Enzo woke with a start. "Where are we?" His eyes squeaked open.

She sat back in the seat, looking straight ahead, her mind blank, then tried the key. Not even a click.

"It overheated!" he yelled. "You should've stopped for water!" She let the accusation echo along the dusty woodland road.

He jumped out and stormed back to open the deck lid and said, "There's no radiator!"

Sylvie grabbed her hair and barretted it to her head then helped Diana out of the car. Enzo plopped down on the ground. He unfolded the map and laid it open in his lap, then took out a filmy plastic bag and sprinkled marijuana into a cigarette paper and rolled the joint. He inhaled deeply and held his breath, glaring at her across the road. Diana picked up pebbles and threw them into the woods.

A slow-growing hum intruded into the silence. Enzo stood in the middle of the road, looking toward the sound. Heat shimmering up from the red dust made the approaching form waver until taking shape, a pickup truck coated in dull house paint tilting in and out of potholes, pulled as close as it could to Enzo and stopped. A man with black-rimmed glasses leaned on his arm against the open window.

"Hymie?" he squinted at Enzo. "Is that you? It's me! Gus!"

Enzo's dark, curly hair and beard obscured his facial features. He didn't miss a beat. "Hey, Gus," he answered and sidled over to his window.

Gus climbed out, barefoot and in bib overalls, leaned against the truck, took a joint from his pocket, lit it, toked it, and handed it to Enzo.

"It's good to see you, man . . . if you're Hymie, I mean." Holding his breath and pinching the twisted cigarette, Gus proffered it toward Sylvie, raising his eyebrows. She shook her head. He went and felt the deck lid. "How long you been driving?"

"Days," Sylvie said.

Gus laughed. "Shit, man. You're lucky you got this far."

"By the way, where are we? We're looking for Mokelumne Hill," she said, stressing the "lum" rather than the "kel."

"You ain't nowhere near Moke Hill, man. This is Bearmat Creek. You're twenty-thirty miles from Moke."

The hollow drilling of woodpeckers echoed from the cedars.

Gus inspected the engine. "This thing ain't going nowhere. C'mon. I'll take you to my place."

Enzo bowed slightly. "Very nice," he said.

"Thanks," Sylvie said, watching Enzo manipulate Gus. She grabbed underwear, toiletries and Diana's books, and stuffed them into an overnight bag. This crimped her plans—strike one.

"C'mon, man! Hymie?" Gus insisted, narrowing his eyes. "God, you look like Hymie, man."

Sylvie and Diana climbed into the cab and Enzo into the bed and they wound through the forest on a two-lane road.

"I toss the *I Ching*. You know?" Gus said.

"What's that?"

"Chinese Book of Changes? Things come together in the right place at the right time. You can't predict." They were now driving along cleared land.

"You think things happen for a reason?" Sylvie asked.

"All the time, man," Gus said. "'Fellowship with men at the gate.' That's the Trigram I tossed today. Might not've noticed you otherwise."

It would've been hard not to notice them, but maybe without his coin toss he wouldn't have given meaning to their meeting. He pulled up to a small ranch house. "There must be a reason your old man looks like Hymie. That's why I stopped. I saw him from way back. Same curly hair, same beard. Thought I was seeing a ghost. Last I heard he was in New York." Leading them into his living room, he said, "The john's over there."

Enzo collapsed into an easy chair. Gus left the room and came back with an old copy of the *I Ching*. To Enzo he said, "She never heard of this book, man. Can you believe it?" He showed Sylvie how to toss the pennies and look up the hexagrams whose poetic images illuminate this moment now, free it from life's whimsy, and link it to centuries of guidance.

Gus provided blankets, pillows and the living room couch and said they could stay as long as necessary. Such generosity toward total strangers. Or did he think of them as strangers? He didn't seem to mind that Enzo was nothing like his friend Hymie.

In the morning Gus invited Enzo to try to get a job with him and told Sylvie, "It's a road crew with an independent contractor." He also gave Sylvie a stack of paper. "In case you want to write letters. Or if Diana wants to color."

That evening Enzo came home saying he'd gotten the job. To celebrate, Gus invited over his neighbor, Amina, who arrived in a long India-print skirt and flowy top.

"Got your India clothes on," Gus said.

Addressing Sylvie, she said, "I learned in India how to beat the heat."

"How's the ceramics biz?" asked Gus.

"I got into more shops," she said, "so I need to go to Golden Market for boxes."

When the men were at work the next day, Amina invited Sylvie and Diana along with her. She went into Golden Market general store while Sylvie and Diana entered the post office, an old clapboard building. Inside, three men sat talking in straight-back chairs around a cold potbelly stove, turning to watch as Sylvie mailed her letter notifying Janis she was there.

During the ride back, Sylvie said, "I have an old friend in Moke Hill, married to a guy named Cory Bassett who grew up around here. She's been writing me for years about their farm. I'm dying to see it."

"Wow, Cory Bassett?" Amina said. "Your friend's old man shows at art fairs. I need to go to Moke. Saturday, in fact. I'll take you."

INTO THE NET

As Amina drove to Moke Hill, she said, "Everyone out here looks like a hippie but don't let that fool you."

Sylvie thought about kind strangers and disappointing friends. "It's been a while since I've judged people by appearances."

The windows were open. "You OK back there, little girl?"

"OK," said Diana.

"Good. Sometimes it's too windy." Amina was quiet a while then said, "I mean, this one time I flew next to a guy who kept peeking at me. I felt him stereotyping me and wanted to teach him a lesson. I said, 'I learned in India to detach. You know what I mean?' and he said 'No.' Just 'no.' I said, 'To let go. To live in the spirit.'"

Sylvie liked Amina's voice, slow and mellow with a deep undertone, like a smoker. When she imitated the man, she lowered it further.

"He said, 'That's bullshit' and 'You're too young to lecture me about life.' I said, 'What does age have to do with wisdom?' He said, 'If my daughter spoke to me that way...' and nodded toward the two women across the aisle, the daughter looking out her window and the wife gazing into her compact mirror. He tells them, 'This woman—

sorry, I don't know your name?' I said, 'My mom calls me Cynthia.' He goes, 'Cynthia has just been in India.'"

"That rhymes!" said Diana.

"Yes it does," Sylvie said. Looking in the mirror, Amina winked back at Diana.

"The mother looked me over—my bare feet, my nose ring. She says, 'Bonny is a finalist in the Miss Teenage America beauty contest.' I was like, 'Oh, wow! I won that crown three years ago!'"

"You're joking!" said Sylvie.

"That's what the guy thought! He says, 'Enough of your teasing.' So I gave details, the local and regional contests that led up to it. Even showed him my passport. He compared my name to the list of past winners and saw it was true. He gazed at the picture of me with long shiny hair and said, 'That's you? Why do you make yourself so ugly? Are you on drugs?' I laughed so hard I couldn't speak. I said, 'The first time I got high was with the other finalists. We were under such pressure. Imagine—a contest to see which of us was the most beautiful. We all smoked pot and laughed about how absurd it was.' He said, 'You're making fun of us.' I said, 'No. We'd all become friends, and only one would be chosen. What do you suppose that did to our friendships? Especially when I won a shitload of money for it.' 'OK,' he said. 'You rejected all that. Took the money and ran. I bet men don't look at you the way they used to.' 'They shouldn't,' I said. 'I'm married. Our guru paired us up so we could pursue spiritual growth together.'"

"So you decided beauty contests are shallow and you felt bad and went to India to find your soul?"

Amina paused. "Something like that. And it helped. For a while. So, anyway, I say to the guy, 'What's your daughter's talent? I was a singer.' So I sang my song, 'Tra-la, it's here, that shocking time of year / When tons of wicked

336

little thoughts merrily appear . . . .' Everyone on the plane applauded when I finished so I stood up and bowed."

"You're really good," said Sylvie.

Amina drove along silently. "That was ten years ago. Now I'm divorced and married to my work. He left me 'cause I like drugs too much. Doing all that spiritual work got old."

Sylvie said, "I envy you for having a husband who wanted to do spiritual work."

"Yeah, but when I got high, I laughed at how absurd it all is. When you're born rich, you already know what money does and doesn't mean." They passed a for-sale sign and continued to the end of a long dirt road. Amina stopped at a rickety cabin of uneven boards. "I'll wait while you check out the scene then come tell me when to pick you up."

Sylvie helped Diana out of the car and went and knocked on the door. Then again louder. It opened slowly to reveal an overweight Janis with dull eyes.

"Hey!" Janis said and they hugged each other tightly. "Oh, it's so good to see you!"

"You too! When should my friend pick us up?"

"An hour? How's that?"

Sylvie felt slighted. "Really?"

"Hour and a half?"

Amina called, "I heard. See you at 1:30!"

"Sylvie, I'm sorry," said Janis. And to Diana, "Hi cutie. Come in. I'm making tea." It was a tiny one-room cabin with two beds lining one wall and another disguised as a sofa. The postcard Sylvie had sent was taped to a window.

Sylvie asked, "Where are your boys?"

"With their dad."

"I was hoping Diana could play with them."

"I'm sorry," said Janis, tears filling her eyes. "We're separated. I'm moving to town." To Diana she said, "Sweetie, there's toys in that box over there."

"So, no more homestead?"

"I haven't even gardened since my last pregnancy. Look at all this weight I can't lose!" She started tearing up. "Cory calls me 'fatty' all the time. And then I found out he was sleeping around that whole year."

"Oh, Jan! What a complete ass! I've been pretty dumb too."

They sat watching Diana flip through the toy box and pull out cars and trucks. "I loved your letters about picking cherries and everything. What happened to all that?"

"It's what I wanted to do—my neighbors were doing," Janis started sobbing. "I was ashamed at the mess I'd gotten into." She wiped her eyes and looked up. "I'm really sorry."

She felt light-headed. Sylvie had pinned her hopes on a fiction. She longed for a body of water that would ground her.

"God, so am I." You have no idea, she thought.

Janis said, "I'm going on General Assistance. It'll keep me and the boys alive, anyway."

"What about Cory?"

"He's a child. He plays with art. He kept saying he was about to strike it big and just be patient. But so far . . . ."

Sylvie slowly sipped tea, watching Diana play. "Remember 'Bail me out?'"

"How could I forget?" Janis smiled. "Remember the gum?"

Sylvie laughed and mimicked her younger self saying, "Mr. McComb? What's this?"

Janis's familiar laughter bubbled up. "We should've paid attention during that film on men-stroo-ay-shun."

Gasping through laughs Sylvie said, "Why didn't they . . . have a class about . . . not marrying . . . shitty men?" They caught each other's eye and soon were laughing uncontrollably. When there was a lull they'd make eye contact and start again.

Diana called out, "What's funny?" which made them laugh so hard tears streamed down their faces and they were sobbing and hugging each other and rocking.

"Oh, Sylvie," Janis said. "I've missed us." Now she was bawling.

Sylvie held her and said, "Me too." She sat back and said, "But mailing that pig ear was really violent! We should've gone to reform school." They laughed all over again until Sylvie's sides ached.

Driving back, Sylvie told Amina how she'd hoped to move in with Janis and now saw how impossible this was. "There's not even enough space for her and her kids. And she's moving to town."

After a beat, Amina said, "Just so you know, I slept with her old man. So foxy!"

Sylvie felt personally violated. Now she saw Amina as a stake in the heart of the idealism of their generation that had swept Sylvie up.

She hoped the van could be fixed and offer a way out. Gus gave her his mechanic friend's name so Sylvie called and asked him to check it out. He picked up her and Diana and drove to see it, still sitting where it had stopped. He took a look and said the engine parts had fused together. This officially killed her plans. How could she leave? Besides, Enzo could still access the rent money as easily as she, and there wasn't enough for carfare to get away and settle somewhere. Could she ask Gus to let her and Diana live with him? But how would she keep Enzo from kidnapping Diana again? She knew police didn't get involved in domestic issues. She was trapped. Did it make sense to buy cheap land and build a small shelter as they'd planned to do in Wolford? That would keep Enzo tied to a place while she slipped away, as he'd done to her in Vermont. Maybe it was a revenge fantasy, but that's all she had for now.

Every day Gus brought home a newspaper, so while he and Enzo gossiped about work, Sylvie found ads for property sales. She thought, whatever happened, they could make a little money and said, "We can't afford to leave. And no car." They had no choice, like the destiny Gus talked about.

"Looks like this place chose you," Gus affirmed.

He let her use his phone to call a real estate agent, Chester, who picked them up on Saturday to see a five-acre parcel, exiting the highway onto a red clay road pocketed with deep holes that snaked through a field into woods of arrow-straight giant pines and cedars. As they climbed, the ruts deepened, making Chester swerve, his furrowed brow suggesting he wasn't used to such roads. At the first bend was a pond whose water level—judging from the bare dirt strip around its rim just below the ring of vegetation—had evaporated by a foot. At the next sharp turn, a log cabin attached itself like a growth on a dust-covered green metal caravan, a flat parking pad beside it and a picnic table across the road from it. They continued past one makeshift cabin then another, both clinging like loose teeth to the edge of the hill, their backsides facing an unending forest sloping below. Sylvie was amused by how such teetering shacks sat on the street just like in colonial towns back east.

Chester parked where the road ended just past the third dwelling and escorted them through the woods around the perimeter of the parcel, Enzo with Diana on his shoulders. The soil sparkled with feldspar and a hint of rosy quartz. Sylvie was awed by the virgin trees, their tips lost in the sky and trunks wider than she could reach with arms outstretched. Standing beneath one was like gazing up the side of a skyscraper. The pungent cedar smell underscored this alien terrain.

"These trees are hundreds of years old, I'd say," said Chester.

"Beautiful!" said Enzo, slowly inhaling air that was much warmer than in Vermont right now.

"That plant sticks to my legs," said Diana.

"That's bearmat, also called mountain misery. Misery, 'cause it's sticky, too smelly for animals to eat and you can't get rid of it."

Back at Gus's they discussed the land. For Sylvie and Enzo, discussing plans and pursuing dreams was something they did well, generating an excitement that flared like a fire splashed with gasoline. Ignoring the churning in her stomach, Sylvie saw the investment as a possibility.

"Toss the coins," Gus suggested.

SQUATTING

They negotiated a deal that let them camp while saving for the down payment, but until closing they shouldn't cut trees greater than twelve inches in diameter. They pitched tent on a flat clearing. Sylvie set up an outdoor kitchen like they'd had in Wolford and learned that soapy water attracted yellow jackets that she had to sift out to keep from getting stung. She mailed her parents her new address and told them Janis lived nearby.

Enzo continued working with Gus and had plenty of cash for Sylvie every week, and always pot for himself. Gus picked him up where dirt met asphalt and followed the winding hilly lane out to Bearmat Road. One evening after work, he and Sylvie carried Diana by turns to explore the neighborhood and chanced upon Gerard reading on a rocking chair outside his house.

"What's the book?" Sylvie asked.

"*Alaric and the Fall of Rome,*" he said. "Here, take it, then we'll talk." Later she'd visit him and discuss how that rich and powerful city fell to barbarians. Gerard also bragged about his beautiful girlfriend Theresa who sometimes stayed with him. Sylvie rarely saw her.

Outside the middle house, Mattie's, they encountered a stack of branches piled on the road. Witt, in the first house in the queue, greeted them warmly. Scrawny like a seasoned alcoholic, he was at his picnic table with one leg crossed over the other, the point of an elbow resting on a knee, one hand cradling the bowl of his corncob pipe. His thin, gray hair was gathered in a rubber band at the nape of his neck. He invited them to share some rice.

Sylvie asked, "Was that pile of branches supposed to be a roadblock for us?"

"Who knows?" he said.

"Think this land is worth buying?" asked Enzo.

"It's a damn nice property," Witt said. "Good price. Why the hell not?"

Witt had attached log structures to the old green Airstream caravan he'd hauled from Texas, and added a counter with a sink but no running water and a living room where a swing hung from a rafter. Wide wooden planks comprised the floor, covered with worn-out rugs, dirt nestling in their thick pile. Sylvie glanced inside and realized the fuzzy gray pillow and the black scarf on the floor were cats.

Diana was tired so Witt suggested she nap in the hammock hanging between two pines. Sylvie climbed on with her and rocked her to sleep by pushing a foot off a nearby live oak to keep it moving then dipped down the hammock sides carefully so Diana, snoozing, balled up in its middle, wouldn't roll off.

"There's water all around here," Witt said. "Springs. You just gotta find 'em."

"How?" Enzo asked.

Witt sucked hard on his pipe. Behind his thick lenses, his eyes looked distant and tiny. "Ferns," he managed to say, holding his breath to keep the marijuana smoke in. "Green grass." He kept his lips tight.

Sylvie recalled the spring in Wolford, near the ferns and blueberries. "Have you seen any on our land?"

He exhaled. "Prob'ly. Don't recall where. Just walk around. You'll find it. You can try witching for it." He uncrossed and recrossed his legs. "Until then, use my spring."

Locals called this area "Hippie Hollow," a term Sylvie hated, with connotations of mindless burnouts, which many in the area weren't. People nestled in makeshift houses in wooded enclaves, eking out livelihoods off the grid. You had to be strong and inventive to pull it off. A true hippie was more likely to be homeless.

Witt had sold vacuum cleaners door-to-door in Texas. Once he visited a posh neighborhood where he imagined people would spend money on a vacuum simply because they could. He targeted the richest man in town, a beef farmer. A maid led him to the living room.

"The guy said, 'Let's see what you got there, boy.'" Witt began vacuuming the carpet. As he moved around the room, the man pointed out dirt with his toe. Inspired by his interest, Witt showed how the wand attachment worked, moving it up the door trim as high as the crown molding and down along the baseboards.

"He said, 'Nice job, son. Thanks for showing me your machine. But, see, I've got one that works just fine. Now you have yourself a wonderful day,' And he showed me the door. I decided people are bastards, mostly, and the way to cope is learn as much as possible and avoid people."

Selling vacuums was also how he'd met Charlie, who bought one and befriended him.

* * *

Charlie owned this land as investment property and invited Witt out to watch over it. So Witt drove out in his Airstream.

Sylvie said, "You got here by chance, like us."

"Yep. Charlie owns these fifteen acres and wanted someone to make sure no one squatted on it. Funny thing was," he chuckled, "I'm squatting!"

"How did he choose Bearmat?"

"Heard about the gold. Every now and then someone finds a nugget. Sometimes a mother lode."

"There's gold here?" Enzo asked.

"This place used to be called El Dorado. I know spots in the creek to go panning. Sometimes it feels like paradise here."

The gold was gone but Sylvie understood the rest—he grew provisions, paid no rent, lived on his pension and entertained visitors from all over.

Witt's friend Jennifer came outside and sat on his lap, but he shook her off and shooed her away. Sylvie laughed inwardly about this scrawny old guy, disinterested in sex, having attracted this beautiful woman. He toked his pipe and told Enzo, "I feel for women. They grow up knowing men are jerks and have learned to cope with that."

Sylvie felt Enzo looking at her, but didn't turn her head.

Referring to Mattie, Witt said, "Hey, here comes my 'daughter.' That's what I call her anyway." Mattie was approaching with her nine-year-old daughter Serena.

"Hey, Dad! Having a party and didn't invite me?"

"Course you're invited. We're welcoming the new neighbors, Enzo, Sylvie and Diana."

Enzo held out his hand in greeting. Mattie closed her eyes and put a joint to her lips. "The lady is supposed to extend her hand, not the man." She exhaled. "I learned manners at home—what silverware to use when. Proper table setting. My mother sent me to my room when I screwed up, especially when she was throwing a dinner party. I ran away from such rules. That's why I like it here. But," she added—incongruously, Sylvie thought—"I remember what's proper."

"Mattie's been like a daughter to me. I brought her out here, didn't I? We met in Frisco."

Ignoring him, Mattie said to Enzo, pointing, "I paid for this road here—it's mine. But there's a road from right there up onto your land." Sylvie looked where she pointed but didn't see any road.

"Hi, Mattie," said Jennifer.

Mattie continued confronting Enzo. "Think you cut some of my trees."

"No, we cut our own small trees," he said.

Diana had been coloring a picture at the picnic table and handed it to Serena.

"That's ugly!" Serena said, crumpling it and throwing it to the ground and wiping her feet on it, then took her mother's hand and they walked home.

Diana ran to Sylvie, who hugged her and said, "Some people's eyes don't see art."

Jennifer said, "She's pissed 'cause I'm here."

"Now, honey, that's not true," said Witt. "Though I gotta say . . . ."

"Or 'cause we're here," Sylvie said. "I'm sure that roadblock's for us."

"Who knows?" Witt said. "So use that overgrown road she pointed to."

Enzo asked again, "Up the middle over there?"

"That's it," Witt said. "Her place is so close to the road, she likes to leave chairs and shit, the TV out there. Hell, it's the flattest place she's got. TV runs on propane." Witt drew on his pipe. "She's not as unfriendly as some around here, like the pot growers in the area. Like, don't step on that place across that road on the downhill side of your land. He buried explosives there."

Witt said he dispensed with bastards, but Sylvie thought he'd found a nest of them.

THE NEIGHBORHOOD

Standing by the tent and looking into the canyon, Sylvie was overwhelmed by its pristine beauty. Seduced by it. It was the ideal place to hide out. She inwardly smiled, thinking how Mom would appreciate the irony of her hiding in the wilderness with the man she wanted to flee. Mom and Dad didn't know her current predicament and hadn't known any of her predicaments since that day she was five years old so how could they guide her? Now there was so much to tell she wouldn't know how. If she ever saw them again.

They finally found someone to tow the dead van—her supposed passage to freedom—to rust away at the end of that overgrown road. Two steps forward, two thousand back.

Sylvie pushed for buying the land with a down payment from the rent money and a monthly mortgage—she was investing in her financial security the only way she could figure while her personal security was at stake. More irony!

Walking through the woods to find a shorter route to their mailbox, Sylvie came upon a modular house, a chicken coop, a shed and a long, flat driveway leading to Bearmat Road. She went up the front walk and rang the doorbell. A short, chubby woman opened the storm door but stood behind the screen.

"I'm Sylvie and this is my daughter Diana. We bought the land behind you and are camping there until closing."

"Oh, my goodness! Won't you come in? I'm Melba Stout. I'm sorry Becky's not home from summer camp yet. She'd be happy to know another child lives nearby."

Sylvie was happy to feel the air conditioning. The only other place to cool off was a mile away where the spring-fed stream met Jesus Maria creek where boulders trapped water in a frigid pool big enough to swim a few strokes, deep enough to dive into.

Melba related how her husband Alvin had been laid off just shy of the thirty-year benchmark when his pension would be vested, forcing them to sell their house in San Isidro and find a more affordable lifestyle. Land here was cheap as were modular homes, so they bought five acres and towed a house, each half carried and deposited by flat-bed trucks. Melba stressed they'd left a comfortable neighborhood to come to this middle-of-nowhere.

"If it weren't for my church family, I'd be in the looney bin," she said. "Bring your husband to meet Alvin on Saturday. Becky will be home then. Oh, and feel free to cut through our property to reach the road. And your mailbox."

On Saturday when Diana and eight-year-old Becky saw each other, they instantly ran off to play. Sylvie noticed how when Enzo said hello, Melba winced.

"Mexican?" she asked.

"Italian," he replied. Scrutinizing him, Melba recounted how bobcats prey silently at night and take what they need, leaving a neat hole in the chicken coop, like a human would. Sylvie thought Melba was right to suspect him, but for other reasons.

Enzo showed Alvin the diagram he'd drawn of a cantilever on a downhill-facing house and Alvin said, "If you need tools, I've got it all."

"Wonderful," said Enzo.

"We've got a month before frost, so if we work fast we'll get you fixed up in no time," said Alvin. The next afternoon he brought over a post-hole digger, chainsaw and bark peeler. He felled some pines as thick as thighs and pointed out fallen cedars they could also use.

"See how the wood's still fresh?" he explained.

Sylvie helped carry logs, gripping as tightly as she could, straining the ligaments of her thumbs. Then she switched jobs—the men carried logs to her to peel the bark. Diana played nearby with plastic horses Becky had given her.

They built the cabin using a long pole and crossbar propped together and bound with rope. And per Witt's suggestions, Enzo bought inky black creosote. He and Alvin dipped the poles' tips in it and stuck them directly into the ground in a row, with the end pole nailed to a live oak that anchored one corner of the house. The structure looked like a handful of sticks tossed in the air and tumbled in a pile. Inside they built a double-wide bunk bed, also attached to the live oak. The top bunk had a ladder and its own window. The roof was sheets of metal Witt had given them, saying, "Just the top ones in the pile are rusty. I ain't ever gonna use the rest."

Alvin said, "By the way, you're welcome to use our water spigot. It's behind the tool shed."

"Thanks," said Enzo. "That'll make life easier."

When Diana went to bed that night, Sylvie, exhausted, lay cooling on the ground outside the tent. Enzo lay beside her. Their bodies drew together; their sex was sweaty and raw. They fell asleep on the red dirt.

* * *

When Enzo got paid, Witt drove him to Golden Market to buy plywood for a loft. He also gave them a woodstove he'd once crafted from a manhole cover and sundry boards to make a partial floor leaving the other part dirt which quickly compacted like sheet vinyl. Sylvie joked it never needed sweeping and would wear it away if she did. Enzo dug a pit for an outhouse and surrounded it with walls and a roof.

The cabin crouched beneath the giant live oak attached to its corner. A twisted manzanita concealed its door, trunks interlacing, twigs like underwater coral, leaves shimmering like tumbling coins, purple bark so smooth Sylvie loved petting it. They covered cantilever logs on the downhill side with a sheet of thick plastic they rolled up during the day for air.

Despite her plan to flee, Sylvie was stuck with Enzo more than ever and unnerved by being so remote with him. She rarely saw Janis. Witt was too much of a blabbermouth to confide in, Mattie too hostile, Gerard too spacey, Melba and Alvin wouldn't help deceive a husband, no matter how unsavory.

When Enzo was working on road crew, Sylvie gathered wood and water and went to the spring to wash clothes that always smelled of wood smoke. She was constantly on edge, yet the ancient woods dwarfed her concerns, mesmerizing her. She tried to make Diana's life as structured and fun as possible. She enrolled her in kindergarten in San Andreas; the bus picked her up by the Stouts' where Becky also boarded. At night, Sylvie delighted Diana by hooting to attract owls. And, with the nearest public streetlights miles away at Golden Market and the treetops disappearing into the thick, black night, she took her to lie on a blanket in a clearing and look at the whole Milky Way. She taught Diana to look for slow-moving satellites and meteorites speeding silently to their doom. She'd heard news on the radio about Skylab and how it'd soon fall to earth and mused that if it should fall here, she could attract tourists and charge admission and make enough money to leave. She thought about her place in the vastness of space and the eons of evolution that led to her lying here thinking how she'd stored up so much unique information to pass along to her daughter.

She sometimes rode with Witt to the Moke Hill library to rent picture books to read to Diana in the evening as they sat together on the stuffed chair rescued from the roadside, balanced on a wood block, an idea borrowed from Strong Hawk. Sylvie would gaze out at the green sea of trees bubbling through the canyon and relish the breeze softly flowing through the window and out the door like waves onto a shore, cooling her skin, rustling the manzanita leaves. And she tuned the transistor radio to symphonic music far away in space and time, its tasteful audience consuming the refinement of synchrony and motion, the tide of feelings rising through musicians' breath and fingers.

Melba invited Sylvie to Bible studies which she attended since she'd loved discussing parables in Sunday school, and brought Diana to play with Becky. Alvin was leading a discussion about the book of Revelation. He read, "The twelve gates were made of pearls—each gate from a single pearl! And the main street was pure gold, as clear as glass."

Sylvie said, "Maybe this is symbolic?" creating a long pause.

Then Alvin continued, "Imagine how beautiful! How grand!"

A parent in the group said his children attended a home school up toward Sheep Ranch. As he glowed about the Bible-based curriculum, she asked, "What other kinds of classes do you have?"

"What do you mean?"

"Like, literature. Do they discuss ideas?"

"Well, that's why we've created this school, Sylvia. To protect them from the many corrupt influences that pollute the world."

"You mean, like Shakespeare?"

"Nothing but dirty jokes!"

It turned out that some of the teachers were dropouts from high school as well as from a hedonistic Haight-Ashbury life a few years before.

* * *

Sylvie discovered the hidden county road Witt had said not to cross. It extended along the far end of their land and the Stouts' and fed onto Bearmat Road.

"Witt says the county might extend electricity along that road. Last night I saw lights on in a house at the hilltop over there."

"Do we need it?" Enzo said.

"That reminds me of Strong Hawk's wife, the one doing laundry by hand. Do you know what that's like?"

"Whatever," Enzo said.

Sometimes Enzo stayed with Diana while Sylvie hitched to Golden Market. She walked some along Bearmat Road before hitching, stopping to chat with Mrs. Hinkey who was sometimes out front. Sylvie continued visiting and eventually Mrs. Hinkey invited her inside. Entering the house felt like falling into a vortex: newspapers blasting bizarre headlines were stacked in columns on the floor; piles of clothes—a different color scheme at each visit—consumed space where chairs could have been; dishes caked with dried bits of dinners and cigarette butts perched on glossy end-tables; stained upholstery peeked through granny-square afghans in dime-store yarn; the TV light danced with perpetual game shows watched by her special-needs adult son; the cat litter box filled like a magic pitcher, its odor visiting every room.

Mrs. Hinkey was always eager to discuss news she'd read, so Sylvie asked if she could borrow any recent newspapers and took home a stack of supermarket tabloids. Their stories were grounded in enough fact they might actually be true, and if they were false, what difference would it make other than disrupting one's sense of order? Could Rita Hayworth have been a zombie for two years and returned from the dead? What kind of mind would it take to not just invent the stories, but want to publish them as fact?

Best of all, Mrs. Hinkey had a telephone she'd let Sylvie use. And when her laying hens were ready to sell, Sylvie bought four. Unfortunately, she'd been right to doubt Enzo's chicken coop design, screened on all sides like a rabbit hutch—feed fell from the dish to the ground below the cage where wild birds ate it. After a few weeks he let the hens out, saying they needed to scratch. The two arucanas flew into the trees at night, descending only to eat the feed in the daytime. And Sylvie couldn't find any eggs. "What's the sense of letting them range free and also feed them? Do you know how many eggs we could've simply bought?" Eventually she found several weeks' worth of eggs under leaves where they'd rotted.

Once when Sylvie came home from hitching to Golden Market, Diana ran up and hugged her knees tightly. Sylvie started caressing her head and flinched. "Did you cut your hair?"

"Papa did," Diana sobbed. Enzo approached, scissors still in hand.

"Why?" Sylvie asked him.

"She looked ugly. She still does!"

Diana wailed and ran to her bed and lay face down.

"What is wrong with you?!" Sylvie glared at him. He just turned and climbed up to the loft and came down holding his baggy of pot.

"You," he said. "You're what's wrong with me." And took off.

Sylvie sat with Diana, assuring her the haircut was cute, stroking her hair until she calmed down.

"Come, let's go get water."

They each carried an empty plastic milk gallon and followed the trail along the hilltop toward the Stouts'. Acorns crunched underfoot as they picked their way over the roots of live oaks whose branches were adorned with mistletoe hanging like molting antlers.

Stepping across a crumpled and rusty fence, Sylvie was surprised to be facing an elderly man who smiled and said, "I don't want to be a stranger with just empty hands to lend. I want to be considered your confidential friend." She stared, speechless, as he continued, "Blessed are you who are poor, for yours is the kingdom of God" and held out his hand saying, "Good morning. I'm Pastor Anderson, Melba's father. And you are . . . ?"

"Sylvie. This is Diana. We live over here."

"Why hello, Diana. My, you're a pretty girl."

The most perfect thing he could've said, Sylvie thought. "Melba kindly shares water with us."

Pastor Anderson escorted them to the faucet. "I live here," he said. "Melba likes me to stay indoors."

"I guess you could get lost in the woods?" She put down one container and held the other under the faucet. "Where are you a pastor?"

"Oh, that was years ago on radio in Alabama. Now I write poetry. Here's one I'm working on: 'I heard them say, please show the way; I bade them pray, they turned away.'"

"Nice," Sylvie said. "Do you share this at Melba's church?"

He considered a moment. "Let's just say my daughter and I live separate lives."

Sylvie finished up the second gallon. "That should be hard if you're living in the same house. Is that why you don't attend her Bible studies?"

Pastor Anderson jumped at the sound of a car pulling up the driveway. "I have to go. Perchance I'll see you later." He started walking away, then turned and said, "Don't tell her we met!"

* * *

In this neighborhood, Sylvie relied on Witt and enjoyed talking with Gerard and even nutty Mrs. Hinkey. Melba had been less friendly since the time she was getting into her truck to drive Sylvie to Golden Market and suddenly yelped and thrust her left hand in Sylvie's face to show her the diamond was gone from her ring. Sylvie helped her look for it, both pacing along the driveway then kneeling down to sweep their hands over the gravel. Melba kept one eye on Sylvie as if she'd made the diamond fall and was hiding it.

One morning when Enzo and Diana were still sleeping, Sylvie headed over to see Witt before getting to work. She waved hello to Gerard who was out reading on his porch. He quickly put a pillow on his lap to cover his nakedness and waved back.

Now that it was June, Witt—except for his black-rimmed eyeglasses and the green rubber flip-flops—would also sit naked, with his penis tucked between his crossed legs. Jennifer came outside, pudgy and topless, and sat on his lap putting her arm around his shoulder. He grimaced. "C'mon honey, find another seat," he complained. "It's way too hot." Jennifer frowned at Sylvie as she went back inside.

Mattie and Serena also came over, cooling themselves with fans made of magazine pages. Both wore what looked like kitchen curtains, long, sheer pink fabric wrapped around them like transparent saris. Mattie eyed Jennifer and Sylvie, kissed Witt on his cap and she and Serena turned back home, mooning all as they went.

Sylvie wanted to be the kind of person who made things better and thought about those she'd met who did, especially ones who kept peace in the neighborhood by being kind to everyone: Rosie in the apple orchard, Griselda and Olga in Nogare, Strong Hawk at Wildrose and now Witt. Some repelled outsiders, like Dwayne in the schoolhouse, Giovanni in Bussana Vecchia, and Yvette in the tutoring group. She reflected about how she and Enzo had wanted to unify their tenants but failed, and was sorry they'd disturbed the peace in Bussana Vecchia.

"I know I can physically survive anywhere," she told Witt. "But I don't know how well I do socially. I've done so much that now seems reckless; moving to Italy, taking that magazine job, buying the van with Enzo—heck, even marrying him!—believing my friend Janis, ending up here in the middle of nowhere—no offense—with no car. I could go on." She held back tears.

Witt said, "Honey, those things happened not because you're reckless but because you're open to people. Too open. You don't question anyone's motives."

"Yeah," she nodded. "I take them on face value."

Witt said, "But that's OK. You assume that what they do, think and say are all the same 'cause that's you."

In April, Sylvie had planted vegetable seeds that had swollen to life, but had forgotten about the annual drought. Witt lent her a witching rod he'd broken off a cherry tree in town and showed her how to rest it lightly atop her fingers and look for water. She'd walked slowly, stopping near some ferns where she noticed the rod point down, then bob one, two, three, four—she counted—ten feet deep for each bob. Maybe electrical energy flows from water underground and conducts through water in the branch and bodily fluids. Or is it all in your head, where you make connections and it depends on what you want it to be?

After a beat Witt said, "How'd you like a bathtub?"

"For what?"

"Usually people fill them with water to take a bath," Witt said, "but I s'pose you can plant vegetables in it. Or sleep in it." He winked at her.

"I mean, wouldn't it take forever to fill up?"

"I bet if you put it in the sun and poured in ten gallons, it'd warm up pretty quick."

"I guess we could set it next to that water tank that's caught some rainwater," Sylvie said. It'd be a lot of work, but so was everything here.

* * *

Always pondering her escape, Sylvie thought they could sell trees for lumber and she'd be able to buy tickets out of here. Witt said there was one big logging company in the county. Next time he drove her to the library, she found the phone number. She used many plants for their potential as food, fiber or medicine. But consuming trees was different because they took more time. To sell lumber made her uneasy but it would provide her ultimate survival.

Enzo agreed with the plan, so Sylvie arranged for someone to come give an estimate. The logger said legally they could only cut six large trees on a five-acre parcel. But even then, they'd earn half what they owed for the land. Sylvie felt guilty exploiting the woods this way but what else could she do? She asked the company to write two checks, one for each of them, and secretly gave her parents' address for hers.

Dad wrote the startling news that, "your mother now teaches family planning to women downtown." Sylvie wondered if Mom appreciated the irony. He then quoted an article in *Time* magazine about drugged-out hippies. His final words, "You've thrown your life away. Good luck with it," were so venomous Sylvie was shocked. He ended with his cliché, "Write when you get work." She'd made a mess she wanted to fix by herself but needed help, always believing deep down they'd help if she really needed it. After all, they'd given her the opportunity with the rooming house, a situation that had led to their undoing, but still. But she realized that they communicated with each other so superficially, all of them believing their feelings were understood, as though the very family structure said everything that needed saying. Sylvie could see how such unspoken assumptions had guided her life.

She also could see now, with a jolt, that she'd been lying to Diana about the reality of this family. On some level, little Diana must know the truth. Sylvie thought how she'd known at a young age that Mom couldn't protect her. Had that been healthy for her?

* * *

Enzo surprised her with, "Witt gave me seeds," he said. "I'm going to grow pot."

"Oh no! If you get caught, we're screwed. Besides that seems hypocritical, considering you threw my plants out of the car."

But she had to face her own contradictions—she tolerated his pot smoking because it domesticated him. The last time he ran out of pot, he flew into a rage and threw a stovepipe at her, its sharp metal edges cutting the web of her thumb when she raised her hands to protect her face. Later as she walked toward the pines to gather kindling, he threw a rock that hit her shin. Both times she muted her cries so as to not alarm Diana nor allow him to know he'd hurt her. The day after the rock incident, her leg had swollen and Witt drove her to the hospital where it would've been pointless to report to the old male doctor how it happened. He didn't ask any questions and she figured it wouldn't be worth it, just as it wasn't worth reporting crimes to the Burlington police. If Enzo thought she was leaving, he'd steal Diana again. Enzo was mainly interested in his own comfort and to him, she and Diana were just props, not people.

June was approaching and the rental contract would be up, so Sylvie encouraged Enzo to fly to Burlington to check on the house and rent it out another year. After he left, she culled and organized clothes, packed books, burned the excess and put the necessaries in her suitcase. Witt was away with Charlie so she went to the Hinkeys' and called Janis to ask for a ride to the Greyhound station in Sacramento.

"I can't get the car until Wednesday. Cory needs it for a craft show until Tuesday."

But Enzo returned home on Tuesday. Escape had eluded her.

OUTCAST

Sylvie parked the wheelbarrow beside the uprooted daffodils' wilted corpses she'd rescued from a bulldozer on Bearmat Road. Enzo sat on the roof, bringing the cigarette to his wide mouth dotted by a dimple, a can of Drum tobacco nestling in the triangular space between his crossed legs. She was annoyed by him watching her work, self-conscious about her tank-top clinging to her sweaty body; she didn't want to attract him. She wrapped her hair in a rubber band to keep it off her face, wiped her arm across her forehead, streaking it with mud then plopped down by the cabin door, hugging her knees to her cheek.

Back in April during a break in the rain, Enzo had peeled off shingles, rubbery under the hot sun, and removed too much. Then the rain had restarted. Today he'd been hammering nails into rusty tin sheets, the pounding echoing through the canyon. He flicked his cigarette, hooked the crowbar on the roof's peak and took out of his jeans pocket a leather pouch bulging with marijuana. He rolled a joint and burst into "Io ca vule bene assai," the song that had won Sylvie's heart, bellowing with increasing volume the more stoned he got. Sylvie knew he sang it when lost in a haze, as important chores like fixing the roof lost their urgency—even became funny—until it would rain and Sylvie would have to empty the jars on the floor. Enzo quipped that letting rainwater fall into the kitchen saved trips to the Stouts' spigot. He stood up suddenly, both legs shaky on the slippery metal, causing the can of tobacco to roll to the ground.

"Someone's coming!" he said.

"Your friend, the roof guy?"

"No, a woman, smartly dressed."

Sylvie strained to look through the thick trees. "Melba mad about something? Did you turn off her hose?"

"She's pulling something."

"Rebecca and her dumb horse?"

"Smaller."

"I see her," Sylvie said. "She's wearing a dress."

The woman entered the clearing and was looking around as if she'd arrived at the end of the earth. "*Che cazzo!*" Enzo cried, his voice trailing as he leaped from the roof and ran toward the visitor crying out in Italian, "What are you doing here?"

Sylvie went inside to wash.

"Sylvia!"

She flung open the door and gaped stupidly at Mamma standing there, implausibly, in a white blouse trimmed with pink embroidery, a beige linen skirt and leather pumps. They grasped hands and kissed cheeks until Mamma let go and pushed into the cabin, Enzo behind. Mamma's face froze as she looked at where the floorboards stopped halfway to the wall, exposing bare ground below where a cat clawed the earth. The commotion awakened Diana who climbed down from her bunkbed and stood watching.

Mamma exclaimed, "*Mamma mia*, Diana! How you've grown!" and bombarded her with hugs and kisses. Then she looked around and said, "So! This is your house." She tightened the corners of her mouth and dusted off the chair.

"How'd you find us?" Sylvie spoke in Italian, settling on the bench.

Mamma winced at the board propped on tree stumps for a table, a smaller board for the bench. She said, "I waited in the station in San Francisco and took the bus to San Andreas."

Enzo laid tobacco strands into an open paper. "Babbo wrote me about you," he said.

"Puh! Babbo won't let me type so I clean homes." She crossed her legs. "He steals my pension."

"He's frantic," Enzo said. "It strains his heart."

"When did you leave home?" asked Sylvie.

"Weeks ago. I was in Switzerland, working. Enzo, give me a cigarette." He eyed her, then complied. She looked around. "No one in Europe has lived like this for five hundred years! Where's the bathroom?"

Enzo and Sylvie exchanged glances.

"Outside? *Madonna!*"

Sylvie showed her the path and Mamma followed it to the outhouse, saying when she returned, "A chicken sat watching me."

"Enzo freed them and we haven't been able to catch any."

"*Ei*, what do you two know about farm animals?" Mamma said.

"Babbo's letter said he wakes up from his nap and you're gone," Enzo said.

"When I think of the sacrifices I made for you! *Madonna mia!* And Babbo. He trusted everyone but me, the fool. Twenty years ago, after his heart attack, everyone but me said it was natural. He was only forty! I knew they put something in his coffee. It was *I* who kept this family from being trampled in the gutter by pigs."

Enzo said, "She's nuts, Sylvia. Be careful what you believe."

"I, *cari*, am the sanest person you'll ever know. Thank God I can type! A hundred words per minute, no errors. I posted signs and got business. I slaved day and night while Babbo sat like a lump, never changing his old T-shirt or his pajamas. Just shuffling around in those slippers."

Sylvie hated having cigarette smoke in the house. "Maybe we should get you settled."

"You know that market in Fuorigrotta, Sylvia? Makes me sick. The stink. *Che puzza*! Those vendors with their hands all over the scales. And the butcher with those fat slabs of flesh dangling from the ceiling like hanging men, and the flies dancing all over. Disgusting!"

Sylvie said, "We'll talk later. There's your bed."

Mamma looked across at the mattress resting on a frame of two-by-fours and plywood. Beside it, ants walked in single file along the wall of split cedar logs all the way to the plastic kitchen sink. Sylvie took off her shoe and used it to smush them.

"This looks gross," she said. "But can you smell the dead ants? Kind of like vinegar? Keeps live ones away." She put her shoe on and sat back down.

Mamma reached over to stroke her cheek and clucked at her then heaved herself out of the chair, picked up her suitcase and tossed it onto the bed.

"Where can I bathe?"

"When Enzo gets more water, you can pour some into the sink. We'll go to the creek tomorrow." Sylvie paused. "We live self-sufficiently."

Enzo said, "Yes, outside the system."

"*Madonna, che pazzi*! You've lost your minds!"

Mamma went to bed and slept through the rest of the day and the next one, too. She lay so leaden that Sylvie listened for breathing now and then. While she slept, Sylvie walked to the school bus stop to meet Diana then to see Witt, who recounted what he'd heard about how Mamma had hitchhiked to their place.

"My buddy Stan saw her sitting on a suitcase in the Greyhound lot and he pulled up to her and said, 'What are you doing?' and she said, 'Enzo' and he said, 'Italian dude? You looking for him?' So she smiles and he recognizes Enzo's dimple on her face and says, 'You a relative? Shit, I'm going that way. Climb in.' He said she didn't understand a word, but got in his car anyway."

Witt poured more coffee and raised his eyebrows at Sylvie.

"No, thanks," she said.

"So when Stan got to the Stouts', he looks her in the eye and says, 'Follow this driveway to Enzo. Go behind that house and keep walking, OK?' but he saw her go up and ring the bell and could hear the exchange. Melba came out and asked if she was Enzo's friend and she pointed to herself and said, 'I Mamma.' Melba pulled her arm and pointed behind her house and said, 'Back there.'"

* * *

The days sweltered. Low tree branches cracked off easily. The mountain misery, choked by drought, was so venomous with resin a lit match could set it ablaze. The pilot-light blue sky held no trace of vapor. The water drum had lain empty for weeks and the pond had shrunk to a mud hole. Mamma shut down behind her eyes, blue like a glass of ice. She hadn't brought clothes suitable for the intense daytime heat so she'd been wearing Enzo's old cut-off pants and a strip of cloth ripped from a sheet to wrap around her chest.

Sylvie went outside to build a fire as usual, away from the house and trees. She had left yeasted dough to rise overnight and heated oil in a cast-iron pan to make fried bread then brought it all inside and sat with Mamma drinking coffee while Diana had fried bread and milk. As they were finishing, Enzo descended from the loft and picked up the empty water container saying, "Gotta go work."

"Where?" Mamma asked.

"Construction site."

"All that schooling and you're a laborer? *Madonna!*"

They all accompanied Enzo down toward where Gus would pick him up. Deep down, Sylvie wasn't sure where he actually went all day.

"Tell me more of your story," Sylvie said as they walked.

"Well, Babbo feels better after six months and what does he do when he gets his strength back? Smoke. He went out for tobacco and saw my posters and came home and accused me of all kinds of things."

"Like what?"

"Like . . . like how my skirt rose up when I hammered, how my bottom shook. All he could think of was men who must've seen me, maybe jotted down the phone number so they could call and say they had work for me. Did he thank me for keeping him alive? Never! He complained he felt faint when he imagined me tacking up the posters." She exhaled cigarette smoke, squinting.

"I ignored him when he thrust a poster in my face. My customer would be back soon, but my pace was broken. I asked, 'How do you think we've been eating while you sat there?' And what do you suppose he said about that?"

Enzo said, "He said the only women who advertise are whores. And you said, if a whore kept dinner on his table while he lay dying, he'd be grateful."

"Dear boy, you were paying attention! You remember?"

"Yes. He'd hit you and chase you and you'd try to jump out of reach on a little chair."

She laughed. "So, who does he enlist as his agent? Little Enzo who has to go rip down my signs, the ones he'd posted. He brought home twenty but I knew there were five more. Can you believe, Babbo told that little boy that his mother's a whore?"

"Mamma, he made me!" Enzo's voice trembled.

"Made you? No one can make you! You're just weak. You could've lied and said they were gone."

"He'd know."

They'd followed the bend in the road beyond Gus's place where the pond was getting smaller each day.

"Now look at you. Bringing your family to live like animals. Weak, like your father."

Sylvie was shaken. Her heart warmed to the little boy in her husband, realizing how badly he needed therapy. But he was her sworn enemy whom she was plotting to leave.

Diana said, "Don't yell at Papa!"

Sylvie said, "It's OK, sweetie. Papa's OK with his mother."

"You're his mother!" said Diana.

Sylvie smiled. "I'm his wife," while thinking, sometimes I feel like his mother. She was beginning to see that besides Babbo's violent example, Mamma's chiding had damaged young Enzo.

Mamma seized the attention. "Babbo took over my typing business. He booted me out but expected me to do the work while he flirted with the customers. That's how men are."

Enzo set the container near the spring where he could fill it when he got home and took off to meet Gus on the asphalted road. Sylvie, Mamma and Diana continued back home beneath the sheltering trees.

* * *

Sylvie awoke to the odor of Pine-Sol wafting from the floorboards. Cool mountain air had brought relief during the night, cool enough where Sylvie decided to build a fire indoors then wait as water worked toward a boil.

Seeing that Mamma's bed was made and her corner tidier than ever, Sylvie went out and glimpsed her behind some manzanitas.

"Thanks for scrubbing the floor, Mamma. You didn't need to," she said, then saw the overhanging branches above flames that leapt up amid a column of heat.

"Mamma, no!" Sylvie kicked dirt on the fire.

"I was cold."

"You can't make fires like that out here!" She ran and got a shovel. "Come on! Kick dirt on it!"

The nearby mountain misery was quickly turning black like melting plastic, its resin sizzling. Without conviction, Mamma tapped at the dirt with the side of her shoe.

"Dammit, put out the fire!" Sylvie ran inside for a jug of water and ran back to douse the flames. When the fire was out, she slumped to the ground and cradled her head on her arms.

Enzo ran out, buttoning his shirt and called, "Everything OK?"

"Under control," said Sylvie.

Oblivious to the commotion she'd created, Mamma said, "I never told Babbo what happened in those homes. I worked hard, everywhere I went. I wondered who these people were and how they'd earned so much money. Then I knew: Mafia. That scared me so I'd flee back to Babbo. But he'd start with the accusations. It got so I couldn't get out of bed. I'd get up to go to that Godforsaken market only when he went out. I'd cook dinner and he never praised the food I slaved over in that pitiful kitchen. So I'd do a bad job on purpose. Too much salt in the greens. Not enough in the sauce." She laughed. "He complained. He yelled. So I went back to bed."

No wonder Enzo was so messed up. "You were depressed," she said.

"To put it mildly," said Mamma.

Sylvie got up and Mamma followed her inside, saying, "I was suffocating. Dying. He took my life away. I loved having my own money, not depending on him. So what do you think he did?"

"Locked you inside?" said Sylvie.

"*Cara*, far worse." She plopped into the chair. "Do you have an ashtray?"

"Not indoors, please," Sylvie said.

Mamma hesitated before returning the cigarette to its pack.

"If it weren't for me, he wouldn't even have a home. Last year I went to Switzerland and—oh horrors!—didn't leave a note. When I was gone, he saw a lawyer who declared me legally incompetent. *Me!* That let him put his name on my house, the one paid for with my pension money. He gets my monthly check! I saved his life, so I'm crazy!"

Sylvie was aghast at Mamma's story and even more outraged at Babbo. She wondered if her conflicts with Enzo were about his self-absorption rather than cultural differences. She poured boiling water into the coffee filter and let it drip.

"After breakfast, we'll go to the swimming hole. By then we'll need cooling off," Sylvie said.

"Yay!" said Diana, who was up and dressed and coloring with crayons.

* * *

The road coughed dust as they descended toward the canyon floor and its cooler air. A woodpecker worked on a tree somewhere and animals made waves skittering through the brush. They followed the bend in the frigid creek, pregnant with spearmint and watercress, and spread out their towels, mindful of rattlers that loved curling up behind the hot, smooth boulders huddled around a pool deep enough to swim. Sylvie dipped slowly into the water where, when she stood still, fish swarmed and touched their noses to her feet. Diana jumped in and Sylvie supported her as she blew bubbles and kicked her feet. Mamma dangled her feet in the pool.

"Sylvie, you're special to me. Enzo is a difficult man, a child really, but a good-hearted one."

Sylvie was touched. "He gets violent like I've seen Babbo do."

"Men are like that." Mamma inhaled her cigarette. "I wanted California for Enzo—and you gave it to him." All his life Mamma had guided, prodded and nagged Enzo to emigrate to California and this is the California they got. "Come to Naples with me," Mamma said. "This is no life for my granddaughter." Mamma to the rescue, Sylvie thought.

Next morning when Sylvie went for water at the Stouts', she was disoriented by how big the sky was. Then she realized the pile of smoking rubble was the house! The chickens and pony were gone. The outdoor faucets still worked—she felt ashamed to feel glad about that. Back at the cabin she told Mamma to watch over things while she asked Witt for a ride to Golden Market. Along Bearmat Road, he slowed down at the Stouts' place.

"It happened the other night," he said. "Melba drove over and asked about you."

"Was Pastor Anderson with her?"

"Who's he?"

"Melba's dad. She basically kept him locked up."

"I told them you had nothing to do with that fire."

"What?! Why would they even think that?"

Witt winked. "Ain't you just dirty hippies? Damn foreigners too!"

"It's not funny. I'm sick of that attitude," she said. "They should look closer to home."

CRIMES

As Mamma prepared to boil water on the woodstove, Sylvie took Diana to Witt's spring.

"What's Nonna doing?" Diana asked.

"Making a fire indoors so she doesn't burn up the woods. We're going to Witt's to stay cool."

Jennifer was on Witt's picnic table. "They ripped up his plants and went looking for him." She adjusted the strap on her tank top. "I told the cops he was down the canyon, and then found and warned him." She sipped water. "He'd tossed coins and got something about 'straying into a gloomy valley' so I knew he didn't go that way."

"Why were cops here?"

"They got a tip about him growing pot. Like he's a big dealer." Then she added, "I know it was Mattie."

"Mattie ratted him out? But he treated her like a daughter!"

Jennifer sighed, "Some daughters really hate their fathers. I don't know the whole story. But they used to talk about being growers together. Maybe she thought Enzo was replacing her?"

Sylvie continued to the spring, worried about Witt. How would such a scrawny guy fare in jail? But his life here was hard anyway. He'd been so generous with them, sharing the spring and materials and knowledge of the woods. She and Diana were heading back up when Enzo caught up with them.

"Those guys who sit around the post office heard Witt turned himself in, telling the cops he was too old to be scraping around on the forest floor."

"That's so like him," laughed Sylvie. "He works hard but really just wants to relax."

Coming into the clearing where Sylvie had tended her garden the past few months, she saw the goat Enzo bought from Mrs. Hinkey nibbling the few remaining plants she hadn't yet obliterated. Mamma sat smoking on a nearby log.

"What the hell have you done?! Why'd you untie her?"

"I grew up on a farm. She was bleating. You're not supposed to tie goats."

"Do you know how long that took to grow?"

"*Ei*, it's California! Get more seeds."

"Right. And you'll get the water," said Sylvie.

Mamma looked into the distance, smoking serenely.

Sylvie was too enraged to speak. Enzo never said anything to cross Mamma. And with Witt gone, she'd lost the only person in this damn place who listened to her and knew what the garden meant to her—her partnership with nature, destroyed by Mamma.

Jennifer contacted Witt's friend Stan to help arrange a fundraiser for bail money. They reserved the high school gym for a square dance potluck dinner on Saturday. Sylvie wanted to attend but didn't want to take Diana and didn't trust Mamma alone with her. Enzo was in a mood so she gave up the idea. She visited Jennifer in the morning for details.

"Can you believe Mattie had the nerve to show up? Probably just so no one would suspect her," Jennifer said. "At least she didn't dare wear that stupid curtain."

The next day Jennifer came over to report they'd raised bail so after six days in jail Witt would be free by afternoon. Later when they heard a car coming up the road, Sylvie, Enzo and Diana all went to welcome him home.

"I'm sorry we couldn't attend the fundraiser," Sylvie said. Witt looked smaller, more bent. Had he lost another tooth?

"I want to thank you for letting me stay there," Witt said. "Really, I'm . . . ."

"I mean it!" Witt said. "Hell, I haven't eaten so well in years."

* * *

Enzo drove home in an old Plymouth convertible he said he'd bought cheap from a coworker. Though relieved he'd brought home a car and not an animal, Sylvie worried. "You got the title this time, right?" she asked.

"Of course. They'll deliver it," he said. "Don't be a stickler. Let's drive to San Andreas."

She suspected he'd acquired another stolen car but felt too weary to protest. Besides that, Janis had written to say she and the boys had moved to San Andreas where they lived with her new boyfriend and Sylvie wanted to visit.

Just past Golden Market she saw a woman hitching. "That's Theresa! Stop!" Though Sylvie recognized her, they hadn't really spoken together. Theresa got in but said nothing except goodbye when they parked. Enzo said he was going to the hardware store but Sylvie suspected he might look for pot. She took Diana to buy shoes and then went to see if Janis was home. No answer.

Driving back home, Enzo pulled over to pick up a hitchhiker who climbed into the back next to Diana.

"OK back there?" Sylvie turned to ask.

The man fidgeted. Then indicating Diana's doll lying face down on the floor, he said, "Is that a real baby?"

Chills ran down Sylvie's spine. This guy was crazy. He frightened her so much that when Enzo came to a stop sign, she said, "You can get out here."

The man seemed confused but got out, cussing as he slammed the door. Back home, Enzo drove up the overgrown road and parked next to their dead van. Mattie intercepted them as they got out of the car.

"Did you happen to see Theresa?"

"We gave her a ride."

"That's what I heard."

"From who?"

"You better watch it. Gerard was chasing her with an axe, and if he knows you helped her, he'll go after you, too."

Sylvie saw the irony of her closest contact with Theresa being potentially life-threatening. She had never seen Gerard get angry, but maybe that was because they only had intellectual discussions about politics and history. Mattie said he was a speed freak, that when he received his monthly disability check, he disappeared to buy the drug. This month when he was high, Theresa announced she was leaving him, which enraged him. Sylvie was shaken that she'd befriended someone so volatile. Like Hank.

And Enzo.

WHAT GOES AROUND

Enzo hadn't returned home last night. It was dawn when Sylvie heard leaves rustling. She went outside to see Gus supporting Enzo by an elbow, his clothes torn, his hand cupping a blood-soaked bandage on his ear.

"What's going on?" she cried.

Gus whispered, "A goon bit off his earlobe."

"Did what?? How's that even possible?"

"I'd just gotten in my truck and saw Enzo come out of the bar and light a cigarette. This huge guy out of nowhere pounced on him—I'd seen him at work."

"Road crew?"

"What? No, he farms over there," Gus nodded.

"Farm?" Sylvie looked to Enzo, who was clearly on strong painkillers.

"Over there—the marijuana farm across the canyon road."

"You dare put us at such risk?!" She glared at Enzo.

Gus said, "There's a rumor Enzo wants to start his own business, now that he learned their techniques. That's a big no-no—there's pros here from Colombia who don't tolerate that shit."

Mamma had been standing by the door listening.

"The sewer rats followed you here!" said Mamma. "Is nowhere safe? *Madonna!*"

Gus said when they asked at the hospital how it happened, Enzo answered in Italian. "They couldn't translate. I couldn't either."

Enzo went to bed, as did Mamma, but Sylvie stayed up thinking. Planning. When Diana and Mamma were both awake, Sylvie headed to the Hinkeys' to call her parents.

"Mom? Dad?" There was silence. "Can Diana and I stay with you a few days?"

"Not a good idea," Dad said.

After a pause, Mom got on the phone. "Hello?"

"Do you think I could stay with you?" She flashed on Sticky saying these same words.

After a longer pause, Mom said, "Your father and I are enjoying intimacy for the first time. I'd rather you don't."

Gross, Sylvie thought.

The phone was passed again. "The letters you've sent," Dad said, "I don't think we need this."

"What do you mean? What letters, Dad?"

"It's me," said Mom.

"Mom, please? Just for a few days."

"I thought we hadn't earned your respect?"

"God, even that crazy Urantia book says civilized man loves his grandchild!" She hung up, shaking. Were they gloating about the mess she'd made? Showing how hip they were to follow the "tough love" fad designed for addicts? Addicted to what? She stomped home fuming.

* * *

Mamma said, "You can't stay in this hellhole. You need to come to Naples. *Madonna!* I hope Italy doesn't become so barbarous."

Sylvie said, "I went to Italy to escape the political violence here but I need to tell you that your boy Enzo is a violent man."

Enzo said, "Me? I never hurt you."

"Want me to give details?"

"Those little taps? Come on!"

"Forget it, Sylvie; that's how men are."

Sylvie continued sorting and packing the trunk. "Enzo, remember when you said, 'How much fun with a little baby playing around?' This is terrifying. Not fun."

Enzo slowly rolled a cigarette then stood and started packing.

Mamma said, "I'll write Babbo and say how I came here to rescue you. He'll buy the tickets."

"I'll go with Mamma. We can get Diana into school. You stay and sell the land."

Enzo said, "Put her in the Catholic school."

Sylvie saw she could leave with Mamma in plain sight and Enzo wouldn't stop her.

* * *

They had a four-hour layover in Los Angeles. After they'd collected their luggage Sylvie said, "Mamma, why don't you go wait for us where we're departing. I need to do something."

"I'll follow you."

Sylvie kept Diana close while she headed to the airline desk and exchanged her tickets to Rome for two to Chicago. The attendant said her check for the price difference would be mailed. Although it was Babbo's money, she gave her parents' address.

She found Mamma nearby sitting on her suitcase and tearfully hugged her, saying, "I want—need—to make Diana's world better and I really want to thank you for helping me do that. But to really do it, I have to leave Enzo. I'm going to my parents'."

"I don't blame you," said Mamma.

IN COMMEMORATION

Below was a surprise package, waiting to be opened. Or a bomb about to explode: If they turned her away, she had enough from the overseas ticket to maybe get a room. She'd find a grunt job and enroll Diana in school. She'd called from L.A. to say they were coming for a couple of days and quickly hung up. The plane pierced through fields of silvery clouds that disintegrated nearer to ground.

As the taxi arrived in her town, she mused how familiar old structures now housed strangers where she'd previously known everybody on this block, across the alley, on other streets. Her old home's facade had frozen in the past but inside would be wearing new tiles, new fabric, new colors. She had to go in. And they had to let her.

"Here we are at Grandma's house, honey."

"I like that house."

"You know who used to live here?"

"Who?"

"Me."

"Where was I?" asked Diana, as if for the first time.

"That's a big mystery," Sylvie said, realizing this was the kind of answer Mom used to give her.

Dad appeared behind the glass front door, looking gray, awkwardly opening it, standing aside to let them in.

"Hello, Sylvie," he said. At least he didn't slam the door, she thought. Maybe because Enzo isn't here?

"Hi, Grandpa!" Diana greeted, hugging his leg.

"Hello there." He stiffly patted her head, shooting Sylvie a warning look.

"Where's Grandma?" Diana asked.

"Coming along shortly." To Sylvie he said, "Your mother just had the house cleaned. Have a seat on the side porch." Sylvie and Diana went to hang their sweaters in the closet where Molly still lived, growling from her bed.

Dad returned to his recliner in the family room and sat to read the *Wall Street Journal* and watch stock market reports. Sylvie squatted down to pet Molly who licked her hand, then her tail thumped the pillow and soon she was in Sylvie's lap excitedly licking her face.

"Who's a good dog?" Sylvie repeated, motioning Diana to come greet her too.

As Diana hung up her sweater, Sylvie saw she wore two dresses, one over the other, and pink corduroy pants.

Sylvie asked, "Sweetie, are you afraid you'll lose your clothes?"

"No, Mommy. It's so if I spill."

The back door slammed. Mom's long, sure steps carried her briskly through the kitchen. Diana ran to meet her, followed by Sylvie and Molly. "Hi Grandma!" she said, hugging her knees.

Mom patted Diana's head saying, "You're so big!" then patted Molly's head. To Sylvie she said, "What've you done to your hair?" Sylvie had quit answering this question when she'd quit getting haircuts fifteen years ago. Mom unpacked a paper grocery bag. "For dinner we're having tuna salad and potato chips. I don't cook much since I've been working."

"I'll make dinner if you want." As a teenager, Sylvie could make cakes from mixes and heat frozen vegetables and cans of soup. Then there was the millet. "You don't seem surprised I cook, Mom." She tried to bridge the gulf between them. "Have you lost all sense of wonder about me?"

"I supposed a married woman should know how to cook."

"I didn't know how until I lived in Italy." She hoped Mom might like trying new things.

"You certainly had ample possibility to learn." She paused. "Why don't you take Diana to the porch?"

"Can we have something to drink?"

"It's where it always was."

Sylvie poured milk for Diana and water for herself. Mom fixed herself tea and joined them on the porch. Outside the screens, a breeze ruffled the yellowing leaf tips of the spiraea bushes.

Mom cleared her throat. "Your father thinks you haven't lived up to your potential."

She'd always interceded for Dad, something that saddened Sylvie. Mom's interference hadn't let her and Dad work out their issues. Sylvie knew she had descended into a lower social class. To punctuate this point, Mom, later joined by Dad, recounted her classmates' successes, reminding Sylvie her lifestyle didn't fit with their notions. Sylvie realized she needed to navigate back into the mainstream for Diana's sake but knew she'd never again feel a part of it. Or maybe never had.

After dinner she took Diana upstairs to play old board games, read stories and, best of all, take warm baths in the clawfoot tub. Sylvie smiled at how Diana seemed fascinated with switches and knobs, not just the faucets but also kept switching the lights on and off. When Diana went to sleep, Sylvie soaked in a bubble bath, as hot as she could stand, closing her eyes and stilling her mind.

Using her parents' address, Sylvie enrolled Diana in first grade, just now gearing up. She didn't know how long they'd let her and Diana stay but would find a way to keep Diana in that school. And despite Mom's overt hostility, whenever she saw Sylvie looking at apartment ads she said, "You don't need to leave just yet."

One Saturday Mom was preparing for a dinner party and the evening outdoor temperature dropped to near freezing. Even the house was so cold that the dinner guests crowded together in the living room, their teeth chattering. When Mom went to check on the pork roast she found it was raw. It turned out that "someone" (Diana, of course) had lined up the oven knobs "to make them look even," and had flipped a wall switch that turned off the furnace. ("I turned on the light," she told Sylvie, "but it didn't work.") Sylvie had wanted Diana to feel part of the natural world but now realized she needed to learn about the manufactured one. As angry as Mom was, the guests, fortified by hours of cocktails, found the incident adorable and clucked over Diana's cuteness, exclaiming how lucky Mom and Dad were to have Sylvie and Diana stay there, which Sylvie hoped would soften them.

* * *

Enzo called from the Hinkeys'. "What are you doing?"

"Living in peace," she said.

"You can't just leave me."

"I can. I did." She hung up.

The phone rang again and she instructed her parents not to answer. It sounded fifteen rings then stopped and rang twenty times more. Dad shouted, "This is nonsense!" and slammed the door to the family room.

Sylvie started divorce proceedings. Lyman's gave her a job, just blocks from home and from Diana's school. A neighbor was selling an old Chevy Nova that belonged to their son who'd gone to college and said Sylvie could buy it in installments.

Mom made clear she wouldn't babysit but to Sylvie's amazement, Jim volunteered, telling the parents, "Hey, folks. Diana's your flesh and blood. Get over yourselves." He'd often come over to play board games with her in the dining room until her bedtime.

Dad kept reminding Sylvie she was a guest in the house and Mom started charging monthly rent. Yet whenever Mom saw Sylvie circling apartment ads, she'd say, "You don't want to leave, do you?"

This baffled Sylvie who said, "Don't worry. No one will rent to a single mom with a kid."

* * *

Sylvie sent her Vermont friends her new address and phone number and was excited when Annie called to say she'd have an upcoming layover at O'Hare and wondered if they could meet up. The following week Sylvie and Diana ran outside to greet Annie, who emerged from her cab in skin-tight leopard-spot pants and a shocking pink top, her hair cropped and bleached nearly white. Dad had been watching through the front door until he turned and disappeared into the house.

"Annie! Wow!" Annie hugged them both, picked up Diana and carried her all the way to the third floor. "I need a cigarette," she said.

Sylvie made her sit close to the window and said, "Exhale through the screen so my parents don't smell it."

"I brought you something." Annie handed her a record album with her group's picture on the cover.

"Oh my God! You punk rocker!" Sylvie recognized another face in the picture.

"Yeah, that's Brian. You might say we make beautiful music together," Annie laughed. "We've been together a couple years."

"You were just learning guitar and now you've got a record!" She remembered thinking Annie had no talent. And Brian was a carpenter who played guitar. "That's amazing."

"I know, right?"

"God, Annie. So much has happened in a short time."

"You only live once. Gotta follow those dreams, whatever it takes."

"Yeah," said Sylvie. "But dreams take some strange turns."

"California didn't work out?"

Sylvie said, "Enzo was abusive. I didn't know about wife abuse and couldn't understand it. I think my dad thinks I'm a masochist."

"Wow! Enzo? No way! We all adored him!"

"Yeah, that's why I couldn't confide in you."

"But he was a sweetheart!" said Annie. "So much fun. So you stayed married because your religion says to love everyone or what?"

Sylvie laughed, now certain Annie wouldn't have believed her. "Well, it also says to use wisdom. It takes a while to gain that, though, and figure out what matters most." She wanted to add, didn't you ever notice my agony?

"No kidding," said Annie.

"What about Florie?"

"Split custody. Kinda sad at first but now it's great. Rick's floozie isn't all that bad, really. Better for him than I was."

Sylvie thought how hard she'd worked to hold her family together, how much she'd struggled, even suffered. She admired how Annie followed a personal dream even though it meant partly removing herself from her daughter's life. Sylvie knew Diana's childhood wouldn't last forever and wanted to accompany her through it.

It was a warm, calm September day, so after Annie left, Sylvie wanted to show Diana the Bahá'í temple and the beach. She drove down and parked in the lot and they strolled through the gardens. She gave Diana three pennies to toss, each in a different fountain. They walked up the many stairs into the sanctuary and sat in the middle row of chairs where she showed Diana how to tilt back her head and look up into the three-story-high filigreed dome. Afterward they walked around outside and again that sentence struck her, "The source of all learning is the knowledge of God." I know God is love and have been learning what love is.

Next she drove as close to water's edge as she could get in Gillson Park.

"Let's leave our shoes in the car. You're going to like walking on the sand."

Watching Diana play tag with the waves and throw pebbles into the water, Sylvie tried sorting through all the people she'd met in the past decade, looking for a simple rule she could tell Diana about how to choose friends. Why hadn't she realized sooner that the trustworthy ones weren't necessarily the funny, exciting, smart, attractive, creative, interesting, compatible ones, but the sincere ones?

* * *

Although they ate together every evening, Sylvie found it impossible to recount her experiences and her parents didn't ask. After dinner one evening when Diana had gone to bed and Dad was watching TV, Sylvie and Mom sat drinking tea in the dining room.

Sylvie said, "Mom, I need to know something. Remember back on Isabella when I told you about the man who molested me?"

"You mean, the man who exposed himself?"

She then told Mom the entire story, how he commanded and she refused and was scared for her life. Choking back tears, Sylvie ran into the powder room. In the mirror she saw how her face was red and contorted.

Mom followed behind and said through the closed door, "Sylvie, you don't have to tell me all this."

"Mom, I need to!" She turned on the tap so Mom couldn't hear her crying, the years of fear and tension flushing through her pores. She hadn't looked into mirrors in the woods and now she noticed faint lines starting to form on her forehead. "I'll be out in a minute."

Mom was back out in her dining room chair, drinking her Lipton's tea. Sylvie sat down and continued, "He ran off and I thought I'd won. And I just realized that's why I never let people know when they hurt me."

Mom sat in silence, her eyes brimming. She whispered, "I didn't know that . . . . I called the police when you weren't listening. I didn't want you to be alarmed and tried to act calm. I couldn't believe this would happen in Wilmette!"

Sylvie was stunned and pleased to hear Mom had tried. She took a breath. "Gee. I wish you'd told me this."

"I suppose I could say the same thing," Mom said, "and I was relieved you didn't seem frightened. The man had run down the street and over to Laurel Avenue where he tried the same thing on another little girl whose father called the cops. They came and nabbed him and he went to jail."

Sylvie said, "Yeah, there was something Halloweenish about it. Something unreal."

Mom studied her a moment and said, "I always thought you were an old soul."

Sylvie was stunned. So many years of blaming Mom, thinking her negligent. To Sylvie's five-year-old mind, Mom's lack of awareness meant Sylvie had seen a part of the world her parents couldn't fathom. But she now realized Mom had behaved appropriately for someone who believed such things couldn't happen in their town. What might Diana have witnessed and didn't know how to talk about? How long will that take to be resolved?

Sylvie now saw it wasn't Mom but that worm of a man, that child molester who had taken residence in her mind, inserted his will into hers, infected her feelings and worst of all derailed her spirit. She scorned him, cursed him and—at last—exorcized him from her head.

* * *

One evening Enzo called and said, "I have money for you. From the land sale. Come to the Evanston Y and I'll give it to you."

That he was nearby frightened her but she drove there after work. His ear had healed though his lobe hadn't grown back. He gave her a check in her name for several thousand dollars. That plus the tree check couldn't compensate for all her anguish.

The next day when Sylvie arrived to pick up Diana, the office secretary said Enzo had been there a half hour before. "He said he was taking her to an appointment."

How had he figured out where Diana's school was? Sylvie's heart leapt to her throat. They could be anywhere in the world by now! She ran back to her car and drove around looking in playgrounds, and as far as Gillson Park. At last she went home and was set to call the police. As she walked inside, Dad met her and said, "Enzo called and wants you to pick up Diana."

"When?"

"Just now. They were at Central School playground and had gone to get ice cream."

Sylvie's lawyer filed a restraining order. Enzo had his own lawyer through Legal Aid and asked for custody. The case became difficult because according to his lawyer, Enzo knew men who'd swear Sylvie had slept with them during their marriage.

"Litigation like this gets complicated. This case is *pro bono* and you know I can't devote much time to it," her lawyer said, adding that if Sylvie could find witnesses to the abuse, she'd have no problem getting full custody.

She called Judy and Gary, Miriam and Linda in Burlington, all of whom insisted they knew nothing about it and implied she was making it up—she'd hidden it well. "We're sorry you're having such difficulty," Gary said. "We think of Enzo as our friend." Enzo didn't deserve such loyalty.

Enzo called Dad, saying he'd kept track of all the hours he worked on the house and had a sum he said Dad owed him. Dad scoffed and said, "You're damn lucky I didn't have you deported, you ingrate!" and slammed down the phone. Enzo called several times and Dad resisted answering until he finally gave up. Enzo screamed at him that he was going to set fire to the house. Sylvie's lawyer used this ammunition and stressed to Enzo's lawyer that he had a history of drug abuse, had been hospitalized and wasn't stable.

But the lawyers worked out that Enzo could have unsupervised visitation in Illinois, which meant Sylvie had to leave Diana alone with him. This amazed her since he was unemployed and probably lived off his land money— enough to buy tickets to anywhere. So much for free legal aid, Sylvie thought. She was starting to see that Enzo maybe wasn't all that interested in kidnapping and raising Diana by himself, but had just done that to control her. Still, she sewed contact information into all Diana's clothes and made her memorize their address and phone number and her grandparents' full names. And she packed food for Diana and told her she had to eat it all and not eat anything from Enzo's kitchen unless it was from a brand-new package. She also insisted that Diana stay near the Y and not travel farther away. "Anyway, don't you usually play in the gym or go with Papa for candy at Woolworth's?" she said. "Besides, honey, he doesn't have a phone and I want you to be ready when I pick you up."

When Sylvie came for Diana, Enzo usually seemed very stoned and Diana would be playing alone with dolls while he slept on the sofa. Once Enzo called because when he was pushing Diana on the rope swing, she fell on her head, so Sylvie rushed over to take her to the ER. Every day Sylvie's stomach was in knots.

Soon Diana complained she didn't like going to the Y, saying, "There's nothing to do!" She wanted to play with neighborhood kids. Sylvie told Enzo she wouldn't force Diana to visit. Afterward he rarely called to speak to Diana but occasionally called to accuse Sylvie of turning his daughter against him. But Sylvie didn't talk about him unless Diana asked and then avoided saying anything negative.

One day before she was to drop off Diana, Enzo called and asked, "Sylvie, why do you break up the family? We're still married in the eyes of God."

"God watched you hit me!"

"C'mon. That was nothing."

"That rock could've hit my head."

After a long pause she said, "Hello?"

"I should've killed you then."

She slammed down the phone, shock buzzing through her. When it rang again, she knew it was him and when it stopped ringing, she took it off the hook. She told her parents she wouldn't speak to him. She didn't care if he tried to sue her!

Away from him now and seeing who he decided to be, she regretted things she'd done—cutting down those beautiful trees, pocketing Babbo's airfare money and more—putting gum in the fetal pig, giving Paul the old-man cactus, getting the Hare Krishna to quit wearing glasses. Was it street theater? Had she helped people see things differently? Or was she obnoxiously mocking them? It was safe now to feel such shame, in this comfortable home cosseted by the well-oiled system. And yes, she thought, I rescued Diana and me from her father who wanted to kill me.

Kill me!

The next day Dad fielded a call from the school secretary who said Enzo had shown up and since she knew about the restraining order, she called the police. Enzo wasn't charged but was warned not to show up again. Sylvie felt like a hypocrite who had rejected the system when she jumped outside it but used it now that she could. Dad answered the phone that night and Enzo just said, "Tell Sylvia I'm going to Italy," and hung up.

Sylvie lay in bed thinking that being a father was just a game for him. He used Diana to get back at her for imagined wrongs. When would he have started beating his daughter? She remembered his qualities she'd admired that signaled to her he'd be a good dad. He'd seemed so different from boys she'd known and she'd believed he was going to be something great but he was just an unworthy man and she'd been obtuse. And she hadn't respected herself enough.

* * *

They all sat down together for dinner. Sylvie hadn't realized in adolescence—when she'd professed to despise Dad—how alike they were: Both stubborn and argumentative, and political opposites, which blinded her, if not both of them, to their similarities. Battles had been waged at dinnertime, where she'd sit at his left elbow. Each evening she'd prepared the battlefield with the appropriate tableware, setting the deceptively placid table with the accoutrements they needed as an excuse to sit next to each other. Civil rights, Vietnam, all related topics set them off. A wiser family would have steered the conversation away from controversial topics, like their neighbors the Szwinskis who played word games throughout dinner. Once when Sylvie had eaten dinner there, Mr. Szwinski kept everyone laughing. Of course, she hadn't known that both parents were alcoholics and probably couldn't carry on a coherent conversation. It didn't strike her at the time that their word games had such arbitrary rules.

Now a year had passed. Enzo was gone. Diana had finished first grade. Sylvie's divorce was final; she'd been promoted to assistant manager and would get her degree in another year.

At dinner now, Dad said, "Maybe you'll start thinking about law school."

"Dad, really," Sylvie said. "I don't think lawyers are interested in justice. They're just into winning." And that's how he saw her! "Plants are much nicer. I'd rather study them."

Dad scratched his chin, patted his pocket and looked at Mom.

"May I be excused?" asked Diana.

"Yes. Carry your plate into the kitchen," said Mom, "and stay out of the living room!"

Whenever Diana stepped into the kitchen, Molly lay in wait and barked at her. And whenever she did, Mom and Dad laughed. Traitor, Sylvie thought. She was my puppy, how dare she! Well, it's so predictable it's funny. Sometimes. But they laugh every single time. How must Diana feel?

Something under Dad's jacket bulged where he'd been patting. He cleared his throat. "Well, Sylvie, in recognition of your progress this year," he said, "I've gotten you a little something."

Sylvie looked at him stupidly. This is the man who, when she'd desperately called and begged to stay with him a few days, had said, "I don't think so." She looked into her wooden salad bowl and forked a lettuce leaf and remembered how she hated rinsing these bowls. They're always sticky. God, she thought, I've been independent for ten years, and Mom still won't share the kitchen. She brushes me off with, "I can't work in here when it's so crowded," or "Why don't you make the salad?"

"Your father wants your attention, Sylvie," said Mom.

Again, Dad cleared his throat. "You've made great progress this year—managing at Lyman's, working on your degree. So we wanted to give you this." He lifted a box from his inside pocket and passed it to Sylvie.

He's kidding, she thought, taking the box. It was long and green with Marshall Field's written on top in white script. She took off the lid and dug through a bed of tissue. Deep within, she felt something hard and cold. She lifted it out. It was a gold watch! Her fork clattered off the table and onto the carpet.

"That must've cost at least a hundred dollars," Mom said. "I always wanted a Hamilton watch."

"Oh my God!" Sylvie exclaimed. "This is beautiful!"

Dad was grinning. "Well, we didn't want your accomplishments to go unnoticed," he said.

My accomplishments? she thought. Well, they didn't like when I dropped out of college and moved to Italy. Do they like that I'm studying plants? They certainly didn't like when I married Enzo. So was that sarcasm? I never predicted I'd be here again, or for this long. But Mom acts so hurt when I look at apartment ads. I don't get her. I don't think she enjoys us being here, but she makes it hard for me to leave. Well, thank God Lyman's likes me and I still have friends in town who can help me out by sitting with Diana.

The watch was the most elegant thing Sylvie had worn for years, and it made her feel rich. She even started to paint her fingernails and would get a manicure as soon as she could afford it. She often felt her wrist for the watch and lifted it to her ear to hear it tick. It was mechanical, the kind she wore as a kid, that Dad knew how to fix. It kept perfect time. But sometimes she felt it release its grip on her wrist.

She was driving one spring day when the earth smelled rich. Her window was open, and her left arm was out, her fingers in the gutter of the car's roof. When she brought her arm in to turn the wheel, she noticed the watch was gone!

In a panic, she pulled into the next gas station and got out of the car, thinking she'd have to go search the street for it. She looked inside the car, felt between the seats and cushion backs. Finally there it was, on the floor.

At dinner she said, "The watch is great, Dad! Keeps perfect time."

"Hamilton made clocks for the train stations," Mom said.

"Really great," Sylvie said. "But sometimes the clasp opens up. Once I caught it falling off."

"Well, of course it falls off," Dad said. "Otherwise I never would've found it."

Sylvie was bewildered. The watch had been his peace offering, a token of his love. But now it felt like receiving stolen goods.

"You found it? But someone must be looking for it! Shouldn't you find the owner?"

"I put an ad at the golf course and after two weeks no one claimed it so I got to keep it."

Mom said, "You didn't think he paid for it, did you?"

Sylvie eyed her. "Well . . . ," she said. Should she check inside it for flies? Should she look for New Zealanders?

Her appetite gone, she got up to carry her dishes to the kitchen, the plate and salad bowl in one hand, glass in the other. As she balanced the dishes, she could feel the watch clasp, loosening on her wrist. Molly barked as Sylvie rushed to put the dishes on the counter but not before the watch slid off and fell to the floor. The barking and clattering must have sounded funny from the next room. She wasn't sure but thought she heard them laughing. Then she laughed too, like she used to with Janis, until tears flowed.

Through the kitchen window Sylvie could see Diana lying on the grass, looking up at the sky. She went out and sat with her for a few minutes then said, "C'mon, I know where we can go." She took Diana's hand, helped her up and they headed to the lakeshore where the temple was.

BOOK CLUB QUESTIONS

1. How would you cast the main characters in a film?
2. Sylvie is learning to discern when people are being authentic or artificial. Talk about your own experience with this.
3. How does Sylvie's childhood trauma affect her psychology?
4. What misunderstandings exist between Sylvie and Mom? How does Sylvie resolve them?
5. How is Sylvie different from her family? Her classmates?
6. Does Sylvie's inclination for pranks manifest itself as she matures?
7. How would you describe her relationship with Dad?
8. How do you understand Sylvie's attraction to Danny, Saul and Enzo's brooding "dark" side?
9. What warning signs does she fail to see in Enzo? How obvious are they?
10. What inspires Sylvie to understand different religions?
11. Why does Sylvie leave the USA?
12. How does living abroad change Sylvie's thinking?
13. What are some similarities and differences Sylvie notices in the various communities where she lives?

14. Discuss the covert and overt racism in the book. What about sexism?
15. What kinds of abuse—to self and others—occur throughout the book?
16. Sylvie thinks women in her family had lost touch with their true selves. What are some examples of this concern throughout the book?
17. Why does the idea of "water line" resonate with Sylvie?
18. Have you ever had a friendship like Sylvie's with Janis?
19. How does Sylvie's interest in gardening and wild plants resonate with you?
20. How difficult would it be to live off the grid?
21. Diana is always accounted for. What are Sylvie's dreams and fears for her?
22. What issues does the book raise about parenting?
23. What different factors make it difficult for Sylvie to leave Enzo?
24. How do those times compare/contrast with now?
25. What does Sylvie finally realize in the end?

CPSIA information can be obtained
at www.ICGtesting.com
Printed in the USA
BVHW031256240221
601012BV00005B/62